Rae Norridge was born and educated in South Africa but re-located to the United Kingdom in the early nineties and is now living in rural Leicestershire. She is the creator and author of *Hilmy the Hippo* children's series. *Wonderful Mr Boon of the Bushveld* was publish in South Africa. Rae is an artist by profession, selling her paintings through galleries. Central to her work is her love of nature and wildlife.

She is married, with two daughters and three grandchildren.

The *Apricot Tree* is dedicated to all the women who have been victims of war.

Rae Norridge

THE APRICOT TREE

AUSTIN MACAULEY PUBLISHERS™

LONDON • CAMBRIDGE • NEW YORK • SHARJAH

A CIP catalogue record for this title is available from the British Library.

ISBN 9781398440098 (Paperback)
ISBN 9781398440104 (ePub e-book)

www.austinmacauley.com

First Published 2022
Austin Macauley Publishers Ltd®
1 Canada Square
Canary Wharf
London
E14 5AA

I wish to express my gratitude to the many people who supported me along my journey of writing *The Apricot Tree*.

Firstly, to my husband, Bruce, who was my sounding board. His multiple rereads of the manuscript gave me on going and valuable critiques in making this book a better read.

Among others who gave me unswerving support is Robert Simpson, who encouraged me with great enthusiasm. I am eternally grateful for the many books he gave me relating to this conflict.

Warner Bastion and Val Wadge who generously gave their time to edit the manuscript.

With a Dutch grandmother and a very English grandfather who fought alongside his British compatriots in the Boer war, I am well placed to understand and offer a balanced view of the 1899-1902 South African War.

I owe a special debt of gratitude to my late father, Robert Stephens, a keen historian and numismatist who first sparked my interest in this controversial chapter of the British Empire.

Prologue
1881

Distorted shadows of the midwives danced across the candle-lit walls of the African farmhouse. Johanna Van Vuuren groaned weakly with each contraction. Two women attended her, Hetta Els, a stalwart white Boer, the other Palesa, a young Sotho woman.

All through the hot African night, Palesa watched disapprovingly at the strange methods of white childbirth. With each cry of pain, Hetta Els would drop to her knees, and with her face turned to the heavens, wail a fervent prayer to her Lord. Johanna Van Vuuren had been in labour for more than 25 hours.

In the voorkamer, front room, Hendrik Van Vuuren sat with his two daughters. This time he prayed for a son, a son to carry on the Van Vuuren name and to inherit the family farm, Doringspruit. A son, and only a son, could secure the next generation.

He looked at his two young daughters in the glow of the flickering candle. Marike was the eldest. Her eight-year-old face was red and swollen from crying. Sannie, two years Marike's junior, played cheerfully with a ball of wool stolen from her mother's sewing basket. Despite an abundance of thick, golden hair, both girls were plain to look at.

Hendrik sat with the family Bible open before him, listening to his wife's cries in the stillness of the night.

Johanna gave a loud, animal-like groan. Palesa moved swiftly and with strong, experienced hands caught the infant as it slithered into the world.

Hetta Els dropped to her knees once more and began to pray to her God with the Bible clutched against her large heaving breasts. She prayed that this new child of Johanna Van Vuuren would be a good, God-fearing child, a child who would respect its mother and its father, a child who would not bring disgrace to this Christian family. She prayed that God might bestow upon it such virtues as obedience and loyalty. She then opened the Bible to Psalm 23, and began to read softly.

It was the soft, gentle singing of an African lullaby which brought Hetta Els back to the earthly world.

'Hou stil, be quiet,' she snapped, as she watched the black woman gently swaddle the infant in soft, clean sheeting. 'I'll not have those heathen songs in this good, Christian house. Do you hear me?'

Hetta stood up and placed the Bible on a small table, and then turned towards the bed. Johanna Van Vuuren's face was as white as the pillows on which her head was cradled, and a river of blood flowed between her lifeless legs. Johanna Van Vuuren was dead.

Hendrik stood up when he heard the door to the voorkamer open. Hetta entered, cradling the screaming infant.

'Oom Hendrik,' she said respectfully. 'I am sorry, Oom, your wife was very weak, she had been in labour too long. She simply was not strong enough.'

'The child?' he asked, the words withering from grief on his lips. 'What about the child?'

'I am sorry, Oom, it is another girl,' replied the midwife. 'But she is strong and healthy.'

Hendrik's large hands, callused and veined from working the soil, reached out and took the swaddled bundle from Hetta Els. He stared down at the small pink face and said, 'She will be named after her mother, Johanna Marie, but we shall call her Hannah.

Chapter One
1897

Hannah tethered the horses to the lower branches of the apricot tree. She examined the saddles carefully, and then checked the stirrups. Overhead, the shrieking cries of a flock of ibis broke the silence of the lilac dawn as they flew, necks outstretched, to a nearby dam.

Marike stood at the window of the voorkamer, which overlooked the front yard of the farmstead. She stood with her feet apart and her hands on her wide hips, watching her young sister tend the horses.

'It's not right, Pa,' she said softly. 'Pa should not allow a young girl to go out hunting with strangers.'

Hendrik sat at the large dining table hunched over a bowl of mealiemeal. He wiped his mouth on the back of his hand and replied in a voice he reserved only for Marike.

'Ag, my liefie. Oh, my love. Hannah is still a child. You must not worry your kind heart with such matters. These men who come today are not strangers. No, we've never met them, but they're not strangers. They are Hans Badenhorst's nephews. I have known Meneer Badenhorst for nearly thirty years, we are good friends and he is a good man.'

Marike turned from the window and faced her Pa.

'Hannah is not a child, Pa,' she said with respectful conviction. 'Hannah's now sixteen years old. Nature has told us that she's a young woman, and she should dress as such and be treated as such. Riding out on the veld like a young boy, dressed in breeches and a rifle slung on her back, is not right. It's not right at all.'

Hendrik ran a thick finger around the walls of the bowl scooping up the last stubborn fragments of the mealiemeal. 'Hannah is still young,' he replied gently.

'Besides, you wouldn't want to deny your sister a day of good hunting. There is plenty of time for her to grow up and be a woman.'

Marike, in her slow cumbersome way, left the room. An obedient daughter never questioned her father's judgement.

At that moment, Sannie, Hendrik's middle daughter, came into the room from the kitchen. Colour was high in her cheeks and a smile played at the corners of her small, thin-lipped mouth.

'I have packed Pa some biltong and some rusks,' she said, placing two large saddlebags on the table.

Hendrik was pleased to see that Sannie had done her hair differently that morning, and that she was wearing a new, sage green, floral print dress with a lace collar. He smiled quietly to himself, remembering the morning of the last nagmaal, communion, when he spoke to Hans Badenhorst. Hans had told him that his two nephews, who had made their fortunes in the ivory trade in Portuguese East Africa, were returning to the Pretoria district to buy a farm.

Immediately, Hendrik knew that if a man wanted a farm, then he needed a good wife, for what is a farm without a good woman? Hendrik had taken the opportunity to arrange a day of hunting on Doringspruit, so that he could acquaint Hans Badenhorst's nephews with his two eldest daughters. It was time for them to marry, to give Doringspruit the heirs he so desperately wanted.

Over the years he had carefully nurtured domesticity and Boer traditions in his family to ensure that his daughters would make good wives. Sannie and Marike were good Christian girls ready for marriage. They were accomplished in the kitchen and could work wonders with a needle and thread. Above all else, they were strong and healthy and would bear many sons. What more could an honest man want?

Satisfied everything was in order, Hannah gently patted the rump of her filly and then crossed the yard and headed towards the house with her dog Honnie, a bitch of dubious and mixed ancestry, trotting devotedly at her side.

The smell of coffee and the soft chatter of the servants in the kitchen greeted her as she entered the house. Hendrik looked towards the door of the voorkamer when he heard the ring of Hannah's boots on the wooden floorboards.

'The horses are ready, Pa,' she said, dropping down into a chair at the dining table.

'Good. Now eat,' bellowed Hendrik, with jocular enthusiasm. 'It will not be long before our guests arrive. Sannie, bring Hannah some coffee. We have a long day ahead of us.'

Hannah drank her coffee while Honnie lay at her feet. As she placed her empty mug on the table, Honnie began to growl softly. The dog jumped up and ran out into the yard to bark.

'Our guests have arrived,' cried Hendrik excitedly, and hurried out on to the front veranda.

All three girls were aware of Hendrik's intentions. Each one sat alone with her thoughts, while Hendrik's loud enthusiastic greetings drifted into the house.

Marike sat heavily in the chair, her fingers twisting the cloth of her apron on her lap. She was Hendrik's first-born and the dearest to his heart. Her cumbersome body and shy, reticent nature had not invited the attention of would-be suitors. Some considered her simple; others regarded her as the product of a home without the love of a mother. Her tastes were simple and her interests were limited. In Marike's narrow world, marriage was not an option. To leave her family home was unthinkable. The welfare of her Pa and her sisters was all that mattered in her insular life.

Sannie's face glowed with anticipation and excitement. At 22, the offers of marriage had been few. One such offer came from a Trekboer who had spent several weeks on the far borders of Doringspruit. Trekboers led a nomadic life, roaming the countryside in their wagons, never putting down roots, a lifestyle that invited suspicion and penury. The offer had been repugnant to both Sannie and Hendrik. Other offers for her hand in marriage had been unsuitable, as the men were either too old or too poor. Today was another glimmer of hope. She wanted so dearly to have a home of her own, servants who would respect her as the woman of the house and a loving man in her marriage bed.

From the moment Hendrik had announced that two young men were to be their guests, Sannie began to plan the lunch menu and her attire. She spent several hours the day before, in the privacy of her bedroom, in the tin bath filled with water scented with lemon juice and orange rind. She used her very own home-made lavender and calendula soap, and her hair was washed and rinsed in vinegar to give it a brilliant shine. These brothers, she was sure, were in search of wives.

Hannah had reservations about this invitation. Her Pa's overwhelming enthusiasm for prospective husbands for Sannie and Marike was uncomfortable and at times deeply embarrassing. She was grateful that, at this point in time, she was the youngest of the three sisters as it was in the Boer culture that the eldest sibling was to be married first. Her father's guests were, no doubt, aware that Hendrik Van Vuuren had three unmarried daughters who were in need of husbands.

***

Hendrik was not a small man. He stood six feet tall in his stockinged feet with broad shoulders and a large barrel chest on which rested a full, thick, golden beard.

But when he entered the room in which his daughters sat, he looked small in comparison to the two men who followed him. Frans and Petrus Badenhorst both stood several inches taller than Hendrik. The men were almost identical in looks; both had coal black hair and eyes the colour of polished jet. Both had shoulders that sloped down towards powerful arms, a testimony to years of lumbering ton upon ton of ivory.

Hendrik proudly introduced his daughters to the two men, who at once removed their wide brimmed, felt hats and bowed respectfully.

'This is Marike, my first-born. Marike is a wonderful seamstress,' said Hendrik, glowing with pride. 'And this is Sannie. Sannie is the cook in the family. But, of course, you will sample her talents later at lunch. And this is my little lamb, Hannah,' continued Hendrik, with a thick outstretched arm in Hannah's direction. 'She is the baby of the family. She can read a spoor with as much accuracy as she can shoot an apricot from 100 yards. Hannah will be out riding with us this morning.'

Sannie hurried to the kitchen and returned, her face flushed with excitement, with a tray of coffee and some rusks for their guests. Placing the tray on the table, she tilted her head to one side and gave the two men her best and most engaging smile.

Petrus Badenhorst's eyes swept through the room. Hendrik Van Vuuren was not a rich man, but nor was he poor. At the far end of the room stood a stinkwood sideboard, with a fine collection of Delftware. Thick, maroon velvet curtains hung heavily from the windows, and a single kudu skin adorned the floor. Above the doorway leading to the kitchen was a large mounted buffalo head with thick black horns spanning the full distance of the opening. A yellowwood bench stood beneath the window with two comfortable chairs arranged in such fashion that it was the obvious place for intimate conversation.

In turn, Petrus assessed Hendrik's daughters. The eldest, Marike, was a hefty lump of a woman with sallow, pockmarked skin. The second daughter, Sannie, was a little less plain, with small, close-set eyes in a broad, flat face. The youngest was of indeterminable age and a stark contrast to her two sisters. Had it not been for her thick blonde hair pulled loosely into a knot, Petrus would have thought that she was a boy. She wore a pair of riding breeches, something he had never seen a woman wear. His gaze lingered on her face; her extraordinary blue eyes and her smooth, flawless skin excited him. Her features were fine, with a small straight nose, high cheekbones and a well-chiselled jawline. His black eyes moved down towards her ill-fitting, khaki-coloured shirt hoping to see the swell of her young breasts, but the looseness of fabric revealed nothing.

After they had finished their coffee, Hendrik stood up and went across to the rack from which the rifles hung.

'It is time to saddle up, gentlemen,' he said, passing Hannah a rifle.

Petrus' small eyes glittered with pleasure; the girl was joining them on their hunting trip. When the time was right, he would make his move. It had been years since he had sampled the pleasures of a white woman's body.

***

Hannah and Hendrik rode a little way ahead, side by side, knee to knee. Across their saddles they rested their rifles. The Badenhorst brothers rode a little distance behind.

The veld was dusty, as the expected spring rains had not yet arrived. The grass stood tall and yellow, and swayed in the breeze, rustling and whispering as it brushed against the horse's flanks. The thorn bushes stood naked and were silvered by the morning sun. Whydah birds bobbed in flight, long-tailed and heavy in their breeding plumage.

This was Hendrik's Africa. To him the veld was more than a piece of land to plant crops and raise cattle. It was God's gift to the Boers. It was the Promised Land for his people, to cut from this unyielding earth a nation that was proud and God-fearing. Rumours of war, between the British Empire and the Boers, were on the lips of every man. Hendrik knew that when the time came to take up arms he would be ready, for this was his land, paid for in blood by his forefathers.

Hannah reined in her horse at the sound of an alarm call of a guinea fowl. Hendrik reined in beside her, the Badenhorst brothers pulling up alongside Hendrik. They sat in silence and watched the tall grass as it whispered in the breeze.

The guinea fowl screeched once more. Some flew clumsily into the air, while others ran with feathers askew and heads erect across their path, followed by a she-leopard and her two young cubs.

Hannah heard the click of the bolt of Petrus Badenhorst's rifle. The leopard stood frozen, yellow-eyed and beautiful. She dropped from her horse and ran towards the cat with her hat in her hands screaming. With infinite speed and silence, the leopard and her cubs disappeared into the sea of tall, winter grass.

Hannah turned towards the hunting party. Her hair had tumbled down from the loose knot and fell about her face and shoulders in ribbons of gold.

'How dare you,' she spat in outrage. 'This is Doringspruit. We hunt for the pot, not for pleasure.'

Hendrik, shocked at his daughter's outburst, turned to the Badenhorst brothers with embarrassment to apologise.

The words froze on Hendrik's lips. Petrus Badenhorst was leaning back in his saddle with his eyes half-closed and fixed on Hannah, a smirk on his slackened mouth betrayed his lust. Hendrik, not sure of his next move, saw a knowing look exchanged between the two brothers. They grinned confidently with their eyes focused on the young woman.

Frans dug his spurs into the horse's flanks and headed towards Hannah creating a cloud of dust in the morning light. He leaned forward in the saddle and with an outstretched hand grabbed Hannah's arm. The movement was swift and calculated. With the sound of ripping fabric, she wrenched her arm free. Her shirt fell open, revealing her young perfect breasts, with nipples pink from the heat.

In that fleeting moment, Hannah read their thoughts, fear ran through her like small fingers of lightning. Petrus sat in the saddle, raping her with his eyes; his expression so intent that she could almost feel his coarse, oversized hands on her body.

Frans attempted another lunge towards her, the hooves of his horse pounded the dry earth, the cloud of dust became thick, blurring his vision. With the blood hammering in her ears and her eyes fixed on her predator, Hannah swiftly stepped back, out the way of his powerful reach.

Hendrik's hand slid silently to the rifle resting on his thighs, but with the keen eyes of a hunter, Petrus saw the movement and turned on Hendrik, his rifle barrel inches from Hendrik's chest.

'It is time for you, old man, to leave us. Drop your rifle on the ground and go back to the house. Leave the girl with us. We will teach her what she wants.'

Hendrik raised his rifle and threw it in the direction of Hannah. He turned his back on the barrel of Petrus' rifle and slapped the rump of Hannah's horse. The filly bolted and headed towards her mistress. Frans' horse reared as the filly closed in on them. Hannah took the opportunity and scrambled for Hendrik's rifle, which lay several yards from her feet.

Hendrik heard a shot, like a crack of a whip, and saw a spurt of dust beyond Petrus' horse, making the horse rear and snort in fear. Petrus pulled hard at the reins, allowing his rifle to fall from his grip. Hendrik slid from his saddle and grabbed the fallen rifle lying in the sand. With steady hands, Hendrik aimed it at Petrus.

'Get off my land,' he hissed. 'God has witnessed your evil act and you will atone for your sins on your day of judgement. Leave this farm. As the good Lord God is my witness, I will kill you if you ever return.'

Petrus looked down at the barrel of the rifle and smiled.

'We are going, old man, we are going.' He looked in Hannah's direction and called to his brother, 'Come Frans, let it be. There will be another time. Oh yes, there will be another time.'

Frans, with his horse now under control, joined Petrus. With one last glance at Hannah, they dug their spurs deep into the horses' flesh, turned and cantered off.

Hendrik raised the rifle to his shoulder and watched the two men through the sights until they disappeared into the distance of the open veld.

Hannah, stunned by the shameless act these men had been about to commit, stood in silence for several minutes. The world around her seemed to have changed in that moment, the sky overhead seemed darker and the warm air had taken on an unnatural chill. She watched her Pa with his head tilted to the side as he unswervingly studied the men through the rifle sights. She pulled at her torn shirt as best she could to cover her naked breasts, and then remounted. For her Pa's sake, she gathered herself together. He was not to know how shaken she was, and he was not to know how repulsed she had felt the first time she had laid eyes on the two brothers.

As soon as the two men entered the voorkamer, she had felt uneasy. They were too polite in a crude sort of way. Her father, in his innocence, had been too eager. She had noticed Petrus' eyes swimming around the room, drinking in every detail. She had been further annoyed when they refused to allow Honnie to join them; they believed that dogs were a hindrance. No dog, in their experience, had earned his meal after a good day of hunting. From the moment they rode out of the yard towards the open veld, she could feel their eyes on her. Once the leopard appeared, she had acted on instinct—protect the beautiful creature from the ruthless intentions of her Pa's guests.

In silence Hannah and her father made their way home, their thoughts running wild in their heads. In the distance they saw the smoke spiralling from the kitchen chimneys of the farmstead. The smoke rose into the flawless blue sky like a talisman of love and security.

Hendrik, deeply ashamed and shaken by the Badenhorsts' behaviour, tried to gather his thoughts into some semblance of order to find an explanation for Sannie and Marike of their early return. As he rode, his thoughts turned to Marike. Marike, the daughter who could never master her letters, the daughter who everyone considered slow, was the daughter astute enough to understand that Hannah was no longer a child. He was deeply ashamed and guilty that he had seen his daughter's naked breasts, a sight no Christian father should see. But it was this sight that told him that Hannah was no longer a child. Why had he been so blind? Why had he not heeded Marike's warning? What had occurred that morning would never be discussed, it was a private matter between himself and his youngest daughter.

As the cool shade of the eucalyptus trees washed over them, Hendrik signalled to Hannah to stop. He removed his hat, leaving an invisible band pressed into his thick golden hair, then wiped his brow with the back of his hand, and began to speak.

'Hannah…'

'I know what Pa wants to tell me,' she interrupted. Her hands still trembling, she fiddled with the reins avoiding her Pa's eyes. 'I understand what happened today, Pa.'

'No, my child, there are things that I must tell you.'

'Pa has nothing to tell me,' she said, trying hard to spare her Pa the agonies of an explanation. She had clearly understood the intentions of the Badenhorst brothers. The gossip of the servants had taught her many things. It was not in the servants' culture to whisper. Their intentions were never to be disloyal or hurtful, but their voices often carried across the orchard with unsavoury tales of misfortune.

'There's no need to explain,' she continued, 'I understand that certain things happen between a man and a woman, and sometimes these things are not right.'

Hendrik, appalled at her frankness, spluttered, 'My child, where did you learn such things? Not in our house, surely. Your sisters would not know of such things.'

'No, Pa, such things have never been meant for my ears. I hear the servants gossiping. Sometimes out in the orchard or in the kitchen when they were unaware of my presence. Many times Palesa has warned me not to be too trustful; not all men have good intentions.'

Hendrik sat silently on his horse; in the space of a few short hours, his vision of his perfect life had come to an abrupt end. White men, whose past was not known, could not be trusted. Servants spoke unashamedly of sins of the flesh beneath his roof. He was ashamed to think that Hannah had learned such things from idle gossip. Was he right not to discuss with them the evils of this world? How was he to know that in his clean Christian life men like the Badenhorst brothers existed? Hannah had been the only daughter to learn the language of the farm workers and house servants. Never had he given any thought to what might be discussed in the kitchens by these heathen women. Yes, they were good, hard-working people, but none-the-less heathens.

'My child, are you telling me that such sin is spoken about under our Christian roof?'

'Pa mustn't be angry. They never meant ill towards me. Perhaps I shouldn't have been listening to things that were never meant for my ears.'

Hannah sat quietly and reflected on how much a mother was needed in this world. What experience did Sannie and Marike have? They too, were raised only by their Pa. It had been Palesa who had taken on the motherly role and taught her the facts of life. Hannah had never forgotten that warm afternoon beneath the apricot tree, how Palesa explained, in a gentle mothering tone how nature reproduced, and that it was the most natural thing in the world.

Hendrik watched Hannah as she stared into the distance. For him, she had been neither a daughter, nor the son he never had; she was simply just his child. It was like owning a dog, the gender never came into the love; it was merely a dog.

'Tomorrow we will travel to Pretoria and from there we will take the train to Cape Town. I am not happy for you to be here at Doringspruit. It's no longer safe. I fear that these men will return. You can spend time with your Tante Magda. She will take care of you. I will cable her once we're in Pretoria and tell her we will be on the next train.'

Hannah leaned forward and rubbed the filly's neck. Leaving Doringspruit and her family did not rest easily with her. It had been the only life she had known, and beyond those boundaries, the world seemed threatening and uncertain.

'I don't want to stay for long, Pa. I want to come back as soon as possible.'

'It is time for you to learn to be a young woman, and Tante Magda will teach you English.' Hendrik swept his forehead with the back of his hand before continuing with a bitter edge to his voice. 'After all, she married an English officer. Even though he has been dead for 12 years, she still considers herself English. Yes, you will be safe with her.'

It was not Hendrik's wish to entrust Hannah to his partially estranged sister, nor was it to his liking that Hannah would be living in a British colony. But the Badenhorst brothers were unconscionable hunters, taking what they wanted from this earth, and would hunt her down, of that he was certain. Hannah, riding out on the veld, was a free spirit and he would not imprison her with the invisible bars of his fierce protection. He had little choice; he had to put his prejudices aside and take her to a place of safety.

Chapter Two

Hannah leaned out of the window of the train as it eased its steaming iron bulk to a standstill at Cape Town station. Hendrik, with deep foreboding, stared out across the platform, which was teeming with people, people who were of a different ilk to that of the Boers. The station was filled with a cacophony of shouting porters, steam and smoke hung in the air like a cloud of doom, carriage doors slammed and whistles screeched in every direction.

For Hendrik, this was the portal to hell. A British colony, ruled by Imperialists whose greed for power and wealth rose above their belief in the Lord.

For a brief moment, he entertained the thought of returning to the Transvaal without so much as disembarking from the train. The image of the Badenhorst brothers swam before him with their sneering mouths, and their eyes greedy for his daughter's young body. In his mind he saw their powerful bodies enveloping Hannah in a frenzied attack of lust. He knew, without question, that Cape Town was the lesser of the two evils.

Once outside the mayhem of the station, Hendrik, tired and overwhelmed by his emotions, hired a carriage. He fumbled through the pockets of his corduroy jacket looking for Magda's address in Wynberg, and handed it to the coachman. He looked about him with grave mistrust and then turned to Hannah. Her face was bright with eagerness.

'Pa,' she whispered, 'it's all so…so different.'

'Of that you may be sure,' he barked, and began to load their luggage onto the carriage, all the while ignoring the coachman's futile attempts to help.

Through the carriage window, Hannah saw a landscape vastly different to that of the Transvaal. Where the veld around Doringspruit was dry after the short winter months, the Cape countryside was green and peppered with a multitude of wild flowers. The vast skies and the wide-open spaces of the farm now contrasted sharply with the powerful, omnipresence of Table Mountain, which dominated every turn.

She caught her first glimpse of the sea with gulls circling and screeching as they bobbed in the wind above the waves. Along the roadside were fat clumps of arum lilies in full bloom while the proteas, on the slopes of the mountain, flaunted the magnificence of their spiky blooms.

Hannah, though weary from the long train journey south, felt exhilarated by nature's diversity. Never once had she imagined the world to be so rich in colour. She realised from the moment the train pulled into the station, how little she knew of life. For the first time, she felt vulnerable and ignorant. Her father looked oversized and uncouth on the platform, ignoring all the friendly gestures of the porters.

She looked down at the dress Marike had made for her, it looked tired and dull in comparison to the richly textured fabrics the women wore as they paraded themselves elegantly along the platforms. Her Pa had told her little of her Tante Magda. What was she like? Did she have the same forceful nature as her Pa?

As she sat in the swaying carriage beside the snoring Hendrik, she knew, for better or for worse, her life had inextricably changed.

The carriage came to an abrupt halt in front of a cream-coloured house. The house looked inviting and friendly, with a wide shaded veranda edged with a lace work of wrought iron, which was painted in a brilliant white. The windows glistened in the bright Cape sunshine, and behind the panes, she saw neatly draped curtains. Hydrangeas grew either side of the neatly swept footpath that led up to the house. Two large English oaks graced the front lawn and beneath them, in a low flowerbed, bloomed a multitude of spring flowers.

'Wake up, Pa. We're at Tante Magda's house.'

Hendrik jerked himself awake. 'Here already? Magtig,' he said, and quickly put on his dusty, weatherworn slouch hat.

Clumsily, he climbed down from the carriage and immediately straightened his jacket in a vain attempt to look fresh. Hannah sat for several moments gathering her thoughts; everything around her seemed perfect, from the charm of the house to the breath-taking beauty of the surrounding countryside.

Hendrik, flushed from sleep, stood for several moments to harness his emotions. Bitterness ate away at his very being, like a cancer that was all consuming. This was a British colony swarming with Imperialists and he was forced to subject his daughter to the unpalatable ills of the Cape. This was the

Sodom and Gomorrah of Africa. His nation, the Boers, had left the British-ruled Cape Colony and trekked north into the hinterland to find independence. Now, this very nation was threatening to overpower the independence that the Boers had fought so hard to achieve. His hatred scorched his heart. The British Empire, he believed, was drunk with greed.

'Beautiful house,' sang the coachman in an Irish lilt, interrupting Hendrik's thoughts. Hendrik, dismissing the coachman's air of familiarity, ignored the remark with stubborn silence. He impatiently took the luggage from the little Irishman and reluctantly dropped the fare into his upturned hand. Hannah climbed down from the carriage and stood beside her father, she looped her arm through his, and together they made their way up the path to the front door. Once the carriage was out of sight, Hendrik lifted the heavy brass knocker and knocked on the door.

***

Everything about Magda Hetherington was deliberate. From the way she swept her hair from her face to accentuate her high cheekbones, to the flattering cut of her dress, which complemented the narrowness of her long waist. Every movement of her body was played out according to the audience, from the quick flutter of the wrist to the sensuous sway of her hips.

Magda Hetherington knew the power of her beauty and had used it to her every advantage. She bore little resemblance to her brother, whose coarse fleshy features were weather-worn and creased, while Magda's features were refined and her skin was smooth and pale. Hendrik was large and powerful in build; Magda was graciously tall and long-limbed.

'So this is my young niece,' said Magda enthusiastically, after the formalities and greetings were over. 'Hendrik, she's so much like me, I simply cannot believe it.' She leaned forward and lightly kissed Hannah on the cheek. 'Hannah, my dear, welcome to the Cape. I know you are simply going to love every minute.'

Hannah watched her aunt as she moved about the well-appointed sitting room. She tried hard not to look bewildered, for bewildered she was. This was to be her new home for the next year or so, and for a brief moment she longed for the familiarity of Doringspruit and the comforting presence of Marike.

Tea was ordered while Hendrik's demands for coffee were conveniently ignored. Hannah sat with her hands clasped in her lap and took in her new surroundings. Her Pa's large bulk and crude clothing looked incongruous in such a refined setting. Elegant chairs and sofas, covered in cream silk and floral chintz, were placed in a formal fashion around the room. Fine Turkish rugs lay on highly polished yellowwood floors, and on the walls hung intricate water colour paintings of hunting scenes. Against the far wall, either side of a doorway, stood two handsome jardinieres with fat, healthy palms.

'It's not for long, Magda,' exclaimed Hendrik, waving a large callused hand in the air in an attempt to emphasise his words. 'The purpose of this visit, I must stress, is for Hannah's safety. Where else could I take the girl, Magda? Her whereabouts in the Transvaal would have soon come to the attention of the Badenhorst brothers. I know, as the good Lord is my witness, they will return for her. Men like that are relentless, they never give up.'

'She'll be safe with me, Hendrik. Of that you may be sure.'

'I need not remind you, dear sister, that Hannah is a good Christian girl, raised on the Lord's word. After a time, maybe six or eight months, she must come back to where she belongs. In the meantime you can teach her English. Ja, she will benefit if she can speak a little English.'

'Hendrik, Hendrik,' replied Magda, with contained laughter. 'I intend teaching her a lot more than English. We live in a changing world and woe betide the woman who falls behind.'

'Magda, you are not to teach her the heathen ways of the Cape. It is against my better judgement that Hannah should be here, here in this…this—'

'In the Cape Colony, Hendrik,' interjected Magda with some degree of irritation, 'talk of war is everywhere. The British are a force to be reckoned with. Hannah will do well to converse fluently in English. After all, the British will win this war…of that I have no doubt.'

'We will fight,' replied Hendrik. 'Do you think we will sit back and let them seize our land? Magtig, we will fight, and how we will fight. It's greed, that's what it is all about…greed.'

Magda placed her cup neatly into the saucer and then returned it to the tray. 'You've arrived in fine weather, Hannah,' she said, changing the subject abruptly. 'You are fortunate. This time of the year can be a little blustery.'

***

The following morning Hendrik sat at the far side of the breakfast table, sipping coffee from a fine china cup. His large fingers were finding difficulty with the delicate, ornate handle.

'Magda, I do appreciate what you are doing for Hannah. She is a good Christian daughter, and the Lord will protect her from temptation. I trust you will put her Christianity above all else. I will send for her as soon as I think it's safe for her to return.'

'Of course, Hendrik. I will have her best interest at heart. When do you intend returning to the Transvaal?'

'Today, on the afternoon train,' replied Hendrik, buttering another slice of delicate toast.

'Hendrik, don't rush back. Let me show you around our beautiful Cape Town.'

'Magda, my sister, there are things to be done on the farm,' he said, taking a bite of the toast, sending shards and crumbs in all directions.

'You know that spring is a busy time of the year. There are crops to be planted and the cattle are calving. It is too much work for Sannie and Marike. And, of course, Adam and the farm workers must be supervised. Adam is getting very old now; he doesn't have the strength that he used to have. Jonas is a hard worker but needs a careful eye. I need to be sure that all my workers are doing what needs to be done.'

Magda smiled. Hendrik was still Hendrik after all these years and she was sure Doringspruit had not changed since the day she had left. Hendrik was a replica of their father, and their grandfather, unforgiving and resilient, this is what the Boer nation prided itself on.

'I haven't seen you in twenty years. When I received your cable saying you were bringing Hannah, I was so excited. Oh, Hendrik, I know we have corresponded over the years, but it is so good to have you here, in my home. Now tell me about my other two nieces, Marike and Sannie. Marike was a mere baby when I left the Transvaal. And I want to know how the burghers feel about the influx of foreigners to Johannesburg. Hendrik there is so much to talk about. Please stay for a day or two.'

'One day, my sister, when the British have left the Cape, I will visit.'

Magda laughed. 'Then, Hendrik, you will never visit.'

Hendrik stood up from the breakfast table whilst mopping his mouth with his napkin.

'The train to Pretoria leaves at midday. I must be on it,' he said, dropping the soiled napkin onto the table. 'Besides, Sannie and Marike are alone at Doringspruit. It would be inappropriate if I stayed away too long.'

***

Magda ordered a new wardrobe of clothes to be made for Hannah. Her dresses were quite acceptable for the pastoral way of life on Doringspruit but would look crude and embarrassingly outmoded in the sophisticated lifestyle of Cape Town. Shoes, hats and accessories were ordered from fashionable stores on Adderley Street. Music lessons and art classes were arranged. Tickets to the theatre were booked. Dinner parties were organised.

The Cape spring turned into a long, hot, dry summer. Hannah's social skills were honed to match those of Cape Town's elite society. She felt comfortable in her new environment, and this comfort gave her confidence. She began socialising on a daily basis, unlike Doringspruit, where socialising was done only on special occasions, such as nagmaal communion, weddings, Christenings and funerals, or on those very rare occasions when a visitor might pass the farm.

The beauty of the Cape seduced Hannah. She was captivated by the sheer magnitude of the mountains whose imposing presence changed at the whim of nature's calling. Shrouded in mist on the days when the driving rain swept in from the sea, the peaks stood like giant ghosts against the grey skies. On hot summer days, the mountain slopes shimmered silver and green as the leaves of the strange flora shivered in the coastal breeze, and on clear evenings, the vast rocky outcrops glowed in the amber light of the setting sun.

The sea, not to be outdone by the beauty of the mountains, presented itself in different cloaks of mystery and power. The dazzling light shimmered on the wet sands and blurred the distant horizons. The vast expanse of water was an alien element to Hannah. The sea was secretive, revealing only what it chose to reveal, spewing up strange creatures along the shore line after the turbulent waves dramatically crashed and receded back again into its vast depths of its unknown macrocosm.

This plethora of beauty gave Hannah a sense of immeasurable freedom. This, the most southerly tip of Africa, was not tied to the doctrine of the Holy Book. Here, its people were at liberty to enjoy life, to walk in solitude along its pristine beaches, and to meander along the mountainous paths lined with floral abundance. In this corner of heaven, she was answerable to no one.

On cold wet days, Hannah and Magda chose to stay at home and read. Magda's drawing-room was warm and cosy where, on inclement days, a healthy fire always burned in the grate. Her shelves were packed tight with books of all descriptions, from light novels to the English classics, from political volumes to botanical interests. Hannah had never before been an avid reader since the only book at Doringspruit had been the Holy Bible. Unlike Sannie, who kept a Bible beside her bed and never failed to read from it before going to sleep, Hannah found the Bible not to her liking. This rich well of literature on Magda's shelves fed Hannah's thirst for knowledge. It took her into a universe filled with new experiences, exposing the narrow rawness of Doringspruit and her cloistered childhood.

Since the Cape was under British rule, Magda Hetherington mixed with top ranking military officers and was a regular guest at the Governor's social functions. Now with Hannah as her ward, she ensured that every invitation was not to be missed.

Hannah enjoyed the fine clothes and looked forward to their shopping trips. The women of Cape Town were discerning shoppers and would not settle for anything but the very best, imported from London and Paris. She was adventurous with new tastes and flavours of Cape cooking. Fresh herbs and spices were plentiful since Cape Town was at the heart of the Dutch East India Company, whose ships delivered exotic spices from the east. For the first time she tasted fresh fish, since at Doringspruit, fish had only come in tins, and Hendrik had refused to eat anything that was canned.

***

The long hot summer melted into winter bringing with it cold, driving rain. Spring once again returned with bright floral displays and renewed rumours of war.

Hannah sat before her easel, unhappy with her work. Overhead the large domed sky was mottled with cloud and the sea glittered and sparkled in the spring sunshine. She studied her fifth attempt to capture the scene, but her efforts reflected her frustration. She had mixed the cerulean too strong, making the sky too blue; the mountain slopes were too green and the seagulls too cumbersome.

She closed her eyes and saw her Pa sitting at the table in the voorkamer, and Marike bent over a piece of needlework. She saw the dry veld shining golden in the afternoon light and Honnie racing after the crowned plovers, which in turn ran screeching into the long grass. This world of her childhood seemed a lifetime away. Now, Cape Town, with its beauty and vitality, had usurped her affections for the quiet tranquillity of Doringspruit.

But she had grown tired of the shallow chit-chat of the officers' wives with whom they mixed with on such a regular basis. Their conversations consisted of the idleness of their servants or the limited range of fine clothing to be found in the Cape Town stores. They complained about the weather. It was either too hot or too cold, too windy or too stormy. Nothing pleased them. They longed for the pleasant green fields of England and their sumptuous lifestyles.

The jingoistic talk of the officers about their inevitable victory over the Boers began to irritate and annoy her. This hunger for war filled her with uncertainty. Where did she belong in these uncertain times? When these dark shadows of war had passed, she would return to the Cape. But until then, she needed the peace and tranquillity of the open veld, her sisters and her beloved dog Honnie.

'Aunt Magda,' she said, picking up a protea and examining it absently, 'I have been in the Cape for a little over a year now, and I still cannot believe the wealth of beauty. Look at this bloom, it's flawless.'

'Proteas only grow in the Cape,' said Magda, watching Hannah from under the brim of her large, straw hat. 'They were named after Proteus, the Greek god of the sea.'

Hannah swirled the paintbrush in the water and watched the colour bleed from the bristles.

Without looking up, she said, 'I think it's time for me to return to Doringspruit… to Pa, and of course, Marike and Sannie. And I do miss Honnie so much.' Once again she swirled the paintbrush. 'From Marike's letters…well, the letters that Sannie writes for Marike, she misses me. As you know, Pa couldn't teach Marike to read or write, no matter how hard he tried. Marike is the closest I will ever have to a mother. She worries about me and I know she wants me to come home. It's not only here in the Cape that war dominates every conversation, it's in the Transvaal. I think the family feels, that as a Boer, I'll be safer at home.'

Magda adjusted her sun hat and looked at Hannah in a stern, but affectionate, manner.

'You know when war is declared, you'll be far safer here in the Cape than in the Transvaal. The Boers will be outnumbered. There is absolutely no hope for the Transvaal Republic or the Orange Free State, no hope at all. It will be impossible for the Boers to match the might of the British Empire. Think carefully, Hannah, before you make your decision. Think very carefully.'

Magda leaned forward in her chair and reached out and affectionately touched Hannah's arm. 'And besides, you have changed. Your expectations of life have changed. Could you be happy living at Doringspruit now that you've experienced so much in Cape Town?'

'I have no choice, Aunt Magda,' said Hannah softly.

She stared out across to where the deep blueness of the sea met the sky. Little pricks of light danced across the surface of the water, flashing brilliantly in a random fashion.

'I'm living in a British colony; if war is declared, it will be impossible for me to return. Pa and my sisters will be considered the enemy…I will be the enemy. When the war is over, if there is a war, I'll return to the Cape, of that you can be sure.'

A bee buzzed about her face. She waved her hand in an absent manner before continuing, 'Besides, Doringspruit is far from any town. It poses no threat to anyone. We'll be safe on a remote farm.'

'War is inevitable, Hannah,' replied Magda. 'In the heat of war, there is no place to hide. No matter how remote the farm, no matter where, war reaches out and whatever it touches, it destroys. Don't be naïve, my child.'

'I can't stay here, Aunt Magda, knowing Sannie and Marike will be left alone at Doringspruit if Pa joins the Boer commandos.'

'Again, Hannah, not if but when Hendrik joins the commandos. In fact, I think he wants this war. The Boers want to flex their muscles against a mighty power. It's so foolhardy, they are minnows fighting the sharks.'

Hannah sat in silence with her thoughts. She recalled the passion and fervour with which her Pa had spoken of his hatred for the British. He was dogmatic in his belief that God was on the side of the Boers.

'Whatever you decide, my child,' continued Magda, 'I will stand by your decision. But should you decide to return home, you must give me time to find suitable travelling companions. It is not seemly or safe for a woman to travel alone.'

It took Magda only two days to find what she was looking for. With her network of connections, she learned that four nuns were leaving the Cape to set up a convent in Irene near Pretoria. After a brief meeting and a handsome donation to the new convent, they were delighted to be Hannah's chaperones.

***

Hannah moved about her room packing her stylish new clothes and the gifts she had bought for everyone at Doringspruit. There was an intricate brooch of seed pearls set in silver for Sannie, and a pretty tortoiseshell clasp for her hair. For Marike, she had bought a fine, porcelain doll dressed in lace, satin and silk. Hendrik's gifts were a silver brush and comb set and a new novelty mouth organ. For each one of the female servants, Hannah had bought a bright, colourful scarf, and for Adam and the other male farm workers, boxes of snuff.

Outside the Southeaster blew in from across the sea and buffeted the sash windows, its power and force reminding the world that the fairest Cape was not perfect. Hannah crossed the room and drew the curtains, shutting out the menacing, dancing shadows of the trees.

There was a soft tap at the door.

'Come in,' she called.

Magda entered the room dressed in her dressing gown. Her golden hair hung loose about her shoulders giving her a youthful and softer appearance. In her hands, now naked of jewellery, she carried a box clad in velvet.

'What a frightful night outside,' she said, looking about the room at Hannah's trunks and boxes. 'Tomorrow I'll count the damage. I've already heard two of my plant pots on the front veranda fall and break.'

She stepped between the mayhem of clothes and sat down on Hannah's bed. 'Come, sit next to me,' she said, opening the box. Inside were several smaller boxes, one of which Magda took out.

'I want you to have this, Hannah,' she said softly and lifted the lid.

Nestling in plush black velvet was a necklace of diamonds. The central diamond was the size of an acorn and oval in shape.

'Aunt Magda, I couldn't possibly—'

'I have never worn it. It was a gift to me from a gentleman friend. Before I could return it, he had set sail for Europe. You see, he had hoped to marry me.'

Magda replaced the lid and took a small leather pouch out the box. 'I want you to have these as well.'

She tipped the contents of the bag out onto the bed. Diamonds of all shapes and sizes rolled out and lay like raindrops on the bedcover.

'When I had a small, but exclusive, boarding house in Kimberley, my guests often settled their accounts with diamonds. The stones were nothing to them, there were so many it simply didn't matter.'

'Pa didn't tell me you were in Kimberley.'

'Hendrik doesn't know, and he would never have approved.'

Magda scooped up the stones in her slender hands and poured them back into the pouch.

'The war will come soon, Hannah. At the Governor's garden party last month, a good friend of mine told me that it is not only the grievances of the Uitlanders, foreigners, that are at stake, there are many other factors which will benefit the Empire if there is a war. Chamberlain and the Tory Prime Minister have made it quite clear that they need the gold to underpin sterling. Kruger will not give in to the British Government's demands, and the war office in London is losing patience. So, quite honestly, my dear, it's only a matter of time.'

Magda pulled the silken strings of the leather pouch closed and tied a neat knot. 'Take care of these, Hannah. In times of war, you will need every resource you have.'

'What will you do, Aunt Magda? Won't you need the diamonds?'

'I have plenty, and I have property. Plus Harold, my late husband, has left me financially sound. I have more money than I need.'

'Aunt Magda? Can I ask you something? Why didn't you have any children?'

'I would've loved to have had children, especially a daughter like you. But some things are not meant to be. I was disappointed. Every month when I discovered it was yet another month passing without a sign of being with child, I would weep bitterly. Harold was so kind and sweet, no woman could have wished for a better and more generous husband. I knew then that we couldn't have everything in life.' She tossed her head back and with a smile, continued, 'I have you now, Hannah. Even though you are going home, I feel as though I have a daughter.'

Magda pulled out a few brooches and several bracelets. 'These are more sentimental than valuable. They belonged to my mother, your grandmother, but I want you to have them. And then there are these earrings, I never wear them anymore, but you are young and they will look beautiful against your skin.' Magda placed the pieces into a small biscuit tin.

'Hide them in here, it's not quite as obvious as a jewel case. Hannah... I will miss you. You will write, won't you? Once again I must ask you, are you sure you will be happy at Doringspruit?'

Hannah ran her hand over the biscuit tin pensively. 'I've loved being here with you, Aunt Magda. I will come back, I promise, when all this nonsense of war is over.'

'You have grown up and flourished in this past year, Hannah. You are a very polished and accomplished young woman. Doringspruit holds nothing for you now. I know. I grew up there and I thought I was very happy. But life was so stifling. I couldn't wait to find out what the world had to offer. I wanted to see things and do things.

'Then, one day I met Harold in the trading store in Hemel. He looked so handsome in his uniform. He had joined the British army to escape the tedium of boarding school in England. He had fought at the battle of Majuba and survived, only to die of an abscess on his tooth several years later. Hard to believe isn't it? But I had five good years with him; I loved him very much. He showed me what life was all about. He introduced me to the theatre and many exciting things, things I never dreamt existed while I lived at Doringspruit.

'Our father was strict; everything was done according to the Holy Book. No one approved of Harold, after all, he was English and our forefathers had undertaken great sacrifices to get away from British rule. Now I was bringing an Englishman into the family. Oh, the arguments! But they could see I was in love and I think that, secretly, they thought Harold was a man of his word, so reluctantly, my father gave his permission for us to marry. I've never looked back. Hannah, you must follow your heart.'

'Why didn't you remarry, Aunt Magda?'

'Harold was the only man I loved. I could never have loved like that again. Had I remarried, the man would have been second best next to Harold. No one deserves to be second best. Remember that, Hannah.'

Hannah looked around the room at its plush comfort and welcoming ambience, and felt a chink of regret. Once she was back at Doringspruit, she would be on Boer territory, and Aunt Magda would be considered the enemy.

She sat on the edge of the bed and reflected on the wild insanity of the warmongers, whose breath had tainted every conversation and every newspaper.

In the Cape she had seen them spread their propaganda in the elegant surroundings of the Governor's mansion and across the sophisticated dining tables of Cape Town's elite. In the Transvaal, she knew that propaganda would be extolled at prayer meetings, cattle sales and across the open veld to anyone who was willing to listen.

She took the biscuit tin and placed it at the bottom of her portmanteau. Very carefully, she covered it with a shawl to hide it from prying eyes.

Beyond the windows of Hannah's room, the vengeance of the Southeaster was tamed. The shadows of the trees now stood still and a quietness settled across the night. It was the calm before the storm.

Chapter Three

Willem Prinsloo sat at the large dining table at Doringspruit. Since he had bought the neighbouring farm several months previously, he had been a regular guest at Hendrik Van Vuuren's Sunday table. He was twenty-six years old with dark hair and a pleasant, friendly face. His smile was relaxed and easy, revealing a slightly irregular set of teeth. Willem Prinsloo's gentle manner and engaging personality had made him a popular figure in the district. Since he enjoyed Hendrik's company, he looked forward to his Sunday invitations.

'Magtig,' exclaimed Hendrik. 'Sannie, my child, these sousboonjies are the best I've ever eaten. Don't you agree, Willem? My Sannie is the best cook in the Pretoria district.'

Willem nodded politely, while an unbecoming, puce-coloured blush spread upwards from Sannie's neck and covered her full, round face.

'Thank you, Pa. Pa is always so kind,' she said, and dished herself a second helping of her famous beans.

'More meat, Willem?' asked Hendrik waving a large square hand in Willem Prinsloo's direction. 'Sannie, give Meneer Prinsloo some more mutton. A man must eat well if he wants to run a good farm.'

Sannie sprang into action and took the plate from Willem, while Hendrik carved several thick slices of roast mutton and slapped them onto his plate.

' Magtig, but that dog is barking,' said Hendrik, and stood up and crossed over to the window that overlooked the front yard.

In the distance, in the haze of the heat, he saw an ox wagon making its slow way towards the farmstead with a trail of red dust billowing in its wake.

Honnie ran into the yard and stood expectantly for a few moments, then raced towards the wagon.

'I do believe it's that cheating smous,' roared Hendrik. 'He knows full well I do not purchase anything on the Sabbath.'

Hendrik watched as the pedlar's wagon drew closer and the plume of red dust grew larger. From the window, he could see flashes of light reflecting from the pots and pans that dangled from the sides of the swaying wagon.

Honnie caught up with the wagon and ran alongside it barking with excitement. The wagon stopped and Hendrik saw a familiar figure climb down from the front seat. She bent down and wrapped her arms around the dog, then lifted her skirts and raced towards the house.

'It's Hannah,' cried Hendrik. 'Hannah has come home!'

***

The sound of the crashing plate turned everyone's attention on Sannie. She stood with tears of anger in her eyes and shards of broken china at her feet.

Hendrik, ignoring Sannie's crisis, hurried out onto the veranda and then ran into the yard. Hannah, his little lamb, was home.

Hannah saw her Pa race down the front steps of the veranda. His thick golden hair was wild about his head and his beard was overgrown and unkempt. He was larger than she remembered, and now as he came towards her with his arms outstretched, she saw a wildness in him.

'Pa,' she called. 'Pa, it's so good to be home.'

Hendrik threw his arms about his daughter and embraced her. 'Welcome home, welcome home, my little lamb. Come inside and see your sisters. Magtig, they have missed you.'

Willem Prinsloo watched Hendrik wrestle with his emotions as he ushered his youngest daughter into the voorkamer. Hendrik's eyes were bright with unshed tears and his face glistened with pride.

From the moment Hannah had boarded the train in Cape Town, the excitement of seeing her family again took precedence over everything. She had kept to herself as she found the company of the nuns oppressive. Their prying eyes seemed to watch her every move. They had a constant need for prayers, giving thanks for everything, from the water they drank to the bountiful beauty of the countryside. Once at the station, the sight of Hymie was truly worth giving thanks to the Lord, for now she could escape their constant vigil.

The voorkamer was exactly the way she had remembered it. Nothing at Doringspruit ever changed. She watched Marike lumber her way around the dining table with her arms outstretched ready to embrace the sister she loved so dearly. Marike flung her arms about Hannah and wept. Hannah, after some little time managed to free herself from Marike's emotional embrace, and immediately undid the bow and pulled off her hat, which was adorned with a cloud of pale green ostrich feathers.

She turned to Sannie, who still stood with the broken plate at her feet. Sannie's cheeks were scarlet and her pale blue eyes reflected her disappointment at Hannah's return.

'Hello, Sannie,' said Hannah, with a welcoming smile. 'Oh, the food smells so good. Sannie, I missed your cooking. I missed everyone…it's so good to be home again.'

'You should've let us know that you were on your way home,' said Sannie hotly. 'Pa would've come to the station to fetch you, instead you took a lift from a man without being chaperoned. What will people think, Hannah?'

'Hymie is Hymie. He is a good friend of this family,' replied Hannah, whilst bending down and wrapping her arms about Honnie in an attempt to change the subject. Honnie, who was happily sniffing her skirts with intense interest, looked up at her mistress and yelped.

'You too, Honnie. Not a day went past when I didn't think of you. I know you would've loved the beach.'

Hendrik took Hannah by the elbow and steered her towards their guest.

'Willem, let me introduce you to my youngest daughter Hannah, my little lamb.' He gave a loud chuckle and continued, 'And, Hannah, this is Meneer Prinsloo. He has just recently bought the farm, Soetwater, on our northern border.'

Willem stood up, scraping his chair on the wooden floorboards. He tried his utmost not to stare. Hannah wore a dress of pale green silk, which was tied at her narrow waist with a darker green, velvet sash. Her face was flushed from excitement and the strands of her golden hair, which had escaped the pins, curled neatly against the curve of her neck.

Willem bowed respectfully and said, 'Oom Hendrik has told me much about you. I know everyone here at Doringspruit has missed you.'

Hannah laughed and turned to the kitchen doorway to see the servants jostling for a view of her without crossing the threshold.

'Palesa, Thuli, Louisa. Oh, it's so good to see you all. And little Klaas…you have grown so much.'

The servants clucked and giggled as they greeted Hannah, their eyes bright with excitement.

'Back to work,' bellowed Hendrik, in a good-natured way.

Hannah looked about the room. Its crude, heavy furniture lacked refinement. On Hendrik's plate she saw coarse, thick slabs of mutton swimming in a pool of thick, fatty gravy, which had splashed over the sides and soiled the tablecloth. Marike's and Sannie's clothes were homespun, and their hair was fashioned in a style that only a Boer woman would wear. Her Pa's ill-fitting shirt was stained with gravy, which had congealed into a pattern of misshapen streaks.

She watched him as he gesticulated with his wild enthusiasm at her return. She saw the excitement in his eyes as he introduced her to Meneer Prinsloo, reminding her of the day the Badenhorst brothers had come to visit. Her Pa had not changed, and Doringspruit had not changed. She at once felt a deep sense of shame that her thoughts were so disloyal. This had been her home that had given her succour and love in her childhood, the home her Pa was so fiercely proud of. This man, with his large, callused hands had worked the soil tirelessly so that he could feed and clothe his three motherless daughters.

She tried hard to blink away the tears of shame that stung her eyes.

'Why, Hannah,' gasped Marike, 'you're crying.'

Hannah hurriedly wiped away her tears on the back of her hand, but they began to flow once more. She looked about the room and knew that her tears were not only the tears of shame. In the turmoil of her emotions she knew what she felt was also fear—fear for the future of this simple nation, of which she was so much a part, for they were standing in the long shadows of a looming catastrophe.

The voorkamer took on a festive air. Marike set a place at the table for Hannah, while Hendrik celebrated by opening a bottle of one of his finest wines. Hannah disguised her feelings with false laughter as she related the tale of her tedious journey home in the company of the nuns.

'…And when we stepped off the train in Pretoria, and I saw Hymie Rosenberg standing on the platform, I was so relieved. Sister Bernice wanted me to travel back with them to the convent, and then to notify Pa that I was there, so that Pa could come and fetch me. She was furious when I refused. I assured them that Meneer Rosenberg was a good family friend and could be trusted.'

'You should've taken the nun's advice, Hannah,' interrupted Sannie, with a bitter edge to her voice.

Hannah, ignoring Sannie's remark, continued, 'Hymie had gone to the station to collect his order of tinned goods that had come up from the Cape. I promised him that if he gave me a lift to Doringspruit, the next time he came round to sell his wares, I would buy his finest and most expensive silks, enough for two dresses each. Of course, Hymie wanted to know what was fashionable in Cape Town, and what all the ladies were wearing so that he could order the very latest.

'So you see,' said Hannah, with a knowing smile, 'I got the transport I needed, and Hymie got a lesson in fashion.'

'Well,' said Hendrik, feeling quite sated from the heavy lunch and several glasses of red wine, 'no doubt, the silk he has stashed away in that grubby wagon would've doubled in price now that he knows you are beholden to him to buy it. You know what these Jews are like.'

Hannah gaily chatted on about Cape Town and the sea. She enthused about the mountains, the food and the elegance of the women.

As she spoke, Sannie watched Willem Prinsloo, her eyes never leaving his face. In turn, Willem Prinsloo's eyes were on Hannah. He was intoxicated, not with Hendrik's good wine, but with Hannah's presence. Even when Hendrik replenished Willem's glass, Sannie saw he was transfixed. Like a magnified light on tinder-dry grass, resentment burned into the very core of Sannie's soul. For Sannie, Hannah's return could not have been more untimely.

**

Doringspruit was resplendent after the first summer rains. Hannah led the horses through the peach orchard. The blossoms had gone, and the bright verdant shoots of new growth covered the branches. The orchard had been transformed from a pink, frothy cloud of blossoms to a haven of green, dappled light.

In the distance she heard the sonorous call of the red chested cuckoo, piet-my-vrou, piet-my-vrou, piet-my-vrou. Bright green tendrils of pumpkin vines crept across the furrows of neatly dug earth and the runner beans were twisting their way up the rows of canes. Honnie, with her tail in the air, trotted proudly a few paces ahead of Hannah, happy her mistress was home once more. Honnie was thickset and no taller than Hannah's knee, with a wiry golden coat. She turned and looked back, her tongue lolling to one side, to check if her mistress was still following.

When Hannah reached the front yard of the farmstead Hendrik was waiting for her.

'Hannah, my child,' he called out to her as she came into sight. 'Adam has told me there is a problem with one of the cows. She's stuck in the mud and it's going to take both Adam and myself to get her out, but I'll go out riding with you tomorrow.'

Since Hannah's return, the summer rains had been heavy. The afternoon thunderstorms had been particularly violent with heavy intermittent cloudbursts. For nearly a week, the rain had been unrelenting.

'I'll see Pa at lunch,' she called, as she mounted her horse and cantered off. Honnie barked in excitement and followed.

***

Willem Prinsloo rode out to inspect the damage done to his farm by the torrential rains. Around him the fields were sodden. Branches of the black wattle trees, torn from the trunks with the weight of water, lay in the red mud. One of his small dams had burst its banks taking with it a wall of stone. He needed to repair it and he knew he would need Oom Hendrik's help. He knew his neighbour had generations of tools of all shapes and sizes and was always willing to offer his help and his equipment.

He set out in the direction of Doringspruit. Since that Sunday, two weeks previously, Hannah had walked through his dreams. Every waking hour she had not been far from his thoughts.

Brilliant green shoots pierced the earth like little spears where the veld fires had burned the winter before. Everywhere Willem turned, there was the promise of a new season. The acacia trees were in blossom and were singing with the sound of bees. Small flocks of waxbills moved through the bushes in waves of blue and the thin, mournful call of the bush shrike echoed through the trees.

He crossed the boundary, marked by a row of eucalyptus trees, on to Doringspruit farm. As he rode, the smell of the rich earth filled his nostrils. Like a woman, he thought, it was a smell begging to be enriched with seed.

As Willem turned the bend on the narrow track between the rocks, he saw her. She sat tall and straight in the saddle. Her thick golden hair was half hidden by her hat, which had slipped from her head and hung down on her back. At the sound of Honnie's bark, she turned and saw him.

39

'Meneer Prinsloo. Good morning. What brings you this way?'

Willem smiled and doffed his slouch hat. 'Good morning. I was hoping Oom Hendrik had some tools that I could use to repair my dam.'

Hannah brought her horse up closer to the track. The morning sun caught the sharp angles of her refined face and her eyes were wide and inquiring.

'Did you have much damage from the rains?' she asked.

Willem shook his head. 'Not much, only the dam. The rains were needed.'

He noticed how relaxed her slim fingers were on the reins. Her nails were neatly shaped and perfectly formed.

'I'll ride with you to Doringspruit, if I may?' she said, smiling in her usual friendly manner. 'I've been out for several hours now and I should be heading back.' She pulled her hat back onto her head and continued, 'Pa doesn't stop talking about you. It's so nice that he has a friend so close by. It must be difficult for Pa having women around the house all the time.'

Willem concentrated on her hands, fearful that his thoughts would betray him if he looked her in the eye.

'Oom Hendrik is a good man. I am fortunate to have him as a neighbour.'

***

As they entered the yard, Hannah saw Sannie on the veranda watering the scarlet geraniums which were newly potted. At the sound of the horses' hooves she looked up, the watering can still poised in her hand, spilling water on to the polished concrete.

Willem read Sannie's thoughts and hurriedly excused himself after the formalities of greetings were over, and went off in search of Hendrik.

Hannah tethered her horse in the shade of the apricot tree, crossed the yard, and climbed up the steps to the front veranda.

'Jezebel, that's what you are,' spat Sannie. 'You knew I wanted him and you had to have him. You've brought your fancy ideas back from Cape Town to tempt him with your wanton ways. I bet you lay with him… shameless, in the veld. I can see it in your eyes.'

Hannah stepped forward. 'Aren't you ashamed of yourself?' she whispered harshly. 'To say such things about a sister you haven't seen for so long. Or is it that you are just simple-minded.' Hannah did not wait for a reply. She turned and made her way into the house.

Sannie raced after her. 'It's not over yet. I'm not done with you, Jezebel,' she hissed, her chest heaving and her face puce with anger.

Hannah went into the voorkamer to return her rifle to the rack. Sannie followed. 'Don't think I don't know what happened with the Badenhorst brothers. They saw the devil in you and wanted nothing more to do with this family. They came here to find a good honest woman to take as a wife, I know, because Pa said so. But you had to spoil it all, and now you're trying to spoil it all again.'

Hannah tried to side-step Sannie who was standing close to the doorway. 'You are shameless,' continued Sannie, 'straddling that horse with your legs open like a whore.'

A shadow fell across the entrance to the voorkamer. Sannie spun around and came face to face with Willem.

'I didn't mean to eavesdrop,' he said, with deep embarrassment. 'Oom Hendrik wanted me to stay for lunch. Tell him that I have changed my mind, I am in no need of the tools.' Willem doffed his hat, turned and hurried out the house.

***

'It has been six weeks since I last saw Meneer Prinsloo,' said Hendrik, as he closed the Bible after the evening reading. 'I have sent Adam over to Soetwater with an invitation asking him to Sunday lunch but he has once again declined. Last week he was not at nagmaal, communion, and that is strange for Meneer Prinsloo.'

Hendrik's daughters sat tight-lipped and silent. 'I cannot understand it,' continued Hendrik. 'He's never refused my hospitality and I know he's not ill.'

Marike shifted uncomfortably on her seat. 'Perhaps, Pa, he has found a woman. Meneer Prinsloo is in need of a wife.'

'No,' said Hendrik. 'I saw it in his eyes when Hannah arrived home from the Cape. I thought to myself, yes, I have found a son-in-law.'

Sannie leaned forward in her chair, her lips rolled back in a sneer and anger flared in her pale blue eyes.

'No,' she yelled. 'Pa has it all wrong. Meneer Prinsloo had made it quite clear he was going to ask for my hand in marriage. It all happened two weeks before Hannah returned to Doringspruit. Meneer Prinsloo and I were sitting on the veranda.

'It was after lunch, and Pa had gone to help Adam with the snake in the chicken run. Marike had gone to lie down. He thanked me for preparing such a good meal. He then began to tell me about Soetwater. He told me his plans for the future, and that he had planted several beds of roses because he knew women loved roses and he wanted Soetwater to be a place where a woman could be happy. He then put his hand over mine and looked into my eyes. At that moment Pa came running up to the veranda and Meneer Prinsloo withdrew his hand. Pa asked him for his help. So Willem left with Pa to help with the damage in the chicken run.

'I waited for two weeks, hoping he had managed to speak to Pa. Then he came that Sunday, the Sunday Hannah arrived back from the Cape. Before we sat down to eat, he whispered in my ear that he would speak to Pa after lunch. I do not have to finish my story…we all know what happened after that.'

Silence enveloped the room. The call of the jackals in the distance drifted through the open window, a lonely, desolate sound in the hot African night.

Hannah rose early the following morning. She saddled up, and in the soft, grey light of dawn she headed north in the direction of Soetwater. From the window, Sannie watched her sister in the saddle, slim, fearless and radiant. She turned from the window and collapsed on her bed and wept.

Ever since they were children, Hannah had been the sister that everyone favoured. The servants adored her; nothing was too much for the young Hannah. Her Pa spent time teaching her the ways of the veld. Friends of the family always asked after Hannah, and the eyes of the young men at nagmaal never left Hannah's face.

Over the years, jealousy had crept into Sannie like a slow drip of venom, poisoning every thought and deed related to her younger sister. She saw the look in Willem Prinsloo's eyes the moment Hannah entered the room that Sunday. No man had ever looked at her, Sannie, with such naked lust.

She knew jealousy was a sin according to the Holy Book, but jealousy was also a weakness, and the Holy Book had said that the weak shall inherit the Earth.

Once Hannah crossed the boundary of Doringspruit, she followed the track, which led to Soetwater's farmstead. Willem's crop of mealies was knee high and healthy. In the open veld a few cows stood happily, fat and heavy with milk. In the distance she saw the house peeping through a windbreak of poplar trees. As

42

she drew nearer she saw a wide bed of roses below the veranda, blooming in shades of pink, red, yellow and white.

Not far from the house she saw a small dam beside a clump of wattle trees where Willem and two farm helpers were in the process of excavating some soil. Hannah tugged at the reins and headed in their direction.

Willem looked up when he heard the hooves of Hannah's horse. He stood in silence drinking in her beauty. He watched her dismount and remove her hat, which she then hung on the pommel of her saddle. In the dark blue shade of the wattle tree Hannah's skin looked pale with a warm glow across her cheeks from the long ride. Small strands of hair, which had escaped the single braid, bracketed her face.

'Meneer Prinsloo,' she called, and waved in greeting, 'I wish to have a word with you, if you can spare the time.'

Willem had been reinforcing the walls of the dam. He had removed his shirt and stood naked from the waist up. Beneath his golden skin his muscles were bunched from the physical effort of the repair.

'Mejevrou Van Vuuren,' he said in surprise. 'You are the last person I was expecting to see.' He grabbed his shirt that lay on the rocks, and out of respect for a woman, he slipped it on. With long, relaxed strides, he walked over to where she stood.

'It's about …my sister, Sannie,' she began, with a small amount of uncertainty. 'I had no idea—'

'That I was about to ask Oom Hendrik for her hand in marriage?'

Willem stood inches from her. Hannah saw how green his eyes were, and how his dark hair curled and clung to his forehead from the perspiration.

'Hannah, you must not carry the guilt. Yes, I was about to ask Oom Hendrik. But Sannie has slashed her heart with her own blade. Jealousy has overruled her reasoning. She feared that I had changed my mind and was about to ask Oom Hendrik for your hand instead of hers, but you see, Hannah, I would not have changed my mind.'

He brushed his forehead with the back of his hand wiping away the perspiration. He felt uncomfortable, uneasy with the fact that he had caused dissension in the Van Vuuren household.

'I came here to ask you,' said Hannah softly, 'not to judge Sannie too harshly. She didn't mean what she said. She is a good woman and will make a good wife.'

'I saw her face that Sunday, Hannah. I knew then that she is a jealous woman. There's nothing wrong with that, but malice is another matter.'

He stepped away from her and looked out to where the farm workers were working on the wall of the dam.

'Sannie's needs are my needs,' he said softly. 'She wants to be a Boer wife, cooking a meal for her man when he returns from a hard day in the field. She is strong and will bear a man many sons, that's what our nation needs, many sons. But her scathing words told me that she is not the woman I want to raise my sons. I want a wife who is generous with her thoughts and deeds, a wife who will not judge others, a wife who will make me proud.'

Hannah stood silently, her thoughts with her foolish sister. Willem Prinsloo was everything Sannie had always wanted. She had come here to repair the damage Sannie had done, but the damage was irreparable. Her sister had revealed her true, foolish self.

'Go back to Doringspruit and tell no one you were here,' said Willem. 'Least of all, Sannie.'

'If you can find it in your heart,' replied Hannah, 'give her another chance. I am sure Sannie will have learnt a lesson.'

Hannah mounted her horse, tugged at the bridle and rode off without looking back. As she passed the little farmstead of Soetwater, she saw the roses offering their beauty to the world. Sannie, in her jealous rage, had lost a good man.

Through the gossip of the servants, news reached Doringspruit six weeks later that Willem Prinsloo had married Elsa Cilliers of Irene, in the district of Pretoria.

Chapter Four
1899

'I have enlisted, Father,' said Tristan, standing with his back to the fire in the library at Tylcoat.

Godfrey Dunn-Caldwell drew on his cigar then slowly removed it from his lips. Of all the expectations he had for his son, this was not one of them. Trying hard to conceal his disappointment and shock, he absently examined the burning tip of his cigar which was wedged between his pale skeletal fingers. After a considerable length of time he looked up, narrowed his eyes and said, 'Very patriotic of you, Tristan. Have you thought this through?'

'Of course, sir. I have given this much thought,' replied Tristan, trying hard to keep the irritation he felt from his voice. 'And I feel this is something I need to do.'

The fire crackled and a log collapsed in the grate. Tristan had feared this conversation from the moment he put his signature on the enlistment form down in London. His father, though fiercely patriotic, was a political creature opposing any form of conflict or war.

'Need to do, or wish to do?'

'Wish to do, sir,' replied Tristan. 'There is war fever in London at present and everyone who is able and fit is enlisting. New Zealand, Australia and Canada have volunteered their troops, they are all fighting in the name of the Empire.'

Godfrey leaned back in his chair and examined his son through a cloud of blue smoke. Tristan was a fine-looking man, tall, successful, handsome, everything a father wanted in a son and heir.

'Look at these shelves,' said Godfrey, waving his hand around the room. Floor-to-ceiling shelves were packed with leather-bound volumes collected by generations of Dunn-Caldwells. 'If it's Africa you want,' continued his father, 'then read about it and when this damn war is over, visit it.'

Tristan, uncomfortable under his father's scrutiny, moved across the room to the tall windows, which overlooked the rose garden. Outside the rain slashed mercilessly across the countryside leaving it silvered under the slate-grey skies. The rose bushes stood naked after the first, sharp October frost, which had stripped the last of the summer blooms.

'I have a philosophy in life,' said Godfrey, flicking the ash of his cigar onto the ornate rug beneath his feet. 'War and whores are to be avoided at all cost as they are the downfall of many a good man.'

Without turning to face his father, Tristan replied. 'Up until now, Father, I have managed to avoid the latter, but war is a whore, Father. They both serve the purpose of man's gratification. But since the Empire is in need of good men, I feel I need to serve my country.'

Godfrey eased himself deeper into his winged-back chair. He crossed his long lean legs, and once again examined the burning tip of his cigar.

'When our officers return from campaigns across the world, the talk is of victory and honour, but the truth lies on the battlefields with the broken and bloodied bodies of our good men, fighting in the name of the Empire. Tristan, this is not the game you used to play with your toy soldiers. This is reality. This is life. Some men return as heroes, others return maimed, and some don't return at all. Those that die on foreign soil are buried, and those graves are forgotten. This is not what I want for my son.'

'I understand your disappointment, Father'

'I cannot sanction this move by giving my blessing, but I will pray for your safety and your good judgement.'

Outside the rain had stopped. The fields and the gardens glistened beneath the silver sky. Tristan watched Higgins, the head gardener, stride across the sodden lawn beyond the rose garden, fork in hand and his faithful setter by his side.

'Have you discussed this with Felicity?' continued Godfrey.

'No, sir. I wanted you to be the first to know.' He turned from the window to face his father. ' I have written to her requesting an appointment for tomorrow.'

'You will, of course, make your intentions clear before you leave,' said Godfrey. 'You know how much we have all wanted this match.'

Tristan turned once more and stared out through the long windows of the library. Felicity was the root of his decision. Dear, sweet, kind Felicity. She had been in love with him since they were children. Always inveigling her way into his games, manipulating her way to be seated next him, encouraging such games so that he could be her partner. As they grew into adulthood, her ardour showed no signs of abating. Both families having encouraged the match since their infancy.

Felicity was well educated. She was a gracious hostess and a devoted daughter. But behind her dark brown eyes, there was an emptiness that Tristan found annoying. During his years at Oxford reading law, he was able to mix with young women with enquiring minds and a spirit of adventure. Felicity fell short of these qualities. He loved her like a man would love his sister and no man would dream of making love to his sister. He had become trapped in an untenable situation, a situation that had been taken out of his hands, and the only way out was enlisting and going to war.

'You haven't answered my question, Tristan. Do you intend making your intentions clear before you leave?'

'No, Father. I will not have Felicity beholden to me. I might return disfigured or maimed. She must be free to do as she pleases.'

Godfrey leaned forward and stubbed out his cigar in an ashtray beside his chair. 'This war will be over in a matter of weeks. After all, we are fighting a bunch of simple Dutch farmers. We have the might of the Empire on our side. Before you know it, you'll be back with us.'

The long clock struck the hour. 'I think that is our cue for lunch,' said Godfrey, as he stood up from his chair. 'How long is it before you leave?'

'I sail for Africa in less than a week.'

***

Felicity fingered the choker of pearls that encircled her slender neck. Yes, the pearls were the right choice; Tristan had admired them many times. She studied her reflection and was pleased with what she saw. Her cheeks were glowing with excitement, and her hair was perfectly arranged.

It was unusual for Tristan to be up in Leicestershire during the week. His legal duties kept him in London from Monday to Friday and she had never known him to break this pattern. When she had received his letter requesting a meeting on Thursday afternoon, she had cried with joy. There could be no other reason than the request for her hand.

She planned every detail of the meeting. She brushed and restyled her hair several times, pulling the pins and rearranging her curls so that they lay on her forehead in perfect symmetry. Her dress was the palest of pink, offsetting the creamy colour of her flawless skin. She drank no tea, keeping her breath fresh, nor did she eat anything that might cause offence.

She requested that Yates should show Tristan into the conservatory. The conservatory was flamboyant with her father's collection of orchids, many of which were now in bloom. There was no better place for a proposal of marriage.

Tristan rode across the countryside. The heavy rain from the day before had abated and now the late afternoon sun slanted across the fields. Fat cows, grateful for the warmth of the afternoon sun, stood ankle deep in thick lush grass.

Rooks took flight at the sound of the horse's hooves, flying up in to the leafless trees. Tristan took the short cut through woods on the far boundary of the Tylcoat estate, where he and his sister had chased mythical dragons and searched for the lost kingdoms of the enchanted elves.

Overhead the bare branches of the oaks, birch and elms diced the brightness of the autumn sky into a mosaic of light on the woodland floor. As he rode, the musty smell of dead and decaying leaves rose up to greet him, a smell reminiscent of his childhood. He inhaled deeply, burning the memory of it into his soul so that he could carry it with him across the sea to war. Leaving this land of plenty, its peace and tranquillity would not be easy, for this was where he was born, on these beautiful and bountiful fields of green.

**

Felicity stood up from the small, metal lover's bench and came towards him as he entered the conservatory. He stood tall with his wide shoulders squared; she never failed to see how handsome he was. His dark hair curled in all the right places, framing an almost perfect face. His green eyes were fringed with the same dark, thick lashes.

'Hello, Tristan. This is such a pleasant surprise,' she said softly, her eyes bright with expectation.

'Felicity, you are looking well.'

She moved closer to him and reached up and kissed him on the cheek.

Tristan placed his hands on her shoulders. In some strange way, he felt no guilt about what he had to do. He had never encouraged her. Any encouragement had been in her own, unrealistic, romantic imagination. She had driven him into the arms of the 'whore'. Had things been different he would not be rearranging his life. Backed up by their families, they had given him little choice. He needed a way out, and the way out was by going to war.

'Felicity, I don't wish to procrastinate on small pleasantries, so I'll come straight to the point.' His hands were gentle on her shoulders, thrilling her with his touch. 'There is something I need to tell you…'

'Yes,' she whispered breathlessly.

'This is not easy for me. I am leaving for South Africa…I have enlisted. I leave before the end of the week.'

He felt her shoulders stiffen beneath his hands. 'You…you are going to war?' she spluttered, her eyes round with disbelief. 'Is that what you have come to tell me…that you are going to war? When I received your note…I thought, I thought…' The words floundered on her lips. 'I have waited for so long for your…your request for my hand. But instead you are here to tell me that you have willingly signed up to go to war!'

'I'm sorry, Felicity. I never meant to lead you into thinking I wanted your hand in marriage. Never once have I even suggested a union between us.'

Her dark eyes were fixed on him. 'No, you have not,' she said, fighting to control her anger and shock. 'Nor have you led me to believe otherwise.'

'Your father is a military man. He will understand,' he said quietly. 'Our country is in need of good men and I owe it to my Queen to serve the Empire. I am sorry, Felicity, to disappoint you. I am so sorry.'

The mention of her father, who had recently returned from the Sudan campaign, gave her new hope. Fleetingly, she saw her mother, the dutiful wife, waiting for her father's return from campaigns across the Empire. She would be the same dutiful wife, given the chance.

'I will wait for you, Tristan. I know that in your heart you love me. It's all this talk of war. It inflames patriotism. I know you will come back to me. That's why I will wait for you.'

'No, you are not to wait. God knows how long I will be away. You must be free to enjoy yourself. You are not to wait for me.' His own words sounded abrupt and brutal in his ears.

'I will wait for you, Tristan. I will wait.'

'Felicity, this is not easy for me. It has come as a great disappointment to my father, but sometimes we must do what we wish to do. You are not to wait for me, you must move forward with your life. There is someone out there that will make you happy, and will fulfil your dreams.'

'You have been my life, Tristan. Ever since we were small children you have always been there. Without you, I cannot breathe. It…it has always been…us, you and I together.'

'There will never be a union between us, Felicity. Perhaps we should've addressed this matter a long time ago. I know it has been the dream of both our parents, they have encouraged us right from our cradles. We have never had a choice.'

'My choice was you, Tristan.'

'Felicity, it will never be.'

Her face turned deathly white and her eyes became fixed and distended in disbelief.

'Maybe…maybe after the war.'

'No, Felicity, no. I am leaving for Africa, and at this point in time that is all that matters to me. I'm sorry. I'm so dreadfully sorry.'

'My father says the war won't last long…it can't last long. It will be over in a matter of weeks. Maybe when you've had time to think. I'll be here for you, Tristan, just as my mother has been for my father.'

'No, Felicity. Not now, not ever. I'm sorry. I am truly sorry.'

Not wishing to see the pain and condemnation in her eyes, he turned away from her and headed towards the doors. He came to say what he needed to say; it was not easy for him any more than it was painful for her.

Her humiliation turned to outrage. Colour flared in her cheeks. She wanted to strike him, to tear his face from his head. A cold, calm fury swept through her.

'Tristan.'

He stopped, briefly, at the mention of his name.

'Tristan,' she snapped. 'You came here today and ripped my heart out and discarded it like a used rag. You've humiliated me by reducing me to begging, and now you are going to walk away leaving me to pick up the pieces while you go off to hide in the battlefields of Africa. Going to war is honourable, a mark of a brave man. But you are neither brave nor honourable, Tristan. You are a coward, and there is no place for cowards on the battlefield.'

He knew an element of truth lay in her powerful diatribe. He passed through the glass doors of the conservatory and did not look back. Never look back, his father had once told him, looking back can weaken a man's resolve.

Felicity stood and watched his receding image. She sank to her knees and began to weep. The sickly sweet vanilla perfume of the orchids, which she had so loved, now assaulted her nostrils and caught in her throat. She sat crouched on her knees, with the shell pink satin of her dress engulfing her, and wept. Her life, her future, and her dreams crumbled and vanished in the fading light of the conservatory.

Chapter Five
October 1899

In a cloud of red dust, Hendrik galloped into the yard at Doringspruit. Sannie was sitting in a small square of sunlight on the veranda, drying her thick, golden hair. Marike and Hannah were chatting idly over a pot of coffee and a plate of rusks. At the sound of Hendrik's haste, the three women turned to face him.

'God has willed it!' he shouted, as he hurriedly dismounted. 'There is no hope of peace. I have just returned from Pretoria and spoken with the State's artillery. We are to prepare ourselves and our farms for war.'

Hannah stood up abruptly, knocking over a mug of coffee that was standing at her feet. The dark liquid ran into little pools on the highly polished floor of the veranda. She watched her father as he strode across the yard with excitement in every step. He climbed the stairs to the veranda, where at once he removed his hat and ran his powerful fingers through his thick mass of yellow hair.

'Lord Milner has got his way. He has lusted for war and now he has it. Oom Paul Kruger has given into the British demands, but that is not enough for Milner; he wants war.'

Hendrik sat down heavily on the wooden bench. Honnie, sensing the tension in Hendrik, immediately repositioned herself at his feet.

'Is Pa sure about this?' asked Marike, her voice rasping with emotion.

'Yes, my child. But this is God's will. From the day they found gold beneath the earth in our beloved Transvaal, even before that, when diamonds were found in Kimberley, the British have coveted this land. They disguise their greed with their excuses. As we speak, their soldiers are on the water with their horses and weapons. Forces from around the world have offered their men. Australia, New Zealand, Canada. The mighty British Empire. But we Boers know this land. We will fight, and God will be on our side.'

Marike jumped up from her chair, hurried into the house and began to wail. Hannah went after her.

'Marike, come Marike.' said Hannah gently. 'We must be strong. We must not let Pa know that we are afraid for him.' She led Marike back out on to the veranda, where Marike seated herself beside her Pa and began mopping her round, wet face with her apron.

'The veld is on our side,' continued Hendrik, his voice ringing with passion. 'The grass is tall now that the summer is coming. It will give us good cover. We know this land. We know every rock, every crevice, and every kopje. Magtig! We will fight.' He stood up and looked out across the yard and into the veld beyond. The sun was directly overhead, creating small pools of purple shadow beneath the trees. The cicadas sang in the heat, and the lazy hum of the bees filled the veranda. The air was still.

'How beautiful all this is, how quiet and peaceful. Soon the sounds of war will shatter the silence and the blood of our enemy will stain the veld. God gave us this land, and God will ride with us to fight the British Empire.'

Hendrik looked at each daughter in turn and said, 'God has blessed me. I have fine, strong daughters. I am a proud father.'

Marike began to weep once more while Hannah comforted her. Sannie sat in shocked silence. *War*, she thought, *will I ever find a husband?*

'Doringspruit has been appointed as the place for everyone to assemble when the call comes. Come, Sannie, you must begin to bake some rusks. We are going to need plenty. A soldier needs sustenance, and what better sustenance than that which is baked with the loving hands of a daughter.'

***

The following evening, in the stillness of the night, a messenger banged on the front door of the Doringspruit farmstead. Hendrik leapt from his bed and raced to open it. A young boy, no more than fourteen, stood on the front veranda.

'Oom,' he said excitedly, whilst removing his hat. 'A declaration of war has been announced in Pretoria. All the men in the district will gather here at first light to form a Commando.'

'Magtig!' cried Hendrik. 'Our time has come. The Lord be with us.'

Hendrik watched the youth gallop from the yard. His eagerness for battle was displayed by the speed in which he rode his pony. His boyish shoulders were hunched while his blond hair took on the colour of the moonlight.

Hendrik turned and went back into the house. He stood for a brief moment in the voorkamer, reflecting on the news. War. That is what his nation wanted. The Lord had listened to their prayers. They would now go forth and fight for their independence. Nothing would stand in their way.

He returned to his room and went down on his knees beside the bed, which he and his wife, Johanna, had shared. The bed where his children were conceived, and where his children were born, and the bed in which his wife had died. He prayed for victory. He prayed for the safety of his daughters, he prayed for Doringspruit and all those who worked for him. He then prayed for God to protect him in battle so that he could return, in victory, to his beloved farm.

***

In the soft, pearly mist of dawn the men began to gather at Doringspruit. Hannah had not slept since hearing the news. The words of the British soldiers, who had gathered at the Governor's tea parties, rang in her ears. A handful of ignorant farmers could not match the might of the British Empire. Her fears matched the beliefs of the British. A great sense of unease swept through her as she watched the men gather in the front yard.

Through the night Sannie had slaved away in the kitchen preparing provisions for the Commando, while Marike darned her Pa's socks and replaced the lost buttons on his shirts.

The men rode in on their horses and ponies, saddlebags bulging with supplies. Hannah and Marike stood on the veranda and watched the men gather. Hannah saw the excitement on their faces and the fierce determination in their eyes. Each man came dressed in what he thought was fit for battle. Hannah recognised Oom Piet, a close friend of her Pa. His thick tobacco-coloured beard was neatly trimmed and he wore a business suit and a collar and tie. Dominee Botha wore his corduroy trousers, a waistcoat and a jacket, and Hans Bosman wore a high-crowned hat and a frock coat.

Hendrik stepped out onto the veranda wearing his best black suit, which he reserved for weddings and Christenings. His beard had been cut short, jutting out from his chin like a well-used scrubbing brush. Hannah saw in his bearing his pride and enthusiasm. This is what he wanted, a chance to show the British Empire that the Boers were not be trifled with. She turned her head away when she saw her Pa sling a bandoleer of ammunition over his shoulder. He took up his Mauser rifle and headed towards his horse.

She watched the young boys sitting proudly on their ponies. The pale golden fluff, which sprouted from their fresh faces, Hannah noticed, was left unshaven as a mark of a true man. Willem Prinsloo was the last to arrive. As he reined in his horse he saw Hannah on the veranda. He lifted his wide-brimmed hat in a silent greeting. For a few moments they held each other's eyes. Willem was the first to look away and then dismounted. Sannie stepped out of the house and walked up to where Hannah was standing.

'Look there's Willem,' she whispered. 'I've not seen him since that day. Look, he's coming over to us.'

Willem took off his hat as he climbed the stairs.

'Ladies,' he said quietly. 'I ask you please to take care of Elsa, my wife. She is carrying my child and will need the company of other young women. Her Ma is with her at Soetwater, but her Ma is old. Elsa has heard much about Doringspruit and I know she will welcome you in our home.'

Sannie watched him as he spoke. She wanted to reach out and feel his skin beneath her touch. She wanted to tell him that she still loved him and that she would pray each night for his safe return. But instead she stood silently; her eyes wide with unshed tears.

With brief bow, he turned and went down the stairs to where his horse stood. Marike slipped a comforting arm about Sannie's shoulders. 'We shall pray for his safe return,' she said. 'He is a good man, Sannie. God will protect him.'

Once all the men had gathered, Dominee Botha led the prayers. The men stood with their hats grasped to their chests and their naked heads bowed. Dominee Botha's melodic voice rang out in the cool morning air, speaking the words that were in everyone's heart. Hannah thought of the women across the land weeping. She thought of mothers weeping for their sons, daughters weeping for their devoted fathers, loving wives praying for the safe return of beloved husbands, and lovers weeping for lovers. She thought of the British, the wives of officers she had met in Cape Town. She thought of those who had left the shores of England, and the women they had left behind.

The commandant's rasping call suddenly interrupted her thoughts. 'Opsaal, saddle up.'

The men sprang into their saddles. The horses whinnied and snorted. The dust rose in the morning air and with a thunder of hooves the commando rode out of the yard and across the veld.

Hannah, Sannie and Marike stood and watched in emotional silence until they were out of sight.

***

Sannie placed the large family Bible on the dining table and watched her hands caress the faded, black linen cover. She stared at it for a long while, her fingers tracing the edges till they found the black ribbon bookmark.

She sat down and opened it. The smell of Hendrik's tobacco rose up from the pages like a breath of memories. Sannie saw her Pa as he always sat when reading the evening scriptures, his work-worn hands, palms down, either side of the Holy book while he read, his rich, melodic voice ringing out in the voorkamer.

Sannie thought back to when she was a young child. Never listening to the words, she would simply sit and watch, with love and amusement, the movements of his thick golden beard taking on a life of its own. As she grew older, she began to listen with interest and enjoy the drama the scriptures had to offer.

Outside, lightning flickered in the distance and the shriek of the water-dikkop broke the silence of the night. Sannie dropped her face into her hands and began to sob. Oh, Lord our Father; bring him back to us, she prayed. Bring them both back, Pa and Willem Prinsloo, strong and unharmed.

Hannah sat on her bed reading one of the many novels, which Aunt Magda had given her. The moths and the small, brown beetles attracted to the light of her lamp, circled and buzzed about. The curtains billowed and flapped in the soft warm breeze that blew in from the open window. Tossing the book aside, she stood up and crossed the room to close the window.

On hearing a stifled sob, she stood silently with her hand poised on the handle of the window, and listened. She heard it once more and hurriedly closed the window. She then made her way to the voorkamer where she found Sannie, her face red and swollen from crying, sitting with her clenched fists pressed against her mouth.

'Sannie,' cried Hannah, and hurried over to where she was seated. Sannie, on hearing Hannah's footsteps, banged her clenched fist on the table in a controlled fit of temper, her wet face glistening in the yellow light of the lamp.

'Why, Hannah?' she spluttered. 'Why did our men have to go and fight?' She dropped her face into her hands and sobbed. 'We were all so happy here at Doringspruit. What do they want, these men with greed and blood on their hands? They have fought the Kaffirs and now they are fighting us…for what?…the gold?…the diamonds?'

Marike, on hearing Sannie's angry voice, hurried into the voorkamer. She reached out her hand and placed it on Sannie's shoulder.

'Hush, my sister,' she said softly. 'We have prayed for Pa and the good Lord will deliver him to us, safe and well. Pa said that the Lord will ride out with the Boers, for this is our land. It is the land He has chosen for us.'

'Yes, Marike, but some men will die. That fact we must face. Will Pa be one of them? …Will Willem Prinsloo be another?' Sannie gasped as she spoke, her chest heaving in between her words.

'I also miss Pa, Sannie. I haven't slept since Pa left,' said Marike softly.

Sannie's wet face was contorted with emotion. 'Oh yes, Marike,' she spluttered. 'We have all missed Pa. He's been gone for ten days but neither you, nor Hannah, has mentioned the reading of the Scriptures. Don't you think Pa would have wanted us to continue the nightly readings?'

Marike took Sannie's hand in hers. 'Sannie, the Scriptures simply would not be the same without Pa. We must continue to pray every night to our Lord that this war will end, and Pa will return to us.'

Hannah stared down at the opened Bible on the table and said gently, 'Sannie, if you wish to read the Scriptures you must do so, if it makes you feel better.'

'I want them home, both Pa and Willem Prinsloo,' choked Sannie. 'Yes, I know Willem Prinsloo is a married man, but I want him to return to Soetwater.'

With a gentle hand, Marike lovingly brushed the hair from her sister's swollen, wet face. 'Since I cannot read, Sannie, would you read the Scriptures to us tonight? I would like that.'

Hannah sat down and listened to Sannie as she falteringly read a psalm from the Bible. While the words rang out in the silence of the room, their thoughts were with their men on the veld, sleeping beneath the great black dome of the African sky.

When she was finished, Sannie quietly closed the Holy Book and bent her head in prayer. Silently, she prayed for the two men that she loved so dearly to be protected from the horrors of war.

**

Once again, through the veld gossip of the servants, the Van Vuuren sisters learnt that Elsa Prinsloo had been delivered safely of a baby boy.

Marike immediately rummaged through her chest of fabric remnants to find something suitable to make the tiny infant a nightshirt. Marike could never throw any scrap of fabric away, no matter how small. Their Pa had always been generous with their clothing. When the smous, Hymie Rosenberg, called in at Doringspruit with his pedlar's wagon of goods, Hendrik always allowed the girls to choose whatever fabric they wanted, no matter what the cost, for he knew Marike would turn the flat yards of cloth into well fitting, stylish dresses.

Marike sat on the veranda with her head bent over the tiny nightshirt, her fat fingers working the needle and thread with skilled dexterity. The sharp morning sun slanted across the yard and the air was still. The poplar trees glistened in the distance with healthy summer foliage.

Hannah had gone out hunting for guinea fowl, since it had long since been decided that the chickens were to be spared for the eggs. Honnie had happily joined Hannah, as she never missed the opportunity to be out in the veld with her mistress. Sannie was in the orchard with Palesa, picking peaches. Once picked, they would lay them out in the sun to dry.

At the sound of horses' hooves, Marike looked up from her sewing. A small band of men rode towards the farmstead, a cloud of red dust rising in their wake.

Marike dropped her sewing onto the bench on which she was seated and stood up. As the men neared the house, she walked to the end of the veranda to greet them.

They drew up their horses sharply, and removed their slouch hats. Manoeuvring his horse to the front, the leader of the group cleared his throat of phlegm. He spat a large globule on the ground with considerable force, and then began to speak.

'Good morning, Mejevrou. My name is Bert Vernooten.'

Marike, feeling a prickle of fear run through her, studied the men. They were shoddily dressed and their horses looked tired and undernourished. She noticed

58

the man who called himself Bert Vernooten scanning the yard with his small black eyes. Yes, they were Boers, thought Marike, but that did not mean that they came as comrades.

***

'Good day, gentlemen, Meneer Vernooten. Can I be of any help?' she said, with a voice that showed no hostility yet rang with caution.

'We have been ordered to requisition all the horses and ponies. The Commandos are in dire need of them,' said Vernooten, with an air of authority.

Marike stood with her hands on her wide hips and said with trepidation. 'And Meneer, what do you expect us to use for transport? We cannot offer you our ponies.'

'Mejevrou, it is not a matter of offering us the ponies. We have been ordered to take them.'

Marike's eyes scanned the distance, fearful that Hannah would return, and Jonas too had taken one of the horses into Hemel to fetch the post.

Sannie came out onto the veranda and stood beside Marike. She straightened the lace collar of her dress, and with a sympathetic voice said, 'We have three ponies in the veld that you can have.'

Marike turned to face her. Sannie's willingness to part with their ponies astounded her. The horses and ponies belonged to Doringspruit; they belonged to their Pa. It was not Sannie's position to give their Pa's possessions to whomever she saw fit.

'Do you have any letters of authority?' asked Marike, her fingers fidgeting with the hem of her apron. 'We simply cannot give our ponies to just anyone who rides in from nowhere. What authority do you have?'

'This is war, Mejevrou. War. We have been ordered by our general.' Vernooten looked out across the yard. His face and beard were covered in a layer of red dust. He tugged at the reins, dug his heels into the horse's flanks and headed in the direction of the field where the three ponies stood happily grazing in the quiet tranquillity of the morning.

Sannie's eyes blazed with anger as she addressed Marike.

'Our men need the horses, Marike, or are you too stupid to realise this? How dare you challenge them! It could be Pa who needs the ponies or it could be Willem Prinsloo.'

'Or it could be a loose band of thieves commandeering our ponies, Sannie. We cannot simply trust everyone who rides onto this farm. We have ourselves to protect. If you had told them that Hannah was out hunting, they would have taken Wit Ster as well. Hannah needs her horse to hunt. And Jonas, thank goodness, was out too.'

Sannie turned on her heel and marched back into the house. Her rigid back and squared shoulders told Marike that she was consumed with rage.

That night the three women sat around the dining table listening to Sannie reading from the Bible. The servants had finished in the kitchen and had returned to their huts. Sannie closed the Holy Book and bent her head in silent prayer.

'I feel uncomfortable about the incident this morning,' began Hannah. 'How do we know they took our ponies for the commandos. We have never seen them before. Those ponies would fetch a good price in Pretoria.'

'It is our duty to look after our men,' hissed Sannie, looking up from the Bible. 'I could see they were Boer commandos, Hannah. It is our duty to support our men, no matter how difficult it is for us.'

'Boer commandos they might well be, but that doesn't make them our friends,' replied Hannah. 'Opportunists roam the countryside every day. As women alone on this farm we must be cautious. No one is to be trusted.'

Hannah, with the memories of Frans and Petrus Badenhorst flashing through her mind, shivered in the warmth of the evening.

'We mustn't argue,' said Marike, raising her hands to silence the two sisters.

'We can't let this happen again,' said Hannah, her voice rising with concern. 'We must hide our valuables. Anyone could ride onto Doringspruit and demand whatever they want. Pa has left us to look after the farm. We can't let Pa return and find everything has gone. No, we will bury our valuables, that way no one will know what we've got or where we have hidden it.'

The women sat silently in contemplation. Outside, somewhere on the veranda, the incessant sound of a cricket jangled Sannie's nerves. 'Oh, that cricket! Get outside, Honnie. Find it and kill it,' she said, amidst a new outburst of sobbing. 'If Pa was here, he would not rest until it was found.'

Hannah twirled a loose strand of hair around her finger. The war had only just begun and already, as sisters, they were divided in their thoughts. She reflected on the day's events, and at once knew they were more vulnerable than they had ever realised. They were alone on a farm, hours away from their nearest neighbours.

'We must find a place to bury our valuables,' began Hannah. 'Pa has a trunk in which he keeps his gold sovereigns and I have the diamonds that Aunt Magda has given me. If marauders enter our home, what hope do we have?'

Sannie picked up the large, heavy family Bible and returned it to its resting place on the dresser between two large, Delft vases. She sat down once more and pushed the lamp into the centre of the table. Leaning forward in a conspiratorial manner she whispered.

'We can bury it in the floor of the old stable. No one ever goes in there. The servants mustn't know either; what they don't know, they cannot tell.'

'We must hide some of the gold in the house,' continued Hannah. 'If we need to flee at a moment's notice, we need to take it with us.'

'There is no place in the house that is safe from the prying eyes of the servants, Hannah,' snapped Sannie.

Hannah stared into the flame of the lamp that was casting a golden pool of light on the surface of the yellowwood table. A moth fluttered against the glass burning itself with the heat. It fell to the table and lay with its velvet wings half folded.

'Maybe...' said Hannah softly. 'Maybe we should sew some of the sovereigns into the hems of our coats. We never have the need to wear the coats now that we don't go to Nagmaal, Communion, any more. Who is going to steal a woman's coat?'

Marike looked at Hannah and smiled. 'That's a good idea. I will sew the sovereigns into little pockets in the hem. I'll begin tomorrow. I'll work on the coats in our bedroom. Tell the servants I am ill and mustn't be disturbed.'

'Tomorrow night, we will dig the hole,' whispered Sannie. 'We might have to work throughout the night. We are women, we don't have the strength of men.'

***

Thin wisps of cloud drifted across the moon like remnants of tattered lace. The prickly pears, which stood tall like multi-headed giants, threw shadows across the walls of the disused stable. The Van Vuuren sisters crept across the yard in silence. Honnie, with her ears close to her head, raced off into the blackness chasing a nightjar.

Once inside the crumbling stable, they lit the lanterns. Sannie began digging with a pickaxe while Hannah scraped away the loose soil. They took it in turns. While two of them worked, the third sister rested.

'Ja, I think that's deep enough, Hannah,' gasped Sannie, brushing away the loose hair from her scarlet face. The dust from the soil had risen up and clouded the pale light of the lanterns. Marike stared into the hole. Outside, the night breeze rustled the fine branches of a peach sapling, which had sprung up from a discarded pip. It scraped against the wall of the stable like hands clawing at the lid of a coffin.

'I think it's deep enough,' Marike's words were barely a whisper. 'After all, it's not a grave.'

'For me it is a grave,' retorted Sannie, choking back her tears. 'It's a sad day when you have to hide what is rightfully yours. I wish Hell and damnation on the British. I wish...I wish that all this was over, and every khaki was dead.'

Marike and Hannah lowered the wooden trunk bearing Hendrik's wealth into the dark depths of the soil. Hannah took the biscuit tin containing her diamonds and placed it on top. One by one they began to shovel the earth back into the hole, covering their tangible wealth, like dogs burying their bones, to hide it from the covetous eyes of their enemy. Outside, in the darkness of the night, a jackal barked.

We are burying our possessions and burying our dreams, thought Sannie. Only to be unearthed when this war is over. Until then they must be hidden in the darkness of uncertainty.

Chapter Six

Tristan sat comfortably in the saddle. Overhead, the African sky was flawless, the blue only broken by a hot, pulsating sun. He had ridden out with two regulars to scan the veld for any sign of a Boer encampment. His trained eye searched for the smallest of clues, a mere glint of a rifle butt, or a small spiral of smoke from a campfire, the smell of tobacco.

The horses were in dire need of watering since it was midday. The grass was dry and rustled beneath their hooves. Tristan pressed on, searching for an appropriate place to rest. He found a small stream, which ran between large boulders at the foot of a kopje.

Reining in his horse, he signalled to Trooper Hammond and Sergeant Sherbourne to join him.

Tristan dismounted and left his horse to crop the yellow grass. He pulled off his helmet and mopped his brow with his handkerchief. He had been in this God-forsaken land for six months. He had kept a journal, but there was little to write about. Nothing changed; the sun blistered everything that lay beneath it. Rain was a rarity, clouds were never seen, dust engulfed everything and worked itself insidiously into every pore of his body. This was Africa.

He made his way down to the stream and dropped down onto his haunches and splashed the water on his face. Even the water in the streams was not welcoming. They had been warned of diseases—never drink from still water, drink from the rushing eddies.

He thought of Tylcoat and its lush lawns and civilised gardens. He thought of his father, and the disappointment his father felt with his enlistment. He thought of Felicity. He had no news from home. Letters were heavily censored and, besides, he had been on reconnaissance for three months and post would not reach him until he returned to headquarters. He was thankful for that. He had no wish to know what he had left behind. Felicity had swum in and out of his thoughts, leaving an ever-increasing trail of guilt.

He stood up and made his way along the bank of the stream. He heard the shot at the same time as he felt the pain. A second shot exploded from somewhere close by, ringing eerily amidst the rocks and boulders of the kopje. Some doves took flight, their wings flapping in hysteria. Then there was silence. He heard the movement of Trooper Hammond in the grass nearby.

'Are you okay, Sir?' he whispered. 'I think I caught him, brazen bugger he was, standing on the ridge like God almighty. Fucking Boer.'

'My leg. He got me in the leg.' Tristan looked down and saw the blood seeping from his thigh. It trickled to the ground beside him, the dry earth drinking it up thirstily, leaving nothing but a growing dark stain.

'We need to get him to a field hospital,' said Sergeant Sherbourne. 'He'll bloody bleed to death if we're not careful. All I can do for now is staunch the flow.'

'Who's to say there aren't any more bastards out there waiting to pick us off,' said Hammond. 'We best wait till dark. Until then, we must lie low.'

Tristan lay in the sparse shade of a small thorn tree. He felt the pain and he felt the heat. The flies were quick to gather around the wound; their incessant buzzing a reminder of the hostility of this unforgiving land.

Once again, Felicity drifted into his thoughts, her gentle but characterless face smiling at him. He thought, too, of his sister Katherine. Felicity and Katherine had been best friends and when Katherine died, Felicity was quick to step into the role of comforter. He hadn't thought of Katherine for many years, he could not, her death was too painful to reflect on. It was strange that he should think of her now, beautiful Katherine, his sister and best friend.

Sherbourne and Hammond felled two small trees and with a blanket, made a stretcher. The terrain was difficult and, carrying a wounded soldier, the pace was slow. After the third day moving south, Sherbourne knew they would not reach a field hospital in time.

Tristan's fever began to escalate despite their attempts to keep him shaded. Water was a scarce commodity and therefore was restricted to drinking purposes only. Sherbourne's attempts to staunch the bleeding had been successful, but the wound began to ooze pus, making it difficult to keep it clean and sterile.

Tristan lay on the stretcher, in his delirium, he was back at Tylcoat. The fire in the grate was burning his cheeks, it was hot and he could not move away. He saw his father, the pacifist, seated in the winged chair, his lean legs outstretched and crossed at the ankles. His gaunt face was barely discernible through the blue haze of cigar smoke. 'Some return as heroes,' said his father. 'Others return maimed, and some don't return at all.'

Chapter Seven

'We must ride out to see Elsa Prinsloo,' said Sannie, taking the golden brown rusks out of the oven. The smell of her baking filled the house. Marike stood with her feet apart wiping her plump hands on her apron. She had been assisting Sannie with the kneading of the next batch of rusks and preparing them for the oven.

'Yes, Sannie,' she replied enthusiastically. 'It hasn't been neighbourly of us. Willem Prinsloo asked us specifically to visit his wife, and as Christians we have failed him. The baby must be nearly three weeks old now and as yet we have not been to see if all is well. But we can't all visit; one of us must stay at home.' Marike reached out for flour and spread it evenly on the kitchen table. 'Take the Cape cart and go with Hannah, I'll remain here at the house. It's not wise for all three of us to be away.'

'You're right, Marike,' replied Sannie, whilst pressing her finger on the hot rusks. 'I'll ask Hannah to stay behind and look after the house. Ag ja, these rusks are now done.'

'No, Sannie, you and Hannah must visit. I will visit when I no longer have this nasty cough. It wouldn't be right to visit a small baby, coughing and sneezing like this. Besides, I am sure Hannah will enjoy Mevrou Prinsloo's company.'

***

Hannah and Sannie set out early one morning after making the final arrangements by sending one of farm workers with a brief note. The gifts for the new baby were carefully folded and placed in a basket. Marike had made two small night-shirts and a quilted blanket, using scraps of fabric she kept in an old chest for just such occasions.

It was a perfect morning, the veld was green from the summer storms and the birds were plentiful. As the cart bounced along the track a covey of francolin ran into the long grass, their harsh cries trailing in the morning air. A woodland kingfisher flashed its brilliant blue plumage as it swooped past to settle in a nearby acacia tree.

'I love this time of the day,' said Hannah. 'It's so quiet and clean and untouched.'

Sannie sat in stony silence, her raw, work-worn hands firmly clasped in her lap.

'You've been to Soetwater before, haven't you?' she began. 'I saw you that morning sitting on that horse like a whore with your legs apart and lust written on your face. I knew you were going to Meneer Prinsloo to fornicate.'

'Sannie...Sannie. Yes, I did go to see Willem Prinsloo, but it was to tell him that what he had overheard that morning simply wasn't the Sannie I know. I tried to explain that your reaction was totally out of character and to give you another chance. He didn't want me, Sannie. You, in your jealous rage, let yourself down.'

Sannie's face curled into a sneer. 'Of course, he didn't want you, no man wants a wanton woman for a wife, Hannah. A man is a weak creature, he will lie with a woman and spend his passion, but when a Boer takes a wife, she must be above reproach.'

'Sannie, what are you implying? Are you saying that I came here to Soetwater to...to ...'

'I know what you did, Hannah. I saw you when you returned that day. Your lips were red and swollen from your lovemaking. I saw the carnal want in your eyes.'

Hannah raised her hand and slapped Sannie across the face, forcing her head back with a jerk. Sannie's eyes blazed with unshed tears. 'How dare you suggest such evil,' whispered Hannah hoarsely. 'You have a wicked mind, Sannie. Your jealousy lost you the man you love. No man wants a woman filled with venom. It would be wise for you to control your dirty thoughts of others. Now, we're not far from the house. Pull yourself together so that we can present ourselves respectably.'

Sannie sat with her shoulders squared and stared at the track ahead, her lips pinched together in fury while the mark of Hannah's hand flamed on her cheek.

It was quite clear that Willem Prinsloo did not marry Elsa Cilliers for her good looks. She was a short woman with a square, thickset body. Despite her bold features, she had scraped her brown, almost colourless hair from her face and tied it into a bun on top of her head giving her some height. Her dress was fashionable, and cut in such a way that it cleverly hid the recent ravages of pregnancy. Hannah was pleased that she had worn one of her better dresses given to her by Aunt Magda.

They were graciously received by Elsa Prinsloo, and were immediately introduced to Mevrou Cilliers, Elsa's mother.

'You have a beautiful home, Mevrou Prinsloo,' said Hannah, as she gazed at a large porcelain vase filled with white roses. On the walls hung some good Dutch paintings, and an elegant upright piano stood against the far wall.

'Thank you. When I married Meneer Prinsloo, I brought some of my own possessions with me. I inherited quite a few good pieces from my Oupa, grandfather, Meneer Boshoff.'

Sannie stood with a sullen expression on her face. *Had it not been for Hannah, this would've been my home,* she thought bitterly. *I would have made it equally as beautiful, if not more so.*

Coffee was served in elegant china cups and Mevrou Cilliers, thankful for company, could not stop talking. Hannah was pleased to be able to discuss Cape Town with someone who had been there, and had travelled extensively. They laughed and chatted about the shops in Adderley Street, and where one could buy the best shoes and gloves. They exchanged notes on the best picnic spots, and the finest restaurants. Hannah knew the first threads of longing for the Cape were beginning to weave their way into her heart.

A servant, carrying the new arrival, interrupted their conversation. She placed the baby in a small wooden cradle, which stood close to where Elsa sat. Both Hannah and Sannie stood up and crossed over to peek at the infant.

'I have named him Willem Gideon Johannes Prinsloo. But we call him Gideon' said Elsa, with pride. 'Isn't he a beautiful child? So much like his Pa.'

For the first time in many weeks, Hannah saw a composed expression wash over Sannie's face. Her lips turned upwards and a pink flush lit her cheeks. She stretched out her hand and with a tentative finger, stroked the baby's cheek.

'Yes, he is a handsome child, Mevrou Prinsloo. I know he will bring you much joy,' said Sannie, her eyes fixed on the sleeping infant.

The visit went all too quickly for the women. Hannah had enjoyed Mevrou Cilliers' tales of her travels abroad, and Elsa Prinsloo's creative ideas. Sannie could not bear to be parted from the sleeping Gideon, and Mevrou Cilliers was intoxicated with the fresh pastures in which she could regale all her stories of adventure. Elsa was pleased to have a break in her daily routine. She had always loved socialising when she lived in Pretoria, and now found living on an isolated farm, tedious and lonely.

The women parted with affectionate farewells, promising to visit regularly. In this time of war, which cast long shadows over their lives, friendships were welcomed.

Chapter Eight

'His fever is worse this morning,' said Trooper Hammond. 'We can't keep dragging him on. We have to find somewhere where he can recover, and then get him to a field hospital. It's been three bloody days now and it's beginning to put us all at risk. These fucking Boers are everywhere. And besides, it's hard to keep the bloody jackals away. They can smell the blood from fucking miles away. I swear I saw vultures yesterday. Christ almighty, that would be a dead give-away.'

Sergeant Sherbourne knew this was true. He looked down at his captain and wondered if they would get him to a field hospital alive. He ran his hand over Tristan's forehead. 'There's a farm a few miles from here,' he said, to the uncouth trooper sitting on his haunches beside Tristan. 'It's probably a few miles to the west, I saw the smoke at first light this morning.'

'It'll be a bloody Boer farm, you'll not be welcome,' replied Trooper Hammond. 'They're fucking barbarians; they'll shoot at anything that moves. Bloody savages the lot of 'em.'

'We have no choice. The captain can't go on. If we carry on he'll die, if the Boers are hostile, we'll all die. It's a chance we must take.'

Sherbourne swung himself up into the saddle and cantered off in the direction of the thin trailing smoke, which was spiralling into a flawless blue sky.

As he neared the farmhouse, a dog came racing out. It barked incessantly while circling his horse.

'Honnie, hou stil, be quiet,' called Marike, as she came out onto the veranda. Sherbourne dismounted and put his hand out for Honnie to smell, and then ruffled the top of the dog's head. Honnie was silenced and trotted happily at his side as the sergeant approached the stairs leading up to the veranda.

'I am in need of some help,' he said respectfully. 'One of my men is injured and I need a place where he can rest.'

Marike stared at him blankly. Sherbourne felt uncomfortable confronting this large woman with ice blue eyes and a large, rotund body. A moment later a second woman appeared with a rifle grasped tightly in her hands and a tirade of Dutch flowing from her lips. Together they looked formidable. *God help the Empire,* he thought wryly, *if these are the women folk that are the backbone of the Boer nation.*

Hannah was on the far side of the orchard picking some yellow clingstone peaches. The clingstone were always the last peaches to ripen, and when this crop was finished, it would be the last of the summer fruits.

She heard Honnie barking, but continued to pick the peaches, comfortable in the knowledge that both Sannie and Marike were in the house with the servants. After some time, when the barking continued, she put down her basket, and hurried round to the front of the house where she saw an English soldier, his face red from exertion, standing beside his horse. Immediately, she looked towards the front veranda and saw Sannie standing with the hunting rifle raised against her shoulder, her head tilted to one side as she studied the soldier through the rifle sights. Marike stood beside her, her hands nervously twisting her apron, babbling incoherently.

Harold Sherbourne spotted Hannah as she approached from the far side of the house. Is there no end to these ignorant Boer wenches, he thought? They come creeping out like white maggots from rotting flesh.

'Can I help you?' asked Hannah, in her clear, perfect English.

Sherbourne was quite taken aback by the woman standing before him. Her cotton dress was in the palest of blue, accentuating the vivid blueness of her eyes and tendrils of blond hair that bracketed her flawless face. Relieved that he could at least communicate with one of the women, he cleared his throat and tried to begin his explanation. 'Perhaps you did not understand,' said Hannah impatiently. 'What can we do for you?'

Harold Sherbourne looked towards the two women on the veranda, the position of the hunting rifle had not moved. 'My captain is injured and is in desperate need of care. We've travelled far and, as yet, found no field hospital. His fever is high and I know that if he doesn't receive medical attention, he will die. I must ask you, please, to understand, and give us some help.'

'Where is he? How many of you are there?' asked Hannah with her eyes fixed steadfastly on his.

'Three of us,' he said. 'Trooper Hammond, Captain Dunn-Caldwell and myself. They are a few miles east of here. If you have a wagon that we can use, we can be back by late afternoon. Your hospitality will be rewarded.'

'What does he want?' shouted Sannie, from the veranda. 'Tell him he must leave this farm at once.'

Hannah, ignoring Sannie's demands replied. 'It is not reward that we are looking for. He is a man in need, and as good Christians, we will help him. We do not have any medical supplies that you can take with you.'

'Any assistance will be of great help,' replied Sherbourne.

'Bring your captain here to the farm and we'll do what we can for him, but then you must be on your way.'

Hannah led him round to the side of the house and across to the barn, where they kept a small cart. 'I think this should be suitable,' she said brusquely. 'It is light weight and can be drawn by a single horse.'

He harnessed his horse to the cart while Hannah went into the house to fetch him fresh water and some fruit.

Sannie thrust the rifle into Marike's hands and followed Hannah into the house.

'What are you doing?' screeched Sannie. 'Why are you giving them some peaches. Surely you're not going to give them to that…that…to our enemy.'

'He has asked us, Sannie, and in a very polite and humble manner, to help his captain.'

A torrent of words flowed from Sannie's lips. 'Help his captain? He is the enemy, a blood sucking rooinek, Hannah. He is on our land and needs to be shot.'

'Shot,' retaliated Hannah. 'Then what? The rest of them will come after us. Use your head, Sannie.'

'Will he bring the cart back?' screeched Sannie. 'Answer that. We'll never see that cart again.'

Hannah dropped the last peach into a bag and turned to the puce-coloured Sannie.

'I have agreed that they can bring their injured captain back to the house,' said Hannah, as she brushed past Sannie on her way out to the yard.

Shocked and infuriated, Sannie screamed after her. 'How can you bring the enemy back to our home, Hannah. You have invited him into this house? And who is to say we will ever see the cart again, like Pa's ponies, taken, never to be seen again.'

'Yes, and you were very quick to give the ponies away. Why Sannie, were you hoping they would be grateful enough to marry you one day?'

'How dare you…how dare you say such a thing. I am not the whore in this house.'

Hannah turned on Sannie. 'There are no whores in this house, only those who think uncharitable thoughts, and that is worse than a whore.'

Sannie stood and stared after her sister. She watched Hannah hand the peaches and the fresh canteen of water to the British soldier. She hurriedly made her way back to the veranda and stood beside Marike, her anger flaring across her face.

'How dare she invite the enemy into our home. How dare she!' she rasped. 'He is nothing to us. His bullets are fired against our loved ones, yet we must have him under our roof? The next time a Commando calls in for supplies, I will turn him over to them.'

'Let us get through the first problem,' said Marike quietly. 'We, as Christians, cannot leave a man to die in the veld like an injured dog.'

'Yes, we can when that dog is a British soldier, enemy to our nation,' replied Sannie, with spittle flying from her angry lips. 'He can rot under the blazing sun for all I care. Let the vultures pick his bones till there is nothing left of him other than vulture excrement.'

Marike stared at Sannie in disbelief. 'Sannie, such words are vile. I must remind you that you are a Christian, and like a true Christian, you will speak no ill of others.'

Sannie turned and hurried back into the house, leaving Marike standing on the veranda. Hannah returned to the orchard where she had left the peaches. She gathered up the basket, heavy with large sun ripened fruit, and made her way back towards the house. Sannie came rushing out of the kitchen and raced towards Hannah, her skirts clutched in her hands. She briefly looked over her shoulder to see that Marike was out of earshot, and then whispered contemptuously. 'Is there no end to your wantonness? Is it the fact that they are men? You want them under our roof so that you can flaunt your fancy ways, so that you can fornicate with them like you did with Willem Prinsloo.'

Hannah stepped past Sannie, and without looking back said, 'There is another basket in the orchard. Make yourself useful and bring it in.'

***

73

It was dark when they heard the sound of the cart returning. Sannie left the voorkamer and hurried to her bedroom, which she shared with Marike, and watched through a chink in the curtain, the events taking place in the yard, unobserved in the darkness of the room.

Hannah and Marike went out to the cart, accompanied by Adam and Jonas. Hannah had asked the two farm workers to help with the arrival of the injured English soldier. She also felt comforted by their presence knowing that should this be an ambush, both Adam and Jonas would prove their loyalty to the family.

Since Hendrik's departure, Adam had positioned himself at the top of the hierarchy of the servants, keeping them in line and ordering them about. Adam knew all too well that no black man would take orders from a woman, regardless of colour. There was very little need for Hannah to instruct Adam on the running of the farm; Adam had been Hendrik's faithful servant from the time he had been a young man. Doringspruit was Adam's home, and he knew every stone and every tree, he loved the farm and he loved Hendrik. Doringspruit, he felt, had been good to him, he had many wives each with many healthy children, and he had a good herd of cattle, making him a rich man.

Jonas, too, had been a loyal labourer. He worked long hours for Hendrik, and Hendrik had always rewarded him well. Now that Hendrik was away, Jonas had taken it upon himself to protect the women of Doringspruit, not only the daughters of Hendrik Van Vuuren but also Abraham's family. Abraham, another faithful and loyal servant to Hendrik, had ridden out with the Commando as an agter-ryer.

Adam stood close by and watched the white men lift the injured and unconscious soldier onto the makeshift stretcher. His suspicious eyes noted the highly polished boots and the well-made saddles. He did not understand the words that passed between the soldiers, and felt disquieted in the way the men conducted themselves. He heard sharp words snapping from Hannah's lips, while her arms waved about in concern for the dying man.

Trooper Hammond and Sergeant Sherbourne carried Tristan Dunn-Caldwell into the house. Hannah had cleared her room, moving her belongings into her Pa's room, and made her room suitable for nursing. She could not, under any circumstances, put any Englishman in her Pa's bed, and more so now that Britain was at war with her nation. Her conscience was divided; this was a man who needed help, and who would not help a dying man? Although this dying man was trained to kill and maim on the battlefield, her conscience would not allow her to turn her back on anyone in their time of need.

Tristan was gently laid on Hannah's bed, which had the sheets turned down ready to receive him. She stared down at the young captain. For Hannah, he simply was not just a dying soldier, but a man who belonged to someone, someone's son, someone's brother, someone's husband. His death would make a difference to someone's life. She would nurse him with the dedication she would give to her Pa, for that is what she would expect from others if her Pa were in the same position. With a large pair of scissors, she began cutting away his clothes. Sergeant Sherbourne stepped forward and began to help.

'What is his name?' asked Hannah, as she struggled with the thickness of the fabric.

'Captain Dunn-Caldwell,' replied Sherbourne.

'Yes, that I know, but what must I call him if I am to get him out of this fever?'

'Tristan,' Sherbourne answered, whilst removing the last remnants of Tristan's trousers.

Once all his clothes had been removed, Hammond and Sherbourne turned Tristan on his side for Hannah to look at his injury. As she gently pulled the dirty dressings from the wound, his rotten flesh, which was stuck to bandages, peeled away allowing the thick yellow pus to run free. The stench from the wound rose up, assaulting Hannah's nostrils. She turned her head away briefly, caught her breath, and then examined the wound closely. The flesh was parted like an overripe, burst plum. The exposed bone was fractured and Hannah was able to see the path the bullet had taken.

'This will take some time to heal,' she said, as the foetid smell of the wound filled the room. 'Fortunately, the bullet passed right through, had it remained lodged in the leg it would have created a further infection. So we must be grateful for that.'

Hannah washed the wound with salt water then applied iodine generously. With clean bandages made from old sheets, she packed and dressed the gaping hole in his leg. Carefully they turned Tristan onto his back, and with a piece of clean flannel, squeezed drops of water into his mouth.

'I will sit with him throughout the night,' she said, as she gently dabbed the flannel on his dry lips. 'He's dehydrated and I need to feed him little drops of water. His fever is high and he needs constant cold washes to bring his temperature down.'

'We will help you,' said Sherbourne, pulling a chair up to the bed.

'You cannot remain under our roof,' replied Hannah. 'You can sleep on the veranda or in the yard, even in the veld if you so wish, but not under our roof.'

'We will be no trouble,' replied Hammond, his eyes darting around the room. 'We only wish to be of assistance.'

'I don't care,' retorted Hannah. 'I can take care of this man without any help. Now, if you please, can you leave us? I am going to be busy all night.'

The two soldiers reluctantly left the house, and, only when Sannie saw them out in the yard, did she emerge from her room.

'I forbid them to sleep in this house, the dying soldier is enough,' she said, staring down at Tristan.

'I have already told them, Sannie, I don't care where they sleep.'

Sannie went into the kitchen to make a fresh pot of coffee. If Hannah was going to be up all night, she would need plenty of coffee. While Hannah was awake, thought Sannie, the two English soldiers would not be able to enter the house unheard. She went to the rifle rack, took the rifles from their hooks, and carried them back to her room, where she hid them under her bed.

Tristan's delirious mind was once again back at Tylcoat. He was a boy, running along the paths of the rhododendron walk; a fine drizzle of rain was on his hot cheeks. The rhododendrons were in full flower, the blooms heavy and drooping from the rain. As he brushed past their branches, drops splashed against his clothes and into his face. He ran out of the dell and across the lawns to the gravel path, and then up the wide sweeping stairs, which led to the grand hall.

Then he was older, he was down at the lake with Katherine, her face swimming before him in the mist. She was calling him. Tristan, Tristan, but as he drew closer she disappeared into a diaphanous cloud. He called out to her, Katherine, Katherine. Katherine did not answer, but silently beckoned him with her long slender hands. He reached into the radiance, her face floating before him, pink and smiling, but the light in her eyes was gone. Katherine, Katherine, he called.

'Magtig,' exclaimed Marike the next morning in the kitchen. 'I never slept a wink with that confounded English soldier. Katherine, Katherine, he called all night.'

Thuli giggled as she stirred the mealiemeal in the large cast iron pot on the stove. Sannie, cracking the eggs into a bowl, looked up and said, 'I will not feed them, the English soldiers, Marike, they must find their own food.'

Thuli moved about the kitchen with her baby tied onto her back with a blanket. She hummed as she went about her duties, her lean body moving with the rhythm of her tune. Sannie looked up from her baking to see Trooper Hammond standing in the open doorway of the kitchen, leaning lazily against the frame with his small, grey eyes fixed on Thuli.

'Get out of my kitchen,' she yelled, but knew the words were futile since he could not understand them. She raised her plump arm and pointed past him.

'Fucking peasants,' he mumbled, and with an appreciative look at Thuli, turned and went outside.

Marike went into the room where Hannah was nursing the captain. Seeing the strain on Hannah's face, she said kindly. 'Can I bring you some coffee, Hannah. It's been a long night for you.'

'No, thank you, Marike. I will come and have breakfast with you. Call me when it's ready.'

Hannah looked down at the sleeping man. His high fever had abated, but he was still warm and unaware of the world around him. She noticed how perfect his hands were, his fingers were straight and his nails were cut square. They were the hands of a man, yet they were not worn or scarred, but smooth and lightly tanned. His thick, dark hair curled onto his damp forehead. Despite his square angular jaw and perfect, straight nose, his features were slightly irregular. Hannah had been introduced to many men in Cape Town, some were fine looking men, others good looking in a dandyish sort of fashion.

The English captain, now lying in her bed, was by far the most appealing man she had ever seen, despite the fact he had the pallor of a dying man. She wondered who Katherine was, his wife or his lover. She knew that she had to make this man well, so that he could return to her, for Katherine was a woman waiting, as they were waiting for their Pa, and Elsa, waiting for her husband.

She washed his face with a cold damp cloth and then left the room to find Sannie and Marike, so that they could have their breakfast together.

'I caught him starring at Thuli, Hannah,' said Sannie, as she placed the rusks on the table in the voorkamer. 'It was that younger one with little eyes like a snake. His eyes followed her every movement. I don't like it. They must go. I can smell trouble when I see it.'

'I watched him follow Thuli into the yard,' continued Marike, with a look of concern on her face. 'I agree with Sannie, they cannot be trusted.'

'I'll speak to Sergeant Sherbourne,' replied Hannah, and immediately stood up. 'I'll tell them they must leave at once.'

She went out onto the veranda where the two men were drinking coffee. Sherbourne was seated on the bench, and Trooper Hammond sat on the low wall with his feet up, basking in the sun. As Hannah approached, it was only Sherbourne who stood up. Hammond remained seated, his fingers tapping a silent beat on his thighs.

'I have to ask you to leave at once,' she began. 'Leave Captain Dunn-Caldwell with us and you can return in a few weeks to check on his progress. If the Commandos call in and find you here, you will be shot and they will accuse us of treason.'

'We cannot leave our captain at your mercy,' sneered Hammond. 'Once our backs are turned, you'll have a bloody bullet through his heart, you will. Oh, no, we're staying here until he is well, even if it takes a month or two.'

'In that case,' replied Hannah. 'You must leave now and take your captain with you.'

'We'll go,' said Sherbourne, raising his hand to silence Hammond. 'But I'll be back soon. We are grateful to you, and I must thank you on behalf of our regiment and Captain Dunn-Caldwell's family for the kindness you have shown him.'

Hannah remained on the veranda and watched the soldiers mount their horses. It was only when they were out of sight, she returned to the voorkamer.

***

Hannah remained at the bedside of her patient, but Marike agreed to help out one morning when Hannah needed to go hunting for guineafowl and buck. Her morning proved to be successful, so Hannah returned home sooner than expected. On her return she found bun-size balls of raw dough tied to the inside of her patient's wrists, one on each temple held in place by a bandage wrapped around his head, and one tied to his neck.

'Marike, what is this?' she exclaimed.

'It's a good traditional remedy, Hannah, and it works. The raw dough held at the pulse of a patient reduces the fever. Ma always did it when Sannie and I were children. I remember it well. When we visited Mevrou Joubert last year, her youngest daughter was ill with a fever and Mevrou Joubert said it was a fine way to bring the temperature down.'

'Not in this house, Marike. I know you mean well, but not in this house.' Hannah hastily pulled at the bandages releasing the raw dough. 'I don't want to offend you, Marike, but it makes no sense.'

Long after Marike had left the room, Hannah was still laughing quietly to herself. Even under trying and stressful circumstances there was always something to humour the heart.

During the day when Hannah needed to rest, Thuli sat beside Tristan feeding him small droplets of water. The fever came and went, but his wound showed good signs of healing. The infected area was washed every day and treated with the little remaining iodine.

Tristan was once again lost in his dreams. He was running through the woods on the Tylcoat estate, the damp air fresh against his skin. The sound of the birds echoed through the trees and the leaves rustled beneath his feet. He ran and ran until the woods ended. The brilliance of the sun in the mist dazzled his eyes. As he ran, the iridescent, golden glow grew brighter and brighter. He opened his eyes and with some confusion looked about the room. The afternoon sun shone through an open window and filled the room with yellow light. The whitewashed walls glowed in its brightness. Outside the birds chattered noisily, and in the passage way beyond the room was the rustle of skirts. He had no recollection of where he was, or what had happened.

He looked around the unfamiliar surroundings. On the far wall hung a faded photograph of a woman which was framed in a simple black frame, and beside the window stood a wardrobe, large and crudely fashioned, but the soft yellow sheen of the wood made it a handsome piece of furniture. On the pedestal beside his bed stood a bowl and a floral water jug that was partly chipped. A chair stood close by, made from the same wood as the wardrobe, with strong armrests and a seat made from a latticework of thin leather strips. Lying on the chair was a book with a piece of cream-coloured lace sandwiched between the pages, no doubt a bookmark. The spine of the book faced him, and on it he read, 'Pride and Prejudice' by Jane Austen. A shock of pain shot down his leg bringing back faint memories of the incident.

A young woman entered the room, her violet blue eyes betraying her surprise. He stared at her for some time, unable to ask the questions that needed to be asked. As she hurried over to the bed her skirts rustled, the sound was strangely familiar, a sound that he recognised, like gentle whispers of kindness.

Hannah had left her patient for several minutes. The afternoon was warm and she had gone into the kitchen to pour a glass of peach juice for herself. Outside, in the yard, the grey lourie called as it bounced about the branches in the orchard. No doubt, Hannah thought, if Sannie was in the kitchen, she would've raced outside, arms flailing, to chase the bird from the fruit. Hannah finished her juice and rinsed the glass, then returned to her patient.

As she entered the room she pulled up with a start. During the few minutes of her absence her patient had regained consciousness. His green eyes held hers as she stood in the doorway. Suddenly this man was now a stranger. She had come to know every crease and every line in his sleeping face. She had never heard his voice other than his feverish cries for the woman he loved, nor had she seen the colour of his eyes. As he had lain in the bed, responding to her care, he was without emotion, simply a casualty of war. Now with his searching eyes, he was human. He was suddenly an intruder in her room, a foreigner and the enemy.

Hannah hurried over to the bed and with a brusque edge to her voice said, 'welcome back.'

He raised his hand slowly, his eyes never leaving hers. Hannah took the water jug and poured some water into a mug. She raised his head gently and held the mug to his lips. He sipped thirstily and then gently pushed her hand away. She rinsed the flannel in a bowl of water and wiped his forehead.

'Tonight you must try and have a little soup,' she said, as she rinsed the flannel once again, avoiding the stranger's questioning eyes. 'You've had nothing but a few drops of water over the past week. The soup will make you stronger.'

A large square of sunlight fell across the bed. Tristan's eyes followed Hannah as she crossed the room to draw the curtain to shade it from the hot afternoon sunshine. He saw how the cotton fabric of her dress pulled against her breast as she reached out for the curtain. She had slender arms and small wrists, but her hands showed signs of hard work. He noticed the graceful movement of her neck and the fine angle of her jaw. Her eyebrows arched perfectly above her vivid eyes and her ears were small and neat, and lay close to her head. *She's little more than a girl*, he thought, *and beautiful*. Sensing his gaze was upon her, she turned and gave him a friendly smile.

'I'd better let the servants know that there will be one extra for supper tonight.'

He watched her leave the room and then turned his head and gazed out of the window with the half-drawn curtain. He was in Africa, so utterly different to his native country, England. He thought of the gentle rolling Leicestershire hills, quilted with green squares and stitched together with hedgerows and dry stone walls. Here he lay in a foreign land. There was nothing gentle about Africa. The sun pulsated with merciless heat and the vast endless sky was littered with vultures. Rivers flowed swiftly with unspeakable dangers, or they flowed not at all. Thunderstorms shook the earth violently with lightning that split open the leaden skies revealing the wrath of the heavens. Death lurked around every corner, disease, hostile tribes, wild animals and unforgiving Boers. Africa was a savage land.

His weak body lay heavily in the bed. Sounds drifted into the room from the kitchen, the click of a spoon against a pot, women chatting and then laughing and then humming. The clatter of a plate that was dropped and a sharp word. More laughing and chatting. The smell of cinnamon and burnt sugar mingled with sounds of happy domesticity.

A woman entered his room; she was short with broad shoulders and wide hips. Her full face was plain with round cheeks like scarlet apples either side of her broad nose. She stood at the foot of the bed and spoke in harsh whispers, her foreign words told him nothing, but her eyes were as hostile as the world beyond the window.

Hannah entered the room and Sannie turned and left immediately.

'Your name?' whispered Tristan, speaking for the first time, his dry mouth barely moving.

'My name is Johanna Van Vuuren. But everyone calls me Hannah.'

Chapter Nine

From the bed Tristan could see a blade of light of the pastel dawn through the chinks of the curtains. He had been conscious now for three days and had seen very little of Hannah or her sisters. Hannah had assigned three Sotho women, wives of the farm workers, to attend to him. They were pleasant enough but ruthlessly thorough in washing him and changing the linen. Hannah occasionally brought in a tray of food and asked after his well-being. Her manner was efficient and hurried, which left little opportunity for him to make conversation.

He could hear the now familiar sounds of breakfast being prepared, and the chatter of the servants. He was desperate for conversation. He tried to make himself understood when his attendants were at his bedside but soon gave up. His only link to civilisation was the ever elusive Hannah.

The smell of the mealiemeal drifted into his room. At first the porridge tasted like desiccated cardboard but it grew on him, especially since one of the black women stirred in a spoon of honey and a thick block of butter. He had come to understand that the religion in this house, apart from Christianity, was food. Since there was nothing to break the monotony of the day, he looked forward to his meals.

His day started with a bowl of mealiemeal, followed by two fried eggs, fried tomato and little pumpkin cakes. On his tray there was always fresh fruit and rusks. Coffee was brought in several hours later with either a slice of cake or biscuits. Lunchtime varied considerably, but there was always meat on the plate with vegetables, and a dessert of stewed fruit or cake. Dinner in the evening was always a full meal with either guinea fowl or venison accompanied by a variety of vegetables, some of which he had never tasted before. It was not out of boredom that he enjoyed the food, he liked the subtle use of spices and herbs and the imaginative way in which it was prepared.

The closed curtains began to glow with the early morning sunlight against the window. The small chink now allowed a shaft of golden light to stream into the room. Tristan knew that it would soon be time for his breakfast tray to be brought in, the start of another day.

He thought back to Tylcoat and wondered how long it would be before his father knew that he had been injured. He wondered how long before his regiment came looking for him, and how long he would be a patient in a Boer household. The fact that he was bored comforted him, as he knew that this was a sure sign he was on the road to recovery. Luck and good fortune was on his side.

Thuli arranged the breakfast on a tray. She juggled about trying to fit it all on without the plates overlapping. As she stooped to pick it up Hannah interrupted her. 'I'll take it in this morning, Thuli. Thank you.'

Hannah entered the room and placed the tray on the pedestal beside the bed and hurried over to the window to draw back the curtains. The morning sunshine slanted across the floor in dazzling beams of light. As she swung the window open, the soothing bubbling call of the coucal drifted across the room.

'Good morning,' she said brightly.

Tristan watched her every move. 'That bird, the one calling outside, it's a strange call, yet beautiful.'

'We had rain last night, the coucal always comes out when it's been raining. It's often referred to as the rain bird…Do you need anything else?'

Tristan eased himself up into a better sitting position to receive the tray on his lap. The movement sent a sharp pain down his leg making him wince in agony.

'Yes,' he said, trying quickly to recover, his green eyes still fixed on her. 'I need conversation.'

'I mean, do you require anything in particular to eat?'

'I might not be able to eat conversation, but I desperately need it. Hannah, you are the only person I can speak to. Your servants are excellent and see to my every need, but I can't talk to them, they don't understand English. Social starvation is equivalent to nutritional starvation. Conversation is considered the best panacea for a broken and injured leg. Didn't you know that?'

'This isn't a vacation,' she said, while avoiding his gaze. 'You mustn't forget that you are the enemy, and you are here purely out of necessity.' She straightened the blankets on his bed and patted them into place.

'Hannah…'

'I would prefer it if you called me Miss Van Vuuren.'

'You did say everyone calls you Hannah, and I surmised that I might do the same.'

'It was a little forward of me, I'm sorry,' she said, as she pulled the sheet taut and tucked it tightly under the mattress.

'Miss Van Vuuren,' he said, with a wry smile. 'Will you sit with me for a little while, while I eat my breakfast?'

'There is a lot of work to be done on the farm, I can't be idle and sit around doing nothing.'

'I want to know more about your family and the farm. I've been here for ten days and I simply don't have a clue as to my whereabouts. All I know is what I see beyond that window.' He raised his hand and pointed to the window through which the sun streamed. 'Please Hannah…Miss Van Vuuren, give me some of your time. I implore you. Kindness is like salt, a little goes a long way.'

She took the tray from the pedestal and placed it on his lap, then swung the chair around and positioned it in such a way to make conversation easier.

'What do you want to know?' she asked, as she sat down.

'You can begin by telling me how I came to be here. I remember being dragged across the veld. My God, how painful it was. I remember Sherbourne and Hammond arguing all the time, the heat, the pain, and the thirst…'

'I have no idea how you became injured or who shot you,' she said. 'Sergeant Sherbourne arrived here asking for help, and we offered it. They brought you here. It's as simple as that, if you need further details, you need to ask the soldiers who accompanied you.'

Tristan toyed with the knife on his tray. 'I remember the shot ringing through a ravine. It seemed to reverberate off the rocks, making it impossible to detect where it came from. I think a sniper was positioned on the crest of the hill. The pain, it's impossible to describe. Sherbourne and Hammond did everything in their power to help me. I owe my life to them.'

He took the knife and buttered a slice of bread, then cut it in half, spreading one half with apricot jam. He took a bite and swallowed it down with a sip from his coffee cup.

'The days that followed are a blur. I seemed to slip in and out of consciousness. All I remember was Hammond and Sherbourne lifting me onto a makeshift stretcher. The pain was so great I think I must have passed out. The thought of it makes me reel. And the flies, constantly at my face, my mouth and no doubt my wound. That constant buzzing. For the rest of my life that lazy sound of flies will take me back to that ravine.'

The coucal stopped its hypnotic call, and the black collared barbet took that as its cue and began to call from the apricot tree, which grew outside the bedroom window.

'So many strange bird calls,' he said, taking another sip from his coffee cup. 'That's a new one, I haven't heard it before. At home I always took an interest in the birds. We have a fine collection of ornithological books in the library. My uncle travelled extensively around the world and is considered an authority on some species. Waders and the ducks have always caught my attention. We have a variety on the lake. As children, my sister and I would sit and count how many species visited the lake at any one time. I think the record was ten, I'm not sure.'

Hannah listened. She did not want him to stop. The sound of his voice was refreshingly new. Against her better judgement, she began to ask him questions and found for the first time, since her return from Cape Town, she was enjoying herself.

Tristan polished his plate with a small piece of bread, mopping up the yoke of the egg.

'You speak English very well, you are quite comfortable with the language,' he said, as he popped the fragment of bread into his mouth.

'My aunt in Cape Town taught me. She was married to a British officer who fought at the Battle of Majuba. That's her photograph over there,' she said, pointing to the faded sepia photograph hanging on the wall. 'I spent a little over a year with her in Cape Town.'

Tristan looked in the direction of the photograph. The woman in the picture bore a striking resemblance to Hannah.

'Why don't you look at me, Hannah?' he asked suddenly.

The colour flared in her cheeks, but still she kept her eyes averted. She did not reply. As she hurriedly stood up to lift the tray from his lap, he grasped her wrist.

'Hannah, look at me. I know I am the enemy. I know that puts you in a difficult position. But I would never, never harm you nor any member of this family.'

Hannah pulled her arm free. She tried desperately to hide the effect of his touch, praying that her eyes would not betray her. Hurriedly she lifted the tray and left the room.

The following morning, against her better judgement, Hannah once again took Tristan's breakfast tray into his room.

'I was hoping to see you today,' he said softly. The joy of seeing her was quite evident in the expression on his face. 'Hannah…Miss Van Vuuren, I want to express my gratitude to this family. As I said yesterday, I would never do anything to put you or your sisters in any jeopardy whatsoever. Once I am fit to be moved to a field hospital, I will go, but my gratitude to you will never, be forgotten.'

Hannah moved over to the window and pulled back the curtains. Outside, a gentle breeze whispered through the leaves of the apricot tree.

'What is the name of this farm?' he asked, as he watched her slim form reach out for the faded curtains.

She turned to face him. The soft light of the morning sun caught the gold of her hair, which had been pushed haphazardly from her face into a knot in the nape of her neck. 'Doringspruit,' she replied. 'The direct translation is River of Thorns. A beautiful name.'

'Please sit for a while, Hannah. I am not asking for much, just a few moments of your time.'

Hannah moved back to the chair, which stood close to the bed. She pulled it back, straightened her skirt and sat down. 'This is a simple farm, Captain Dunn Caldwell, and we are simple people.'

'This might be a simple farm and your sisters might be simple people, but Hannah, you are different. For a start, you speak the Queen's English like Queen Victoria herself, which sets you apart from your sisters.'

'Captain Dunn…'

'Tristan. I am Tristan.'

'Well Tristan, this is a working farm, and every minute is precious. We have crops to attend to, cattle to care for, and we need to be self-sufficient in these hard times. There is no time for idle chit chat. We each have our duties, and my duty is to hunt. That brings me back to the point that I have no time to sit about and be idle. And besides, you must not forget who you are in this household.'

Hannah stood up, and as she took the tray from his lap, Tristan reached out and brushed her arm.

'I am forever indebted to you and your sisters,' he said softly. 'I will never forget what you have done.'

She took the tray and without replying, hurriedly left the room. She left the tray beside the stove in the kitchen and hurried out the back door and went into the orchard. The last of the peaches hung from the branches, most of them half eaten by the birds. With her cheeks aflame, she headed in the direction of the vegetable garden. The pumpkins sat on their dead vines like white, headless Buddhas, round and obese. The runner beans were finished and young Klaas was busy digging them back into the soil. The summer, with its generous gifts of rain, would soon be over and the dry season would start. Honnie spotted her and came racing towards her, her tail high and wagging. *These feelings I have for him are absurd*, she thought, *and utterly dangerous*. She had been introduced to many Englishmen and British soldiers in Cape Town, all of them showering her with attention. She knew she only had to snap her fingers and there would be a willing party. But Tristan's green eyes were intent, and followed her with an intimacy that aroused a dangerous willingness in her. She knew it was wrong to enter his room. The servants could provide all that he needed, but his open door was like a magnet so powerful, that it was impossible to resist.

She bent down to pick up a piece of broken branch from the fig tree, and threw it for Honnie to race after. She wished the war would end and life would be normal once again, making her free to talk to anyone without insidious feelings of guilt. She made her way back to the house with Honnie at her side.

As she entered the kitchen, Sannie turned on her. 'Why were you so long in his room, Hannah? What were you talking about?'

'Merely small talk, Sannie. Is that a sin?' she snapped back, while pouring a glass of milk for herself.

'He is the enemy, and as your sister, I forbid you to enter that room,' she shouted, with malignant hatred in her eyes. A fierce surge of temper rose up in Hannah like an erupting force. Sannie, always Sannie who placed demands on the family. It was always Sannie who ruled those around her, in a despotic manner. Hannah took the glass of milk and threw it across the kitchen. The creamy, white liquid flew through the air showering everything in its wake before the glass crashed noisily to the floor.

'I will do as I please, Sannie,' hissed Hannah. 'You will not tell me what to do, whom to talk to, and what I should do. He is someone's husband, someone's brother and someone's son. I will not let your vicious mind rule this house. If you dare bring this up again, Sannie, I will ride to Hemel and find a place to live.

Then you can do your own hunting on the veld, and bask in your own malicious thoughts.'

Marike heard the raised voices and came hurrying into the kitchen. 'What's this all about?' she asked, her eyes round with shock and her face red with concern.

'Marike,' began Hannah. 'I am saying this now and I intend keeping my word. If Sannie continues this talk of vengeance, I will leave Doringspruit and find a residence in Hemel. I will not tolerate it any more. I intend doing as I please. If I wish to speak to the English captain all day, I will do so. If I wish never to speak to him at all, I will do so. It is not for Sannie to say what I can, and cannot do. Is that clear to you both?'

Hannah turned and left the kitchen and hurried out onto the front veranda and sat down on the bench. She dropped her head into her hands. What am I telling them? She asked herself. She had no intention of ever leaving Doringspruit, what made those words rush to her lips? She threw her head back and brushed the loose hair from her face. The morning was still young, yet the veranda was already engulfed in the heat of late summer.

Marike came out onto the veranda; she stood for several seconds then crossed over to the bench and sat beside Hannah. 'Hannah, we must not fight. I wish this war was over and Pa was home with us. I hate everyone who has caused this war and taken Pa from us.'

Hannah looked down at Marike's clenched hands, which were bunching her apron in her lap. Her face was wet with tears. 'I know Marike, I miss Pa. But we can't live on wishes. This is a war and we don't know how long it is going to take. We are sisters, we can't let our personal problems divide us.'

'Even though he is English, he's a handsome man, Hannah,' said Marike, her eyes staring into the distance. 'I'm not a fool. I've seen you passing his room, wanting to go in but thinking better of it. My sister, remember he is the enemy.'

'Thank you, Marike,' said Hannah placing her hand over her sister's, 'for being so understanding. Even though we cannot live on wishes, I wish I felt differently.'

Hannah stood up and went to Hendrik's room. She lifted the lid of the old wagon chest and took out a few books, which she had put there when she moved her things from her room. They were books, which Aunt Magda had given her to read. She briefly checked her appearance in the mirror, straightened her bodice, and made her way to Tristan.

She knocked briefly before entering the room, as she knew Palesa was busy with his morning ablutions.

'Come in,' he called. Hannah found him seated upright in the bed with thin strips of shaving cream on his face and a bowl of water on his lap. Palesa stood with a large mirror in her hands in which Tristan could see his reflection. He looked up as Hannah entered the room, his razor poised in his hand. With deft fingers he brushed the razor quickly in downward movements, erasing the last of the white strips, and then dropped his razor into the water.

'Thank you,' he said to Palesa who immediately returned the mirror to the vacant hook on the wall, and then hurriedly left the room.

'I've brought you something to read,' she said, placing the books on the bed. 'I'm afraid you can't be fussy, there is very little English literature in the house. These are two of the books my aunt gave me.'

He ignored the books and looked at Hannah while wiping his chin on the towel, which had been draped around his neck. 'The argument? It was about me wasn't it? Hannah, I understand if you can't talk to me. I don't know what was said but I gathered it was a heated argument. I don't want to divide this house, you must do what is best.'

Hannah looked at him directly and said, 'I am my own master, no one rules me in my own home. I will talk to whom I wish.' Realising that the embers of her temper were still smouldering, she dropped her voice before continuing. 'But you must understand, Captain Dunn-Caldwell, that Sannie does not see you as a man but only as the enemy. We are all struggling with our own thoughts and fears.'

'I have told you, Hannah, I will never put you in a dangerous position. When I'm well enough, I'll leave. As you can see, I'm not in a position to do so right now. But as an officer of the Queen's army, I give you my word that the Empire will never harm you or your sisters. Our fight is with men in arms, not with women.'

'But my sisters don't see it that way, you are fighting our nation.'

'Hannah, many Boers have joined up with the British forces,' he said, as he combed his fingers through his dark hair. She noticed how perfectly it curled and sprang back into place. As he spoke there was intensity in his voice. 'I was in Johannesburg when the Uitlanders, foreigners, panicked and tried to leave for Cape Town or Natal. Their desperate need for gold was forgotten. All they wanted was a safe passage back to where they came from. The scenes were horrific. People crammed into trains and open cattle trucks, women and children screaming and crying while the Boers jeered and pushed them into the overcrowded carriages. Everyone sees the battles from their own angle.'

Hannah stood silently. She thought of the Badenhorst brothers and their crude hands and lustful eyes. She knew that on every tree that bears fruit, some of it would be rotten. Her nation was not perfect. Her Pa believed that they were the chosen race, but Hannah had been open-minded enough to know that all men were equal.

Her thoughts went back to when she was a child. Her Pa had taken her and her sisters to Meneer Volskenk's farm. They had gone out walking after lunch and Meneer Volskenk took the sjambok with him in case they encountered snakes. They found a young boy, no more than nine or ten years of age, the son of one of the farm workers, picking a bunch of grapes. She vividly remembered Meneer Volskenk grabbing hold of the boy and taking the sjambok to him. The boy cried that he was sorry but the whip sailed ruthlessly through the air several times, striking the child across his back and forearms. Hannah had turned away and buried her face in her father's chest, but it did not block out the pitiful cries of the young boy or the sinister hiss of the sjambok. When she had looked again the child had run off, and all that remained was a small bunch of purple-green, under-sized grapes, lying half-eaten in the dirt.

She knew, with quiet discomfort, that her God-fearing nation was tainted with cruelty. Meneer Volskenk was no better than the Badenhorst brothers. *Yes*, she thought bitterly, *we all see things in different ways, and war was no exception. The Boers believed they were beyond reproach, but they had lusted for this war, and that did not rest easy in her mind.*

'I am going to ask Palesa to help me lift you out of this bed and get you into a chair,' she said, changing the conversation.

***

The chair was placed beside the window and it was a welcome relief to Tristan. His bedroom was on the side of the house; therefore, the views were not obscured by the front veranda. He studied with interest the variety of birds that visited the apricot tree; they came singly, or in pairs, and very often in small flocks.

From the window he could see Hannah ride out, at one with her horse. She was lean and graceful, moving in a sensual rhythm with her hair flying like a golden pennant in the wind. His eyes would remain fixed on the path that she took, waiting for her return. His feelings for her were growing every day. He did not welcome this powerful attraction, but now the attraction had grown into an obsession that consumed every waking hour. Their conversations together had built a friendship, and the friendship had given birth to something much deeper.

He wanted to feel her skin beneath his hands and run his fingers through her thick, silky hair. He stared down at his broken leg, immobilised by wooden bench planks, which served as splints. How long before it was healed and he had to leave? How long before the war ended and he could return to this farm, not as the enemy, but as a lover?

What was this war about, he asked himself. Empire greed? Where was Chamberlain's sense of justice declaring war on a nation such as this? A white man's war, Christian against Christian. A futile war against a poor nation happy to sit on their verandas and watch their crops flourish and their cattle multiply, while their simple womenfolk dutifully bore the fruits of their husbands' seed, securing the next generation. These were people who did not need the shackles of titles, but were divinely grateful that their God had delivered them to this Garden of Eden. And now the mightiest Empire on this earth had waged war, so that they could bleed from the soil its immense bounty of gold and diamonds.

Tristan heard the soft humming of a female servant in the kitchen. And these innocent farm labourers, he thought. What of them? Where do they stand amidst all the hatred and greed?

He readjusted himself in his seat, the boredom now seeping into his bones. Was it the boredom and the isolation that had nurtured these feelings for a woman, whose culture and customs were as diverse from his, as day was to night? He thought of the women he had known, dressed in their finery, so frivolous in their thoughts and coquettish in their ways, and Hannah, a natural beauty, unaware of her sensuality, whose fine porcelain features belied her strength. Putting Hannah in the crowd of all the women he knew, she stood apart, vital and spirited, others paled into insignificance like a colourless vapour with little or no substance.

He wondered how long it would be before Sherbourne or Hammond would return to the farm, to take him back to his regiment, or to a field hospital where he would be among his own kind. He would hear the language of his birth, and everything around him would be familiar. But he knew he was a changed man. The driving force to fight this war was gone. It was a senseless war where there would be no winners. Every man, woman and child, of every colour and every race, would feel the heavy weight that war inflicted. The Grim Reaper was riding the waves of war on the sea of destruction, which he knew was sweeping across this land.

Chapter Ten

Hannah heard Honnie barking in the distance and went out onto the veranda, where she saw Hymie Rosenberg's wagon trundling slowly along the dirt track towards the house, with a long red plume of dust trailing in its wake. There was always something comforting about Hymie's visits to Doringspruit as it was their tenuous link to the outside world. The sisters enjoyed peering into the dark, cavernous interior of his wagon, which carried everything and anything, an intriguing insight into the material needs of others. Hendrik did not like nor trust Hymie for two reasons, firstly his unconventional, nomadic lifestyle and, secondly, he was a Jew.

This visit of Hymie's was dangerous. He was not to know that they harboured a member of the British forces. Hannah trusted Hymie explicitly, but what he didn't know, he couldn't tell. She turned and ran into the house to find Sannie. From the passageway, she saw the open doorway of Tristan's room, with Tristan sitting in the chair beside the window, his leg propped up on a stool, reading. She hurried inside and whispered urgently while pulling the curtains closed.

'The smous has come to visit. He must not suspect that you are here. Keep very quiet and still, and I will get rid of him as soon as possible.'

'The smous? Who or what is the smous?' he asked with amusement.

'The smous is a pedlar,' she replied hurriedly. 'He travels across the country selling his wares. We know him well, but we can't risk Hymie finding out that we are harbouring a British soldier.'

Tristan watched her frantic movements as she raced out of the room to find Sannie, swinging the door shut behind her.

Hannah found Sannie in the kitchen, preparing the cooked pumpkin for pumpkin fritters. Her muscled forearms were covered with flour, while her hands pummelled the mixture with a large, wooden spoon. Sannie turned when she heard Hannah's hurried footsteps behind her.

'Sannie,' began Hannah with urgency. 'Hymie Rosenberg will be here any minute now. He must not know about the English captain.'

Sannie's eyes held Hannah's, sensing the power she now had over her sister.

'That Jew is a British sympathiser,' she said, her face red and glistening with little beads of sweat. 'But being a Jew, he will sell any information to anyone, for a price. That's our Hymie Rosenberg.'

'Sannie, he mustn't know. Please keep the servants from talking to him.' Sannie wiped the perspiration from her forehead on her forearm, leaving a smear of flour. 'You have put us in this danger, Hannah, now you get us out of it.'

'Where's Marike?' asked Hannah, looking out of the kitchen window. 'I must explain the situation to her before he gets here.'

Marike had gone round the side of the house to see what Honnie was barking at. The sight of Hymie's wagon made her run to the kitchen, where she heard the raised voices of her sisters.

'Quick, it's Hymie,' she said, her eyes wide with fright. 'What are we going to do, the servants will talk to him.'

'No, they will not,' demanded Sannie. 'Once we have purchased all we need, he must be on his way.'

The sisters went out into the yard to meet Hymie's wagon as it came to a standstill in a cloud of dust. The clatter of his goods, which hung from the wagon, rang out in the afternoon sunshine.

'Good day, ladies,' he called, as he swung down from the front of the wagon. He removed his faded, black bowler hat and threw it onto the seat. 'It's hard times, I warn you, hard times.'

'In other words,' retaliated Sannie, her hand shading her eyes from the sun. 'You are going to charge us even more for your already expensive goods.'

Hymie chuckled as he moved round to the back of the wagon. He was a small man with refined features and his ready smile revealed even white teeth. Hymie's flamboyant personality reflected in his clothing. He wore tight fitting navy blue and maroon striped trousers with a multi-coloured, paisley waistcoat over a crisp yellow shirt.

'Well, you know, I have to move through the military lines. The British think I am a spy for the Boers, and the Boers think I am a spy for the British. I have a hard time. But that's the price I pay for my good customers.'

'Hymie,' said Hannah. 'Would you like something to drink before we decide what we need. You have travelled far and I'm sure you must be thirsty.'

'Now that would be nice,' he replied, glancing at his gold pocket watch. He tucked it back into his waistcoat pocket and continued with a gleaming smile. 'Hannah, you are the angel the good Lord sent us.'

Marike at once hurried to the kitchen to tell the servants to prepare a pot of coffee while Hannah and Sannie made their way to the front veranda.

'I see you have sold your oxen,' remarked Sannie, the smear of flour still evident on her forehead. 'And now all you have are donkeys to pull the wagon.'

'I wish I could've sold the oxen, but they were taken from me by a band of Boers. They said they need the oxen for their own supply wagons. Not a penny they paid me. "It's my livelihood," I said, but what do they care? I was grateful that they didn't rob the wagon and my goods as well. I must be thankful for that. But…the donkeys are good. I don't think I will have oxen again. But the wagon is not as laden as it normally is, so the donkeys are fine.'

'Have you any news on the war, Hymie?' asked Hannah. 'We are desperate to hear anything, we have no idea what's going on.'

Hymie seated himself on the bench and began to mop his brow with a handkerchief. 'I heard news of your Pa from Meneer Jordaan. You know Pieter Jordaan of Rooiplaas? Well, Meneer Jordaan was with your Pa at the battle of Elandslaagte. Your Pa was injured, but only a minor injury to his left arm, so he was able to escape after a dreadful night on the veld in the rain. But he is safe.'

Marike walked out onto the veranda carrying a tray with coffee and a plate of fresh, newly baked biscuits. On hearing the news, she hurriedly put down the tray and began to weep.

'Pa has been lucky this time,' said Sannie, as she lifted the tray and placed it on the bench. 'We must continue to pray for his safety.'

She began to pour the coffee and, without looking up, she asked, 'Is there any news of Willem Prinsloo of Soetwater?'

'No, Sannie. I know Meneer Prinsloo was with the Hemel Commando, same as your Pa, but I have heard nothing of his welfare. I do know that at the battle of Elandslaagte many were killed, both Boer and British. The British won the battle, but I do believe it wasn't an easy victory.'

Silence enveloped the veranda, only the distant call of the black-collared barbet could be heard. Sannie stood up and handed Hymie a cup of coffee, followed by the plate of biscuits.

'The siege of Ladysmith ended last month,' said Hymie, noisily sipping his coffee. 'I was in Pretoria when they marched the British prisoners from

Ladysmith through the streets. It was a sight to see, everyone cheering and waving.'

'Have you any newspapers, Hymie?' asked Sannie.

'Yes, yes, plenty. But it is old news. Every day things change.'

Hannah stood up and offered the smous another biscuit, which he readily accepted. With the biscuit still poised in his hand, he said gravely. 'I must warn you. I've recently passed through Hemel. Several miles north of the town, some farms have been raided by loose bands of natives. On one farm, all the women were murdered. You must be very careful. This is happening everywhere.'

The sisters sat silently, visions of such atrocities flaring in their minds. Doringspruit, in all its tranquillity, their haven, seemed so remote and cut off from the nightmare world that surrounded them.

'Trust no one,' continued Hymie. 'The English shopkeeper in Hemel, Mr Farrell, was shot by the Boers. They claimed he was a spy. There was no proof. The Boers simply needed an excuse to loot his shop. Mr Farrell had served them well for many years, often giving families credit when he knew they were too poor to pay him. He was a good man. There is no accounting for what men do in times of war. Good, honest men of all races and colour become the devil's disciples. Aye…where will it all end?'

'Why have you not joined up, Meneer Rosenberg?' asked Marike. 'Oom Paul Kruger said every man in the Republic must do so.'

'Aye,' exclaimed Hymie, dunking his biscuit into his coffee. 'I know that you fine people are Burghers, but I am not one of you. When I call at the farms with my wares, I know what everyone is thinking. 'There is that dirty Jew again'. I know that's what they think of us Jews. I cannot fight alongside men who think that. I cannot join the British, I am not British, I'm from Lithuania. Yes, I lived in both London and Glasgow as a child, but that does not make me British, so why must I fight for an Empire that knows no other law other than pillage?'

Honnie, who was lying at Hannah's feet stood up and moved over to Hymie, hopeful for a small piece of biscuit. Hymie rubbed the wiry hair of Honnie's head with his well-manicured, delicate hand. With a chuckle, he said to Honnie, who now had a long string of saliva running from her mouth, 'Aye, aye…you gave me many, many sleepless nights, yelping and whining in the back of my wagon all the way from Natal.' He reached over and took a biscuit from the plate and gave it to the grateful Honnie, who immediately trotted off to eat it in private.

'Do you remember us all squabbling, who was going to hold the new pup first?' said Sannie.

'And Pa held her first,' laughed Marike. Hymie drained the last of his coffee and, once again, leaned forward to put his empty cup on the tray.

'Your Pa, Meneer Van Vuuren, his rough hands are as gentle as a sparrow's wing. "Her name is Honey," I said to him. "Honnie," he said. "No Honey, Meneer," I replied. But your Pa simply could not pronounce it properly, so she became Honnie.'

They all laughed at the fond memories of their Pa, but Marike's laughter was peppered with her tears.

'Now, kind ladies,' he said as he stood up. 'We must decide on your purchases. Anything in particular? I'm short of a lot of things, but on the other hand, I have a lot of luxuries which I bought from the British Army. Many of them would sell their own mothers for a bottle of gin or a flagon of whiskey.'

'Flour and sugar,' said Sannie. 'And seeds, any vegetable seeds that you have.'

'Iodine and bandages,' said Hannah. 'We have no idea when we'll see you again, Hymie. We need to be sure that we have everything.'

They gathered around while Hymie hauled all manner of goods out of the hot recess of his wagon. 'Sugar for you, Sannie,' he said, lowering a heavy sack down into Sannie's waiting, outstretched arms. She turned and carried it across the yard. Marike then took the heavy sack of flour and followed Sannie into the house.

'I have iodine, Hannah, and Vermaak's druppels, drops. The drops will cure anything from fever to constipation.'

'Only the iodine,' replied Hannah. 'I don't trust the drops.'

'Bandages, you say?'

'Yes,' replied Hannah. 'Large and small.'

'I have all sorts of medical items, Hannah. Crutches, slings, things that people want to get rid of, once they are well. A few pennies to them is better than the stuff lying about. One soldier gave me his crutches for a packet of cigarettes.'

Hannah looked back at the house to see if Sannie and Marike were about to return and said quickly. 'Hymie, I'll take that pair of crutches, if you still have them. One never knows who will need them in the future. The farm workers are always injuring themselves.'

Hymie scratched through his things. From the interior of the wagon Hymie called out over his shoulder, 'my goodness, I have so many crutches, I'll be pleased to offload a pair or two.' On finding a matching pair, he scrambled out the wagon and handed them to Hannah. With a furtive look towards the house, he said quietly. 'Be careful Hannah, servants talk.'

Hannah, unsure of what Hymie was implying, replied, 'I'll put the crutches away for safekeeping. God willing, we'll never need them.'

'Remember what I told you about Mr Farrell, the English shopkeeper in Hemel? Servants, in their innocence, gossip.' He glanced towards the house again and on seeing Sannie and Marike crossing the yard, he whispered. 'Be careful my child, be careful.'

Hannah took the crutches and the bottles of iodine and made her way to the house. Sannie called out as she approached the wagon. 'Hymie, don't sell all your rubbish to Hannah, you know she will buy anything.'

Hymie, with great agility, jumped down from the wagon and watched Hannah cross the yard. Her slim back was straight while her skirts, flaring from her narrow waist, moved in a gentle rhythm to her walk.

Hymie dusted himself down, and with his eyes still fixed on Hannah, said to Sannie. 'If I weren't a Jew, I would marry Hannah. There is not a man in the district that is not in love with her.'

'Well,' snapped Sannie. 'It is fortuitous that you are a Jew, Meneer Rosenberg, for what kind of life would a woman have being dragged across the veld in an old wagon pulled by donkeys?'

'Oh, if Hannah were my wife, I would build her a palace of gold and ivory. See how that dog follows her? That would be me, at her side, day and night.'

'You are a fool and a dreamer,' sneered Sannie.

'Aye, a dreamer I am. But dreams are the shields that protect our souls from the weapons of this harsh life. Without dreams, we will never survive. It's a cruel world, Sannie, a cruel world.'

He is above himself, thought Sannie, affronted by his familiarity. If her Pa were here, he would chase him off Doringspruit for being disrespectful to her, and for speaking about things that should not be spoken about.

Marike walked up to the wagon to help Sannie with the last of their goods. Hymie jumped up into the back of the wagon to find the last remaining bag of coffee beans.

'I'm sorry, ladies. It's only a small bag of coffee beans, that's all I have. But Marike, what do you want? Do you have anything special in mind?'

'No, my needs are the needs of my sisters,' she replied shyly.

Hymie reached into his pocket and pulled out a packet of Zinnia seeds, and handed them to her.

'Plant these, Marike. It will add a little splash of colour to our sad world.' He disappeared into the back of the wagon, appearing a few minutes later at the opening. He leaned over and handed Marike a yard and a half of fine lace.

'This is a gift from me, Marike. In these hard times, who will buy my lace? Take it, it will bring you luck.'

Beneath her bonnet, Marike's face flushed a deep red as she took the lace from Hymie's hand. 'How very kind of you, Meneer Rosenberg,' she said softly, 'but it is such a generous gift, I couldn't possibly accept it.'

'As I have said, Marike, who will buy lace in such hard times? It's Nottingham lace, the best you can buy. I know what a good seamstress you are, your Pa is so proud of you. You will put it to good use.'

'I certainly will, Meneer Rosenberg, I certainly will.' Marike rolled the fine oyster-coloured lace around her hand and then, lovingly, put it into the pocket of her apron.

Hannah returned from the house and joined her sisters. Together, they said their farewells to the smous, who had brought more than precious necessities; he had brought them news of their Pa.

They stood in the yard and watched his wagon sway and bounce over the rough ground. He leaned to one side so he could look back and wave. The three women stood alongside each other. Marike stood square and solid, with her feet apart; her large pleated bonnet shadowing her round, plain face. Sannie stood with her arms at her sides, her thin lips pulled down at the corners, while her eyes followed the wagon with bitter intensity. Hannah waved freely with her one hand, while the other fondled the dog, which stood beside her, like a devoted servant.

What will become of these daughters of Hendrik Van Vuuren? thought Hymie Rosenberg. Aye, what will become of them?

Sannie stood alone for some time watching the wagon disappear into the golden glow of the late afternoon. Hymie Rosenberg's words echoed through her mind. There is not a man in the district that is not in love with Hannah. *Perhaps*, she thought bitterly, *if I encourage these feelings between Hannah and the*

English captain, he will take her away, far away, and then perhaps another man will look at me. Tante Magda left Doringspruit in 1880, the last time the British fought us, to marry an English soldier and she never returned. I will make history repeat itself. Yes, I will do everything in my power to encourage this liaison.

Chapter Eleven

'Look what I've managed to buy for you,' laughed Hannah, as she held out the crutches to Tristan, who was still seated in the chair. Hannah brushed past him and opened the curtains, allowing the sun to flood the room.

'Help me up onto these things,' he said enthusiastically, whilst examining the crutches for any signs of cracking.

'Steady yourself on your good leg while I support you,' she said, as she slipped her hand under his arm.

Tristan grasped the crutch and heaved himself out the chair. For one quick moment he seemed to lose balance while reaching for the second. Hannah steadied him. She could feel the warmth of the taut muscles of his arm beneath the cotton nightshirt as he leaned on the crutch. She saw how tall he was, and for the first time, it was Tristan who was looking down upon her.

'You know what the problem is with these things? My arms aren't free.' He readjusted the crutches so that they fitted comfortably under his arms, while Hannah still held onto him. 'I only need one arm free to sweep you off your feet, Hannah.' He tipped forward and Hannah reached out and grasped his other arm. For a fleeting moment, her breasts brushed against his chest. He could smell the perfume in her hair, like sweet scented herbs. She tipped her head back and looked into his eyes and saw the seriousness reflected in his.

'Don't do too much today,' she said too hastily, and moved away, leaving him standing unassisted on the crutches.

He walked a few steps, like a man that was well accustomed to crutches, and then returned to his chair.

'That was well done, you'll be up and running in no time at all,' said Hannah, clapping her hands in an affected applause. From the kitchen, they heard Sannie's laughter as she jested with the servants.

'I am jealous of this man you call the smous,' said Tristan.

'Why?' laughed Hannah. 'Hymie Rosenberg is his name.'

'Well, to begin with, it's the first time I've ever heard your sister Sannie laugh. He must be a magician.'

'Oh yes, I expect you could imagine him to be a magician. But why be jealous of him.'

'He has brought something into this house, happiness. I have brought nothing but dissent.'

At that moment Sannie entered the room, on her face was a beaming smile.

'Does the English captain like our gift to him?' she said, pointing to the crutches.

'As a matter of fact,' replied Hannah. 'Tristan believes that Hymie Rosenberg is a magician. He has made us all laugh.'

Tristan watched Sannie's expression; her smile had transformed her face. She looked softer and her features seemed more defined, but the look of shrewd determination still lingered in her eyes.

'I have learnt today that women the world over are all the same. A little bit of shopping and they are in high spirits. Africa, England, they are all the same.'

Hannah quickly translated for Sannie and everyone laughed.

'I must help Thuli in the kitchen,' said Sannie, and hurried from the room. 'I'll cook something special for us. After all, we have had good news today about our Pa.'

Tristan heaved himself up onto one of his crutches and then with his other hand steadied himself on the arm of the chair. He released the chair and reached out for Hannah's hand. Gently he pulled her towards him.

'I am in love with you, Hannah,' he whispered.

Hannah pulled her hand free and stepped back. 'Don't play games with me, Tristan. I deserve better than that, and I expect more from you. Don't use me as a pastime…as entertainment to fill your days until you are ready to return to your duties.' With that she turned and hurried out the room.

'Hannah…you're wrong,' he called, but she was gone.

***

He did not see Hannah for three days. The servants brought in his food and, occasionally, Sannie would enter his room bearing a tray and wearing an empty smile. If he wasn't pacing up and down the room on his crutches, building up his lost strength, he was at the window waiting for a glimpse of Hannah. He was powerless to ask after her, as he knew both the servants and Sannie were at a loss understanding him.

With his new found skill on the crutches he found his room too confining, so one afternoon, he ventured out into the passage. The various odours of the house had become familiar to him. He knew without looking at his watch what time of day it was. The different calls of different birds at different times of the day were nature's timepiece, a timepiece he began to read. But now, as he tentatively broke the invisible boundaries of what had become his prison, the surroundings were foreign to him as he made his way towards the kitchen.

Thuli turned from the stove when she heard the creak of the wooden crutches. From behind her hand, she laughed at the strange man in a nightshirt that was too large, while Palesa clapped her large, capable hands silently and grinned. Tristan moved over to the stove and peered into the pot which was boiling furiously, and through the steam he saw that it was wild spinach. He made his way to the back door and looked out into the orchard and saw that the leaves on the fruit trees were beginning to turn. He stood for several minutes, drinking in this new view from the house.

He turned and passed through the door way into the voorkamer. The large dining table with its ten chairs dominated the room. On the sideboard, amongst the fine collection of Delft plates, was a Bible. It lay like a sleeping Deity, once opened, it would wake and speak from its silent pages and every word would be obeyed.

He made his way across the room and exited through the door leading into the front hall. As he passed, he saw a rifle rack with two hunting rifles hanging from it. He looked back across the room and noticed the giant buffalo horns above the doorway leading into the kitchen. The room was infused with the history of the Boer nation.

From the hallway, he stepped out onto the front veranda and saw Sannie and Marike sitting at the far end. Marike sat with her head bowed over a small item of clothing that she was sewing, and Sannie was leaning back on the bench combing her thick, wet hair. He stood for some time before Sannie noticed him. Abruptly she stood up, and made her way towards him, her loose damp hair bouncing about her shoulders. She took his arm and steered him back into the house, whilst at the same time, chastising him in her gargling, coarse language. She led him down the passage and into his room. Once he was seated in his chair beside the window, she took his crutches and placed them, out of reach, on the bed. With a nod of her head and a smile, she left the room.

From the window that evening, he saw Hannah returning in the shadowless twilight, riding effortlessly on her chestnut filly, her hunting rifle slung over her shoulder, and a brace of guineafowl tied to the pommel of her saddle.

***

Sannie stepped out onto the veranda. The ink-blue evening sky was shot through with vivid, scarlet streaks of cloud, which hung low on the horizon, remnants of the dying sunset. The breeze was cool and carried with it the fading crepuscular calls of the roosting francolin. She stood for several minutes looking out across the yard and into the veld beyond, her arms hugging her chest to keep out the cool air. As she turned to go back into the house, she saw Hannah sitting on the bench on the far side of the veranda.

'Where have you been, Hannah?' she asked, making her way towards her sister.

'Hunting,' replied Hannah, with her hunting rifle resting against her leg.

'It has been three days now and we have seen nothing of you, even the English captain is asking after you.'

'How would you know, Sannie, when you can't speak English?'

'Of course I can't understand what he is saying, but I understand when I hear your name in his sentences, and I can see the question in his eyes.'

'I'll speak to him tomorrow,' she replied. 'It's only a matter of time before his regiment sends for him, and it will be a good thing when he has gone.'

Sannie stared into the distance. The scarlet streaks in the night sky had faded and the moon, crescent in shape, appeared from behind the distant poplar trees. A breeze swept across the veranda, cool, and carrying with it the smell of the wood fires from the farm workers' huts.

'Why this sudden change of heart, Sannie?' asked Hannah. 'It wasn't long ago you forbade me to enter his room. Now, you are encouraging a friendship.'

'The smous' visit, Hannah,' replied Sannie. 'When he spoke of Pa and the battle of Elandslaagte. I thought if Pa was injured and lying in an Englishman's house, nursed by hostile women, I would not be happy. I would want them to be kind to Pa, and to make him feel comfortable and happy. It says in the Scriptures that we must love our neighbours as we love ourselves. I have thought about it, Hannah, and I know I must be a true Christian.'

Hannah stood up. *Since when have you been a true Christian, Sannie*, she thought, but kept the words locked behind her tight lips. 'It's cold out here, let's go in,' she said finally. 'I'm frightfully hungry.'

***

Hannah rose early the following morning and prepared Tristan's breakfast tray herself. She knocked on his door, and after entering saw that he too was up and about on his crutches.

'Hannah,' he said, with surprise lighting up his face. 'Where have you been? Why have you stayed away?' Without answering his questions, she placed the tray on the small table beside his chair. To her surprise, she noticed another chair had been brought into the room.

'Who brought this chair in? It belongs in the voorkamer.'

'Palesa brought it in yesterday,' he replied. 'I have no idea why, but I'm pleased that she did.'

Sannie, thought Hannah. It was Sannie's idea. Something about her sister's new viewpoint disturbed her. Sannie's bitterness and hatred for the British could not have been cleansed by a single visit from Hymie. Something was eluding her. Sannie's thoughts and deeds were always to her own advantage. In some way, Sannie believed that a tryst between her and Tristan would be of benefit to her. But what would she gain? Willem Prinsloo was married, Hannah was no longer a threat. Something had made Sannie have a change of heart, and she knew it definitely was not Christianity.

Tristan's voice interrupted her thoughts. 'Hannah, why have you stayed away?'

'I've been out hunting, we need the meat. And besides, I enjoy being out on the veld.'

Tristan moved near to where she was standing beside the breakfast tray. His face was close to hers; she could see the flecks of amber in his green eyes. He tucked the crutch beneath his arm and reached out his hand and touched her shoulder, his eyes steady and questioning.

Hannah met his gaze and whispered. 'Who is Katherine?' Fear of the answer surged through her veins, while every fibre of her being pulsated with his touch.

He stepped back as if slapped, and turned away so that she could not read his expression. Then just as quickly he turned back to face her.

'Katherine?' he said incredulously. 'Katherine. Who told you about Katherine?'

'When you first arrived…you were delirious. You called her name over and over again. Is she your wife? Your betrothed?'

Tristan eased himself into a chair and stared out through the window to the apricot tree. He sat silently for a few moments. A small flock of Cape white eyes busied themselves amongst the branches. The morning sun reflected on the leaves fluttering gently in the soft wind, which blew in from the veld.

Without turning back to her, he said, 'Katherine was my sister…my twin sister. We were inseparable. She took her own life. I am the only one who knows, and now you. I'm sure her fiancée must suspect, but thankfully my parents believe that it was a dreadful accident.'

'I'm sorry, Tristan. I didn't know.' She moved over to the chair opposite him. He kept his eyes averted, still staring out at the flock of little white-eyes.

He sat silently for a short while, steeped in his thoughts. 'She was only seventeen… we were only seventeen. I ran down to the lake that morning, I wanted to tell her that the Springer spaniel, Josephine, had whelped during the night, six pups in all. All alive and healthy. I was so excited…like a child. She wasn't in her room; the chambermaid said she had seen her leaving the house, heading towards the lake. I ran. The mist was beginning to lift. It is always so misty at that time of the year in Leicestershire. I took the short cut across the lawns, cutting through the thick shrubbery on the east side of the lake. Then I saw her lying in the water, her beautiful face blue and distorted in death.'

He closed his eyes. The image of that day he had revisited many times. Her dark hair spread out on the surface of the water like seeping ink, the bodice of her dress clinging to her in its wetness, while her skirts billowed beneath the surface.

He turned and faced Hannah. The sun slanted through the window, highlighting the plane of his cheek.

'It was a passage of rites. I ran down to the lake a boy, and returned a man. I raced back to the house; emotion seemed to tear my lungs apart. I ran along the path through the rhododendrons with their big showy blooms, heavy with moisture from the mist, splashing against my face. I will always hate those flowers, so vulgar in their profusion. I would tear them all from the soil of Tylcoat if I had my way.'

Hannah reached out and took his hand. 'I'm so sorry, Tristan. I'm truly sorry.'

'The day before the funeral, I went into her room and found the small wooden chest of her childhood treasures. In it, I found a letter from her fiancée ending their two-month betrothal. Peter Thornworthy had apparently fallen in love with someone else. I was sure that someone else was his long-time friend, Thomas Fairfax, and, the truth be known, so did Katherine. I burnt the letter and took the box downstairs to be buried with her. Of course, Peter was at the funeral putting on a magnificent display of grief. At his side was Thomas Fairfax.'

He turned and looked out through the window once more; the small flock of the little Cape white eyes were gone.

'After Katherine's death, my mother took to her bed with some sort of malaise. She never recovered; she died six months later. I had known that the time was coming when Katherine and I would be going our separate ways. She had been planning her big wedding to Peter Thornworthy, and I was preparing to go to Cambridge to read law. I achieved a first, so it was only natural I would go to Cambridge and follow in the family tradition. Once I was at Cambridge, I was able to come to terms with her loss. I had a good circle of friends, some new and some old. It was expected that I would join my uncles' law firm, Dunn-Caldwell, Hadley and Hadley, after my studies were completed. They have their chambers in London. Following that, I had hoped to follow my father's interest in politics, and one day sit in the House of Lords. But after two years in the firm, I felt I needed to break away. I have no idea why I felt that way. I simply needed time to evaluate my life.

'So I enlisted with the Royal Leicestershire Light Cavalry. I have no idea how my father truly felt, you see, he's a pacifist. We have a strong military history in the family, so I expect it was no surprise. My father had hoped that I would make Felicity Langsby my fiancée before I left for Africa. Both families had pinned their hopes on it since we were children. Her father was a General serving with Kitchener in the battle of Omdurman in the Sudan. Unfortunately, Lord Langsby contracted malaria and was ill for months, he later retired. Our families have strong connections so it seemed natural to everyone we would be a suitable match.'

'And is it?' Hannah asked quietly. 'A suitable match?'

'Before I left England, I went to see her. I broke off our relationship. I can't even be sure what kind of relationship it was. Felicity was expecting a proposal and, I must confess, I did little to make her think otherwise. I was… or am… fond of Felicity, but I could never have her as my wife, it would be impossible for me to love her. I am grateful for the comfort she gave me after Katherine died, but even she didn't know that my sister took her own life.'

Hannah withdrew her hand and said softly, 'Your breakfast is getting cold.'

He lifted the tray onto his lap and began to eat.

***

It was after lunch when Hannah took Tristan a slice of Sannie's apricot cake. He sat quietly in the chair and reflected on the morning's conversation with Hannah. He had tried many times to put Felicity out of his thoughts, but his efforts eluded him. He knew now, more than ever, he could never have married her. Now, the memory of Katherine came to haunt him. He tried to read, but after a few lines, his mind was back at Tylcoat. At the sound of Hannah's gentle knock, he called out for her to enter.

'I've brought you a slice of cake,' she said, as she entered the room. 'It's fresh from the oven and still warm.'

Tristan took the plate from her hand in silence. His confinement was playing games with his mind. He needed freedom and he needed to feel the fresh air against his skin.

'You can remove these things now I'm sure,' said Tristan brusquely, his hand patting against his make shift splint. 'It's been five weeks and I'm sure the bone has healed by now. I know full well it should be six weeks, but circumstances are different.'

'I'll call Thuli or Sannie to come and help me,' she replied, as she turned to leave the room, 'and I'll also need a good pair of scissors.'

Hannah returned with Thuli, and together they removed the long strips of torn sheets that held the bench planks in place. Once his leg was free from its restrictions, Tristan tried to flex his knee. The leg was stiff and the movement did not come easily. 'You'll need to exercise your leg to get the strength back into it,' said Hannah, studying his limb, which was thin and white from its incarceration. He stood up, took a single crutch and made his way, stiff legged, towards the wall. Thuli giggled and smiled then hurried from the room. Tristan once again took a few faltering steps.

'Is it painful?' asked Hannah, concern furrowing her brow.

'A little, perhaps I'll need a walking stick for a few days. Or maybe you can assist me, which would be nice.' They both laughed. He came and stood close to Hannah, the laughter in his eyes changed to a deep intensity. He slipped his hand into the small of her back and drew her close until her body curved against his. He looked down into her startled eyes and then kissed her, like a lover, with urgency and passion.

The sound of Sannie's voice in the passage jerked them apart. She came hurrying into the room, her face flushed and her skirts bustling about her feet.

'Thuli says he no longer has his splints, I must see for myself.' She clapped her hands in feigned shock and admiration. 'Magtig, but he must be a strong man.'

Hannah had turned away in an attempt to regain her composure and to hide her flaming cheeks. 'Yes, indeed Sannie, isn't it wonderful. He can be gone within a few days.'

'Ag, he must rest,' she said, and she turned to leave the room. 'A leg must be in splints for six weeks, it's only been five. He must take it easy, Hannah, for his own good.'

In the darkness of her room, later that night, Hannah was unable to sleep. She had relived the kiss a thousand times over in her mind. Tristan's recovery meant he would be gone soon. Would she see him again? Would he be killed, and if so, who would let her know? Who would tell her if he was injured or maimed? Would he come back after the war? Would he want to come back and find her? She was in love with him, and the thought of him leaving was like an insidious shadow creeping across her soul. Life in the house without him, and Sannie's constant barbed tongue, would be unbearable. How long before this war was over? She lit the lamp beside her bed and turned the flame low.

She went across to the window and pulled the curtains back. The room overlooked the veranda, and Hannah saw the faint flicker of lightning in the distance, followed by a soft rumble of thunder. The leaves on the veranda lifted in the breeze and danced across the floor, swirling around until they collected in the corners. It must rain, she thought. We are desperate for rain.

The quiet creak of the door handle made Hannah turn abruptly. The door opened silently and Tristan stepped into the room. He crossed to the window to where Hannah stood and pulled the curtains shut. She showed no surprise, only joy as he came towards her. Her hair hung loose about her shoulders in a thick, silky mass, shining like spun gold in the yellow light of the lamp. Tristan could see her nakedness beneath the thin cotton of her nightdress. He took her hand and led her towards the bed. At last, he could feel her skin beneath his hands and the texture of her hair between his fingers. His body was taut with the want of her, but he was gentle and understanding, for he knew, for her it was the first time.

She reached out to turn out the flame of the lamp, but Tristan's hand stopped her. 'I want to see your golden beauty, I want to see that it is you, Hannah.'

The rain began to fall. It slapped against the corrugated iron roof, like applause for the love beneath it.

Sannie heard the soft click of Hannah's door. She smiled into the darkness and turned over and went to sleep.

***

'Take the captain down to the dam, Hannah,' said Sannie, at breakfast the following morning. 'You can take the cart, the change of scenery will do him good.'

'He might be seen,' interjected Marike, raising her hand in surprise. 'What if a commando calls in and sees them? It's not wise, not wise at all.'

Hannah stared into her mug of pale coffee. The coffee was growing weaker each day in an attempt to keep their supplies going for as long as possible. The idea of her and Tristan alone at the dam appealed to her. 'I think I'll do just that, Sannie. I'll get some of Pa's clothes out of the kist. They'll be too big for sure, but we'll make a plan.'

'It's wrong,' exclaimed Marike. 'I am telling you both it's wrong, and it is dangerous. No good will come of it.'

Sannie and Marike stood on the front veranda and watched the cart roll out of the yard. Hannah held the reins and Tristan sat beside her, dressed in their Pa's clothes, while Honnie raced behind.

'Honnie!' yelled Sannie. 'Honnie, come back here!' The dog obediently stopped her chase and stood with her ears tipped forward, watching with disappointment at a lost opportunity for adventure.

'Why are you doing this dangerous thing, Sannie?' asked Marike.

110

'She is not one of us, Marike,' spat Sannie, her eyes shining with the shrewdness of her thoughts. 'She is like Tante Magda. Everything about her is English. Even the Boer blood that flows through her veins has now turned traitorous.'

'But it is wrong to encourage this liaison,' retorted Marike. 'What would Pa say, what would Pa think?'

'She is a British sympathiser, a joiner. I know that, even if I tried to stop her, she would still give herself to him. She can rather lie in the veld with her shame than practise her filthy ways under Pa's roof...in Pa's bed.'

'Sannie,' gasped Marike in shock. 'Of this you can't be sure. You are being unkind to our sister.'

'Oh, I'm sure Marike. I've never been more sure of anything in my life,' replied Sannie, as she watched the cart turn and bounce down the small overgrown track, which led down to the dam, until it was out of sight.

As the cart passed through the sweet, scented shade of the gum trees, Tristan saw the dam lying in a shallow hollow of the veld. Hannah took the cart round to the far side of the dam, where the weeping willows stood with their supple branches brushing the silver surface of the water. It was quiet, only the soft call of the turtledove breaking the silence of the morning.

They stepped down from the cart, and Hannah reached over to the back and took out a blanket and a basket of fruit. She laid the blanket down under the canopy of the willows and sat down. Tristan stood for some time in the quietness of the moment, drinking in the tranquillity. Here he stood, an officer for Her Majesty, at war with this country, but at peace with himself in this small piece of Heaven.

'They will call for me soon, Hannah,' he said looking out across the dam. He turned to her; his face was grave and intent. 'There might not be time for us to say goodbye, so I want to tell you now, that I will be back for you.'

She sat hugging her knees, the dappled shade moving across her face. She rested her chin on top of her knees and looked up at him before saying. 'I know. Every day I ask myself, is today the day?'

He came and sat down next to her. Gently, he pulled her back onto the blanket and lay beside her, propped up on one elbow. Looking down at her, he brushed a strand of hair from her flushed cheek. The blacksmith plovers on the far bank of the dam cried their metallic call and then were silent once again. The breeze sighed through the yellowing leaves of the willow while the dappled light danced across the blanket.

'Whatever happens, Hannah, I will be back for you. Never doubt that.'

'God willing, I'll be here waiting for you,' she whispered.

'Doringspruit is safe,' he said quietly. 'You have trusted servants who will look after you.'

'How long will this war last, Tristan?'

'I have no idea, a month, two maybe, another six months.'

'Maybe it's over and we have no idea,' she said hopefully. 'What news do we get here at Doringspruit?'

His fingers trailed the outline of her chin then moved softly down her throat and lightly traced circles around her breasts.

He took her without the restraint of the night before, but this time with more fervour, releasing his love for her with passionate urgency. Forgotten were the war and the talk of his departure. Forgotten were Sannie's blistering words and sneering innuendoes. Forgotten was the turbulent world around them; all that mattered was the pure ecstasy of the moment.

Chapter Twelve

Sannie crossed the orchard and headed towards the vegetable garden. Each day, she set out to take stock and check that nothing had been eaten during the night by nocturnal animals, or stolen by the servants or other uninvited intruders. It was a perfect autumn morning, warm and bright. The sun was already high in the sky, casting short, fat shadows across the grass. As she rounded the hedge of prickly pears, she noticed a horse tethered to an iron ring on the wall of the barn. From the design of the saddle, and the helmet hanging from it, she knew at once that the absent rider was a British soldier.

She stood for a moment, fear and uncertainty flooding through her while she gathered her thoughts. A choking cry coming from the barn of little Lettie, Thuli's baby, told her that something was dangerously amiss. She bunched her skirts high in her hands, and ran back to the house, the blood pounding in her head. Entering through the kitchen door, she ran into the voorkamer to where the hunting rifles hung from the rack. She grabbed the rifle nearest to her, and with trembling fingers checked the breech. It was loaded. She opened the drawer of the sideboard and took a handful of ammunition and dropped it into the pocket of her apron.

Fear fuelled the speed of her fat legs and sharpened her senses. She ran through the orchard and headed in the direction of the barn, the rifle clutched under her arm. As she neared the barn, she stopped running and began to tread carefully, picking her way between the fallen leaves. She crept along the wall. Her foot snapped a twig, but the cry of the infant made it barely audible. With the confidence of an experienced hunter, she lifted the rifle to her shoulder and entered the barn.

In a beam of light, cast by a missing sheet of corrugated iron from the roof, Sannie saw Thuli pinned to the floor with Trooper Hammond on top of her, his trousers gathered around his ankles and his face red from exertion.

The shocking impact of the first glimpse of the horrific scene was branded into her mind, photographed against her will. For an infinite moment, she saw the details, like a picture in a book. She saw his pink, freckled hand with its fleshless fingers curled around a pistol. His shirtsleeves had been rolled up, revealing his forearms where the dust of the barn floor clung to the whitish hairs that rose up out of the pale freckled skin. His small eyes were glazed and fixed on her, staring, and his mouth pulled back in a triumphant sneer. A vein bulged blue on his forehead with a small rivulet of sweat running down, tracing its outline. He grunted and heaved. His buttocks, blotched and transparent like white marble, were taut with his movements.

Thuli's arm was flung out from under him, outstretched and helpless, her youthful hand upturned, revealing the pale skin of her palm. Her face was turned towards Sannie. Thuli's dark eyes were round with shock, and the smooth polished skin of her cheek was broken and bleeding, the dirt from the floor clinging to the scratches.

He rose up on his arms and stared unflinchingly at Sannie, but it was enough to give Sannie, the marksman, the chance she needed. She bent her head and aimed through the sights of the rifle and squeezed the trigger. The shot reverberated through the barn. Trooper Hammond's body jerked involuntarily, then collapsed on Thuli. Half his head was unrecognisable.

Thuli, with Hammond's blood and brains covering her face, blindly pushed the body from her. She began to scream, tearing at her face and shoulders in a frantic attempt to free herself from the warmth of his blood. Sannie dropped the rifle and ran to her, pulling off her apron. She pushed it into Thuli's hands, the spare cartridges spilling onto the floor.

'Sssh, Thuli. Sssh,' she said softly, trying her utmost to control the wild fear that was running through her mind. Thuli took the apron and rubbed her face hysterically.

Nothing in her cloistered life on the farm had prepared her for the abomination of what she had just witnessed. Trooper Hammond's ecstatic sneer and Thuli's face, which was contorted in horror and disbelief, revealed the true brutality of war.

***

The rifle shot brought Adam in from the nearby fields. He appeared at the entrance to the barn, and stood in shock at the scene before him. No words escaped his open mouth. Sannie ran over to Thuli's baby and lifted the crying child into her arms. She turned to Adam and said, 'Go quickly and fetch Miss Marike. Tell her to come at once, and then fetch Jonas. Don't tell anyone what you have seen here, do you hear me? For Thuli's sake, this man is an English soldier.' But Adam stood rooted to the spot.

'Gou, quick.' she yelled, and Lettie began to cry once more.

Marike stood white-faced at the entrance to the barn; Trooper Hammond's body lay on its back with his khaki trousers down, exposing his bloodied and slackened genitals. Sannie pushed baby Lettie into Marike's arms. 'Take the child into the kitchen and calm her down, and I'll take care of Thuli. If Hannah returns from the dam don't tell her what has happened. Keep her busy…make up a story. Just make sure she doesn't come to the barn.'

Marike stood with the screaming infant in her arms, her feet were rooted to the spot while her eyes consumed the grotesque scene. Trooper Hammond's blood seeped into the floor of the barn, creating a dark stain around his corpse. A sickly, metallic smell hung in the air.

'Marike,' called Sannie impatiently, in a harsh whisper. 'Take the child to the house. We need to act quickly. We don't know if he is alone…and we don't want Hannah returning to find that we have killed a British soldier.'

Marike turned from the scene in silence, and with the child clutched tightly in her arms, hurried across the orchard towards the house.

Sannie turned to Thuli and steered her out into the sunshine and across to the water furrows in the vegetable garden. Thuli tore off her clothes and stood naked in the furrow, her body doubled over and wracked with grief. Sannie ran to the far end of the vegetable garden from where she could see the track to the dam.

Every day for the past five days, Hannah and Tristan had gone to the dam, returning shortly after mid-day. Sannie squinted into the distance, but there was no sign of the Cape cart. She ran back to the barn with every step ringing in her ears. The grey and white striped blanket, which held Thuli's baby on her back, lay some distance from the bloody remains of Trooper Hammond. She hurriedly examined the blanket, and only when she was satisfied that it was free from blood, she returned to where Thuli stood bathing herself in the shallow water of the furrow.

'Here, Thuli. Cover yourself and go home,' she said, handing her the blanket. 'We will look after Lettie. When you are ready, come back to the house.' Thuli took the blanket and covered her nakedness; calm had at last washed over her.

Sannie hurried over to where the horse stood tethered in the sharp sunlight of the morning. She untied the reins and led it into the barn, where she hurriedly tied the reins to a broken wagon wheel leaning against the wall. She turned and saw Adam had returned with Jonas, who stood staring at the bloody scene before him, his young face cast in an expression of shock and hatred.

Jonas had worked for Hendrik for the past five years. He had been working hard to acquire the cattle to pay the lobola, the bride-wealth, to the father of the woman he loved. One Christmas, Hendrik had given Jonas a cow in payment for all the extra work he had done the previous harvest, and much to Jonas' delight, the cow had calved three times. These daughters of Hendrik Van Vuuren were now his responsibility; he would protect them in his master's absence as a mark of gratitude.

Jonas walked over to the corpse and softly kicked the legs together, and then, with the toe of his shoe, pushed the arms against the body.

'What is Jonas doing?' rasped Sannie. Adam stood and watched Jonas, knowing the anger he was trying to temper.

'It is easier to bury the body when the limbs are together,' said Adam. 'We must do it before it goes stiff.'

'I had no choice but to kill him,' said Sannie softly. 'And we must get rid of the body as soon as we can. No one must know what has happened here today. I don't want the British army coming here and asking questions. They will kill us all if they find out that we have killed one of their men. You must explain this to Thuli.'

'You did the right thing, Miss Sannie,' said Adam. 'Even the hyena that lusts after rotten flesh would not do such a thing. No, he must lie beneath the soil and the spirits will fetch him and punish him for this evil deed.' He rubbed the back of his head while deep in thought, then continued, 'We will bury him tonight.'

'We'll bury him in the mealie field,' said Jonas. 'The mealies are finished now, but their stalks stand high. No one will see us.'

'Let's go now,' replied Adam, his eyes glowing with respect for Sannie. 'We'll start digging at once.'

116

'And Adam…' called Sannie as they turned to leave. 'The horse. We must get rid of his horse. The saddle and his helmet we'll bury with him, but no one must find his horse. We can't shoot it and bury it. It's too large.'

'I will ask Solomon, my sister's first born, to take the horse into Hemel,' replied Adam eyeing the well-groomed charger. 'It will fetch a good price.'

'No Adam, everyone will think he's a horse thief and he will be whipped, or worse at this time, now that there is a war on, he'll be shot. No, he must take it far into the veld, as far as he can, and leave it. That way no one will ask any questions.'

Jonas and Adam left Sannie standing alone in the barn. The events of the morning flashed through her mind, the horror and injustice of it all. Nothing in life had prepared her for what she had done. No matter how she looked at it, she would do it again, if need be.

She turned and saw the man, lying in the dimness of the barn, grotesque and bloodied, the flies already buzzing and settling about his head. She hurried out and crossed to the far side of the vegetable garden, and to her relief, there was still no sign of the Cape cart.

Hurrying back to the house, she found Marike seated in the voorkamer rocking the sleeping infant. Marike's ashen face turned to the doorway when she heard the click-clack of Sannie's footsteps on the wooden floor.

'Sannie,' she whispered, in horror. 'Take those clothes off and burn them.'

Sannie looked down at her blood stained dress with revulsion. She began tearing at the buttons in a hasty attempt to relieve herself of her tainted clothes. Marike took the sleeping Lettie and placed her on her bed in her room, and hurried into the yard to fetch the tin bath. Palesa and two young wives of the farm workers, Miriam and Aletta, were making their way across the orchard towards the house.

'Help me fill this bath for Miss Sannie,' called Marike, gesturing with her arms for them to hurry. Together they half-filled the bath and carried it into the bedroom, where Sannie sat in stunned silence, reliving the events in the barn. Marike lifted the sleeping infant and placed her in Palesa's arms saying, 'take her back to her mother. Thuli will want to feel the comfort of her child.'

As the women turned to leave the room Marike said, 'there is to be no gossip. If the English Captain finds out what has happened here today, he will send for his soldiers to kill us all. Miss Hannah must not know either, she is a friend of the captain and she might tell him. Do you understand?'

Palesa nodded her head and all the women conferred in their own language, talking gravely among themselves.

Sannie sat in the bath of lukewarm water and scrubbed herself until she was pink. The scene flashed before her eyes over and over again, and each time she would resume her scrubbing. The moment she had pulled the trigger, his head snapped back and seemed to explode in a shower of bone and blood. Life on Doringspruit had prepared her for many things, but killing a man was not one of them.

She thought of Thuli, her instinct telling her that the man was taking what he thought was rightfully his. He was a soldier with all the ceremony and trappings, and Thuli was just a simple servant. *Oh, God in Heaven*, she thought, *I hate these people. Let Hannah fornicate beneath the sky with her English captain. God was watching and God would punish*. She stood up and stepped out of the tub. *After tonight*, she thought, *I will put this behind me. God willing, the British army won't come looking for him, and we'll carry on as though he never existed.*

Marike bundled Sannie's blood-stained clothes into a ball and hurried out to the orchard where the farm workers' wives and Palesa stood talking beneath the fig tree.

'Burn these,' she said, thrusting the bundle into Aletta's arms. 'I don't want to see you wearing them, they must be burnt. We want no reminder of the sinful thing that happened here today.'

Honnie raced into the orchard, her tongue lolling to one side and her tail betraying her excitement.

'Go quickly,' Marike whispered to the women. 'Miss Hannah is back.'

Marike heard the wheels of the cart grind to a halt round the side of the house. Hannah's laughter and Tristan's words drifted across in the afternoon stillness. She heard them off-loading the baskets and their intimate chatter as they made their way towards the orchard. Marike met them half way and smiled uneasily.

'Oh, I'm so sorry we're late, Marike,' said Hannah, her face flushed. 'But we saw so many interesting things down at the dam today. We saw a serval. It came down to the water's edge to drink, and we saw a pair of secretary birds.'

Tristan walked on ahead, conscious not to look too familiar. 'I showed him what a barbel looks like. I think he is changing his mind about Africa…I think he's seeing it through new eyes.'

They entered the kitchen but Tristan had already disappeared behind the closed door of his bedroom.

'Where's Sannie?'

'Taking a bath,' said Marike. Looking furtively down the passage to see if Tristan was out of earshot, she continued in a conspiratorial whisper. 'She has her curse. It's come early this month and she's bleeding very heavily. She's not feeling well today.'

Hannah went out onto the front veranda and sat down on the bench. She looked across the yard into the veld beyond, and reflected on the magic moment when the serval, tentative and shy, came down to drink, its spotted coat shining in the morning light. Tristan's eyes were wide with wonder. 'I never knew such a creature existed,' he had said, reaching for her hand. Together they had sat transfixed by the world of nature and its beauty, the panacea to all the ills of mankind.

Marike came out onto the veranda carrying a tray of coffee and some biscuits.

'I heard a shot this morning, Marike. What happened?'

'It was Sannie,' replied Marike falteringly, while offering Hannah the biscuits. 'She thought she heard the baboons in the vegetable garden, but they ran off.'

'Did she see them, or did she hear them?'

'She thought she heard them, so she fired a shot in case they were near.'

At that moment Sannie came out onto the veranda, her face was pale and her hands twitched nervously at her sides.

'I was telling Hannah about the baboons,' said Marike, turning to face Sannie. 'You fired a shot to scare them off.'

'Yes, you should've seen them run,' continued Sannie, all too quickly.

'Oh, so you did see them, Sannie? Marike wasn't too sure.'

Sannie sat down. 'Please Marike, pour me some coffee.'

Hannah sensed that something strange was taking place. Sannie was clearly out of sorts, her eyes appeared sunken in her head and she spoke distractedly. Marike, for once, was in charge.

'Is everything all right, Sannie?' asked Hannah kindly.

'Yes, of course,' replied Sannie, not meeting Hannah's eyes.

Marike took the mug of steaming coffee and put it down beside Sannie. Hannah saw a knowing look pass between her sisters.

'Are you sure everything is alright?' she said, leaning forward with concern.

'Don't make a fuss over nothing, Hannah,'

Hannah felt uneasy. Something had transpired whilst she was at the dam with Tristan. Did that something have anything to do with the shot that she had heard? Marike and Sannie's stories did not match. That in itself made it, just that, a story.

'I'm not feeling well, Hannah,' continued Sannie, her eyes filling with tears. 'It's just that…that…everything is getting to me. This war. I fear for Pa, I fear for us, after all, what we are doing is treasonous. If we are caught with a British soldier under our roof, Hannah, what will happen? Will we be shot? Will our own men shoot us?' She dabbed a linen handkerchief across her eyes. 'I panicked this morning, that is all. There was activity in the vegetable garden, I wasn't sure if it was baboons, so I fired a shot, but it was merely a band of mongoose. They went scurrying when they heard the shot from my rifle.'

Marike lovingly wiped the damp hair from Sannie's forehead. 'Yes, we are all fraught with worry. I pray every night for Pa's safe return.'

Hannah sat silently and watched her sisters who were bonded in secrecy. She had been shut out, she was not trusted enough to hear the truth. Marike, in all the years had never once kept the truth from Hannah, nor held any secrets. *War changes the destiny of man,* thought Hannah, *it also changes the heart.*

***

Sannie waited till Hannah had turned in for the night. She was relieved when Hannah had excused herself early, exclaiming she was tired from the day at the dam. She waited till the house was silent, then whispered in the dark to Marike. 'Keep Honnie here in the room with you. I'm going out to check on Jonas and Adam. We can't afford for them to overlook any detail.'

Sannie slipped from the room silently on her bare feet, carrying an unlit lantern in one hand, and her shoes in the other. Once outside the back door, she sat down and slipped on her shoes.

The almost full moon painted its silver light across the orchard. The water dikkop screeched into the night, and the smell of the dying wood-fires was on the chill of the autumn wind.

She hurried through the fruit trees with their autumn leaves scattered beneath their trunks.

Soft scurrying sounds rustled in the grass at the sound of her footsteps. An owl swooped down and then lifted into the air in one quick, practised movement with the tail of its small prey curling against the motion of flight. She crossed the vegetable garden and saw her pumpkins gleaming white in the light of the moon. She stopped to light the lantern, then hurried on towards the barn. The voices of Jonas and Adam drifted through the night air; she was relieved that she would not be alone with the corpse in the shadowy darkness.

As she entered the barn, an arc of light from her lantern swung across the corpse now lying in a blanket. Sannie turned away at the sight of it, but the brief image was seared into her memory. What was left of his face was blue and unrecognisable as human, only the exposed teeth were an indication that this was at one time a living man. Sannie hurried out of the barn and vomited into the grass. Palesa appeared out of the shadows and spoke comfortingly to her. 'He will be buried soon, never to be seen again, and then we can forget. Thuli will always be grateful for your bravery.'

'But what if the British army comes looking for him, Palesa?' whispered Sannie, as she brushed her mouth with the back of her hand. 'I've put us all in terrible danger. The British will want to know where he is.'

'No one will speak of it, Miss Sannie,' whispered Palesa. 'The secret is safe with us all. Look, the men are coming now with the blanket. I will carry the saddle.'

Sannie leaned against the wall of the barn. Her head was spinning and the smell of her vomit stung her nostrils, while the acid taste of it burned at the back of her throat.

She watched as Adam and Jonas carried the blanket, no more than a foot off the ground with its sagging weight. Palesa followed behind with the saddle and a lantern. Sannie picked up her own lantern and walked several paces behind as they made their way, like some primeval procession, to the field of dying maize.

The dry strappy leaves of the maize rustled in the darkness and brushed against their clothing, stalks snapped beneath their feet and broke as the body swayed in the blanket. The moon rose like an eye of judgement as they floundered through the forest of a past harvest.

They came to a clearing where Adam and Jonas had dug the grave, the rich red soil standing in mounds close by.

Slowly the men lowered the body over the grave, then released the corners of the blanket. A heavy dull thud rose up from the darkness of the hole as Trooper Hammond landed in his resting place, in a field known by only a few, in a foreign land. No Christian words were spoken to mark his passing, only the call of the jackal and the scraping of the spades was heard as Adam and Jonas covered his earthly remains.

'When the summer comes again, the mealies will grow tall and strong, and no one will know what lies buried beneath,' said Adam.

'No,' replied Jonas in anger. 'The mealies on his grave will never grow tall and strong. They will be small and weak, like the man's penis on which their roots will feed.'

Palesa and Sannie left the men and headed back towards the house. Once they reached the vegetable garden, Sannie turned to Palesa and said, 'I'll be fine now, you can go home.'

A bond was forged. Sannie had protected what she needed to protect, a woman's rights, rights that knew no colour, age or religion.

She could not bring herself to extinguish the flame in the lantern; the soft pool of yellow light offered her comfort in the darkness. She took off her shoes and crept into the kitchen. Softly she padded across the floor. As she stepped into the passage her eyes met Tristan's as he was silently closing the door of Hannah's room. For one fleeting second they were comrades in secrets, no words were said. Sannie moved silently past him and went into her room and shut the door.

Chapter Thirteen

The air was cool on their cheeks as they rode out to the dam the following morning. Tristan sat silently beside Hannah, their thighs brushing against each other. He had pulled the tie from her hair and it trailed in the wind, like long feathers of an exotic bird. As they neared the dam, a flock of ibis lifted into the air, and disappeared into the blueness of the morning sky. The surface of the water glistened in the sunlight and the soft boughs of the willows waved like ribbons in the breeze.

Hannah pulled up the cart and they sat in silence watching the hammerkop moving about in the mud shallows of the dam, every step designed to flush out creatures lurking unseen in its darkness.

Without turning to Hannah, Tristan spoke; his eyes focused on the strange bird. 'Last night, when I left your room, I saw Sannie.'

'Sannie?' she replied, the colour draining from her face. 'Did she see you?'

'Yes, but she said nothing.'

Hannah sat speechless; thoughts of the consequences reached out like hands at her throat. That morning at breakfast, Sannie had been pleasant and polite. It was strange that she did not take the opportunity to scream her hatred, berating Hannah for her scandalous ways.

'I wonder what her next step will be,' she said, turning to Tristan. 'What rotten luck, it's so seldom that Sannie gets up at night, she usually takes a glass of water with her to bed.'

'It wasn't water she was looking for,' replied Tristan. 'She was fully dressed and carrying a lantern. Her hair was dishevelled. She must have been somewhere…somewhere outside. She had her shoes in her hand and they were wet with dew.'

'Outside?' Hannah ran her fingers through her hair, sweeping it from her face. 'Outside?'

'Something else I found strange,' continued Tristan. 'Yesterday, after we returned from the dam and I was on my way to my room, I saw Marike taking Honnie to their room, she pushed her in and closed the door. At the time, I thought nothing of it, and then later I wondered why Honnie needed to be locked up.'

'Something happened yesterday,' said Hannah. 'Both Sannie and Marike were acting strangely, Sannie in particular. We are sisters, and as sisters, it's almost impossible to keep secrets from each other.'

They stepped down from the cart and walked along the bank of the dam. Tristan slipped his arm around her waist. The events of the night before were temporarily forgotten. They walked a little way in silence before Tristan stopped and turned Hannah to face him.

'These are difficult times, Hannah,' he said, brushing a strand of hair from her cheek. 'None of us knows what the future holds. I can't stay here until someone comes for me. I need to make my own way back to the British lines.'

'You can't leave here without a horse, Tristan,' she said. 'How far will you get on foot? There are Boer scouts everywhere. This is Boer country. They will shoot you.'

'I must take my chances, Hannah.'

Hannah reached up and softly cupped his face in her slender hands. 'Promise me you'll wait,' she whispered. 'Wait another week…two weeks. If no one has come by then maybe….maybe you can try your luck. By then you'll be stronger.'

Tristan took her hands in his and pulled her against him.

'Last night,' he said quietly, 'when I saw Sannie, I knew that my time at Doringspruit had ended. I have no idea who she might have spoken to, or who she saw last night. It's not fair on you, Hannah. It's not fair on any of us.'

He pulled away so as not to see the fear and sadness on her face. He stooped and picked up a stone and threw it across the water, watching it bounce across the surface. 'I'll wait another week, Hannah, but no longer.'

They took the blanket from the back of the cart and spread it out on the grassy bank. The corners fluttered and folded back in the wind.

'There must be bad weather on its way,' said Hannah, as she pinned the corners down with a few small rocks.

She sat down and wrapped her arms about her skirts and watched Tristan as he sat on the blanket beside her, his lean body and wide shoulders inviting thoughts into her head. Another week, that's all they had, another week.

***

They came riding across the veld four days later, two British soldiers from The Royal Leicestershire Cavalry, with a spare charger.

Marike had gone out early to collect the eggs from the fowl-run when she saw them. She stood frozen, staring into the distance beneath the peak of her pleated bonnet, the basket of eggs clutched tightly in one hand while the other reached up to her mouth. Her first thoughts were for Sannie. Had the British Army learnt about the death of Trooper Hammond? She watched them, harbingers of heartache, making their way towards the house. She turned, and in her clumsy, heavy way, ran towards the house, the basket of eggs swaying precariously in her hand.

'Sannie, Sannie, they come. Sannie, they come,' she wailed, as she ran up the steps to the veranda.

Sannie rushed out of the kitchen and stood beside her, pale-faced, and watched in fear as the riders cantered along the track in the soft light of the early morning.

Hannah heard Marike calling from the veranda. The moment she had feared had finally come. She hastily looked out her bedroom window, and then ran to Tristan's room.

Tristan had heard Marike's cries and, almost immediately, Hannah's urgent knocking on his bedroom door. As the door swung open, he saw her face, ashen with despair.

'They've come…your regiment has sent for you.'

He moved over to Hannah and took her in his arms, 'I will come back for you, Hannah. Whatever happens, hold on to that. When this war is over, we can move forward with our lives.'

He stood back to look at her. 'You are incredibly beautiful, Hannah, in so many ways.'

She moved back into his arms and clung to him. 'I love you, Tristan. Life without you is going to be unbearable. I wish… I wish this war was over and we could be together, free to do as we please. Not hiding away like…like spies or traitors.'

'I will be back for you. I will be thinking of you in each waking hour,' he whispered against her cheek. 'I love you, Hannah. Keep safe until we can be together again.'

'Promise me, Tristan, promise me you'll take care. Oh, this war…this war, what is it doing to us, to our families, to every one?'

'I've left a few addresses on a piece of paper, which I have put in the top drawer in your wardrobe. One is the address of our London townhouse in Kensington; the other is our country home in Leicestershire. If anything happens and we lose contact, you'll be able to contact me through my father.'

He kissed her, then buried his face in her hair and whispered, 'Oh God, Hannah, I love you.'

The door opened and Sannie stood staring into the room, her face drawn and her eyes filled with terror.

'The English soldiers are here, Hannah. They seem to be asking for Captain Dunn-Caldwell and Trooper Hammond.'

'I'll go out to see them now, Sannie,' he said.

'He'll be out shortly, Sannie,' translated Hannah. 'But I'll come with you and explain to them that he is here and doing well.'

Together, they left Tristan standing alone in the room and made their way out to the front yard.

Tristan looked about the room; it had been his sanctuary and his prison. It was here where he fought the gravest battle of his life, the battle to defeat death. It was in this room that he had learnt many things. He had learnt about the enemy and their Christian hospitality and simple ways. The enemy against whom he was now going out to fight, to conquer and to rule, the same enemy who had shown him nothing but kindness. And Hannah, this was her room. He would remember every detail; the small crack in the wall, the photograph of her aunt hanging in its simple black frame, the curtains faded from the sun, the yellowwood floors, and the chairs where they had spent so many long hours talking and laughing.

He walked down the passage and into the hallway. He stopped for a brief minute to gather himself, then stepped out onto the veranda.

'Sherbourne. My goodness man, you do look good,' said Tristan, with false enthusiasm.

'And I can say the same about you, Sir. The last time I saw you, I thought you'd never live to drink another brandy,' replied Sherbourne, removing his helmet. 'I must say Captain, you've made a remarkable recovery.'

Tristan smiled and said, 'I had excellent nursing, the best hospitality a soldier of Her Majesty's Service could wish for, better than any field hospital. They have been good to me, Harry.'

'Any news of Trooper Hammond? He was sent on ahead to notify you. Is he here?'

'No, not to my knowledge,' replied Tristan.

Sannie and Marike stood listening, amongst the words that were foreign to them; they heard the name Hammond and a brief glance, unnoticed by everyone, passed between them.

'No doubt he'll show up somewhere. But in the meantime, we've brought you a fresh uniform, and some toiletries,' said Sherbourne, as he ran down the steps and untied a cloth bag strapped to his saddle. He returned to the veranda with the cloth bag clasped tightly in his hand, leaving the accompanying regulars standing vigil beside their horses.

Tristan took the bag from him and disappeared into the house. Hannah, Marike and Sannie stood silent, offering no refreshments nor inviting conversation.

Tristan stepped out onto the veranda and stood tall and immaculate in his uniform, a British Captain, the enemy. The uniform was a stark reminder that he had another life, and Doringspruit had simply been a short interlude in that other life. Looking at him, with her emotions locked deep inside her, Hannah saw a man so different to the man who had worn her Pa's clothes, which Marike had haphazardly adjusted to fit. He was now a soldier, no longer her patient or her lover, but a stranger.

He turned to Sannie who stood expressionless, her arms at her sides and her lips clenched tightly together. 'Thank you for all you have done, Sannie. And Marike, thank you,' he said gently, noticing that Marike's eyes were moist with unshed tears.

He dropped down on his haunches and ruffled Honnie's head. 'My little friend and dinner companion,' he said. 'Take care of these good women, Honnie. I will miss you.'

Turning to Hannah, he could not trust himself to speak, he merely nodded, but she saw the anguish in his eyes. Briefly, he raised his hand and brushed her arm, and then abruptly turned on his heel and raced down the steps to his waiting charger.

Sherbourne nodded his goodbyes at the three women standing together in the shade of the veranda, then followed his captain down the steps to their horses. As they rode across the yard, Sherbourne turned back and waved, but Tristan looked ahead. Never look back, it can weaken a man's resolve. He did not see Marike cradling Hannah in her arms.

Chapter Fourteen

The cold winter winds swept across the veld bringing with it British victories. The Orange Free State was annexed and its name changed to The Orange River Colony. The victors marched on to Johannesburg, and on 31 May 1900, the town was captured without resistance. Lord Roberts and his men swept into Pretoria, the capital of the South African Republic, and on 5 June raised the Union flag in Church Square.

On hearing the news, Hannah and Marike decided to take the Cape cart into Hemel to replenish their supplies, and hoping to hear the latest news on these recent turn of events.

They set out after breakfast, since it was nearly an hour's ride into the little town. Along the way, they met disheartened burghers on their return home from Pretoria, many of them still sporting the ribbons of the Vierkleur, the national flag of the South African Republic.

'Now that the war is nearly over, I'm sure Pa will be home soon,' said Marike, with a gentle smile on her face. 'That is all that matters to me.'

But Hannah sat silently deep in thought. If the war was nearly over, it meant Tristan would soon return to Doringspruit and they could be together. She did not let her mind wander down the belligerent paths of her father's feelings. She knew the outrage he would feel, and the disappointment. Sannie would speak out before he had time to dismount, taking great delight in slandering her name. On their Pa's return, a new war would rage with a vengeance in their home.

The corrugated iron roofs of the little town of Hemel shimmered in the dusty, winter sunshine. Hannah and Marike made their way to the trading store, which was now run by Mr Farrell's widow. The bell on the door rang as they entered.

'Hannah, Marike. This is such a pleasant surprise,' said Mrs Farrell as she came round from behind the counter.

'We were very sorry to hear about Mr Farrell,' said Hannah, removing her hat.

'There was no truth in it you know,' she replied quickly. 'That is, I mean Mr Farrell was no spy. He had taken the wagon to collect supplies from the station, and for no reason, no reason at all, he was accused of giving information to the British.'

'Well, hopefully the war will soon be over, and we can all get on with our lives,' said Hannah, moving about the store.

'I believe the khakis are camped in and all around Pretoria,' said Mrs Farrell, struggling to keep the joy from her voice. 'The Boer Commandos will have to surrender. I believe both Johannesburg and Pretoria are empty. Those burghers that have remained have changed allegiance. But enough of that, do look around ladies, my stock is limited, but there might be something of interest.'

'I wonder if your English captain is in Pretoria?' whispered Marike, rather loudly behind her hand.

Hannah shot Marike a warning look, and continued to look around the shelves, which were practically empty.

'The women here in Hemel are still wearing the Vierkleur ribbons,' continued Mrs Farrell. 'They say their men will fight to the bitter end. How can they? They are so outnumbered. And the British army is so superior. Besides, who will take charge, now that Kruger has gone?'

'Kruger has gone?' repeated Hannah, in surprise.

'Yes, haven't you heard?' continued Mrs Farrell, a smirk creeping across her face. 'When the Khakis arrived in Pretoria, Kruger and his government had already fled.'

'Do you have any newspapers, Mrs Farrell?' asked Hannah.

'No my dear, the minute they arrive, they are snapped up.'

'In that case, we'll take what coffee you have, and flour,' said Hannah, rather irked at Mrs Farrell's smug attitude.

The trip home seemed quicker than the ride into Hemel, mostly because Hannah and Marike discussed, in great detail, the news they had heard from Mrs Farrell. Would the men be driven back to war? Who would take over from Kruger? What did all this mean?

'Sannie,' called Hannah, as they entered through the back door of the kitchen. 'Sannie, we're home. Unfortunately we have no newspapers.'

Sannie came into the kitchen happy to see the meagre supplies they had managed to buy. 'What is the news in Hemel? Is the war almost over?'

'It sounds like it,' replied Hannah, pouring herself a glass of water. 'Kruger has fled and the British are camped out in Pretoria. According to Mrs Farrell, the Boer women have stated they will encourage their men to fight to the very last.' She drained her glass and put it down on the kitchen table and went into the voorkamer. Her eyes immediately fell on the rifle rack.

'Sannie, there's a rifle missing. What's happened to it? When I left for Hemel this morning, all three rifles were there.'

Sannie came in from the kitchen. She stared at the vacant hook where the third rifle should have been hanging. 'I have no idea, Hannah. Are you sure you didn't take it with you this morning?'

'No,' replied Hannah, looking about the room to see if it had been discarded somewhere.

'I thought about taking it into Hemel in case there were problems along the way, but I changed my mind. That's how I know it was here this morning. Did anyone come into the house while we were out?'

Sannie's mind went back to the events of the morning, and it slowly dawned on her that Jonas had been on the veranda digging out the dead geraniums from their pots.

'No, Hannah,' she said. 'I can't recall anyone being close to the house.'

'Well, it's gone. Someone must have taken it. A rifle simply doesn't just disappear.'

'Who would do such a thing? There must be a mistake, surely,' exclaimed Marike, whose face was still flushed beneath her bonnet from the long ride home.

Sannie left the voorkamer and hurried out to the orchard, where Thuli was sitting in the winter sunshine with little Lettie toddling about her feet. She looked up when Sannie approached.

'Did Jonas take the rifle?' she whispered, while looking back over her shoulder.

Thuli shook her head. 'No, Miss Sannie. Jonas would not take a rifle.'

Sannie hurried to the vegetable garden where she found Jonas turning the compost.

'Jonas,' she called, as she hurriedly made her way across the furrows. 'Jonas, did you take the rifle?' Jonas continued what he was doing, not looking up when he heard her approaching, pushing the fork deep into the leaves and flicking them over. He wore one of Hendrik's old shirts that had been patched over and over again, with brown trousers which were rolled up to mid-calf.

With his head bowed over the garden fork he said, 'I took the rifle.'

'But you cannot simply take what you want, Jonas,' said Sannie, with anger flaring in her blue eyes, 'things that don't belong to you, things that are not yours to take.'

Jonas stopped what he was doing and leaned on the fork. Slowly he turned to Sannie, his dark face beaded with perspiration.

'Other men do,' he said, looking across the vegetable garden towards the barn. 'So I will take what I want. These men in uniforms are swarming across the land like ants. And like ants, they go where they please and destroy what they want to destroy. You have rifles to protect what is yours. I need a rifle to protect what is mine.'

Sannie stood rigid, her face puce with anger. 'You must return it at once. I won't tell Miss Hannah that you have taken it. I'll tell her I mislaid it somewhere. That will give you the opportunity to return it without her asking questions.'

He straightened his back and began turning the leaves once more. His head was bent in false concentration with the job at hand. 'If I must return the rifle, I will tell Miss Hannah why I need it.'

She turned abruptly and hurried back across the dry, sandy soil of the vegetable garden. Jonas' arrogance infuriated her, never once did he address her directly, or look her in the eye with the respect she felt she deserved. He was blackmailing her; that was the gratitude for what she had done for Thuli. Oh, how she wished her Pa was home. He would know how to deal with the farm workers and their heathen attitudes.

She entered the kitchen, hot and flustered from her encounter with Jonas. She turned to Hannah and said, 'I have asked the servants. They have denied all knowledge of the missing rifle, but one of them has taken it. There is little we can do about it, after all, they too have a right to protect themselves from these imperial scavengers.'

***

The veld was silvered by the first winter frost. It lay on the ground like powdered diamonds in the pale light of dawn. The migratory birds had long since gone to the warmth of Europe and the veld was silenced by their departure. Tristan rode in the grey light, his breath and that of his horse, misted in the cold air.

132

England would now be in its full glory of summer, thought Tristan. The roses at Tylcoat would be in their first flush, their heady perfume filling the downstairs rooms of the house. The swallows and house martins would be nesting in the eaves once more, swooping through the air, feeding on the wing. The long summer days, picnics down by the river, the sound of the village church bells in the distance, the damson trees heavy with fruit and the strawberries scarlet and sweet. He longed for home and the gentleness of the countryside with its verdant cloak.

War, with its victories and its defeats, left men changed. The loss of life for greed was an enigma to Tristan. He was now torn between his feelings and his allegiance. He had grown to understand this nation of raw farmers and their needs, and had begun to question the rights of the Empire. What was their quest? Was it the riches that lay beneath the soil? Or was it the power of Rhodes' dream to paint the map of Africa in Imperial red?

He could not believe his luck when his unit was ordered to join forces with Lord Roberts on their march north to Pretoria. Once in Pretoria, he knew he could slip away to visit Hannah as Doringspruit lay approximately 15 miles from the town, an easy journey to make.

Now his horse picked his way along the over-grown track, its hooves ringing on the hardened frozen ground. He was steering clear of the main route, preferring to take the small isolated tracks and cutting through areas of dense bush. If caught by the Boer Commandos he would be taken prisoner, and if caught by the British, he would be questioned about his reasons for visiting a Boer farm. Either way, it was a frightening prospect.

The sun rose in the distance and Tristan could feel its warmth against his skin. The winter sky was cloudless and the air was clear and bright.

He approached Doringspruit from the south, where the farm workers had built their huts and their kraals. As he drew closer he saw the children playing, round and chubby, running happily amongst the chickens and the goats. The smell of the smouldering cooking fires was carried in the winter air.

Tristan dismounted and walked towards the first group of neat little huts, hoping to see Thuli or Palesa. The children gathered around and stared, round eyed with trusting curiosity. A dog growled from somewhere behind the group of children, and then began to bark. An old woman came out of a nearby hut and turned back and spoke to someone inside. To Tristan's relief, the familiar figure of Palesa emerged from the open doorway; instant recognition lighting her face as she hurried towards him.

'Dumela, Palesa. Miss Hannah?' he said, pointing in the direction of the farmstead. He signalled with his hand, indicating that she must bring Hannah to him. Palesa nodded, but took him by the arm and steered him away from the prying eyes of the children. She pointed towards the old disused stables in the distance, and then hurried off in the direction of the house.

Hannah sat on the veranda, chatting idly to Sannie while Marike busied herself with her endless needlework. The warmth of the slanting sunshine was a welcome relief from the chilly morning air.

Palesa hurried round the corner and mounted the steps of the veranda pulling her blanket over her shoulders. She greeted the three women with her usual relaxed smile, and then broke into Sotho, speaking to Hannah alone.

Sannie watched Hannah's expression as she leapt from her chair; the conversation did not need translating. Hannah's face told Sannie that Tristan was back.

'I do wish you wouldn't speak that heathen language, Hannah,' she spat.

Hannah, ignoring Sannie's predictable remark, hurried to her room and changed into her riding clothes. She glanced at herself in the mirror and, with shaking hands, quickly tidied her hair. He came back, she said to herself. He had promised he would and he has kept his word. She ran into the voorkamer and grabbed her rifle. Her eyes were bright with excitement when she popped her head around the door calling to her sisters. 'I'm going out hunting, I don't know how long I'll be.'

Sannie glanced at Marike once Hannah's footsteps disappeared inside the house.

'He's back,' whispered Sannie. 'That look on her face, full of lustful thoughts, told me he's back. She's gone to fornicate with him shamelessly before the eyes of God.'

Marike looked up from her sewing.

'Sannie, don't be so unkind. He is a good man and I am sure Hannah would not betray her Christianity. She is a good sister, and a good daughter to our Pa. It's no surprise that the English captain is in love with her.'

'When a woman opens her legs, a man will love her, for that is what they want,' hissed Sannie. 'She is no better than the foreign prostitutes that can be found on the streets of Johannesburg.'

'Sannie, I cannot let you speak of our sister in such a manner, it is not Christian.'

Sannie turned to Marike, her eyes carefully concealing her hatred, and retorted with a sneer. 'What is Christian about her behaviour? It is a sin to lie with a man before wedlock, and Hannah has lain with many men. I know she gave herself to Willem Prinsloo, that is why he would have nothing more to do with this family. He did not want to be a part of a family that is tainted, a family that has the ways of the devil in it. She robbed me of a loving husband.'

'No, Sannie,' replied Marike in a shocked whisper. 'It is not Christian-like to slander our sister. Of this you have no proof. Hannah is a good woman, she has a good heart and she has values, her morals are beyond reproach. I will not listen to any more. Hannah is a Van Vuuren, and she must be treated as such. In times such as these, the bond of sisterhood is of utmost importance. That is how Pa would want it.'

***

Tristan stepped out of the shadows as Hannah approached. He stood tall and proud in his uniform, yet his face told her that he was still the same man that she had nursed, and the man who had made love to her with tenderness and passion. He waited for her to dismount, and then took her by the hand and led her into the stable.

'This is madness, Hannah, I know, but I had to come even if it was for a few brief minutes. I could not be so close and not see you.'

'It is so dangerous, Tristan,' she said, her eyes round with fear. 'But it's so, so good to see you.'

'Oh God, Hannah, I've missed you,' he whispered, burying his face in her hair while his arms pulled her hard against his chest. 'Just for a brief few minutes, let us pretend there is no war, there is no danger. Let it be just you and me in our own piece of heaven.'

Outside the Boubou shrike called from the branches of a nearby tree while the dry leaves rustled and whispered in the gentle winter wind. They made love beneath the decaying roof of the old stable with the urgency of lovers who had been parted, every minute and every second valuable, not to be wasted. Who knew where the war would take them, and when they could be together again?

Hendrik rode across the veld. His veld, his land. The land that pulsated with the same heart beat as that of the Boer nation. Their forefathers were the life-giving blood that surged through this wild land, taming it with their Christianity. They had fought long and hard; men had died in their fight for independence and, this was no different, they would fight till the bitter end. *The British Army,* thought Hendrik, *with their bayonets and sabres shining brilliantly under the African sun, would learn a brutal lesson.* His nation would fight on with obstinate determination. With God on their side, they could achieve anything. De Wet had given them time to visit their farms and their families, a morale boost, to fuel the flames of patriotism.

The veld was brown and rendered almost lifeless with the winter winds and early morning frosts. But it would spring to life again when the rains came, just as his nation would spring to life after their victory against the British.

Willem Prinsloo rode with Hendrik. His thoughts were filled with images of the baby son he had never seen, and of Elsa. Soetwater and its crops were resting, waiting for his return, victorious and jubilant. He would plant again the seeds that would flourish, giving sustenance to his family, just as his nation would rise up and flourish, delivering a bitter blow to the British Empire. His roses would bloom again in the spring, and Elsa too, God willing, would bloom with the glow of another child kicking in her womb.

They came to the rocky outcrop that stood sentinel between the two farms. The men parted, Willem swinging his horse north on towards Soetwater farmstead, while Hendrik rode straight on to Doringspruit.

As Hendrik cantered across the vast expanse of his land his thoughts were with his daughters. Times would have been hard for them, but they were strong women, he had reared them and they had pure, untainted Boer blood in their veins. Ja, thought Hendrik, Doringspruit was all the richer with his three daughters. In time, when the war is over and with God's blessing, thought Hendrik, I will have three sons-in-laws and countless grandchildren. What more could a man ask for?

In the distance, he saw the farmstead, its roof shimmering in the sunlight and the smoke curling from the chimney. The tall poplar trees to the west stood barren and the little dam to the east sparkled beneath the winter sky. God had shielded him in his battles, and now God had delivered him safely home.

Tonight, with his daughters around him, they would pray and give thanks to the Lord.

Sannie stood up from the bench on which she was sitting to look out across the veld to the horseman, who came riding towards the house. It did not take long for her to recognise the large frame of the rider and his posture in the saddle.

'It's Pa,' she screamed, tears of joy filling her eyes. 'Marike, come quickly. It's Pa. Pa has come home.'

Marike rushed out onto the front veranda, her eternal sewing trailing in her hand, and stood beside Sannie. 'It's true,' she cried. 'Pa has come home. The war must have ended.'

They ran down the steps and into the dusty front yard and began waving their arms in greeting. Hendrik raised his arm; his vision blurred by the joy of seeing his daughters, and spurred his horse into a full gallop.

'Thanks to our Father in Heaven, I am home,' he said, as he dismounted. He reached out and embraced the two women. 'Where is young Hannah?'

'She has gone out hunting, Pa. She will return home soon,' said Marike, mopping her copious tears with the corner of her apron.

'Yes, with a hare or some guinea fowl, we hope,' continued Sannie, as she slipped her arm through Hendrik's.

Hannah headed back to the house; her mind filled with thoughts of Tristan and when they could be together again. As she rode, she could still feel his touch on her skin. Their reunion was brief but passionate, their feelings and bodies galvanised into one. *When the war is over*, she thought, *there will be nothing to keep us apart.*

He had given her some books that he managed to buy whilst in Johannesburg. There were only three, that was all there was to be found in the city that was empty. Most of the foreign shopkeepers had fled at the beginning of the war and very few had returned. But Tristan had been fortunate in finding a shop run by an old German, which sold everything and anything. Amongst the dusty bric-a-brac he found a shelf with a few books in various languages, a good representation of the many nationalities that had flocked to Johannesburg with the discovery of gold.

As she approached the house, she stopped and dropped the books behind a clump of rocks near the vegetable garden, and then made her way round to the front. As she rounded the corner she saw a horse tethered in the front yard. Immediately she felt a prickle of apprehension as she dismounted. Then the bellowing, rich laughter of Hendrik drifted through the open window of the voorkamer. Her heart lifted and she ran up the steps and into the house. 'Pa,' she cried. 'Pa. Oh Pa, how wonderful to see you.'

Sannie sat in the corner of the room, her eyes observing every nuance of Hannah's movements. From the arms of her lover, to the arms of her Pa, reflected Sannie with cloying anger. The warmth of the enemy's passion must still be upon her body, and now she is locked in the embrace of her father, the man who is fighting for the rights of their nation. Has she no shame?

Hendrik was a little thinner than when he had left, but his beard and hair had grown like a mighty mane about his weatherworn face. His clothes had taken on the colour of the veld and were crumpled and ill-fitting. But his blue eyes sparkled with pride as his beloved daughters fussed and rallied around him.

He thought of his fallen comrades, lying in graves across the battlefields, and those who had been captured and never seen again. He thought of those wounded and maimed, lying broken in the veld, some young, some old, crying for their mothers or wives in their time of need. He had been one of the lucky ones. God had blessed him.

That night, Hendrik sat in his chair, the family Bible open before him, his hands, palms down, either side of the Holy book, just the same as it had always been. His voice rang out the holy words while his daughters listened with shawls wrapped about their shoulders, shutting out the cold of the winter night.

The flame in the lamp flickered, sending shadows of the Van Vuuren family dancing across the room. Hannah stared out beyond the window, her thoughts not within keeping of the Holy Scriptures, but with her lover. Now that her Pa was back, could they meet again?

'Let us pray,' boomed Hendrik, bringing Hannah back to the present moment. They bowed their heads while Hendrik started with the Lord's Prayer. He then went on to thank the Lord for his mercy, and for everything, from the food they ate, to the love and joy they shared as a family.

Hannah briefly lifted her eyes and met Sannie's cold, accusing stare from across the table. Hendrik then prayed for the sick and the dying, he prayed for those who were captured to be spared, and for their wives and widows. As Hendrik prayed, he became more ardent, for he was truly thankful for the Lord's mercy.

'How is Willem Prinsloo, Pa?' asked Sannie at long last, without a hint of that fleeting, hostile moment during the prayers between her and Hannah.

'He is home now with his wife and child. We rode together all the way from Lindley,' replied Hendrik, filling his stained pipe with tobacco. 'Ag ja, we have both been blessed by the Lord.'

'What is going to happen now, Pa?' asked Marike. 'Is Pa going to stay home?'

Hendrik threw back his lion-like head and roared. 'No. We are going to fight on. We are going to crush the mightiest Empire on this earth. We know where they are vulnerable and we will attack.'

Sannie shot a look across the table to Hannah. Whatever was planned, Hannah must not know; she would carry the news to her lover. She was Judas; she would betray her Pa, not for thirty pieces of silver, but to quell her lust.

'War is a terrible thing,' continued Hendrik. 'The waste of life, not only human life, but the lives of so many horses and oxen. To shoot the enemy's horse is a difficult thing; after all, the horse knows not what side he is on. To see beautiful horses wasting away, through lack of fodder and overwork, is a hard thing. The screams of young men dying, and the sheer terror on the faces of their beasts, will live with me forever. The smell of death becomes a part of war but you learn to live with it; it no longer repels you. It's simply a reminder that you are alive. Strange thing, that the smell of death should remind you of life.'

***

Hannah rose early the following morning, saddled her horse and rode down to the dam. The winter sky was cloudless and blue, and the air was crisp against her face. The blacksmith plovers called as she dismounted, disturbing the silence of the veld. She walked across to the willow, which stood in its winter nakedness. She sat down and leaned back against the trunk and, in the distance, saw Honnie racing towards her. Honnie, her best friend and companion. Honnie who did not judge; whose love was unconditional.

The morning light cast its brightness across the land. Her thoughts were filled with the moments she and Tristan had shared at that very spot, remembering his eyes, intense with love, and his passion. She thought of how his hands had brushed her face and her breasts, with the gentleness of an attentive lover.

She dropped her face in her hands and began to weep. She thought of her Pa, a man who was as strong as a buffalo, but had raised her with the gentleness of a woman. She thought of his unswerving dedication to his children, which had prevented him from taking another wife.

Have I betrayed my father, my family, my nation? She asked herself, with guilt washing over her like a sobering bath. Have I betrayed myself? Sannie's eyes of the night before flashed across her mind. Sannie had every right to despise her, knowing she had made love to the enemy, under their Pa's roof, in their Pa's bed. A true sin before the eyes of God. Tristan was an intoxicating power; his presence and his touch demanded from her things that were pure, exhilarating madness.

Hannah watched the rippling light across the water. The hammerkop appeared from nowhere and began his dance, seeking out his unsuspecting prey from the mud shallows. After this war, I cannot stay here at Doringspruit, she reflected. This is Sannie's and Marike's home. There is nothing here for me except hatred; Sannie's hatred for me and the hatred that burns deep in Pa's soul. If Tristan doesn't return after the war, I will go back to the Cape, to Aunt Magda.

Hendrik rode across his farm, filled with the pride of a man fighting for his beliefs. One day, reflected Hendrik with passion, Doringspruit will be passed down to my grandsons, for them to build our nation. Ja, that is why we must continue to fight. We cannot let these khakis defeat us; we must fight on for our children and their children. We will build a nation free from Imperialism. We will fight to maintain our independence, we will fight on regardless, again and again, if need be, till we have rid our beloved land of their avaricious touch.

He looked across the veld, the bright winter sunshine glistening on the thorns of the naked bushes. A sunbird settled close by, his feathers flashing iridescent greens in the light of the morning. Lord God our Father, prayed Hendrik, I give thanks to You for Your bounty. This is our Promised Land and we will be invincible.

***

Hendrik sent Jonas with an invitation to Soetwater, asking Willem and Elsa Prinsloo to Sunday lunch, which they readily accepted. Both Elsa and Mrs Cilliers, Elsa's mother, took the opportunity to dress in their Sunday best for the occasion. A sheep was slaughtered and Sannie's best pickles and preserves were served, accompanied by Hendrik's favourite peach brandy.

Sannie was a gracious and attentive hostess. She had selected from her wardrobe her finest dress, and had arranged her hair in a flattering coronet of braids. She had taken time to lay the table, using the best lace tablecloth, which was used only on special occasions, such as Christmas and Easter. The food was arranged carefully and served on the delftware platters, which usually took pride of place on display on the stinkwood sideboard.

Hannah, too, had dressed carefully for this special occasion, by wearing one of the elegantly designed day dresses Aunt Magda had bought for her. She and Mrs Cilliers spent the day discussing books and travel, Mrs Cilliers being the most vocal and Hannah the devoted listener.

Marike devoted her time to her Pa, waiting on him for his every need. Her loving eyes never left his face and she was oblivious to all the chatter and laughter. Her Pa was here in the voorkamer, and that made her world complete.

Hendrik leaned back in his chair, drinking in the homely atmosphere. At times, when he was lying out in the veld beneath the stars, with the sounds of sleeping men around him, and the occasional snort from the horses, he would dream of the laughter of the womenfolk filling the voorkamer, and the softness of their touch. When encamped on some strange kopje with the sounds of the night different to those of Doringspruit, Hendrik would long for the voice of one of his daughters.

The food was not always unfit; their resources were good. Neighbouring farms were generous to the commandos, always offering their best. More often than not, there was a fresh supply of meat and chicken, which was roasted over the campfires. At times, when they weren't so lucky, their saddlebags swelled with goods, such as biltong and rusks.

The camaraderie amongst the fighting men was good, each one looking out for the other. Songs were sung and stories were told, but nothing could compare with the warmth of the family, a home cooked meal, and sitting on the veranda with peace across the veld.

Hendrik watched as the day took on a festive air. At times it seemed as though everyone was talking at once, there was so much to tell. Putting aside their fears for one day, the women feasted on conversation. There was much laughter and little Gideon moved from one loving lap to the next. The servants in the kitchen chatted happily; there was little need for them to whisper to each other as the cheery chatter from the voorkamer filled the house.

141

After lunch, Palesa brought in a tray of coffee and biscuits. Hendrik reached for his pipe and very carefully began to fill it from a small pouch of tobacco. He tapped the pipe with deep concentration and then put it between his lips.

'Magtig, it is so good to be home with our friends and family,' he said, with the unlit pipe clenched between his teeth. He withdrew it from his mouth and said, 'This is only the beginning. We are drumming up support and rebellion in the Cape and Natal. The burghers will rise and fight with us. And we plan to destroy the enemy lines of communication and supplies. Without supplies they will surrender. They simply do not understand how determined we are.'

'Oom,' replied Willem Prinsloo. 'I would rather die in battle, fighting for independence for my son, than be ruled by a bunch of red-necks. They are nothing but vultures.'

'You echo the sentiments of us all,' said Hendrik, as he absently pressed the tobacco into the bowl of the pipe with his thumb. He tapped it once more and continued, 'They are arrogant, and it will be their arrogance that will bring them down. Magtig, they are arrogant.'

Sannie glanced across the room at Hannah, her eyes fixed and threatening. Secrets were being exchanged, and Hannah would carry them to her lover. Hannah pushed back her chair, and with a pretence of disinterest, she lifted the empty tray and went into the kitchen. Sannie heard her joking with Palesa, the Sotho language rolling so easily off her lips. Then she heard the sound of Hannah's shoes on the back steps and knew that she had gone out into the orchard.

Hannah sat down on the small bench beneath the naked, yellow clingstone peach tree. The sharp winter sunlight sent a network of shadows, cast by the leafless trees, across the yellow grass. The voices from the voorkamer drifted through the kitchen and out across the orchard. Hendrik's voice was softened by the distance, but his passion was stamped on every word. These were her people, yet as time passed, she began to feel like an ill-fitting link in a complex puzzle. She was torn between patriotism and reality. The British Empire was the mightiest Empire on earth; the Boer nation was outnumbered, and with each passing day more Boers were surrendering. The fight was futile.

Before Willem Prinsloo and his family departed, Hendrik read from the Scriptures, followed by their prayers to their Lord, thanking Him for the mercy He had bestowed upon the two families.

With little Gideon clutched tightly in her arms, Elsa and Mrs Cilliers, climbed onto the Cape cart and seated themselves beside Willem. Tears were shed with their parting. They knew that the war was far from over, it simply had taken another turn; it was now guerrilla war.

***

Two weeks later, with the winter chill on their cheeks and the fire of determination in their hearts, Hendrik Van Vuuren and Willem Prinsloo rode out to join General de Wet. Tactics and strategy had changed; this was to be a new and dangerous phase in the war.

The cold winter winds turned warm as the spring of 1900 made its ethereal visit to Doringspruit. Marike planted the zinnia seeds that the smous had given her in a flowerbed beside the steps to the front veranda. The rain, which blew in from the south danced across the veld like a magician, transforming the ravages of the dry season into a carnival of colour. The migratory birds returned, feasting on nectar and insects, or anything the new season had to offer.

Summer came and Marike's zinnias grew tall. The orchard was once again filled with warm, sun-ripened fruit. The servants worked together, picking and drying the fruit, while Sannie worked tirelessly, bottling the peaches and making pickles and chutney.

The first year of the new century had passed, and had brought with it nothing but repugnance and fear. The Van Vuuren sisters celebrated Christmas of 1900 by slaughtering a sheep and sharing it with the servants. On Christmas day, they prayed to their Lord for the safety of their Pa and an end to the war.

The summer dragged on into the year of 1901. Hannah watched the horizon for the familiar figure of Tristan. She went out riding and hunting, and frequently visited the dam with her mind filled with memories.

Sannie went out onto the front veranda each evening and watched the setting sun, her mind filled with what could have been if she had married Willem Prinsloo. And Marike, with her slow, heavy body moving about, feeding the chickens and collecting the eggs; her mind was with her Pa. She would return each morning with a basket full of eggs and a heart full of prayers.

Life at Doringspruit continued with its own pastoral routine, while the three sisters in their own way dealt with their confused and conflicting ideas of war. Commandos called in at regular intervals for supplies and any information the women might have to offer. The stories the commandos told them in return, cast dark fears over the Van Vuuren sisters for their future; news of rape, pillage, murder and farm burning.

Chapter Fifteen

A small flock of grey louries took flight as Hannah approached the fig tree. She stood in the pale, grey fortress of branches, searching hopefully for one last piece of fruit that might have escaped the attention of the ever-hungry birds. She found a fig, untouched by the louries, and pulled it from the branch. With the warmth of the sun, the softness of the fruit felt almost flesh-like as it lay in the palm of her hand.

She wiped her fingers on her apron, ridding herself of the sticky white milk that oozed from the stem. Gently she tore it open, exposing the sweet, pink seeded flesh. It was February, and almost all the trees in the orchard had given their summer offerings and were now waiting for autumn.

Hendrik had had very little luck with autumn fruits. Apple trees bore nothing but moth infested fruit so he chopped them down, but apples were not Hendrik's favourite fruit. Time and energy were too precious in Africa to waste on anything that did not yield rewards. It was the same with grapes. Doringspruit did not have the ideal conditions for grapes with its summer rains and dry winters. Some farmers enjoyed the challenge of grapevines, but Hendrik was not one of them.

She left the shelter of the fig tree with its large scalloped leaves, disappointed that the summer fruit season was now drawing to an end. In the distance, she heard the cows lowing and then the sound of a muffled shot. Honnie left her side and raced across the orchard. The colour drained from Hannah's face; she lifted her skirts and ran towards the house. Another muffled shot was fired, followed by another and then another. The moment had come. The horrors of the farm burning had now spread to Doringspruit; the hoped-for reprieve was gone.

As she entered the kitchen, she saw Marike standing, her back pressed against the wall with her hands spread across her breasts, almost in a desperate attempt to protect her heart. Her mouth hung open in mute terror, but the scream was reflected in her eyes.

'Marike, where are they?' cried Hannah, as she ran into the voorkamer. Sannie stood beside the large dining table, her white face twisted in fear. A sergeant turned to Hannah as she entered the room.

'What is the meaning of this?' snapped Hannah, in her perfect English. 'What are you doing on this farm? We have protection from the British Government.'

'Oh, yeah?' replied the sergeant, raising his eyebrows in mocked surprise. 'Who ordered it and why haven't we been told? We've been instructed to burn this farm; it's been reported that commandos visit it regularly and that you have been supplying them with military intelligence. So I must instruct my men to carry out their orders.'

'No,' screamed Hannah. 'It's unjust. We have nursed one of your men, one of your officers. I ask you, as a reward, please to leave us alone. Otherwise, I will report you to Captain Tristan Dunn-Caldwell.'

'Well, Miss,' smiled the sergeant. 'The commander-in-chief has ordered the destruction of the Boer farms, and the women and children are to be taken to refugee camps.' His eyes swept across the room, the expression on his thin, pinched face was one of disdain. He studied Hannah, his eyes running down the full length of her body, his lips curled into a sneer. 'I doubt very much if this Captain holds much sway over the mighty Lord Kitchener.'

Outside, the shots continued. Through the window, she saw an open wagon standing in the yard, waiting to carry them away from their home and their treasures, their reasons for living. Honnie barked hysterically, trying desperately to ward off these foreign invaders. Her duty was to protect these women, this was her territory, and she would fight to the death.

'You have ten minutes to gather a few belongings. I must remind you that there is very little space on the wagon, and what you take with you will have to be carried to the camps. So pack sparingly, pack only the necessities.'

Four troopers entered the house; their faces flushed from the heat.

'Go out into the garden and destroy the crops,' said the sergeant. 'Leave nothing standing. Hack every fruit tree, leave it bare. If there is a vegetable garden, destroy it.'

Hannah signalled to Sannie to follow her. Marike emerged from the kitchen and hurried after her sisters. The sergeant followed Hannah into her room and stood at the window looking out. Hannah dragged a trunk and a large carpetbag out from under her bed.

'I would prefer some privacy whilst I'm packing,' she said, her voice betraying her fear.

'Sorry, Miss,' he said, 'but privacy you ain't gonna get. This isn't a fairy story.'

Hannah opened her drawers and hurriedly threw in some undergarments and nightdresses. She pulled a few day dresses from their hangers and pushed them into small bundles in the trunk. From the bottom of her wardrobe, she retrieved her small collection of books, and threw them onto her clothing. She dragged the sheets from her bed, hurriedly folded them as tightly as possible, and placed them on top of her dresses.

All the while, she felt his eyes on her, hungry and lustful. The last item of clothing Hannah took from her wardrobe was her coat, the hem heavy with the weight of the gold sovereigns. She hurriedly pushed the small piece of paper, with the addresses Tristan had given her, into the pocket of the coat.

No sooner had she slammed the lid of the trunk and fastened the clasp, the sergeant wrenched open her wardrobe and riffled through it. He pulled the drawers from a chest and turned them over, spilling the contents onto the floor. Then he took his bayonet and ripped open the mattress, sending feathers into a cloud about the room.

'What are you doing?' rasped Hannah, in shock.

'Looking for hidden weapons or secret documents; after all, this is a war, not a bloody picnic.'

Two troopers had followed Marike and Sannie into their room. They watched as the sisters carefully packed their belongings. Marike moved about the room; her movements slow as she fumbled through her clothing.

'That's not a necessity,' snapped Sannie, when she saw Marike lovingly placing her porcelain doll in a hollow of clothing in the trunk.

Marike stared back and merely continued her packing in mute silence. She dragged out her bag of rags and began to scratch through it.

'Leave it alone, Marike,' she said impatiently, and snatched the bag from Marike's hand. 'We don't have time. Just pack what we need.' The bag dropped to the floor scattering the rags like fallen leaves. Marike dropped to her knees and fumbled mutely with the oddments of fabric, picking up one piece after the other and casting it aside in a stupefied manner. Sannie bent down and tugged at Marike's shoulder.

'Get up, Marike,' she said harshly. 'Get up, I'll pack your rags.' Sannie quickly gathered up Marike's scraps of fabric and pushed them into the trunk, forcing them down in between their clothing.

Marike stood up and moved to where her open trunk stood on the floor. Sannie watched as Marike opened her fist, and the length of fine lace Hymie Rosenberg had given her, unfurled and fell from her hand.

'I'm going into the kitchen,' said Sannie, as she pushed her way past the trooper standing at the door. 'I want to take some soap and a few items from the pantry.'

The trooper stepped to one side and let her pass, then followed her into the kitchen. Sannie grabbed a few bottles of pickles and bottled peaches, and dropped them into a large basket. She reached for the tin of dried fruit and emptied its contents onto the bottles lying in the basket. The tin itself would take up too much room.

She grabbed as much soap as they had, and the last remaining supply of candles. There were several sticks of biltong hanging from the pantry ceiling, which she hurriedly pulled from the hooks and dropped into the basket.

The soldiers had opened a tin of rusks and biscuits; nothing was left but a mess of crumbs. Sannie hurriedly grabbed a few enamel mugs, a small coffee-pot, and several plates. She moved about the kitchen, hurriedly snatching anything that she thought would be useful.

From the window in the kitchen she could see across the orchard and the men savagely hacking the branches from the fruit trees. Honnie barked as she circled them; the wiry hair on her back stood up in a ridge, and her ears were pulled back in a show of suspicion.

Sannie returned to the room and found Marike seated on her bed, her eyes staring sightlessly at the opposite wall. She wedged the plates and the kitchen utensils down the sides of their trunks, and rolled the candles and soap in one of her nightdresses.

'Let's take your little sewing basket,' she said to Marike, and reached into the back of the cupboard. 'You know your sewing always makes you so happy, and happiness is what we are going to need. And here, we'll simply pour the buttons into your trunk like this.' But Marike took no notice, her eyes remain fixed on the wall, vacant and empty.

As the sisters packed, they heard the soldiers rifling through the cupboards in the kitchen and the voorkamer. Jars and dishes were smashed on the floors. Each sound was a violent aberration on their God fearing world.

Jonas had seen the soldiers riding across the veld towards the farm. Six riders veered off and rode into the pasture where the cows stood lazily grazing the sweet summer grass. Jonas watched with horror as the first unsuspecting victim fell from the bullet that entered its brain from the close range shot.

The beasts began to scatter; the sound of the shot and the smell of the blood sent them stampeding across the veld. The soldiers raced after them, whooping and jeering, as one by one, the beasts fell, either by bullet or by sword.

Jonas turned and ran back to the cluster of huts he called home. These white ants, these destructive termites from across the sea, would not touch his cattle, his hard earned wealth, his lobola for his beautiful bride. He ran, his naked feet skimming across the veld and his brow furrowed from fear. He dashed into the darkness and cool of his hut and grabbed the stolen rifle, which was loaded and ready to fire.

As he emerged into the bright sunshine, he was faced by two troopers sitting on their horses. They had seen him running and had followed him like hunters riding with the hounds. As Jonas emerged from his hut, they saw the rifle in his hand. They raised their rifles and fired. Their bullets hit their mark instantly and Jonas fell, the expression of anger on their victim's face was obliterated by blood.

Women and children, terrified and wailing, emerged from the huts. The soldiers dismounted and began to shout at them in a language they did not understand. The dust from the horses swirled around the neatly swept compound while chickens ran, heads erect, in all directions. Two thin, brindled dogs, sensing the fear, barked with their tails between their legs.

The soldiers entered the huts one by one, turning out personal belongings such as bedding, clothing and intricately woven mats and baskets. One by one, the huts were torched. The women ran screaming from the compound, babies strapped to their backs, their little heads bouncing as their mothers ran. Young children followed, barefoot and dusty. Old men, stooped and wizened, stood and watched the barbaric acts that were being played out before their faded eyes.

The sergeant, satisfied that Hannah's room harboured no secret ammunition or rifles, moved into Sannie's and Marike's room. He pulled open the wardrobe and tossed out its contents. With great effort, he pulled it over and it smashed onto the floor, sending echoes of destruction reverberating through Marike's soul.

'God is watching,' spat Sannie. 'God will punish. Come Marike, leave Lucifer to do the Devil's work.' She took Marike by the hand and led her from the room.

The sergeant called to Hannah as he followed Marike and Sannie into the passage. He signalled to Hannah to follow him as he made his way into Hendrik's room.

'Is there a husband, or, husbands on commando?'

'No,' replied Hannah, with her hand on Sannie's arm, a silent gesture asking her not to leave her alone with this man. 'We are sisters, none of us have husbands. Our father is on commando.'

The three women left the sergeant alone in Hendrik's room to desecrate their Pa's belongings. There was little they could do; to the English sergeant, their Pa was the enemy.

Once back in the voorkamer, the sisters stared at the wanton destruction. Hendrik's beloved Delftware collection lay in shards about the floor and the handsome stinkwood sideboard lay on its side, the cupboard doors broken. Drawers had been tipped out and cutlery lay strewn across the floor. The Van Vuuren family Bible lay open on the table, pages torn from it, the ultimate act of disrespect.

Wordlessly, two troopers ushered them out onto the front veranda. From where they stood, they could see the carcasses of the cows lying in the field, and soldiers riding wildly in all directions slaughtering the sheep.

Slowly the sisters moved across the dust-filled front yard. The English soldiers' horses stood tethered to the back of the waiting wagon. On each saddle hung chickens, their chickens, their necks wrung and their feet bound together. Sannie stopped and stared out from beneath her pleated bonnet. The feathers of the chickens were bright and iridescent in the sunshine, but now seemed gaudy and gay against the lifeless remains of the once contented birds. Sannie thought of her Pa and his endless hard work on the fowl runs, securing them against the jackals, and the never-ending war against snakes. In return, these fowls had rewarded them with a bountiful supply of eggs, which enabled them to bake and cook almost anything their heart desired.

Their trunks, filled with their few chosen possessions, were loaded onto the wagon. Hannah, Sannie and Marike turned to look at the farmstead, a squat, sandstone building with a corrugated iron roof, and a wide shady veranda. It was a house that had sheltered them from the harsh African elements, and the home that had given them a childhood free from fear.

Behind the windowpanes of the voorkamer, they saw the shadowy images of the sergeant putting a match to the curtains. He stood for a few seconds with the glow of the flames illuminating his thin face, and then turned and hurried out of the house.

The flames crept up the curtains like a swarm of tongues. They curled and stretched into the rafters, and like a marauding army, they swept across the roof.

From the wagon, the Van Vuuren sisters watched this cruel act of war. The rafters cracked and the roof collapsed along with the Van Vuuren heritage and the Van Vuuren dreams.

Thuli, with baby Lettie strapped to her back, and Palesa came running towards them, their faces streaked with tears.

'Miss Sannie, don't leave us, Miss Sannie,' cried Thuli. 'Shoot them, shoot them like you did the other one.'

Sannie stepped forward and slapped Thuli hard across the cheek. 'Take hold of yourself, Thuli,' hissed Sannie. 'Palesa, tell her to be quiet.'

Thuli threw her arms about Sannie and hung onto her like a child. 'Please don't leave us,' sobbed Thuli. 'They have shot Jonas, they will shoot us too.'

Sannie tried to prize Thuli's arms from her neck. The sergeant walked up to them and pulled Thuli back. He turned to Sannie and said, 'We must leave now, get onto the wagon.'

Thuli began to wail. The sergeant relented and signalled towards the awaiting wagon and said, 'go with them if you must.' Thuli staggered forward and grabbed Sannie's sleeve.

Honnie was pressed against the folds of Hannah's skirt. Softly, she nuzzled Hannah's hand seeking reassurance. Hannah turned to Palesa, and with words that were barely a whisper, said, 'look after Honnie. Please Palesa, look after her well.'

Once the four women had climbed onto the wagon and seated themselves between their trunks and carpetbags, it began to roll out the yard. The smoke from the burning farm rose into the sky, curling wickedly in black twists of fury. As the wagon began to gain momentum, Honnie raced after it. Palesa called out, but the dog believed her place was with her mistress. Through the rising dust,

Hannah saw Palesa running slowly with her arms outstretched, stumbling after Honnie.

A shot rang out and Honnie fell to the ground. Hannah leapt up from where she was seated, and jumped from the moving wagon. The driver reined in the horses and the wagon came to a standstill. Hannah lifted her skirts and ran to where her dog lay. She dropped to her knees, and cradled Honnie's head in her hands. For a brief moment, she saw recognition in the dog's eyes, then it was extinguished like a light, and was gone.

'No,' she screamed. 'You filthy, simple minded, cruel…cruel…' She choked on her words. She buried her face in the coarse, yellow fur for a few precious moments, and then gently placed Honnie's head down. Even the love and devotion of a dog did not escape the horrors of war.

'All this cruelty and destruction and for what?' she sobbed, dropping her face into her hands.

She felt someone touch her shoulder. She looked up at one of the English troopers. He dropped down onto his haunches beside Hannah.

'It's for the best, Miss. She would've pined and fretted, and there's no place for her at the camp. You couldn't leave her here to fend for herself amongst all this madness.' His hazel eyes were moist with tears.

'I know how you feel, Miss. I've dogs of me own back home. English pointers they are. They're like me children. They mean everything to me, Miss.'

The trooper ran his hand along Honnie's lifeless body.

'I'll bury her for you, Miss. I won't let her lie here and rot. I promise you, I'll bury her. You must remember one thing, very few of us like what we are doing. We've been given orders, and as soldiers, we have no choice but to carry out those orders.'

Hannah stared at her little companion's lifeless body. Honnie had always been at her side, fearless and faithful. 'Where do you come from in England?' The question seemed foolish, her words stilted and barely audible.

'Do you know England, Miss?' Hannah shook her head in silence.

'I'm from Liverpool, Trooper Harry Smartt.'

Hannah rested her hand gently on Honnie's head, and softly whispered goodbye. She climbed onto the wagon, and it began to move down the dirt track. Sannie reached out and took Marike's hand, and with her eyes fixed on the burning farm, she said, 'The walls of our farmstead are made of stone. They will stand strong against the flames; they will not crumble. Like those walls, we sisters will stand strong and defiant against the enemy.'

Marike sat in silence, her eyes unseeing and vacant. Sannie watched the birds circling around the smoke, feeding on insects disturbed by the flames. There were always creatures that found opportunity in everything.

Hannah, with hopelessness and despair clawing at the very fabric of her being, watched the lifeless body of her beloved, little friend recede into the distance. The wagon trundled across the carcass-strewn veld, black smudges of smoke marring the blue of the horizon, as crops and homesteads burned across the land.

Chapter Sixteen

'Where do you think they are taking us?' whispered Sannie, as the wagon bounced along the dirt tracks.

'I have no idea,' replied Hannah, the images of destruction still in her mind.

'I can only speculate that they're taking us to one of the camps. When I rode into Hemel a few weeks ago, I heard Mrs Farrell discussing the camps. The commandos have been blowing up railway lines and cutting telegraph cables. The British want to punish the wives and families of those who are committing these crimes. They believe the Boer women folk are supporting the commandos by supplying them with food and information.'

'These filthy animals…and to think we nursed one of them back to health,' hissed Sannie. 'We should have poisoned him. No one would've been any the wiser.'

Little Lettie began to cry. Thuli undid the tight restraints of the blanket holding the child on her back, and tried to comfort her.

There was no respite from the heat of the late afternoon; the wagon was open, offering no shelter from the merciless sun. As it lumbered across the veld, the putrid smell of rotting flesh filled the air. They passed farm after farm; each one burnt, some still smouldering, while others stood cold and black.

Of all the things they could have taken from the farm, none of them had thought of water. Sannie dug into the basket and opened a jar of bottled peaches. They drank the syrup and ate the fruit, but the stickiness it left on their hands, added to their discomfort.

The long afternoon shadows stretched across the land. To Marike, they seemed distorted and threatening, like the hands of the devil reaching out to them. She sat in silence, shutting out the world with her vacant eyes.

'I'm worried about Marike,' whispered Sannie. 'She hasn't spoken since the soldiers entered the house.'

'She's in shock. Give her time, Sannie,' said Hannah, reaching out and taking Marike's hand in hers. 'We have all been traumatised; what we've witnessed in one day, many people never get to witness in a lifetime. It will live with us forever.'

'But she wouldn't even take a peach. It's almost as if she was dead.'

'She has crept into her own world,' replied Hannah, trying hard to hide the concern she felt. 'She knows that we are with her and hopefully that'll give her comfort.'

The wagon pulled into Pretoria station as the last rays of the sun slid behind the hills, leaving a distinctive chill in the air. The station was filled with wagons off-loading their stricken victims and their belongings. It was abuzz with voices, children crying, men shouting orders and horses whinnying.

Their trunks and carpetbags were thrown down onto the ground amidst all the mayhem. Once the wagon was empty, it pulled away without the driver so much as looking back. The Van Vuuren sisters stood dazed, uncertain of what to do.

'Hannah, Sannie,' called a voice from the depths of the crowd. They looked round and saw Elsa Prinsloo, with little Gideon on her hip, waving her arm frantically.

'Wait here,' said Sannie. 'Don't leave our things unattended, we don't know what might happen if our backs are turned. I'll go to Elsa and help her. Come with me, Thuli.'

Sannie pushed her way through the people and found Elsa zealously guarding her few small possessions. 'Come and join us Elsa, we must stick together,' said Sannie. 'Thuli, take Miss Elsa's things and put them with ours.'

'Where is Mrs Cilliers?' asked Sannie, as they made their way through the crowds.

'She fled. When she saw the soldiers, she told them that if they were going to take her, they would have to take her corpse.'

Elsa stopped briefly and turned to Sannie. 'You know....' she said, the words choking in her throat. 'She ran from the stoep. She took nothing with her. The soldiers simply let her go. My English is poor but I can understand a little. Do you know what those soldiers said? "Let her go, she's an old woman. Let the natives have their fun with her. The British Government will have one less mouth to feed." I called after her, but she ran like a meerkat. I tried to chase after her but the soldiers held me back.' Elsa paused for a brief moment, her recollections of that afternoon played before her eyes, the small farmstead of Soetwater, with all their possessions, in flames. She saw her mother, small and agile, running across the veld like a child in fear.

'Sannie, where will she go? Who will look after her?'

'Elsa,' replied Sannie gently. 'She will probably make her way to Hemel or somewhere where someone will take her in. Her English is as good as those rooineks.' Sannie's words offered little comfort; Africa was a savage land for the old and the weak.

Night fell and the wind blew in threatening clouds masking the moon. Lightning flashed vividly across the sky and the slow roll of thunder rumbled in the distance. Soon, great sucking drops of rain began to fall, slowly at first, and then a great deluge of water fell from the sky. Frightened to leave their belongings, no one moved. The small shelter on the platform was full, leaving the majority of the families open to the ravages of the summer storm.

For Hannah the rain was a relief. The dust and the dirt had crept into every crevice of her clothing, and it offered her the opportunity to wash Honnie's blood from her face and her hands. Sannie took the empty peach jar and stood it upright to catch the rain. They had learnt a valuable lesson; every drop of water they could save, save it they must.

The train pulled in the following morning. It came to a stop with loud rattling of couplings in a cloud of hissing steam. Everyone on, and around, the platform stared in shock at the open cattle trucks. Once again there was no shelter from the elements, but it did not matter for they believed God would protect, and God would provide.

They gathered their belongings, each one helping the next, and climbed into the cattle trucks.

'Look,' spat Sannie in disgust. 'They didn't even have the decency to wash out the trucks. Look at the floor, it's covered in dung, and it's still wet from last night's storm.'

The five women and two infants sat huddled together. The train pulled out from the station, the couplings rattling and clanking like giant chains of slavery, and headed south. Sannie stared out as the blackened countryside flashed by. Where was her Pa? Was he safe? Was Willem Prinsloo safe? Marike sat silently staring into the distance with vacant eyes. Anaesthetised by trauma, her mind was shut off from the world.

Hannah thought of Tristan. Where was he? Did he know of this barbarism? Did he know what his country was doing? Did he know that the family who had nursed him, who had given him back his life and cared for him, had now been wrenched from their home and suffered at the hands of his fellow countrymen? Was he doing the same? Was he tearing women and children from their homes, destroying their lives?

The wheels rhythmically clattered along the track, Tristan, Tristan, Tristan, they screamed as the train steamed across the land now denuded of life.

It was mid-afternoon when the train pulled into the station and disgorged its cargo of dispossessed humans. Close by, and running into the distance, were hundreds and hundreds of white bell tents that stood in neat rows across the dusty veld, like dots on the wings of the guineafowl. Along the barbed wire fence stood children, with haunted faces and ragged clothes, watching with bored detachment.

Bewildered and exhausted, the women dragged their luggage from the cattle trucks. The station was a sea of bonnets as people jostled and pushed their way along the platform. Soldiers patrolled the fringes of the crowd and steered them towards the gates. The Van Vuuren sisters and Thuli grouped together, and behind them, Elsa and little Gideon.

The late afternoon sun slanted across the crowd as they waited to be processed. Dust swirled around their shuffling feet, coating their shoes and clinging to the hems of their dresses. From somewhere deep in the crowd, a woman began to sing a volkslied, the notes rising into the air like the song of a bird. Children cried from the heat while their mothers cried from uncertainty. The ubiquitous buzz of flies and the stench of sewage, inseparable companions, swept down the queues.

From nowhere appeared an English sergeant and singled out Thuli.

'She is with us,' said Hannah, her hand reaching out and resting on Thuli's arm. 'She is our faithful servant, and we must take care of her.'

'I'm sorry,' said the sergeant. 'She must go to the native camp. It's not far, it's on the other side.'

'Tell him, Hannah,' sneered Sannie. 'We will not part with her.'

The soldier turned to Sannie, and in impeccable Dutch replied. 'She can come into the camp on a daily basis, if she is prepared to work. That is the best I can do.'

Thuli called out as she was led away. 'Don't let them take me, Miss Sannie, you know what they will do to me, you know, you saw. Help me, Miss Sannie, help me.' Her big, round eyes were filled with terror as she looked back. On her back was little Lettie, her sleeping head drooping to one side. Sannie raised her hand to wave, but Thuli had been swallowed up in the restlessness of the crowd.

Once all the details had been processed, and a khaki blanket issued to each, the Van Vuuren sisters and Elsa Prinsloo followed a young English officer as he made his way down the rows of bell tents.

The early evening light of the dying sunset splashed across the peaks of the white canvas. Long black shadows cut across the paths, creating sharp patterns of contrasting light and dark. Some internees stood in the glory of the light, soaking up the warmth it had to offer before the chill of the night settled over them. Others skulked in the shadows, watching with suspicion, whispering amongst themselves. Each new arrival was viewed as a possible friend by some, and by others, a possible enemy.

They came across a small group. A mother was sitting on a trunk with her sick child across her knee. Those around her were crouched on the ground weeping uncontrollably. The child was no older than little Gideon; his small, emaciated face was flushed with fever. It was clear to all that the child was sinking rapidly. Sannie turned away from the hopeless scene, but the sounds of the weeping women trailed in the air like a tragic symphony. What would happen to them all? Where did their fate lie?

Marike, with heavy movements, silently followed her sisters and Elsa Prinsloo. She looked neither left nor right, but straight ahead like a condemned prisoner being led to the gallows. She shut out this hostile world she was entering, by shutting it out, she felt she would not be a part of it.

Sannie's eyes darted about with bitterness. Every woman and every child that stood along the rows of tents had been swept away from their farms, just like they had been. Each and every one had witnessed the savagery of war in all its destructiveness.

They stopped outside the bell tent that was to be their new home for goodness knew how long. Hannah was the first to step inside. Immediately she stepped back outside, and said to the soldier who had escorted them. 'I think there is some mistake, this tent already has an occupant.'

'Mrs Katrina Harmse and her young daughter, Sunette, live in this tent, and have been here for three months. You are to share it.'

'But there are four of us and one baby, that makes five. There clearly is insufficient room for us all,' retorted Hannah indignantly.

'Look lady, in most camps there are 12 to 15 people per tent, so consider yourself lucky. This trainload of refugees will stretch this camp to its limits, and we are expecting another trainload tomorrow.'

'We are not refugees,' replied Hannah hotly. 'We are prisoners of war, and there is a difference. We have been taken from our homes by force.'

Hannah brushed past him and stepped into the dimness of the tent. Once inside, she met the hostile gaze of a woman sitting on a khaki blanket. Beside her sat her child Sunette, with eyes knowing beyond her years.

'I'm Hannah Van Vuuren,' she said apologetically. 'I'm sorry, but we've been ordered to share this miserable tent with you and your daughter. We have no choice in the matter.'

The woman stood up, her green eyes bright with anger. She brushed past Hannah and left the tent. She briefly glanced at the women gathered outside and, with her waif-like child clinging to her skirt, disappeared down the pathway between the tents. Hannah watched her hips sway beneath her skirts and her thick plait, the colour of dark honey, bounce with every step. Katrina Harmse was a handsome woman.

Darkness swiftly descended on the camp. The Van Vuuren sisters unpacked their belongings and tried, to the best of their ability, to organise themselves for the months ahead. Elsa prepared a small bed beside her own for little Gideon. Sannie, clucking all the time about the injustice, busied herself with her chest of clothing, arranging and rearranging her items.

Katrina and her daughter, Sunette, returned, and silently prepared themselves for sleep. The Van Vuuren sisters donned their coats, fearful that they would be stolen while they slept. They lay down; the hard earth beneath the khaki blankets was a harsh reminder of their privations. The sounds of the night were different, no owl called nor the nightjar, just the discord of hacking coughs and the cries of hungry infants.

Sannie woke to the sound of someone scratching in the basket of food which stood beside her. She reached out into the blackness, her hand falling on the arm of the child, Sunette.

'Leave our things alone,' hissed Sannie, in a harsh whisper. 'Go back to your bed.' Sannie released the child and reached for the matches beneath the blanket and lit the candle that stood in the mug beside her. She raised the mug, and in the dim glow of the candle, she saw Katrina leaning on her elbow. Her dark golden hair was wild about her face and her green eyes flashed with anger.

'The child is hungry, that's all,' she said, in a hostile whisper. 'If we have to share a tent, you must share your food.'

'Tomorrow,' said Sannie, tossing the child some dried peaches. She blew out the candle and lay down. Sannie stared into the blackness; she vigorously rubbed her hand trying hard to rid herself of the feel of the child's wrist, so dry and fragile, like the wing of a bird. With a sense of deep foreboding and one hand on the basket, she drifted into an exhausted sleep.

***

Tristan stood beneath the night sky, which stretched across the vast African veld, encompassing everything in its darkness. The cool evening breeze rustled across the encampment. A nightjar sang, lending harmony to the incessant call of the crickets. In the distant kopjes, a jackal barked reminding him of Doringspruit and of Hannah. He saw her in everything; the sensuous sway of the grass, the perfumed smell of fresh lemons, the bright flash of a wing of a bird. Hannah, where was she?

He had heard of the farm burning and feared for her safety. Doringspruit lay only a few miles from the main railway line that carried vital supplies up from the Cape to Pretoria, for the British troops. These farms were the most vulnerable. He was powerless to protect her, and her family. After that cold winter morning when he had ridden out to see her, he knew the risk was too great, to both Hannah and himself, to go again. What excuse could he give for visiting a Boer farm? The Boers themselves would have shown no mercy to the Van Vuuren sisters if an English officer was caught on the farm. The Boers were ruthless with those they believed to be traitors. They, too, burned farms as an example to others if they betrayed their nation. He had no way of telling her that he could not see her again. Letters were censored, and eyes and spies infiltrated every minute of every day.

He had been in the Bloemfontein district now for six months, far from Doringspruit and too far from Hannah. Since he last saw her, seven months ago, he could've resigned his commission; he had served his time. He could have sailed back to the safety and comfort of Tylcoat. But with the new guerrilla warfare and its devastating implications, he knew he could not leave the country.

Kitchener's anti-guerrilla strategy had turned the veld into a barren wasteland. The burnt out shells of Boer homesteads stood like decaying teeth amidst the bleached carcasses of cattle and sheep. The land had been swept clean of life.

He looked up at the night sky and the brilliance of the stars. The wind brushed against his cheek. Hannah, Hannah, Hannah. Was she in one of the many concentration camps? What indignities had she suffered?

He had heard his men talking, sometimes with glee, of the farm burning and looting, of the rape, whilst carrying the flag of the Empire. These regular soldiers, born in the back streets of London, Liverpool or wherever, fought in gangs and scrounged the alleys for survival, had taken the shilling for a life of adventure.

He rarely spoke to his men, the individual stories of barbaric acts he had only heard through the thin canvas of the tents, or out on the veld while his men waited for the enemy. The yawning divide between officers and other ranks was a cultural one, even in the face of war, fighting for the same cause. There were always the privileged and the less privileged, the working class, that was the way it was, and had always been for generations. War changed men, what was once the predictable became the unpredictable, and what was the unspeakable, became the acceptable. This was the nature of war.

He had kept a journal with rough sketches of the birds he had seen, and had marked their colourings. It never ceased to amaze him, the vast number of species of birds that could be seen everywhere, with their bright, exotic feathers. It almost became an obsession. He marked the date and place, paying special attention to whether they came singly or in pairs, or whether they came in flocks. This was his panacea, his escape from the brutalities of war.

Chapter Seventeen

In the first few weeks of camp life, shock and disillusionment turned into anger and resentment. Living in such close proximity to strangers was uncomfortable and alien to the Van Vuuren sisters, who always had the freedom of the large farmstead and its surrounding environment.

Katrina Harmse and her child Sunette kept their distance. They left the tent early in the morning and returned just before dark.

Marike, still silent, began to help herself, the light of recognition slowly returning to her eyes. She had dug into her trunk and found her workbasket, and busied herself most of the day with her scraps of material. No one questioned her, no one thought to look at what she was sewing. Sannie had thanked the Lord for giving her the wisdom to pack Marike's sewing items, for without them, Marike would have sunk further into her silent world.

Sannie and Elsa cemented their friendship with the adorable antics of little Gideon, now 16 months old. He was a strong and sturdy little boy, with an easy disposition. He laughed readily and was happy to entertain himself with the small selection of toys Elsa had brought with them from Soetwater. Sannie would sing to him, and she would tell him happy stories about worms and butterflies, enthralling the young child with her avid devotion.

Hannah spent the large part of her day reading. She had read the books many times but there was little else to do. Amongst them, they had designated daily chores. Since she could speak English, it had fallen on her shoulders to fetch the daily rations. On the days when there was firewood to be had, Sannie accompanied her. But very often there was no firewood, and sometimes this shortage lasted for days.

The supplies of food they brought with them, such as bottled peaches, pickles and dry fruit, soon ran out. Two buckets of water were delivered to each tent daily, regardless of the number it housed. This had to suffice for both washing and drinking. Soap was not a part of the rations; it simply was never considered important by the camp authorities. Sannie's supply of soap she had brought with her from Doringspruit was a closely guarded secret. It was only taken out when Katrina had left the tent.

***

Hannah stared down at the ration of raw meat on the plate. It was sticky and green in colour; the smell made the bile rise to her throat.

'This is unacceptable, it simply won't do,' she said to Sannie. 'I am going to the camp superintendent myself to complain. I wouldn't give this to a dog. I am sure even a hyena would turn away in disgust.'

Taking the plate of rotting meat with her, she asked where the camp superintendent could be found. A rotund sergeant smiled and pointed her in the direction of a large marquee. 'He ain't gonna see you, you know, Miss. You're wasting your time.'

'I'll be the judge of that,' said Hannah politely, and hurried on in the direction of the large marquee, which sat squarely in the veld, shining like a bleached giant amongst the smaller official tents. She didn't bother to ask the soldier at the entrance if she could have an appointment, she merely brushed past him and entered.

'Which one of you is Captain Billings?' The camp superintendent looked up and replied. 'I am. Have you an appointment, Madam?'

Hannah walked over to his desk and placed the plate of rotting meat before him. 'This is not fit for human consumption. Would you eat it?'

Captain Billings took off his spectacles and threw them down. 'Madam, of course this meat is rotten. But that is not our fault. The train bringing the meat to us was ambushed by the Boers, by your own people. It had to stand in the sun for nearly two days while the line was being repaired. I'm sorry, but there is little I can do. If you don't like it, don't eat it.'

Hannah, with a hot flush of anger burning her cheeks, turned to leave.

'Oh, and by the way,' continued Captain Billings, 'you speak English very well. Perhaps you can be of some use. We need interpreters in the camp hospital. Some of the women have outrageous beliefs and remedies for illnesses. Perhaps you can persuade them to use more civilised methods as cures for their children. If you are as forceful with them as you have been here this afternoon, I'm sure you will have every success.'

She marched out of the marquee with defeat at her heels. Where was Tristan? Where was he when they needed him?

That night, she thought of what Captain Billings had said. Her people needed her skills and if she could make a difference, then it was her duty to do so. She knew only too well the primitive cures her people believed in. Her recollection of Tristan, with small balls of dough tied to his wrists and head, made her smile. But this remedy was harmless in comparison to some cures her people practised.

Cow dung and goat's urine were popular cures for all ills. Tinctures of drops, which contained all manner of suspect ingredients were in every Boer household across the land. She knew, too, that the gossip in the camp was how the British were not to be trusted. Stories of poisoning and ground glass in food had been bandied about.

Their dying infants were brought in as the last hope and all too often, it was far too late. She knew if she could be of help, her time in the camp would not be in vain. She rose early the following morning, scraped her hair back into a severe knot, donned a crisp, white apron and reported to the camp hospital.

She found the camp doctor, Dr Forester, almost immediately after entering the hospital marquee. Staring down the row of hospital beds, she saw that each patient lay with the haunted look of the sick. Some were mothers who had infants tucked close to their sides, and others lay alone, their eyes staring far into the depths of despair.

Dr Forester was only too grateful to have Hannah on his staff. The language barrier was a huge drawback, and his staff could not afford the time in trying to make themselves understood. His nurses were overworked and took ill frequently. They were mostly volunteers from England, and were not used to the heat and the limited conditions.

Hannah began as an interpreter, but after only a few days, she had her sleeves rolled up and began to take over some basic nursing duties. As the days passed, Hannah's firm voice pleased Doctor Forester, he was at the end of his tether with women who did little to help themselves. She worked from early morning till early evening. The hospital conditions were not ideal, but she knew, out on their farms, these women would have suffered at the hands of ignorance.

One evening, tired and hungry, she made her way to her tent. It was not late, but overwork forced her to have an early night. The days and nights were rapidly growing cooler with the advancing autumn. As she approached the tent, she heard the raised voices of Sannie and Katrina Harmse.

Katrina Harmse was an enigma to Hannah and her sisters. She did little to make conversation and her replies to any question were answered in a short and brusque manner. They knew little of her circumstances, as she offered no encouragement to be friends.

Her daughter, too, was a strange and malevolent child, sneering at strangers as they passed their tent. Sunette was never far from her mother's skirt, her sunken eyes always judging the world around her. She spent her time playing with a small collection of stones, as she had no toys. Katrina was fiercely protective of her child. Sunette ate from their rations before Katrina, as she did with the small allowance of water they each were entitled to. Sunette's welfare always came first.

Hannah entered the tent. Sannie stood with her feet apart and her gesticulating arms were flying about her head in a fit of temper.

'I know you stole them,' screamed Sannie. 'I know, because I hung them out to dry on the ropes.'

'What is going on here, Sannie?' said Hannah, in an attempt to calm the situation. 'I can hear you all the way down the road.'

'Ask her,' replied Sannie, pointing in the direction of Katrina. 'She has stolen my rags. I have my curse and I washed the rags and hung them out to dry. She has taken them. I know.'

Katrina stared at Sannie belligerently. 'What would I want with your filthy, blood-stained rags? If you want more rags, ask that stupefied sister of yours. She has an endless supply.'

Sannie stepped forward, her face close to that of Katrina's. 'Tell me you took them. Tell me,' she screamed.

Katrina moved away from Sannie and sat down on her blanket. She smoothed her dress over the small swell of her belly and said, 'I don't need your rags. I have a child in my womb. A bastard child.'

Sannie, for once at a loss for words, stared at her. Katrina ran her long, graceful fingers through her wild hair, sweeping it from her handsome face.

'It happened the day they came to the farm, to burn the farm. Frederik, my husband, was shot by the British. He was a spy. Spies are shot, as simple as that. He wasn't a good husband, so I can't say I was sad. Our farm was small; we had a few sheep and a few goats. We lost all our cattle during the rinderpest and couldn't afford to buy more. But the goats gave us the milk we needed and I was able to make good cheese.

'I was happy with my husband away as I could manage everything well. I didn't have to put up with his stupid ways and the occasional beating. Ag yes, life was good without him.' She shifted on her blanket, her eyes staring into the flame of the candle.

'Then, one morning the soldiers came. They were strange looking soldiers, many of them were wearing skirts. I had never seen a man wear a skirt before. The one thing I remember so well was their legs, pink and peeling from the sun. I saw the way they were looking at my Sunette. She is a beautiful child.

'I can speak a little English, although it's not very good. My father was a clever man; he could speak English and Kaffir. He taught me English so I was able to make myself understood. I begged them not to touch her. "She is only a child, she is six years old," I said to them. I asked them not to take her innocence. I promised them they could take me instead; they could each take a turn, but to please leave my Sunette alone.

'They took Sunette outside and tied her to the back of the wagon like one would tie a calf. Then, one by one, they raped me, while the rest stood around and watched. Outside, I could hear my Sunette crying, calling for me in fear. These men who called themselves soldiers, were not human. How can a man take pleasure while a child cries in fear, while other men stand and jeer, while they watch a woman being violated?'

As she spoke, Katrina Harmse's green eyes were filled with fiery hatred.

'I didn't scream, as I didn't want my child to know what they were doing. When they were finished, they burnt my house and killed my goats and sheep. Now I carry this bastard child as a reminder of that day. I wish I needed to steal your rags, Sannie. More than anything in the world, I wish I needed those rags.'

The women in the tent sat in silence.

'I'm sorry, Mevrou Harmse. I am so sorry,' said Sannie at last. 'We are all here together, we didn't ask to be thrown together, but we are.' Sannie sat in silence for a few moments. How fortunate they were at Doringspruit. The soldiers came and did the unspeakable, but they, as sisters, were not raped.

She pulled a small piece of soap from under her blanket and handed it to Katrina. 'Here, have this as an apology.'

Katrina took the soap and slipped it under her blanket. A friendship was sealed.

***

Winter swept across the camp bringing with it heavy frosts and icy winds. Elsa was the first to begin with a cough, keeping those around her awake at night. Sannie took little Gideon into her bed to prevent him from catching his mother's chill. Hannah brought Elsa some strange tasting medicine from the camp hospital, but it had little effect. Rations were growing smaller and the supply of firewood became less frequent.

The cold nights made the early morning dew heavy, leaving everything damp and cold. As the sun rose into the pale sky, their blankets and belongings were put out in the winter sunshine to dry. Funerals were taking place on a daily basis, mostly those of infants and children.

'It's unfair, Katrina,' said Sannie, one morning as she saw a small group of women gathering together. 'They are allowed permits to go into town. We can't get permits because our father is on commando.'

'There is nothing in the town to be had,' replied Katrina. 'I have been into town. Even if I had money to spend, there was nothing I could spend it on.'

'How did you get a permit?' asked Sannie.

Katrina smiled. Her eyes looked across the camp to the large marquees that housed the supplies. 'There is a man, Jaap Venter. He is a hands upper. That is something I have never understood, a hands upper, a traitor. How can a man turn against his nation and side with the English? To me, that is treason. But anyway, if you give Jaap Venter, the hands upper, what he wants, he will arrange a permit for you.'

'Did you give him what he wanted?' asked Sannie innocently.

Katrina nodded, 'what is a few minutes, with your legs apart, to get something for your child?'

***

Marike sat in the winter sunshine outside their bell tent with her head bowed over her sewing. While her fingers were busy with her scraps of cloth, she seemed contented. Outside her private, silent world, camp life continued. No one stopped to talk to Marike, and no one took the time to see what she was busy with. The neighbours regarded her with suspicion, as her silence was mistaken for some form of insanity. When someone wanted to borrow a pair of her sewing scissors, a much-prized item in the camp, they came in twos or threes. She sat on her trunk, day after day, with her back to the sun and her sewing basket at her side.

The mid-morning sun had warmed the frozen earth from the night before. Elsa sat beside Sannie on the khaki blanket outside the tent, her eyes bright with fever. Katrina stood brushing her thick mane of hair, her eyes lovingly fixed on Sunette playing with a collection of stones.

Sunette turned her head towards the women, her golden curls shining in the sunlight. At once, she stood up and said, 'Will Ma brush my hair too?'

'Of course, Sunette. Come and sit here and I will brush it,' smiled Katrina.

The child skipped past Marike on her way to her mother's side. Marike stretched out her hand and caught the child's arm. She lifted what was in her lap and thrust it into Sunette's hand.

One of the neighbours was passing at that precise moment; a large woman dressed in black. Ever since they had been in camp, Mevrou Smit had worn nothing but black. She had seen Sunette taking the object from Marike. At once Mrs Smit snatched it out of Sunette's hand before the child had an opportunity to see what she had been given.

'What a waste of fine cloth,' she spat, and threw it down.

Everyone stared in astonishment at the scene. Katrina stepped forward to confront Mevrou Smit, while Sunette scurried over to hide in the folds of her mother's skirt. They all stared down at the object lying in the dust; an intricately made rag doll stared back. The face, made from a piece of peach silk, had two black beads for the eyes and an appliqué of red lint, which formed a smiling, rosebud mouth. The doll's bonnet was exquisitely made from a piece of Marike's white apron, and its pinafore dress was trimmed with a piece of fine Nottingham lace.

Sunette scrambled over to where the doll lay in the dirt. She snatched it up and held it possessively against her chest.

'I think it's best for you to be on your way, Mevrou Smit,' hissed Katrina. 'This has nothing to do with you. If you interfere with anyone in this tent again, you will pay for it.'

Mevrou Smit had been a Trekboer, and nothing frightened her. She had seen it all. Wandering across the veld with an ox-wagon, leading a nomadic life, there was no time for fripperies and such like. Her face was hard from the harshness of the veld, and her constant black attire was little more than rags itself.

'Those rags,' she said harshly, pointing to the doll, 'could have been put to better use. They could've patched and mended our clothes.'

'Instead,' said Marike, standing up. 'Those rags will patch and mend a broken childhood.'

Silence fell over the group of women as they turned to Marike. It was the first words she had uttered since leaving Doringspruit. Katrina moved across to Marike, who was standing with her hands hanging limply at her sides; the white apron she wore, had a large square cut from it.

'That is the kindest thing anyone has ever done for us, Marike. No one has ever given us a gift. I know Sunette will cherish it.'

Chapter Eighteen

In the last weeks of July, the weather turned bitter. The winter wind swept across the veld and whistled its way through the flaps, and sliced under the bottom of the tents creating impossible living conditions. Some internees had managed to obtain wooden packing cases, which lifted their beds off the ground, but in the Van Vuuren tent, they had not been so fortunate.

The overnight frost settled on their blankets. Sannie and Marike curled up together on one blanket and used the other to cover themselves. Hannah chose to work in the camp hospital at night, and slept in the tent during the day, as daytime conditions were fractionally better.

Sannie rose early, gathered their small ration of firewood, and made a fire to boil a pot of water. Frost lay over the camp and shimmered in the dawn light. Wisps of smoke from the small cooking fires and sounds of the awakening camp filled the air—a clink of a pot, muted voices and the distant wail of a sick child. She sat on her trunk before the fire; her hands outstretched over the flame, warming her fingers. In the distance, a pink sun was rising above the far off hills.

Once the water in the pot began to boil, she hurried back into the tent. In the dim light of the morning she saw Elsa, her unseeing eyes staring at the apex of the tent, and her slackened jaw hanging down. In her arm she clutched the sleeping Gideon. Sannie stood transfixed while the colour drained from her face. She turned and hurried to where Katrina lay.

'Katrina, Katrina. Wake up,' she sobbed, while shaking Katrina gently. 'It's Elsa.'

Katrina sat up and brushed her wild mane of hair from her face. She followed Sannie's eyes across the tent to Elsa and the sleeping Gideon.

'She's dead, Sannie. I can see it from here.'

She threw the blanket aside and leapt up. 'We should've seen it coming,' she said, leaning over Elsa's body. 'She has been ill for too long, and it has been too cold. She will not be the last to die in this tent. They treat us like animals. They don't care who dies while they are tucked up in their warm, comfortable beds.'

'Ma,' cried Sunette. 'What is happening? What are you doing?'

'Stay where you are, my child,' whispered Katrina over her shoulder. 'Tante Elsa has gone to heaven.'

Sunette sat patiently on her blanket, her hollow eyes watching her mother lift Elsa's now stiffening arm. Sannie reached out and took the sleeping Gideon in her arms, and hurried from the tent. Once outside, she began to weep, clutching the child against her breast.

'God in Heaven,' she prayed. 'Witness these sinful deeds and punish the enemy. Elsa was a good woman, she did not deserve to die.'

Little Gideon began to wake. 'Mama,' he cried hoarsely, 'where's Mama?'

'I'll go and fetch Hannah from the hospital,' said Katrina, as she emerged from the tent holding the hand of the bewildered Sunette. 'She will know what to do.'

Hannah organised Elsa's body to be taken to the mortuary tent to await her burial. The bitter winter conditions had kept the camp Minister busy; several funerals were now taking place each day.

Mourners at Elsa's funeral were many, for she had been well liked. They all huddled against the wind beside the open grave, singing hymns. Sannie stood and watched her body being lowered into the ground. Elsa was to rest among strangers, hundreds of miles from her home. She shivered at the thought. I will not die here on soil that knows nothing but sadness. I will fight to protect myself and this motherless child of Willem Prinsloo.

***

'We need packing cases, Hannah,' said Sannie, once they had returned from Elsa's funeral, 'or else we will all die. In most tents, they have packing cases to raise themselves off the frozen ground.'

'I'll ask the camp doctor, but he's swamped daily with requests of all sorts,' replied Hannah. 'He really does try his best. He has to meet demands from the camp authorities and internees. He's simply dead on his feet, but I will see what I can do.'

'That's not good enough, Hannah. Your hospital would be only half as full if the camp authorities took some care. I'm sure your Dr Forester sleeps well in a nice warm bed, a proper bed,' snapped Sannie. 'I think I'll go to the storage marquee myself tomorrow and ask for packing cases. I'm sure if I offer a fair sum of money, Meneer Venter will not refuse.'

'You can try, Sannie,' said Hannah, tugging at the bow of her bonnet. The ribbons parted and Hannah pulled the bonnet from her head. 'Even if you find some packing cases, Sannie, there are no guarantees that we won't fall ill.'

After breakfast the following day, Sannie tidied herself up. In the five months they had been in the camp, she had lost her brawniness and her clothes hung on her in a shapeless manner. She pulled the sash around her waist till it fitted snugly, brushed her hair and shaped it into a neat design of braids in the nape of her neck. She would make sure that Meneer Venter did not view her as some simple-minded Trekboer. No, he would see her as a wealthy, sophisticated woman, who knew what she wanted, and had the means to pay for it.

She found the marquee that housed the stores. An English sergeant, fully equipped with rifle and bayonet, stood outside the entrance. Sannie was at a loss for words, since she was unable to express her wishes. She was about to leave when she saw the hands upper, the defector, Jaap Venter.

He hurried over to Sannie. 'Can I help you with anything, Mejevrou?' he said, smoothing down his dull brown hair with the palms of his hands.

'Yes,' she replied, with a pleasant but aloof smile. 'I am Mejevrou Van Vuuren, and I urgently need some packing cases. Yesterday, we buried one of our dearest friends who died of pneumonia, leaving a young child motherless. Unless we can get some packing cases, so that we can make some beds, I'm afraid we will all die.'

Jaap Venter was a shrewd man. He quickly assessed Sannie's clothes and her bearing. He had been in this camp long enough to distinguish one type of Boer from another. This woman who stood before him was not a Trekboer. She showed some refinement.

He disliked the Trek Boers; they were coarse and hard, and their cleanliness was questionable. They led a nomadic life, moving from place to place over the open veld, in wagons they made their home. The camp superintendent had trouble with their toilet habits, as they always fouled outside their tents, never bothering to use the buckets or the latrines. No, this woman was either a town Boer, or, she was from a prosperous, well-run farm.

He could see that she had made an effort with her appearance to see him, her hair was neat and her face was clean. His reputation was obviously spreading.

She was no beauty; her features were too flat and her face too broad, but her teeth were white and evenly spaced. He could see that, under normal circumstances, she would be a handsome, buxom woman. The idea of getting under her skirts aroused him. Very often, these self-righteous women enjoyed rough game play. Once tasted, he knew they would return.

Venter smiled. 'Come over to my living quarters, they serve as an office as well. I can see what's available and I will be able to tell you when the next lot of rations will be unpacked.'

Sannie, with her broad shoulders pulled back in an effort to show her proud bearing, followed him to a row of tents behind the large storeroom marquee. Once outside his tent, he stepped aside and allowed her to enter first.

He stood a few inches taller than Sannie with a face that was browned and hardened by a lifetime in the sun. Down the front of his khaki shirt was a small splattering of oil stains, evidence of a hurried meal. He wore khaki trousers, which were showing signs of an urgent need of laundering, and slung low on his hips was a zebra skin belt, the buckle of which was hidden beneath his corpulent abdomen.

The interior of his tent was cluttered and untidy. To one side stood a desk littered with papers and bric-a-brac, and around the perimeter, every available square inch was haphazardly packed with large wooden crates.

With his eyes fixed uncomfortably on hers, he reached out, and, through the layers of her skirts, she felt him grab her crotch.

'That is not the payment I had in mind, Meneer Venter,' she said, pushing his hand away forcefully. 'I have money and I will pay for the cases.'

'Wooden packing cases are very expensive. How much money do you have, Mejevrou?'

'What is the price, and I will tell you if I have the money?' replied Sannie, stepping back away from him.

Venter stepped forward as Sannie stepped back. She found she was backed against the desk. He placed a thick, muscled arm either side of her and rested the palms of his hands on the desktop.

'Where did this money come from, Mejevrou?' he asked, with his eyes running over her breasts. 'Did you steal it? Is someone from the outside paying you for information about this camp?'

'No, of course not,' said Sannie, leaning back over the desk in a desperate attempt to get his face out of hers.

'I have the authority to have your tent searched if I suspect you are receiving payment from the commandos.'

His dark, fleshy face was beaded with sweat. Sannie felt his breath against her skin; it smelt of tinned sardines.

'We…no, I brought the money with me. It's not much at all.'

'If you have offered me payment, it means you have sufficient money. I am obliged to inform the camp authorities that I suspect money is changing hands. They will act on this information and your tent will be searched.'

The very idea of soldiers rifling through their meagre belongings filled her with fear, their intrusive eyes searching through intimate items of clothing. If they found the sovereigns stitched into the hems of their coats, they would be confiscated on the grounds of false payment. It could be argued that they were spies for the commandos. At all costs, their tent was not to be searched.

'I have a few shillings, that's all. My sister works at the camp hospital and is paid a small amount for her duties. Other than that, we have no money. But the little we have, we are prepared to give you for a few packing cases.'

'Well then, you don't have enough money. As I have said, the cases are much in demand and they are very expensive. But there are other forms of payment that I know you will enjoy.'

With leering authority, he took hold of her, spun her round, and pushed her forward over the desk. She felt him fumbling with her clothing, his rough hands scraping against the softness of her skin. He threw her skirts over her back and pulled down her bloomers. He kicked her feet apart and then fumbled with his trousers.

With a short, sharp pain Sannie felt him enter her. He rode her like the bulls she had seen on Doringspruit. There was no tenderness, no exchange of love, just pure repulsive thrusting. Katrina's words echoed in her mind. 'What is a few minutes with your legs apart to get something for your child?' Gideon Prinsloo was now her child. Tomorrow, she would try and forget this violation. Her anger boiled inside her for she knew that for the hands upper, it was simply another victory in a game of power.

When he was done, she hurriedly pulled up her bloomers and dropped her skirts. 'Where are the packing cases?' she asked, fighting for control of her voice and smoothing down her skirts with shaking hands.

'Packing cases? There's none to be had. All the packing cases are used for coffins and firewood. With this cold winter, firewood is in great demand,' he replied, running his thick fingers over her shoulders.

'But you said…do you mean you took advantage of me, knowing there were no more packing cases?' she hissed, as she slapped his hand from her shoulder.

'No, Mejevrou,' he sneered. 'You offered your cunt so that I would not have your tent searched.'

Sannie spat full in his face. 'You filthy animal, you vile, contemptible snake.'

Venter wiped the spit from his face with the back of his hand and smiled triumphantly. He leaned over and foraged in a box beside the desk.

'Here take these,' he said, thrusting three small tins of condensed milk into her hands. 'And this,' he reached out and grabbed a tin of corned beef from the top of the desk.

'You can have this for your virginity,' he said, his lips curling into a pompous smile. 'Next time it will only be the condensed milk.'

Sannie left the tent. This war had made a whore of her, and by some twist of fate it was one of her own kind that had done it. She knew she could never eat tinned sardines again.

**

The cold July month marked its passing with an unacceptable death rate from pneumonia and bronchitis. August followed with a new devil on its back, measles.

Hannah worked tirelessly at the hospital. Very few patients left the hospital to return to their tents; they arrived too late for the camp doctor to save them. Mothers were refusing to send their sick children to be hospitalised; they felt they were better off in the unhealthy conditions of their tents and with their own remedies practised out on the veld.

At every opportunity, Hannah asked every native she saw of the whereabouts of Thuli. The replies were always the same. No, they did not know of a Thuli. Yes, they would let her know if they found her, but it must be remembered that there were thousands in the native camps and it was hard to find an individual. Maybe she was sick. Many hundreds were sick and many hundreds had died. There was no hospital in the native camp, no doctor or nurse. The food was so poor that you had to find work to be able to eat. Yes, if they found Thuli they would bring her to the white hospital. But, week after week, and month after month, no news arrived of the whereabouts of Thuli or baby Lettie.

***

Hannah left the hospital just as the camp was beginning to wake. The wind swirled between the tents kicking up the dust from the dry winter months. She looked up at the dawn sky; small clouds scudded across, like a flock of ethereal angels waiting to spirit away the tragedies of winter. Spring was on hand, and in Africa, spring passes through in the blink of an eye. Within weeks, summer would arrive, bringing with it a blanket of flies during the day, and at night, the incessant mosquitoes. The summer storms would send a deluge of water across the camp. No tent was equipped to keep the water from flowing under it, saturating bedding, food and clothing.

As she walked down the row of white bell tents, now tinged with pink in the glow of the rising sun, she dreamed of Doringspruit. Spring was a beautiful time of the year, the orchard standing in a cloud of peach blossoms and the veld returning to life with wild flowers and sweet, green grass.

Overhead, a flock of ibis winged their way to a destination unknown. So strange, thought Hannah, that life continued despite the war. Seasons still came and went, birds and creatures of the veld followed their natural instincts, and the sun still rose in the east and set in the west. Now, on this fragment of land, a barbed wire island in the veld, all she witnessed was row upon row of immense sorrow. Beneath each bell tent lived dispossessed families, their faces gaunt with tragedy, cut off from the world outside, the world they knew so well and loved so dearly. Was God truly on their side?

The workload in the hospital was immense. Dr Forester had left to resume his duties as an army medical officer, and a civilian doctor had taken his place. Dr MacNamara was a man of compassion and a breath that betrayed his liking for whiskey. He did not have the energy that an overcrowded hospital of dying patients demanded. Two of their best-trained nurses had died of scarlet fever and one had died of measles; a further three were recovering from exhaustion.

As Hannah approached the tent, she saw Sannie sitting on her trunk in front of a small dying fire, her bonnet casting a shadow across her face, drinking a mug of coffee. Marike was sitting on her folded blanket, with buttons scattered about, playing with Sunette.

176

'Is Katrina here?' asked Hannah, as she dropped down and sat beside Marike.

'She's resting,' replied Sunette idly, as she placed her collection of stones in a neat row. 'Look Tante Hannah, these are my English soldiers, and these here are the Boers,' she said, pushing some stones into a fold in the blanket. 'They are hiding behind the mountain.'

'Katrina must not let Sunette play with the other children,' said Hannah, running her hand affectionately over the child's golden curls, 'for the time being anyway, and keep Gideon away from everyone. Measles is everywhere. The best we can do is to not allow them to mix with others.'

'Here, let me make you some coffee,' said Marike kindly.

'Oh, I'm exhausted,' said Hannah, scratching absently through a pile of Sunette's stones. 'The hospital is packed to capacity with measles. It's rampant. I do wish some of these mothers would listen to us.'

Katrina emerged from the tent, her wild hair falling around her shoulders in a cloud of unruly curls. She bent over the fire to lift the coffee-pot.

'Ah,' she groaned as she straightened up, while rubbing the small of her back. 'Oh, it's so painful. Ah, another one, and so soon. My time has come.'

Sannie and Hannah stood up immediately. 'Keep Sunette busy, Marike,' said Hannah, taking charge. 'I'll run up to the hospital to fetch some clean, boiled water. Sannie, take Katrina into the tent and let her lie down. I'll be as quick as I can.'

After that day when Katrina had opened her heart to the Van Vuuren sisters, she had never mentioned her pregnancy again, and when asked about it, she subtly changed the subject. It was only over the last two months that the swelling of the growing infant inside her was noticeable. She, herself, had made no provisions for the forthcoming baby; it was Marike who had spent time making small nightshirts from one of Elsa's many petticoats. In the last week, a baby's wooden crib had arrived on loan from one of Katrina's camp friends. Katrina had graciously thanked the friend, and put it out of sight in the tent behind her clothing.

Her labour was swift and Katrina dealt with it with little emotion. She was silent apart from the occasional obscenity. Her eyes stayed focused on the roof of the tent, never looking at Hannah or Sannie. No matter how hard they tried, the Van Vuuren sisters could not get Katrina's attention on the impending joy of another child. Her wild hair was spread over her pillow like a large Catherine wheel of gold. Her brow was furrowed with pain, and her flawless skin was running with sweat.

Outside the tent, Marike played with Sunette and kept a watchful eye on little Gideon. Hannah and Sannie knelt before Katrina, chatting excitedly and counting the contractions. Katrina's face contorted with the pain, she groaned and heaved, then bellowed into the muted light of the tent, and finally her bastard child was born.

'It's a girl!' cried Hannah excitedly. 'Katrina, you have another daughter.'

Katrina lay with her head thrown back, drained and emotionless. Sannie took the child and bathed it in the bucket of water that Hannah had brought back from the hospital. Once the child had been bathed, Hannah used the bucket to discard the bloody remains of the afterbirth.

Sannie swaddled the child in some sheeting and handed her to Katrina.

'She is truly a beautiful baby, Katrina,' she said. 'Look how perfect she is. Her head is so round and her little face is flawless.'

Katrina took the infant in the crook of her arm and gazed down at her. 'Yes,' she whispered. 'You're right, Sannie. She is a beautiful baby.'

Marike and Sunette came into the tent to witness the new arrival. Sunette, fascinated by this miniature form of human life, reached out her thin, papery hand and gently stroked the baby's forehead.

'What are you going to name her?' asked Marike, with her eyes fixed adoringly on the swaddled bundle lying beside Katrina.

'I haven't given it much thought,' replied Katrina with detachment, her hand reaching out to brush Sunette's cheek affectionately.

'What about Elsa,' said Marike. 'It's a fine name and I'm sure Elsa would be pleased.'

'No,' said Katrina. 'Elsa was a good woman. I cannot give her name to a bastard child.'

'No one need ever know, Katrina,' said Sannie hurriedly.

Katrina's eyes moved from Sunette to her baby. 'I will know,' she said, with little passion, 'and I will never forget.'

To Sannie there was something wild about Katrina. Her unruly hair, as beautiful as it was, was difficult to restrain, and Katrina made no effort to do so. Her lips were full and sultry and rarely smiled. She was tall and built to perfection, with strong bones covered with firm, muscular flesh. She was secretive, communicating only when it suited her. She would leave the tent on some days, never revealing with whom she was visiting, and returning after dark without mentioning a word on the day's happenings. She carried her pain in the very core of her soul, locked up behind her startling green eyes.

'What about calling her Katherine,' said Hannah tentatively. 'Katherine is very similar to Katrina.'

Katrina eased her arm out from under the baby. 'Do you know a Katherine?'

Hannah reached out and took the new-born in her arms. 'No,' she said, 'not personally, but it is a beautiful name for a beautiful little girl.'

***

Hannah found her work in the camp hospital rewarding. She mixed easily with the English nurses and enjoyed their lively chatter. News of the war filtered into the camp, of battles won and battles lost. Hannah hung onto every scrap of information. When an officer rode into the camp escorting supplies, Hannah eyes looked for any sign that it might be Tristan. Where was he? Was he still alive? Sometimes the news of the war was not encouraging, not for Tristan's well-being, nor for her Pa's.

She befriended Nurse Polly Edwards. Polly was the youngest daughter of Reverend Edwards, a vicar in a small Hertfordshire parish.

When Polly had enlisted, she'd envisaged nursing sick and injured soldiers fighting for the Empire, she had no idea that she would be nursing women and children dying from the ills inflicted on them by her own country. She was passionate about her cause, feeling the injustice of Lord Kitchener's scorched earth policy.

Feeding thousands of prisoners of war was costing her government millions of pounds of the taxpayers' money, something that in her mind could clearly have been avoided. She was a bright young woman who had grown up in a home where politics was a soul mate to religion. Reverend Edwards felt strongly that one was inextricably linked to the other. He had championed the rights of children, and was strongly opposed to the war in South Africa.

Some young women had signed up for the adventure and the opportunity to fraternise freely with the soldiers. Others, like Polly, signed up for honour and dedication.

Polly was a compulsive conversationalist, she jumped at every opportunity to teach or inform others about her country. Hannah's enquiring mind and her fascination with Britain drew her to Polly. They organised that they worked the same shifts, they exchanged books, not that they found much time to read, and spent nearly every waking hour together.

Polly's love for her country was reflected in her descriptions of the countryside, and her vivid stories of her nation's history. Hannah always sat enthralled; it was her tenuous link to Tristan. She never confessed to Polly her involvement with Tristan, she merely commented that she knew an English officer, fighting in the war, as he was a friend of a relative.

Day after day, new internees arrived at the camp. The overcrowding led to more disease, and disease led to an overwhelming number of deaths. Medical supplies and hospital beds were in short supply. Nurses were weary from their onerous duties, and rations were stretched to the limit.

Hannah had never asked Sannie how she had obtained the extra rations for Gideon, but she had seen her outside Jaap Venter's tent, and Venter's reputation was widespread. The camp superintendent, weighed down by more pressing matters, turned a blind eye. Despite the sordidness of the situation, she felt a deep compassion and admiration for her sister.

In snatched moments of solitude, Hannah would sit alone with her thoughts. How often, in her mind, she had walked through the orchard with Honnie at her side, listening to the louries fluttering in the branches laden with sun-ripened fruit. She would hear the familiar sound of the creaking floorboard in the voorkamer, or Thuli's sweet voice humming a lullaby. She would sit on the veranda looking out across the veld at the crowned plovers screaming at dangers known only to them, and Honnie, panting in the heat of the day.

These were memories, carefully boxed away like a precious collection, to be treasured, for those were the things that were no more. These were memories that over the passage of time would turn to sand.

Chapter Nineteen

Marike tossed feverishly on her blanket. The cold she had been suffering with had sent hot surges through her lethargic body. With water being rationed, it was difficult to quench her thirst, and the cough syrup that Hannah had brought back from the hospital did little to ease the rasping pain in her throat.

The night was warm, so the tent flap was left open for the air to circulate. A long wedge of silver moonlight cut across the floor of the tent, illuminating the sleeping women and children. Marike heard a movement; she turned her head and saw Katrina silently leaning over the crib of baby Katherine. There was little movement, and then, silently, Katrina crawled back to her blanket. Marike thought nothing of it and fell into a fitful sleep.

Sannie rose early the next morning and went out to start the fire. Marike sat up on her blanket and looked across the tent. She had kept to herself over the last few days for fear of passing her cold onto the children, especially little baby Katherine. She watched Katrina rise up from her blanket, and without looking down at the crib, Katrina called out to Sannie.

'Sannie, Sannie. Come quickly. It's the baby. I think the baby is dead.'

Sunette jumped up and went over to where the lifeless body of baby Katherine lay in the small, wooden crib.

'Ma. Oh, Ma,' sobbed Sunette hysterically. 'She is so cold.'

'Go outside, Sunette. Gou. Quickly,' shouted Katrina, pulling the young child away. Sunette ran from the tent, her emaciated, bird-like body visible through the thinness of her over-large, cotton nightdress.

'Tante Sannie,' she wailed. 'My baby sister is dead.'

'Ssh, my child,' said Sannie comfortingly. 'Let me go and help your Ma.'

Marike watched Sannie lean over the dead baby. Sannie's face crumpled and a loud choking sob burst from her lips.

'No, it can't be. Last night she was so healthy. She drank so readily.'

'It's one of those things, Sannie,' said Katrina, her green eyes staring down at her baby. 'Some babies just simply die in their sleep, for no reason at all. And, goodness knows, this baby had reason enough.'

Marike's astute eyes followed Sannie and Katrina as they left the tent. She eased herself up from her blanket and went over to the crib, and lifted the baby into her arms. Little Katherine had been a beautiful infant. Cradling the motionless body against her chest, she began to weep, rocking back and forth, back and forth, with her face twisted in grief.

***

The camp photographer arrived, offering to take photographs so Katrina could show the father a picture of the child he would never see. Katrina turned to him, her face hard with resentment. 'I will never see the father again.'

'I am sorry for your loss,' said the photographer, mistaking Katrina's words. 'It's a shame you have lost your husband, and now his child.'

Katrina stared at the photographer, an opportunist, death was his living. She turned and walked away from him as though he had not spoken at all.

The camp Minister came to break the news to Katrina that with the death rate so high there were insufficient coffins. The baby would have to be buried in a blanket.

Marike, on hearing the news, dug deep into her trunk and found the piece of lace Hymie Rosenberg had given her. She cut a length and tied it around the baby's chin, fastening it on the crown of her little head, weeping as she did so. She then wrapped little Katherine in a silk shawl Hannah had once given her. She cradled the dead infant in her arms and once again rocked back and forth, keening as she did so. 'Why? Why did she do this to you, why?'

Not many mourners attended the funeral. So many funerals were taking place each day that people were now only attending funerals of close friends or family relatives.

The women stood beside the little grave under the sweeping African sky. Marike, with eyes heavy with fever, watched as they lowered the tiny corpse into a hurriedly dug hole. Baby Katherine was buried on the distant outskirts of the cemetery, far from the graves of others. Her gravesite told the world that she was buried with shame, the shame of those who had not been baptised.

***

A cool breeze blew in through the open flap of the tent, fanning Marike's feverish cheeks. From the blanket on which she lay, she could see the sharp clear light of the morning, and the shadows of the women as they sat on their trunks. Their idle chatter and the gravelly sound of their shoes scraping on the sand drifted into the tent.

'I'm going to take a walk to the cemetery.' Marike heard Sannie say. 'I want to take Gideon to visit his mother's grave.'

'What does a child know about death and graves, Sannie?' came Katrina's curt reply.

'Elsa was our friend.' Sannie's voice rang with indignation. 'She was the mother of this child and he must remember her grave, as young as he is. One day, he might want to return here to visit her.'

'He's a mere infant, Sannie. How will he ever remember?'

'Why don't you come with us? You can visit Katherine's grave.'

'Death is looking back.' Katrina's voice was muted, as though she was looking into the distance. 'I never look back,' she continued, 'Looking back is the past. We cannot change the past. We must look to the future, because the future is the road we are going to have to walk.'

Marike heard the fading crunch of Sannie's footsteps as she walked away. She eased herself up onto her elbow and, with her weak fingers, wiped the sweat from her face. She stood up, and then went out of the tent into the sunshine. The brightness of the light shot through her head, white-hot with intensity. She put her hands to her face and closed her lids over her aching eyes, to shield them from the sun.

'You killed her, didn't you?' Marike whispered.

Katrina was seated on the trunk and looked up when Marike spoke. Her hair was pulled back and the fine curls, which sprang from her hairline, caught the morning light, creating a fuzzed halo about her beautiful face.

'Yes, I killed her. She was a bastard child.'

'A child, none the less,' choked Marike, as she lowered her feverish body and sat down on the sand.

'A beautiful healthy child. How could you, Katrina? It is a sin before the eyes of God to take a life, especially the life of an innocent child.'

Katrina's face was hard as she looked across at Marike. 'It is a sin to create a life in an act of violence. In simpler words, Marike, to rape.'

'No matter the circumstances, she was innocent.'

Katrina stared into the distance, her face devoid of any expression.

'She was your flesh and blood,' continued Marike, 'a child of your womb, growing beneath your heart. An innocent young child, God's creation.'

'What do you know of my feelings, Marike? Tell me, what do you know?'

Marike closed her eyes to shut out the heat of the sun and the coldness in Katrina's voice. Her head spun with weakness and sorrow.

'All I know is that murder is a sin. I saw you that night, leaning over her crib.' Marike dropped her face into her hands. 'Why? She was so perfect. If you did not wish to keep her, why didn't you give her to me? You know I loved and cherished her. She could have had all the love I had to offer.'

'And how would you have fed her, Marike?' spat Katrina. 'Babies cannot live on love alone. They need food. Where would you get the food? Would you have sold yourself to Venter, like Sannie, to get milk for a child that is not yours? God knows, that is the only way she would've survived in this hell.'

Marike dropped her hand from her eyes. Her mouth opened but was wordless in shock. She gathered herself together and whispered hoarsely. 'The eyes of God are on you Katrina, and He will punish you as He sees fit. And never again will I hear from you such slanderous and unchristian things about my sisters.'

Katrina shrugged her shoulders.

'Believe what you will, Marike. You have always lived in another world, a world where you are safe. I can't blame you for that. We all have our ways of surviving.' She turned to Marike, her face showing no sign of remorse.

'Remember one thing, Marike. What lies between a wise woman's legs, she uses to her advantage, but what lies between the legs of a foolish woman, is her downfall. Sannie is a wise woman.' She picked up a small pebble and examined it absently.

'Don't be naïve, Marike, this world is much too cruel to be naïve.'

'But she was your child, your blood. Did you not feel, as mothers should feel, an overwhelming love for a child so young and so innocent?'

'Every time I looked at that child,' said Katrina, tossing the pebble across the sand, 'I would remember that day. If she grew to be ten, fifteen, thirty, whatever, her face would be a reminder of that day. The day I lost my home, my livelihood and my dignity. The day fear was born in Sunette. Five men, Marike. Five men.

Each taking their turn, laughing, jeering, while Sunette was fettered to the wagon like a rabid dog. Can you understand that?'

Marike sat in silence.

'This war has changed us all,' continued Katrina. 'We do what we do to survive. I did what I did to survive, and to survive, I needed to bury the past. As simple as that, and nothing more.'

She stood up and dusted down her skirt. She turned and walked away, leaving Marike seated in the sand.

***

Hannah walked down the path towards their tent. Grey clouds hung low in the morning sky; the dry season was about to end. Hannah noticed the absence of Sannie seated before the fire, the familiar sight that she had become so accustomed to each morning, after a long night at the hospital. She hurried her step, sensing something was amiss. Marike, it had to be Marike.

She had begged her to go to the hospital, but Marike, like thousands of women before her, believed a hospital to be a place of death.

Hannah's steps broke into a run. The sky over the camp darkened with the threat of the imminent rain. She hurried into the tent and saw Sannie on her knees. She was hunched forward with her face in her hands, while her body convulsed with uncontrollable sobbing. On the blanket beside her was Marike's inert body, her face waxen in death.

Hannah dropped to her knees beside Sannie and reached out her arms. The two sisters clung to each other, united in their grief. Marike had always been in their lives, like a solid rock, always there, guiding her younger sisters.

Hannah reached out her hand and brushed Marike's cold cheek. Marike, her sister, her surrogate mother, her confidant. Marike, who was slow to learn, but wise in many ways. She would never again feel those loving arms of comfort around her, she would never hear her soft chastisement again or see her deft fingers working their wonders with a needle and thread. Hannah's world was spinning in grief.

'I knew she was ill, Sannie,' sobbed Hannah. 'But I never thought she was so close to dying.'

'I woke this morning, Hannah, and she was gone,' wailed Sannie. 'No sound... so silent, just so much like Marike. Slipping away from us, and not reaching out for help.'

Sannie brushed the hair from her wet face with the back of her hand. 'I am so afraid for her, Hannah.'

'There is nothing to be afraid of now, Sannie,' whispered Hannah gently.

'Last night before she went to sleep, she said...she had such fear and anger in her.'

'What did she say, Sannie?'

Sannie reached out her hand and brushed Marike's cold forehead with her trembling fingers.

'She questioned her faith. Marike, our good Christian sister, questioned her faith. "Why?" she said. "Why has our Lord forsaken us? Why has he let little children die such cruel deaths? Why has our Lord let our children suffer? If He were the true merciful Lord, he would not do this to us." I could not console her. Her cheeks were hot and her eyes were bright with fever. I never thought... I never thought she would not live to see the morning. I think...I think, Hannah, Marike died of a broken heart.'

'No, Sannie,' said Hannah gently. 'Our sister had too much to live for. She had been ill for a long while, it's these dreadful conditions under which we live, it leaves no room for sickness.'

'If only...if only,' sobbed Sannie. 'If only we were back at Doringspruit. We could bury her where she was so happy, somewhere where she could always see her home.'

Sannie wiped her nose on her apron. 'But then, if we were back at Doringspruit, Marike wouldn't have died. Oh, Hannah, what will become of us all? Where is your English lover now?'

'Sannie, it's not in his power to help us,' said Hannah quietly. 'That I know. I am sure if he knew how much we are suffering, he would do what he could to help us.'

Hannah lovingly touched Marike's hands, which lay folded across her breasts.

We are women waiting, she thought. *Waiting for freedom, waiting for the war to end, or are we simply waiting to die?*

The hours that followed seemed like weeks. Hannah and Sannie sat beside Marike and reminisced over their childhood. Marike had been the mother to

Hannah, and to Sannie, an inseparable companion. Both sisters knew Hendrik favoured Marike, but this had never fuelled resentment, since no one could harbour ill feelings towards a woman who gave nothing but kindness.

Hannah sat with her chin on her knees and wept; life would never be the same without Marike. She was the calming waters of Doringspruit. Marike, in her heavy and slow awkwardness, had an inner beauty that glowed in her vivid blue eyes. She had been much loved by everyone who met her.

In the dim light of the tent, Hannah dressed Marike in her Sunday best, and Sannie combed and plaited her hair. The remaining piece of Hymie's lace was tied around her head and under her chin, holding her jaw in place, then fastened in a neat bow in the hollow of her temple. Marike's kind and beautiful nature did not deserve to be extinguished in such an unforgiving and crude way. *Tristan*, she thought, *where are you in our hour of need?*

Outside, the rain began to fall. The drops thrummed on the canvas, marking the passing of another dry season.

The rain never ceased, turning the pathways between the tents into thick, sliding mud. Both Hannah and Sannie did not wish for Marike's body to lie amongst strangers in the mortuary, so she lay with her sisters until the funeral cart came to fetch her the following day.

Hampered by the unforgiving torrents of rain, the walk to the cemetery was slow. The mud sucked at their shoes, and clung heavily to the hems of their dresses. Sliding from side to side, the funeral cart laboured through the mire, its wheels flinging mud in all directions. Once at the gravesite, Marike's blanketed body was taken from the cart and lowered into the grave, the bottom of which lay several inches of water.

Hannah stood with her head bent, memories of her beloved sister flooding her mind. The gentleness of her touch and the love she gave to those who most needed it, transcending every adversity that they had encountered.

Hannah sank to her knees and wept. The rain slashed mercilessly across her back, cold and unrelenting. She wept for her sister, whose inner beauty and innocence could never be matched. For the first time in her life, Hannah felt alone, lost in this hostile war with its shadows that crept across her dreams, the war that had robbed her of everything she had held precious. 'Oh God,' she cried out. 'When will this madness end?'

The mourners were few, not because Marike was not well respected, but because of the inclement weather and fear of infection. The internees preferred to keep themselves safe beneath their sodden tents.

The two Van Vuuren sisters, Katrina and Sunette were the only mourners. Standing ankle deep in the mire, they listened to the hurried words of the pastor, which were uttered from memory, as the driving rain made it impossible for the Holy Book to be opened.

The sky above was dark and threatening. Emotion clawed at Katrina's throat. Besides Sunette, Marike had been the only person Katrina had ever grown to love. She stared down into the shadowless grave at the body, which lay beneath the blanket, the image blurred by her tears, and knew that her secret was safe forever.

Chapter Twenty

On 31 May 1902, in a marquee in Vereeniging, all the important Boer leaders voted to accept the terms of a British peace agreement. They had little choice; their situation was hopeless.

The destruction of crops and the slaughter of animals had cut their food supply. The number of men on commando grew fewer by the day, and the condition of the women and children in the concentration camps was pitiful. It was an unpalatable situation for the Boers. De Wet tried to persuade the voters to continue the war, calling for their faith in God. But in the end, even De Wet himself saw the futility of continuing the fighting.

The vote was 54 in favour of accepting the terms, and 6 against. The delegates boarded a special train bound for Pretoria, and the official peace agreement was signed that night, in the dining room of Melrose House.

News of the surrender took time to reach those commandos in remote areas of the country. It was met with disappointment and outrage by most, and among these men was Hendrik Van Vuuren.

Frans Groenewald rode into the camp late Sunday afternoon on June 1st, the day after the official signing of the peace agreement. The Hemel commando was at rest. The morning had started with prayers and hymns, and then lengthy readings from the Bible. The veld was bathed in bright winter sunshine, but a cold, dusty wind swept through the long dead grass, cutting through the bedraggled clothing of the men.

'I have grave news,' shouted Frans Groenewald, as he dismounted from his exhausted horse. 'It is with a heavy heart I have to inform you that a peace agreement has been signed. The war is officially over.'

'Over?' shouted Hendrik. 'On what terms?'

'The terms are these,' replied Groenewald, his voice ringing with despair. 'Prisoners of war are to be brought back. No proceedings to be taken against us. Rifles to be allowed to persons requiring them for protection. Three million pounds to be set-aside for payment of war losses. Dutch and English to be taught in schools…and so it goes on. It is over. We must lay down our arms and swear allegiance to King Edward VII and the British Empire.'

'Never,' spat Hendrik. 'Never will I swear allegiance to the verdomde British Empire. Magtig, we must fight on.'

'Oom,' replied Willem Prinsloo. 'Oom, we cannot go on. Look at the country. Look at our womenfolk. We have no choice.'

Hendrik threw his arms up in outrage. 'With God's blessing, we can achieve anything, and God has blessed us, Willem. We have both survived. Look at these men around you; they are strong fighting men. God is telling us we are strong enough to continue.'

'It has been agreed, Oom. The peace agreement has been signed. We must lay down our arms. We cannot go on, it's now out of our hands and not a moment too soon. Look at us Oom, look at our clothes. God Almighty, I pray that our women folk are safe. We must now consider them. How they must have suffered.'

'We have nothing to lose now, we have lost it all,' shouted Hendrik. 'Magtig, we have lost it all.'

***

News of the peace agreement swept across the concentration camp like rivulets of bright water. Women hurried about the tents exchanging information, some were overjoyed while others shook their fists with fury, outraged that their men had not defeated the British.

Hannah heard the news from a young English officer, who was escorting supplies to the hospital. She stood for several moments, her heart and mind in ecstatic turmoil, the war had ended. God in his mercy had seen fit to end it. Her immediate thoughts were of Tristan. God willing, they would be together again at last. She hurriedly finished what she was doing and quietly slipped out of the hospital marquee.

The long afternoon shadows of the bell tents stretched across the wide, dusty pathways. Hannah ran, her skirts bunched in her hands, carrying the news that they were free at last.

'Sannie, Sannie,' she called, as she approached a small group of women gathered in a knot of heated conversation.

Sannie turned to Hannah, her eyes alive with excitement. 'Have you heard the news, Hannah?' she said. 'It's over, the war is over.'

Mrs Smit, the Trekboer, dressed in her sombre black attire, turned to Hannah and Sannie. 'It's disgraceful, shameful,' she said, her mouth curling into a sneer in her sallow face. 'Our men are cowards. They must return to war and fight till the last khaki is dead.'

'We can go home now, Hannah,' said Sannie, her voice ringing with emotion. 'Oh, Hannah, this is such good news.'

'We must wait till Pa comes to fetch us, Sannie. Sergeant Douglas has said it is not safe for women to return to their farms until their men are with them. We have been advised to stay here till all the mayhem of the aftermath of war is over. It might take weeks, it might take months, we must be patient.'

Hannah left Sannie to the heated discussions of the women and returned to the tent. She collapsed on her blanket and stared up the familiar white canvas. I have survived all this madness and death, she thought. Sannie has survived, and little Gideon. She raised her hands to her face. Let Tristan be alive, she prayed. Oh Lord our God; let him be alive so that he can come back to me.

Sannie left the group of women to argue among themselves. For her, the end of the war meant that Willem Prinsloo would come looking for his son. She had no doubt in her mind that he had survived; a man so vibrant and strong, in her mind, could never die. She felt Elsa's death deeply, but her death had left the door of opportunity open for her once more.

Katrina fell into step with Sannie as they made their way to their tent.

'Have you heard the news, Katrina? The war is over,' said Sannie, the flush of excitement still on her cheeks.

Katrina tucked a strand of hair behind her ear and replied in a bored, distracted tone. 'Ag ja. The war is over, but the hatred will continue. Just look at those women, shouting and arguing as though their voices will be heard.'

'What will you do now, Katrina, now that it's over?' asked Sannie.

'I'll find something. I haven't given it much thought, but I won't go back to the farm. Perhaps I'll go to Johannesburg. There will always be work for a hard working woman. With the mines being in Johannesburg, it'll be a good place to start. There are shops and hotels, so there will be something for me. I am not frightened of work.'

'But what of Sunette? Who will look after her? She is so young.'

'There will always be those women willing to care for someone's child at a price. Maybe a servant.'

Sannie looked at Sunette who was sitting on her haunches, stabbing her bony finger at an insect struggling in the dirt. Despite her emaciated little body, Sunette had defied all the odds and remained healthy, never to be heard coughing, or seen with a runny nose. In the beginning, Sannie had struggled to warm to this strange child. She was secretive like her mother, communicating only when the mood took her. Her birdlike movements as she darted soundlessly around the tent, always scratching for leftover food, irritated and annoyed Sannie, often resulting in harsh words snapping from her lips.

But one afternoon her feelings changed. Sannie had returned from visiting Marike's grave, and as she entered the tent, she heard a hurried, scuffling noise. The dim shadow of Sunette was reflected on the canvas behind Katrina's pile of belongings. Sannie, suspicious of Sunette's devious nature, went over to the child, and pulling her by her thin arm, yanked her out of her hiding place. The child cringed and pulled back. 'I'm sorry Tante, I'm sorry. Please don't whip me.'

Her green marble-like eyes sunk deep in their purple sockets, stared up at Sannie in terror, and the skin on her skeletal face was pulled taut in a grimace of fear. Around her lipless mouth was a sticky white ring, and clutched tightly in her hand was a tin of Sannie's illicit condensed milk.

A sharp sting of guilt shot through Sannie; no child should know such fear. Lying nearby, on the floor of the tent, was the rag doll Marike had made for Sunette. On the red lint mouth of the doll were white smears of condensed milk. The doll's beaded eyes stared up at Sannie, and for a moment she saw Marike.

Sannie released the child's arm, her fingers leaving white impressions on the frail wrist. Sannie was filled with shame. What did this waif know about love, security and all the rosy things a child should know? This was a child, no different to any other; she did what came naturally to her; pretence and games. Sunette was merely feeding her make-believe child, an instinct only a woman would know.

This child was no different to any of the women in the camp; she was fighting for her right to live. She was part of the sisterhood of survival. From that day forward, Sannie felt an overwhelming need to protect this scrap of a child, to shelter her from the harsh realities of life in the camp.

'You must come home with us, Katrina,' said Sannie, after a while. 'You cannot let strangers look after Sunette. She's had a hard time here in the camp. Even if you stay with us for a short while. You might find work in Hemel and we can look after her, we have all grown to love her. Think about it, Katrina.'

***

Tristan had been given orders to escort some recovering troops to Cape Town, where they would board ship and return home to England to rehabilitate in full. He, himself, had been slightly injured, taking a blow to the wrist; therefore, he was exonerated from taking part in active service in the field.

It was Sunday morning when the news reached him that the peace settlement had been signed the day before. Cape Town was jubilant; the word was on everyone's lips. Peace! Cape burghers, colonialists and khakis rejoiced in the streets.

Tristan's first thoughts were of Hannah. He had to get to Doringspruit as quickly as it was physically possible. Cape Town docks were choked with ships, loading and offloading. Ships with livestock would take priority, and then supplies and fodder. Tristan knew it would be days before the Asterleigh Castle could dock and he could see the soldiers safely on board.

How many times had he thought of her, trapped in one of the many concentration camps? He had a vision of her behind the barbed wire fence, waiting for him to come to her. Many a night he had woken to his own cry, her face swimming before him, bloodless and cold in death.

The end to this war had not come soon enough. Some 24,000 prisoners of war were in camps outside of South Africa. These men needed to return to their homes and resume life as they knew it. All the women and children of the Boer nation, who had survived the harsh living conditions in the concentration camps, needed to be repatriated. The land had been denuded of livestock and crops. Men and women, on both sides of the divide, were now weary of war. The war had ended but the dust was yet to settle.

Chapter Twenty-One

Hendrik and Willem Prinsloo rode in silence. The burnt ruins of farmsteads, standing amidst the bleached bones of the livestock, scarred the veld around them. Their emaciated horses were slow, faltering in their weakness. The lack of fodder had taken an unforgivable toll on both sides of the war. Nothing upset Hendrik more than the sight of horses stretched out beneath the sun, dying of starvation. He had seen hundreds, and yet he still could not come to terms with the cruelty of it. More than once he had used a much-valued bullet to put an end to the suffering.

They stopped for a short while beside a small dam to rest and water their horses. Both men sat quietly with their own thoughts; what awaited them at Doringspruit and Soetwater? The sun was low in the sky and sinking fast. The decision to continue their homeward journey weighed heavily on their conscience, for the horses were almost spent. But the pull, like some gravitational force, was stronger than their guilt so they pressed on, leading their horses on foot at a slow pace.

The moon, now in its last quarter, cast a dim light over the veld. A sharp wind rustled through the tall, dry grass, the chill of it stinging their cheeks. They hobbled their horses and lay down to rest. Hendrik stared into the blackness of the night sky, and prayed to his Lord for the well-being of his daughters.

It was midmorning when the two men parted; Hendrik heading east to Doringspruit and Willem Prinsloo swinging his horse north to Soetwater.

The road Hendrik took was a road he had ridden many times before, but never with such fear and trepidation. He saw the small plantation of gums casting their dry shade, like blue stains, upon the veld. As he passed and rounded the bend, he saw the burnt ruin; the charred sandstone walls of his home standing like a chilling ghost against the cloudless African sky.

He reined in his horse and sat for several minutes. Images of what might have taken place flashed before his eyes. His daughters; what had become of them?

What had the enemy done to them? He heard a cry; it took a moment before he realised the dry, choking sobs came from his own lips. He spurred his horse on with his eyes fixed on the destruction, the taste of bitterness deepening with every faltering step of the way.

He climbed the concrete steps to the veranda, his feet heavy and slow. As he entered the house, a rock pigeon took flight, its wings fluttering in the stillness. He watched it rise as it flew above the roofless walls and disappeared. Picking his way between twisted and distorted sheets of corrugated iron, he walked from room to room.

In the voorkamer, he found bits of broken delftware, shining white and blue in the dust. Weeds had sprung up in the far corner growing tall and lanky as they reached for the light.

He moved to the kitchen. A small circle of stones marked a place where someone had recently made a fire, ironically where the stove had once stood. He crossed to the burnt-out doorway, and looked out across the orchard. The fruit trees that had once stretched out their fruit-laden branches like arms offering their bounty to the world, were now merely termite-ridden stumps standing amidst the weeds.

He made his way to Marike and Sannie's bedroom. Through the windowless hole in the wall, Hendrik heard the dry leaves rustling in the chilled winter breeze. In his head he heard the laughter of his children, and the ring of their footsteps on the wooden floors. He bent down and picked up a glass button, glinting like an eye in the debris.

He entered Hannah's room and walked across to the window, through which he saw the apricot tree standing unchanged and strong, the only living thing to escape destruction. A bulbul came to rest in its lower branches. The morning sunlight slanted across the veld beyond, pale and beautiful.

Hendrik slowly picked his way down the passage into his bedroom. Once again, the opening in the wall drew him towards it. This window once looked out onto the wide, shady veranda, the veranda where coffee was drunk, and the girls shook out their wet golden hair to dry. He turned and looked about the room, the room where his children were conceived and where they had been born. The room in which his beloved wife had died.

He pulled at a contorted sheet of corrugated iron. I'll start in this room, he thought. This is where I'll begin to rebuild our lives.

***

Hendrik spent the following day resting. He made mental notes of things that needed to be done. His first priority would be his daughters. After resting his horse for a day and a night, he rode out to Soetwater. Along the way, he saw the bones of his cattle, and his fields lying dusty and barren beneath the winter sun.

The small track to Soetwater from Doringspruit was overgrown, but since Hendrik had ridden it many times, he was familiar with every twist and turn, knowing every rock and every boulder.

Once he had passed the dense plantation of wattles, Soetwater came into view. Doringspruit had suffered greatly, but the walls of the house had stood firm. The walls of the Soetwater farmstead were burnt almost to the ground. No outbuilding had survived the onslaught: the flames of the Empire were too powerful and too strong for the primitive wattle and daub structures. Soetwater had taken a heavy blow.

Hendrik walked around the remains of the house, but Willem was nowhere to be seen. He walked across to the little dam and looked across the barren fields to the veld beyond, the dark foliage of the wattles outlined against the pale winter sky. Hendrik dropped to his haunches and examined the spoor of Willem's horse; his experienced eye told him that Willem must have left Soetwater at first light and headed in the easterly direction of Hemel.

Hendrik mounted his horse and headed back to Doringspruit. The sun was overhead in the cloudless sky, casting precise, squat shadows upon the veld. As he rode, he felt the pulse of the earth beating, and begging for a new beginning. A band of pygmy mongoose ran across his path. The last of the group stopped and looked at him inquisitively, then hurried on and disappeared into the dry grass.

Hendrik felt his senses sharpen with the pure, exhilarating joy of being alive. This was his land, and all around him was God's creation. He looked across his barren fields and saw them as they once were, filled with the shimmering leaves of young, green mealies; cows, slow and sluggish with the weight of their distended udders and his vegetables, growing with eagerness in their furrows. Doringspruit would live again; the Van Vuuren spirit would rise up and be reborn.

In the distance, he saw a man seated in the shade of small acacia tree. The man stood up and waved as Hendrik drew closer, and then began to run towards him. Hendrik saw it was Adam.

Hendrik dismounted as Adam approached.

'Magtig, Adam,' cried Hendrik. 'Magtig, I am so pleased to see you.'

Adam bowed in his usual respectful manner. 'Baas, I am happy to be home, and I am happy to see that the baas is not dead.'

Hendrik bellowed with laughter, 'Magtig Adam, it will take a lot more than a British bullet to kill the old lion of Doringspruit. Come Adam, tell me what has happened. Do you know where my children are?'

Adam shook his dusty head. 'The soldiers, many, many soldiers came. I saw them on the wagon, but then, I do not know. They burnt all our houses, they shoot Jonas. It was terrible, my baas. It was very bad.'

They fell into step as they walked back to the house. The clothes Adam wore were clean and in good condition, on his feet he wore a pair of British soldier's boots.

'So, Adam, where have you been?' asked Hendrik, with a hint of suspicion creeping into his voice.

'When the soldiers came, my baas, they took us to one of the camps. The camps were very bad, very bad. There was no food for us. The children were very hungry. They told us if we want food, we must work. So one day, some soldiers they come to the camp, they say if we are strong they can give us work, and if we work hard, they will give us money and food. They took my brother and me so we could help build the blockhouses.'

Hendrik remained silent until they reached the front steps of the veranda. He sat down and removed his slouch hat. Running his fingers through his hair, he said, 'Do you know where the others are, Adam?'

Adam shook his head once more. 'Palesa went to the camp, but I think she die there. When I saw her, she was sick, very sick. The doctor could not come as there was no doctor, so I think she die.'

Hendrik shook his head. Palesa had come to Doringspruit as a young woman and had been a loyal servant to his wife. Hendrik remembered how she'd wept when Johanna had died, and how she had cradled the little, new born Hannah in her arms. Yes, these people were heathens, but they were still God's children.

'And Thuli?' asked Hendrik.

'I don't know. Aletta, she tell me Thuli went to work in one of the white camps, far away. I don't know why. Some were sent to work on the farms to grow food, but many just die.'

'And now, Adam, what will you do?' asked Hendrik.

'My baas, I want to work here and build my house. Many men went to work in the mines; they tell us it is good money. But baas, I want to see my house every day, and count my cattle. I do not want to work in the stomach of the earth and not feel the sun on my back. That would not be good. When I wake in the morning, I want to hear the laughter of my children.'

Hendrik thought for a long while. He could not condemn Adam for working for the enemy. He knew only too well how the servants on the farms had suffered. At least, Adam had not joined a band of renegade natives who raped and pillaged everything that crossed their paths.

This had not only been a white man's war; the natives had to fight for their own survival. Some, like Abraham, had ridden with the commando as an agter-ryer while others took their chances out on the veld. And what did these simple-minded people know, thought Hendrik. Work was work, food was food.

***

For seven days Hendrik pondered on how to find his family, and how he was going to collect them. He could not go alone with only one horse; they would need transport of some kind. He had ridden into Hemel and had confirmation that families from the Hemel district were in a concentration camp thirty miles south of Johannesburg, situated along the railway line.

Two days later, Hendrik saw in the distance a wagon drawn by four trek-oxen making its slow laborious way towards the house. Squinting against the sunlight, he saw Willem Prinsloo raise his hat in greeting.

'Magtig, Willem. How did you come by this?' called Hendrik, his eyes bright with joy.

'I went into Hemel to visit my sister and her husband, Schalk,' said Willem, as he drew the wagon to a halt. 'They told me to ride into Pretoria and ask the Repatriation Department for a wagon so that we can go and collect our families.'

'Magtig. We must go now, this very minute, to fetch our women. We can't waste another hour. Let's go,' said Hendrik, his voice choking with emotion.

***

As Hendrik and Willem drove through the gates of the camp, shock and disgust overwhelmed them. The sting of disinfectant and sewage assaulted their nostrils, while their eyes were riveted on the overcrowded conditions.

As they climbed down from the wagon, women and children swarmed round like ants at a feast. Hendrik looked from one face to the next, but all were strangers. He asked after the Van Vuuren sisters, but no one seemed to know. 'There are four thousand women and children here, Oom. Van Vuuren is a common name.'

Hendrik and Willem walked down the dusty pathways between the tents. Faces looked out, some with suspicion and some with envy, and some looked out in anger. Every face told a story of desperation and longing. Their clothes were faded and dusty, patched in whatever fabric could be found. Children stared out from behind their mother's skirts, whispering questions with voices of fear.

'Pa, look it's Pa.'

Hendrik spun round. A young woman stumbled towards him with her arms outstretched. Hendrik's heart quickened, but as the light caught her face beneath her bonnet, he saw she was a stranger.

'Pa has come to take us home.' Hendrik turned away, he saw in the young woman's dark eyes that she was insane.

It was Hannah who spotted him first. She saw them moving slowly down a row of tents, her Pa with his hat clutched to his chest and Willem Prinsloo, clean shaven and solemn. Hannah ran, her feet barely touching the ground. She reached out and touched her Pa's arm. Hendrik turned and saw Hannah, relief and joy reflecting in his vivid blue eyes.

'Hannah, my child, my little lamb. Thanks to our Lord, it is you.' Hendrik embraced his daughter, cradling her in his giant arms while he wept.

'Take us to the others,' he said at last.

Hannah eased herself free from Hendrik's arms and said to Willem Prinsloo. 'Your son is doing so well. He has grown and is quite a sturdy little fellow now.'

'And Elsa? How are Elsa and her Ma?'

'Her Ma never came to the camp. But Elsa…I am sorry, Willem. The pneumonia was too much. So many women and children died. It has been a difficult time for us all.'

199

Willem stood and stared into the distance. Hannah saw his jaw clench and his nostrils flare in suppressed emotion. 'Where is little Gideon, my son?'

'Over there,' said Hannah, pointing to the clutch of women at the end of the path.

'And Pa,' continued Hannah, her hand resting on Hendrik's arm. 'Marike...Pa, I am sorry, but Marike is with Elsa.'

Hendrik sank to his knees and buried his face in his hands. 'My first born,' he whispered. 'No, not my gentle Marike. What has the enemy done to our families? Look at this wickedness. What kind of nation punishes women and children, destroys homes and slaughters livestock? And they call themselves civilised.'

Hannah knelt down beside Hendrik, and put a comforting arm about his shoulders.

'Marike is at peace now, Pa. She was so very unhappy. She prayed for Pa's safety each night, but never prayed for her own. We all miss her dearly.'

Hendrik stood up and reached out and took Hannah's hand.

'Come Pa, let me take you to Sannie.'

Willem Prinsloo followed silently, while Hendrik gave vent to his hatred. In the distance Willem saw Sannie; on her hip was his son. God had been kind; He had spared him his son.

As they approached, the group of women dispersed. Mrs Smit called out from beneath her black bonnet. 'Cowards, go back to the battlefields and fight the enemy. How dare you surrender.'

Sannie turned and saw her Pa, and then her eyes fell on Willem Prinsloo. Joy and elation overwhelmed her; he was safe. God had listened to her prayers; Willem Prinsloo had been spared.

After the emotional greetings were over, Willem reached out his hands to take his son from Sannie's hip. The child pulled back, turning his face away and flinging his arms around Sannie's neck.

'He will get used to you. It will take time,' said Sannie, patting the child comfortingly on his back. 'What does he know about men. The only men he has seen have been either hands-uppers or impatient English soldiers.'

'Take me to Elsa's grave, Sannie,' he said softly.

Sannie pointed in the direction of the cemetery, which lay in the distance. 'It's over there,' she said. 'Come, I will take you.'

They walked side by side down the path between the tents towards the veld, strewn with wooden crosses.

Willem stared down at the small, crude wooden cross with its simple inscription. 'Elsa Prinsloo.' He knelt down and prayed, while Sannie kept a respectful distance. When she saw him raise his head, she joined him once again.

'I wish I had some of my roses to put on her grave,' he said. 'She loved the roses, particularly the white ones.'

'One day, when your roses bloom again, you can come back and put them on her grave,' replied Sannie, as she put little Gideon down and sat beside Willem.

The winter wind swept across the veld, cold and uncharitable. She pulled her shawl closer about her shoulders.

'We should not have continued to fight the way we did,' said Willem. 'Our nation was too small to face the numbers we had to face. If we had surrendered when Pretoria fell, none of this would've happened. Elsa would be alive today. Gideon would have his mother.

'Look at all these unnecessary graves. Look at them Sannie, hundreds and hundreds, and this is only one camp. What about the rest? No, our nation could not afford this loss of life. The cost has been too great. What has it achieved? This war has given birth to hatred, hatred that will last for generations. We are not blameless, Sannie. I have seen our own men plunder farms. I have heard of commandos injudiciously burning farms and raping helpless women. No, we are not blameless.'

The wind tugged at the fringing of Sannie's shawl, and at the brim of her bonnet. She reached out and took the hand of little Gideon; she did not trust herself to speak. Willem stood up and looked out across graves, some new and some old, some marked and others nameless.

'I hardly knew her at all,' continued Willem. 'We did not have much time together. But I knew she was a good woman, she didn't deserve to die. She would have been a good wife and a good mother.'

From across the cemetery, Sannie saw her Pa and Hannah making their way to Marike's grave. She left Willem's side and made her way towards them. Together they knelt down and prayed, a grieving family beside a grave, a sight that was common across the land.

They all returned to the bell tent to collect their meagre belongings, when Katrina appeared for the first time, her wild hair unrestrained. She stood at the flap with a look of uncertainty on her face.

'Pa,' said Sannie hurriedly. 'This is Mrs Katrina Harmse. Katrina and her daughter have shared the tent with us. More than that Pa, she has shared our sorrows.'

Hendrik's blue eyes drank in the image of the woman standing before him. Her face was in shadow as she was silhouetted against the brightness of the sunshine outside, but Hendrik could see that she was tall and handsomely built.

Hendrik bowed respectfully, and said, 'Will your husband be coming to fetch you now that the war is over?'

'My husband is dead. I have no husband. He was a spy. They shot him, that is what they do to spies.'

Hendrik was shocked at the forthrightness with which she offered the information.

'I am sorry, Mrs Harmse. I am truly sorry,' replied Hendrik. 'Do you have family to whom you can go?'

'I have no family other than Sunette, my daughter. But we will survive. If you can survive this,' she said, waving her arm about the tent, 'then you can survive anything.'

'Mrs Harmse,' said Hendrik. 'Since you have been a close companion to my daughters, you must come home with us. It is not safe for a woman alone, especially with a child. The war is over but peace is still to come.'

'Ja, Katrina, you must come back with us to Doringspruit, you must,' said Sannie, her eyes bright with the excitement of returning home. 'Sunette will enjoy the farm.'

'It's a good idea,' continued Hannah. 'We have been warned that the country is still quite hostile. It will be best for you both to come back with us, until the dust settles.'

Katrina looked to where Sunette was seated on her blanket, her eyes large and round in her skeletal face. 'Ag, please Ma,' said the child. 'Please can we go with Tante Sannie and Tante Hannah. Please.'

Hendrik watched Katrina move away from the entrance. She made her way to where her belongings stood beside her blanket. She looked back at him over her shoulder. Her green eyes were difficult to read, but Hendrik felt somewhere there was a glimmer of gratitude.

When her packing was done, she heaved up her trunks to carry them out of the tent. Hendrik reached out to relieve her of her burden, but she brushed past him, stooped, and made her way through the flap and into the sunshine.

Willem and Hendrik carefully dismantled and folded the tent and placed it on the floor of the wagon, packing the trunks, carpet bags and blankets on top. The camp superintendent issued one month's supply of rations for each. Inside their wagon, drawn by four oxen, sat three families with their meagre possessions, each touched by tragedy.

The journey home was uneventful. They stopped and outspanned for the night, setting off once again, when the winter sun appeared over the bleak, distant horizon.

The wagon trundled down the dirt track to Doringspruit. The excitement of returning home eased the despair of the burnt farmstead. For a short time, they sat in silence as they reflected on the charred remains of what was once their home, their sanctuary, their history.

'We're home once again and that's all that matters now,' said Sannie. 'I knew those walls would withstand the flames. We will be strong like those walls, and rebuild our lives. We have each other.'

As Hendrik helped the women from the wagon, he turned to Willem and said, 'This is our first day that we are together. Willem, tonight you must camp here with us, for tonight we will give thanks to our Lord and then we will celebrate.'

The wagon was offloaded and the tent erected. Hendrik took his horse and rode down to the dam. An hour later, he returned clean-shaven, and a poor attempt had been made at cutting his wild, unruly hair.

Wood was gathered and a large fire was lit, when the pale winter sun dipped behind the horizon. The women gathered their shawls and blankets around them, and sat huddled beside the flames.

Hendrik led the prayers beneath the stars, praying for the souls of their loved ones, and gave thanks for the mercies the Lord had bestowed upon those who had survived.

Tins of meat were opened, water was boiled and coffee was made.

'The first thing we must do is to buy some chickens,' said Hendrik, hunched over his plate of tinned meat. 'If we have chickens, we have eggs. And if we have eggs, we will never be hungry.'

Katrina brushed her hair from her face and said, 'And we need some goats, for if we have goats, we will have milk. And if we have milk, we can make cheese. And if we have cheese, we will never be hungry.'

'Oh,' said Sannie, with a high spirited laugh. 'We need an elephant. For if we have an elephant, we will have dung. And if we have dung, we will have good crops, and if we have good crops, we will never be hungry.'

Everyone laughed. Hendrik swilled his coffee in his mug. 'The wagon is too small for an elephant,' he replied, bellowing with laughter. 'We will just have to do with goats and chickens.'

'Oh, Pa, it's so good to be back at Doringspruit,' said Sannie, her cheeks shining like apples in the glow of the fire.

Hannah was quiet. She sat with her own thoughts as she stared into the flames. Where is Tristan, she asked herself, over and over again? Will he come back for me?

'You are quiet, my little lamb,' said Hendrik. 'Where are your thoughts, my child?'

Hannah looked up from the flames, and with a false laugh, she replied. 'I was wondering if the hammerkop down at the dam has made another nest with the clippings from Pa's beard and Pa's hair. For surely, there must be enough for that.'

Sannie shrieked with laughter. Being in Willem Prinsloo's company had made her dizzy with excitement. Laughter and jokes were exchanged around the fire. Hendrik took his mouth organ from his waistcoat pocket, and began to play. For a while their troubles were forgotten in the euphoria of their reunion.

Hendrik's eyes continuously strayed to Katrina. He looked down at his hands, weathered and gnarled like the bark of an ancient tree, and then looked at Katrina, long limbed and sensual. She was past her first flush of youth, now she was in full bloom, like a flower flaunting its beauty unashamedly.

She stood up, dropping the blanket from her shoulders, fully aware of Hendrik's gaze. She bent down and moved the logs on the fire. Hendrik watched her hips sway beneath her skirts. The heat of the fire flushed her cheeks, the bones of which were high, giving an upward slant to her green eyes. Her lips, the colour of claret, were full and sultry. She looked up at Hendrik. The orange glow of the flames illuminated her wild curls, which hung about her face in obscene abundance. For a moment, her eyes were inviting, then she looked away and returned to where she was seated.

Hendrik sat transfixed, drunk with the want of her.

***

The first morning back Hannah took her Pa's horse and rode down to the dam. The frost lay heavily on the veld, silvering it with its beauty. The winter sky was pale and cloudless, and as she rode the only sound was the soft cantering of her horse's hooves.

She dismounted, and went and sat beneath the willow, now leafless in its winter attire. The wind whipped across the veld sending the empty weavers' nests dancing on the long boughs of the willow, like puppets on a string. The water in the dam was low; the greyness of it reflecting her mood.

Tristan, she thought, *where was he? Had he survived? Dear God*, she prayed, *send him back to me*.

She remembered their shared moments together at that very spot. She remembered his hands with his long straight fingers and square neat nails. She saw in her mind the way his hair curled against his neck, and the slight irregularity of his features. She remembered his knees, the squareness of them, and how, for the first time she had realised how different a man's knees were to a woman's. She remembered his laugh, his gentleness and his passion.

She pulled her skirts tightly about her legs, blocking the cold wind blowing across the water of the dam. She could never remember days as cold as this, this was by far the coldest winter they had ever experienced. The winter of 1902 would go down in history as one of the coldest winters ever.

She hurriedly mounted her Pa's horse, and rode across the barren fields towards the disused stables where they had last made love, the fierceness of their parting still vivid in her memory. She swung the horse back down towards the track, all the while scanning the distance for the familiar figure of Tristan.

As she neared the plantation of gums, she saw a small grave piled high with stones. She dismounted and knelt down beside it. Instinctively she knew Honnie lay beneath the soil. The soldier had kept his promise. She thought back to that dreadful day, and relived the moment when Honnie had chased after the wagon, her loyalty to the family showing no boundaries. In her mind, she heard the shot, the shot that took the life of an innocent dog.

She wept for her lost companion, she wept for Marike, and she wept for the desperate loneliness that had crept into her soul.

***

In the days that followed, everyone slipped naturally into a routine. Willem Prinsloo left his son in Sannie's care, promising to visit at least once a week, so that the bond between father and son could strengthen. Hendrik's trunk with all his wealth was unearthed, along with Hannah's biscuit tin, containing the diamonds Aunt Magda had given her. They were secreted away, where they were hidden but readily accessible.

Hendrik set out each morning and worked tirelessly on the house, he did everything with Katrina in mind. He reminded himself of the male weaver birds down at the dam, building their nests to win the approval of a mate. He rode into Hemel, and into Pretoria, several times, for building supplies. While he concentrated on work, it kept his mind free from thoughts of sins of the flesh, Katrina's flesh.

From the moment Katrina met Hendrik, she knew he wanted her. Her shadowy plans for her future changed the instant he invited her back to Doringspruit. She knew he was a good man, simply because he had been a good father. The Van Vuuren sisters never tired of their tales about their Pa, and the wonderful man he was.

She, herself, had never experienced the love of a father. Her Pa had found her a distraction and a burden, while travelling the countryside, spreading the gospel, and selling his medicinal tinctures. He was quick to pass her over to the first man who showed an interest, and that same man became an abusive husband.

When she first saw Hendrik standing in the muted light of the tent, strange feelings were roused inside her body. She knew the ways of the world and how to survive its hardships. She had learnt early in life to follow her instincts, and her instincts told her that Hendrik Van Vuuren would give her, and her child, the security they needed.

He was the ugliest man she had ever seen, yet there was a gentleness about him that she found appealing. As the days passed, her feelings for him grew stronger. Everything about him was powerful, from his thick oversized hands to his rich, deep voice; even the hair on his head seemed to have a power of its own. At night, she lay wanting to feel that power inside her, wanting to tame it, as only a woman knew how.

206

He mesmerised her with his flame blue eyes, captivating her with his presence, an enigma to her from a man who was so physically unattractive.

She watched him with Sunette, encouraging her to join in their family conversations, asking her opinion on the day to day things. He took them down to the dam and showed Sunette the hammerkop's nest, which he said, was lined with the golden hair of his beard. Whenever he returned from Hemel or Pretoria with building supplies, there was always a little something for her child, a piece of fruit, a sweet, or a ribbon for her hair.

She knew above all else that she wanted this man as her husband. She staked her claim the only way she knew how, to torment him with her sensuality, which came naturally to her. Every movement was for Hendrik's eyes only; the way she slowly slid the tip of her shell-pink tongue across her full lips before she spoke, the brush of the hand when passing something to him, the suggestive way she caressed her throat with her long fingers. She seduced his thoughts, driving him mad with the sweet promised fruits of the marriage bed.

Chapter Twenty-Two

It was ten days before the Asterleigh Castle docked and Tristan was able to see the wounded safely on board. During that time, more soldiers had arrived and the paperwork needed to be dealt with, keeping him occupied. With each group of wounded soldiers came stories of the war, the tenacity of the Boers and the appalling condition of the women and children in the concentration camps; stories of natives ransacking farms, and murdering those who were wandering homeless on the veld. With each new story came visions of Hannah.

Once his duty was done he applied for leave of absence, and boarded the first train heading north. The train was overcrowded with burghers returning home, their belongings filling the small compartments. Trunks, boxes, and blankets folded and tied with rope, filled every available space on the train. These were the lucky ones; they had been allowed to flee to relatives in the Cape, abandoning their homes and their farms in the Transvaal Republic, in the early stages of the war.

It was late afternoon when the train came to a complete standstill, only a few hours into their journey. Tristan looked out of the window of his compartment, which he was sharing with three other English officers. No station was in sight. He craned his head through the open window and discovered the track was under repair. Several hours later, after the darkness of the winter night engulfed the landscape, the train belched its way back to life.

In the early hours of the morning, Tristan was woken with the sound of couplings and jarring movements as the carriage was shunted back and forth in a small siding. For several long hours, they were once again stationary.

Dawn broke over the Karoo, pink and serene in the stillness. The stark beauty of the open plains stretched into the horizon and disappeared in its vastness. The sun rose higher and turned the landscape from pinks and lilacs to a golden orange in the morning light.

The compartment was layered with a fine coating of powdery dust, which had swept in through the open windows. Once again, as before, the engine jerked to life and their journey continued. No food was available on the train, something that had escaped Tristan's attention, leaving him hungry and thirsty. His travel companions were in a similar situation, only one English captain had thought to carry a hip flask filled with whiskey. Families had packed their own provisions, and the sound of their jubilant breakfasts did little to help their situation.

As the train pushed north, the landscape changed. Soon the visible scars of war became evident; the land was empty of life. Carcasses of cattle, horses, bleached bones and burnt homesteads lay upon the earth in bleak devastation. From the carriage window he saw the concentration camps, built close to the tracks for the easy transportation of their human cargo. He turned his head away; the sight was pitiful, a shameful chapter in the book of the British Empire.

The train stopped at each and every station. The food that was available at the little station shops consisted mostly of biscuits, rusks and coffee and, in some instances, tinned sweets and chocolates.

At Vereeniging, the train stopped for an interminable length of time. The railway guards explained that the tracks further north were under repair, and they had no idea how long the delay would be.

The train finally pulled into Pretoria station on the evening of the third day. Tristan bade his fellow officers farewell, and set off immediately for his military headquarters.

As the grey light of dawn crept through the window, Tristan rose and hurriedly changed into a fresh uniform. On the advice of Colonel Hayworth, he reluctantly spent the night at military headquarters. He was advised that riding alone under the cover of darkness was dangerous. People of all races were desperate, thieving was commonplace and the fine charger, which he had been given, would make him a prime target.

A vivid crack of pink appeared as the dawn sun broke through the thin wisps of cloud which streaked the eastern horizon. Each step was closer to Hannah, and each step was closer to his answers. Had she survived, and if so, were her feelings still as intense as his own? Had the scorched earth policies given birth to bitterness and resentment that would cast shadows over their future together?

The war had dragged on longer than anyone would've thought. Why had this nation of bearded, pastoral men continued to fight? At first, it was their independence, and that he could understand, but it was their pride that kept them soldiering on to the bitter end. Their pride had cost their nation the loss of their women and children in great numbers. Their pride had cost them their fall.

The sun rose higher in the pale sky, its warmth settling over Tristan. A flock of guineafowl ran across his path, an evocative moment as guineafowl were so much a part of Doringspruit. The grass whispered against the flanks of his horse, dry and golden in the winter sunshine. The aloes were now in flower, standing tall like green regimental soldiers; their scarlet flowers like blood stained spears pointing to the heavens.

Africa was an enigma to him, a land of striking contrasts. Vivid sunsets of savage colours would mark the end of another day, and then the morning would yield the gentle mist rising from the rivers, gossamer and pink against the dawn sky. The days had sharp, clear shadows, the nights a brilliant blaze of the southern constellations. Its wildness would tempt only the brave, but it was that very wildness that came with such beauty.

He thought of the seasons at Tylcoat; the spring, with the woods carpeted in bluebells, and the summer, with the heady perfume from the rose garden, and the swans with their cygnets on the lake. The autumn, and the turning leaves of the oak, the elm and the chestnut trees; and then winter, with the warm glow of the hearth on their cheeks while the snow fell, pristine and silent, on the world outside.

The first thing he would do once they were in England would be to buy Hannah the finest filly from the most renowned breeder in the country. He would buy her two black Labrador puppies that could be trained as gun dogs. He had visions of her seated beside the fire, the dogs at her feet, reading one of the many books the Tylcoat library had to offer. Books that had taken generations to collect, and added to, largely by his father who was an avid reader and a collector of fine literature. She would never again have to read the same book twice, unless out of choice.

He reined in his horse on the outskirts of the farm. He could see the plantation of gums, and to the east, the dam shimmering beneath the winter sky. He squinted into the distance for any sign of life; the wind blew cool across the dry veld and carried with it the smell of a wood fire. He touched his heels to his horse and rode on towards the house.

***

That morning Hendrik was in high spirits. Over the past few days, he had demolished a wall in the old stable and was now ready to use the bricks to repair the house.

'It's a good morning,' he said, scraping the sides of his bowl, now empty of mealiemeal, with his index finger. 'I want you ladies to take the cart and ride into Hemel. Buy a few things we need to make life easier, such as some more pans and mugs. You will know what we need. And buy a few things for yourselves, some cloth for dresses or whatever you need.' He put down his bowl and licked his fingers clean, then wiped them on his trousers.

'The way to a woman's heart,' he continued, 'is through a man's gold.'

'We do not need your gold to win our hearts, Pa,' replied Sannie, gathering the plates and bowls to be washed. 'It will be fun for us all to go,' she said. 'Sunette has never been into a shop before.'

'Make sure,' said Hendrik, his finger wagging in the air, 'that Mrs Farrell does not over-charge. She is like a jackal and will find an opportunity in everything.'

'I will stay behind with Pa,' said Hannah. 'I have no need to go into Hemel.'

'You must go, my child,' replied Hendrik. 'You have worked hard. Look at your hands. It will do you a great deal of good to join your sister and Mrs Harmse. Come Sannie, I'll help you get the ponies into their traces.'

Sannie followed her Pa, while Sunette scurried behind, leaving Katrina alone with Hannah. Katrina turned to Hannah once they were out of earshot.

'Join us, Hannah,' she said. 'It will not take away what is making your heart heavy, but it will lift it for a day.'

Hannah looked at Katrina. What did she know of this mysterious woman who had bewitched her Pa and filled the emptiness in Sannie's life, which Marike had left? And her strange, secretive child whose skeletal hands always clutched the doll Marike had made. She had never taken the time to know her. Despite sharing the tent, they were complete strangers, never exchanging more than a few words at a time.

'You are right, Katrina,' she said. 'I'll come along for the ride.'

Hendrik watched the women drive out in his new Cape cart along the dirt track heading east to Hemel. It had been a long time since he had felt such contentment. He waved, and then went to fetch the wheelbarrow piled high with broken bricks.

It was noon and the pale sun was high overhead when Hendrik saw a horse and rider in the distance cutting across his fields. As they grew closer, he saw it was a soldier from the Imperial force. He left what he was doing and hurriedly made his way round the side of the house, out of view from this unwanted trespasser, and retrieved his hunting rifle. He watched the soldier stop, and then after a short time, he resumed his canter. As the rider drew close, Hendrik stepped from the house, the rifle steadied against his shoulder.

Tristan reined in his horse and raised his hand. Hendrik watched in silence.

'Meneer Van Vuuren?' asked Tristan.

'I am he,' replied Hendrik. 'What do you want. The war is over.'

'I have come to enquire after your daughters, sir' said Tristan, as he swung down from his horse.

Hendrik watched as the English captain removed his helmet, revealing his dark head of hair. His accoutrements were polished and shone in the sunlight, his uniform neat and well fitting, cut to every requirement of his lean body. The chestnut charger was immaculately groomed, its coat shining like burnished copper. Tristan extended his hand.

'I am Tristan Dunn-Caldwell, Captain Tristan Dunn-Caldwell.'

Hendrik stared down at the outstretched hand, ignoring it as he spoke. 'What business do you have with my daughters?'

'They took me in when I was injured; Hannah, Sannie and Marike. Had it not been for their kindness and in particular, Hannah's dedicated nursing, I know I would not have lived. My gratitude to your daughters knows no limit, sir. I am so grateful.'

Hendrik felt a suffocating anger. His mouth turned dry and his tongue seemed thick and swollen in his mouth. Since he was not at ease with the English language, each word was an effort.

'No daughter of Hendrik Van Vuuren would harbour the enemy under their Pa's roof.'

'Your daughters were kind to me, sir. No man could have wished for better nursing, or, better hospitality. I wish to thank them all.'

'Get off my land. It is lies that you speak. You are the son of Satan. Every khaki that has left his spoor on our soil has been spawned by Satan,' shouted Hendrik.

Tristan raised his hand in an effort for him to see reason. 'I am greatly indebted to your daughters, sir. Now that the war is over, I have come to offer my eternal thanks. I cannot express my gratitude. Your daughters sacrificed their own security by taking me in.'

Tristan stared at the man before him. He had seen many men like this before on the battlefields; men that fought their battle single-mindedly and without question. Men that lived by the word of the Holy Book. He felt uncomfortable in his presence. 'I am in love with Hannah, and she returns my love. Sir, I wish to marry her.'

Hendrik's vision became blurred as the blood pounded behind his eyes and at his temples. He could not believe what he was hearing. This man was talking of the unspeakable. No daughter of Hendrik Van Vuuren would love the son of the devil. No flesh of his flesh would dare to marry the enemy, an Englishman.

'My daughters are dead, Captain. Dead. All three of them died at the hands of the British in the concentration camp. It was the family of Satan that condemned them to hell. '

Tristan saw the anguish on his face, for a brief moment he thought Hendrik was ready to tip forward into a fit. His face had become so strange, turning from a deep puce to a sickly yellow. His eyes were unfocused and his mouth contorted into an ugly grimace. Then the words slapped Tristan like a blow. Dead. Hannah was dead.

'I'm so sorry,' he said, his words barely a whisper. 'My God, I am so sorry. Hannah…I can't believe it.'

Hendrik stood before him with the eyes of a madman. The rifle was still clutched in his oversized hands, the knuckles of which were white with the fierceness of his anger.

'You cannot know how I feel, Meneer Van Vuuren, you cannot know. I loved her. Believe me, I loved her.'

Tristan put on his helmet mechanically, and mounted his horse. Every movement was done as he had done a thousand times before, automatically, only this time he was blinded by his tears. He tugged at the reins and rode out the yard.

Hannah, his beautiful Hannah. He had not thought to ask the details, details he would want to know. Her father was in no state to ask, and he himself, was in no state to comprehend. He needed to be alone to come to terms with his loss. Hannah, his beloved Hannah. His short time with this woman of Africa was like lost acres in the landscape of his life, acres in which he had planted dreams and hopes, which now would never be harvested.

He never looked back at the man standing where the veranda once stood. He wanted to remember Doringspruit as it was, Hannah with her dog at her side, and the soft wind in her hair.

Hendrik watched him ride away, and then sat down on the makeshift bench he had made beneath the apricot tree. He felt unwell, the world swimming before his eyes.

His daughters had betrayed him. They had taken the enemy in under his roof and nurtured him, like a venomous snake that would turn and strike. It was incomprehensible. He dropped his head into his hands and tried to clear his thoughts, but his heart continued to thunder in his chest, sending the blood pounding into his brain.

God had punished him; there was no greater punishment than the betrayal of a loved one. Yes, God had punished him for his lustful thoughts, thoughts that had haunted him every waking moment. His desires had become the work of the devil. He must marry Katrina. Yes, that would end his longing, he must take her as his wife, and all the unbidden thoughts would leave his mind and God would not punish him again.

For hours, he sat on the bench praying, until the women returned at sunset. He prayed for the forgiveness of his sinful thoughts. He prayed for the forgiveness of Hannah's and Sannie's betrayal, and asked God to grant them salvation. He asked his Lord to look kindly upon them, for they, like Judas, knew not what they had done.

***

The women laughed and joked as they climbed down from the Cape cart and offloaded their purchases. Hendrik watched Hannah. She had become distant since her return to Doringspruit. She went out riding too often, each time on a weak pretext.

Now, it had all become clear, she was waiting for this man, but he had sent the man away and in time she would forget. He would see to it that she met other young men, young men who had ridden with the commando, men who were true men, Boer men.

He watched her as she climbed down from the cart, she looked to the north track and then to the east from where they had come, and only then did she take her belongings and carry them towards the tent. Hendrik knew that the son of Satan had spoken the truth; she did indeed return his love.

It was Katrina who was the first to sense the change in Hendrik's mood. Suddenly she felt afraid that he had time to think, or that maybe she had overplayed her hand.

That night, as they gathered around the campfire for their evening meal, Hendrik was quiet. He did not join in the usual jesting; he sat with eyes fixed on the flames, his elbows on his knees and his thick fingers of each hand pressed together. He made the excuse of being tired so he could turn in for the night, saying he had worked too hard, but Katrina had noticed that very little work had been done that day.

The following day Katrina was out attending their goats. Hendrik had been fortunate in acquiring the goats, for livestock was hard to find. But good fortune had been on his side when, on return from Hemel one afternoon, he came across three goats wandering across the veld. They were in poor condition and no doubt belonged to no one. He coaxed them with some mealies and then captured them one by one. Katrina was delighted and began at once to nurture them back to health.

It was midmorning when she saw Hendrik hurrying across the fields towards her. She pretended she had not seen him, and walked across to the rear of the barn, where she knew he would follow her and they would be out of sight. She undid the top three buttons of her dress as though, by accident, they had worked themselves free.

As Hendrik rounded the corner, Katrina feigned surprise. 'Meneer Van Vuuren,' she said. 'I am sure there are wasps in the crack of this wall over here. I have tried to look but with no success.'

She stood in the morning sunlight with one hand on her cocked hip, and the other arm stretched up resting on the barn wall, emphasising her long narrow waist. Her dress gaped at the neck and Hendrik saw the creamy white swell of her breast. He pulled off his slouch hat and tossed it to the ground. Stepping forward, he took her in his arms and pressed her against the wall, his body hard against hers. He kissed her with hunger, his mouth soft and searching.

Abruptly he pulled back, ashamed of his ardour. 'I am sorry Mevrou Harmse, I came to ask you a question.'

Katrina saw that the top three buttons of his shirt were undone, the first two had not been fastened and the third had been lost. She slid her hand into the

215

opening and lightly brushed his nipple with the tips of her fingers. The other hand reached out to the nape of his neck, her strong fingers working themselves into his thick unruly hair. She pulled his mouth down onto hers, thrusting her hips forward so she could feel him against her once more.

With a sharp intake of his breath, he whispered hoarsely. 'Mevrou Harmse… Katrina. Oh, Katrina. Magtig, you've driven me mad with wanting.'

Katrina cupped his face in her hands, and then reached down to the small of his back and pulled him hard against her.

'Marry me, Katrina. Be my wife,' his words were barely audible. 'Marry me.'

'I will marry you, Hendrik Van Vuuren. Yes, I will marry you.'

'Tomorrow,' he said. 'Tomorrow, we will ride into Hemel and I will find Dominee Theron, he will marry us.'

'I will come to your bed tonight,' she whispered.

'No, not tonight, for it would be wrong before the eyes of God, but tomorrow night, we will be married. We must not tempt the wrath of our Lord. We must wait until we are wed.'

***

'Tomorrow?' exclaimed Sannie, with surprise. 'No, Pa, you must give us time to bake and prepare for a celebration.'

'Tomorrow,' said Hendrik, not looking up from the fire. 'It will be tomorrow. I will ride into Hemel with Sunette and Katrina.'

'We will join you,' said Sannie. 'We can make a day of it again.'

'No,' said Hendrik, too quickly and too harshly. 'No, it will only be the three of us. Sunette must witness her Ma's union. You and Hannah must take care here at Doringspruit. We cannot leave this place unattended.'

Hendrik looked across the fire at Hannah, his Judas daughter. Is this what their nation had fought for, for their daughters to be usurped by the Empire? What had been in her mind when she colluded with this officer? What was in her mind now? Was her lust for her man as great as his was for his woman? What had taken place here on this piece of land, the land that had nurtured her, the land that was her heritage, and the land that she could read so well? She was a child of this soil. Had she tainted it with her carnal lust?

***

News had not reached Hendrik that Dominee Theron had died two days before the war had ended at the hand of a British bullet.

They were married two weeks later after Hendrik had borrowed the Repatriation Department's wagon and ridden into Pretoria to buy a substantial amount of building material.

Chapter Twenty-Three

The implacable cold winter months dragged on into a dry, dusty August. Hendrik looked to the south for rain and Hannah looked to the north for Tristan, but both kept a silent absence.

Hendrik's attitude towards Hannah left her in no doubt that he was deeply disturbed. At first, she thought it was Katrina, the temptress, seductively controlling his mind. She watched him with his new wife, he belonged to her body and soul, slaving for her every need, and in turn, she encompassed him in her world. Their bond with each other excluded all else, only Sunette was allowed to enter their hallowed universe, and then, only by invitation.

Sannie was so involved with little Gideon that she was oblivious to the change in Hendrik. Her life revolved around Willem Prinsloo's next visit to Doringspruit to see his son. Each week, she would present him with something new, a new tooth, a new word, or a new antic. The world passed Sannie by; her life revolved around the motherless child of the man she loved.

Hannah feared to ask her Pa of his troubles for fear he might answer, and the answer might not be what she wished to hear. She was alone with her thoughts, why had Tristan not returned, and why had her Pa become a stranger? The weeks came and went, like waves on a beach, rising on the swell of hope, and then crashing and receding into nothing.

***

One morning, Hannah and Sannie took Sunette and Gideon down to the dam. It was a dry, dusty day with a warm wind blowing in from the east. The weaver birds flew back and forth, streaks of yellow flashing through the air as they busied themselves with their nest building in the willow trees. Rock pigeons took turns drinking from the far bank of the dam, taking flight at the slightest noise.

The children ran barefoot through the shallow mud, the feel of it between their naked toes giving rise to tinkling laughter.

'Sannie,' said Hannah, as she stretched her legs out on the blanket. 'There is a difference in Pa, a remoteness, a sort of distance. What is troubling him?'

Sannie threw her head back, and shrieked with laughter as little Gideon threw a small fistful of mud at Sunette, catching her on her exposed calf.

'No, I can't say I've noticed, Hannah,' she replied, in a distracted manner. 'It's not financial, that I know, as Tante Magda sent him some money to complete the roof. He's hardly touched his savings.'

The words stung Hannah. The fact that she had not been privy to this piece of family information confirmed what she had feared; her Pa suspected a liaison between her and an Englishman.

'Have you told Pa anything, anything at all about Tristan?'

Sannie turned to her. 'If Pa knew what you did, it would break his heart. Why would I tell him?'

'I can't remember when last he spoke to me directly, Sannie. I can sense there is something he's not telling me.'

'What you did, Hannah, is a sin. I know you lay with him in Pa's bed. I saw him leaving your room the night we buried the soldier.'

'Soldier? What soldier?' asked Hannah incredulously.

'The one who came to tell your captain they were coming to fetch him; the thin one with eyes like a snake. I found him in the barn raping Thuli, so I shot him.'

Hannah sat in stunned silence.

'That is what English soldiers do, they rape,' continued Sannie, her eyes staring into the distance as she watched the children playing at the water's edge. 'I wonder how many times your captain has raped. Have you ever thought of that, Hannah, how many homes he has burnt down, how many sheep and cattle he has slaughtered?'

'Why didn't you tell me about the soldier, Sannie?'

'What would you have done, Hannah? You would've gone straight to your lover and told him, and then what? He would've had us rounded up and shot. I couldn't let you know. The day you took him into your arms was the day you were no longer a part of this family.'

Sannie picked up a small stone and tossed it into the distance.

'You and your English ways. You, lying with the enemy while Pa was fighting for our independence. Did you have no conscience? I could not tell Pa of your betrayal. No, it would break his heart.'

'I'm sorry, Sannie, about Thuli. It must have been hard for you all.'

'Look what they have done to us, Hannah,' spat Sannie, with hatred riding on every word. 'Look at that child there.' Sannie's hand pointed to Sunette who was dancing in the mud, her skirts hitched high in her hands.

'Look at her. Have you ever seen a child so thin and yet is still alive? That's what they have done. They locked us behind barbed wire fences and fed us barely enough food for our existence, while their wives and children were safe and warm and well fed, far away from the threat of war. And what did they do with Thuli? Did we ever see her again? No. What of Jonas, Palesa, Aletta? What of them? Where are they? What happened to all the servants on the other farms, where are they?'

Hannah listened to Sannie's tirade of hatred.

'The war has touched us all, Sannie, no matter what our colour, nor on what side they have fought, British and Boer alike.'

In the distance, a black collar barbet began to call. The sound was sweet to their ears, for in the concentration camp, there had been an absence of birdsong.

'I will not judge you again,' said Sannie. 'For it says in the Good Book, judge, and stand and be judged. But remember, he did not come back for you. If he really loved you, he would've returned to you, or sent word.'

Sannie stood up and went over to where the children were playing, leaving Hannah alone with her thoughts.

She had always been her Pa's little lamb. There was a bond between them as there always is when a child has never known a mother. She was always the one who went out riding with him. She was the one he had taught to hunt. She was the one who was at his side while he worked in the fields, while Marike and Sannie took care of the kitchen and all the domestic chores.

She knew every nuance and every expression. She knew how to read the maps of his mind, knowing what roads led to laughter and what roads led to sentiment, and those roads which were private. Now the windows to that map had been inverted, never facing her, putting a distance between them.

***

Hannah offered to ride into Hemel to fetch the monthly food supplies. She went alone, since Sannie was expecting Willem Prinsloo's weekly visit, and Katrina never ventured off Doringspruit without Hendrik. Willem Prinsloo's visit was Sunette's highlight of the week, so she was vehement in her decision to stay at home.

The little town of Hemel had come to life with spring flowers winning the battle over the cold winter days. The spring sunshine reflected off the windows of the small shops that were scattered about the town.

She dismounted from the Cape cart and dusted down her skirts. As she turned to enter Mrs Farrell's trading store, she saw the familiar figure of Hymie Rosenberg on the opposite side of the dusty street.

'Hymie,' she called, and made her way in his direction. Hymie, on hearing his name, spun round on his heel and saw Hannah crossing the street.

'Holy Mary, sweet mother of Jesus, is it really you, Hannah?' he cried, and hurriedly made his way towards Hannah, his waistcoat flapping at his sides like fledgling wings. His small black eyes danced with joy at the sight of her.

'It's me all right, Hymie,' replied Hannah laughing.

'Aye, it's a sight for any weary traveller. I'll be damned. Sweet Jesus, it really is you.'

Hymie took off his dusty black hat and hurriedly patted his wavy, greased hair into place.

'You look so surprised, Hymie,' said Hannah, feeling uncomfortable with Hymie's enthusiasm.

'I am surprised. Sweet Jesus, I am surprised. I thought, well I thought…'

'Whatever you thought, Hymie,' said Hannah interrupting him. 'I am still here, and Sannie too. But Marike…Marike died of the measles in the camp. Oh, Hymie, we miss her so.'

'I am so sorry, Hannah. I did like your sister. Marike was so welcoming. But I was led to believe…Jesus, Hannah. I thought…I was told that all three of the Van Vuuren sisters had died in the camp. It was the soldier; he must've made a mistake. He said your Pa had said…'

'What soldier, Hymie?' interrupted Hannah. 'What soldier? When?'

'The captain. When you travel like I do, you stop and talk to anyone on the road. It breaks the tedium and, of course, information is a business in itself.'

Hymie's words swam in Hannah's ears. She felt the ground tilting upwards. Reaching out her hand, she steadied herself on Hymie's arm.

'Aye, Hannah, you are white. Come, you must sit down.'

'Take me to the cart, Hymie, and you can tell me everything.'

Hymie pushed his hat back onto his head and took Hannah's elbow and steered her over to where the cart stood in front of the store. He helped her up, and then with the agility of a monkey, he swung himself up and sat beside her.

'Tell me what you know, Hymie. All of it, from the beginning.'

'Well,' began Hymie, removing his hat. He stared down at it, twisting the brim round and round as he spoke.

'About three weeks after the war ended, maybe four. Yes, it was about the end of June. I took the wagon out to Doringspruit hoping that you and your family had returned. But about a mile north, I saw this English captain. A magnificent charger he rode, chestnut it was.

'Of course, I greeted him and asked him what he was about, did he require anything from my wagon. He just looked at me. Blank like, as though he didn't quite hear what I was saying. I asked if he needed any help, directions or something. He shook his head. "No," he said. "I have just come from the Van Vuuren farm, Doringspruit, and Mr Van Vuuren has just broken the news to me that all three of his daughters died in one of the concentration camps." Honestly, Hannah, the news came as such a shock to me. "Did you know them?" he asked me. I told him I had known you since you were knee high to a donkey.'

Hannah stared down at Hymie's hands as he rotated the brim, then she looked up at him and saw the anguish in his face.

'I was stunned, Hannah. Aye, it was a sad moment for me to hear of such tragedy. I asked him if he wanted a nip of whiskey because I was sorely in need of one myself. He dismounted and climbed onto my wagon. "Are you the man they call the smous?" he asked me. I said I was, and opened the bottle of whiskey. Honestly, Hannah, when I poured the stuff, my hand shook. Aye, war is a dreadful thing.'

'Did Pa tell him we had all died?' she asked incredulously.

'Aye, he did. The captain said your Pa was very distraught at having to tell him such news. He said your Pa turned a sickly yellow. The captain said he was so upset at the news he simply left, he didn't even ask any details. He told your Pa that he had intended to marry you, that you were both in love.'

The lynchpin dropped into place, locking all the pieces together. Hannah stared down the street. An ox wagon of Trek-Boers was trundling slowly towards them; in the front sat a family with two small children. Peace had come to this country, but private wars would still be fought behind closed doors. She rubbed her hands on her skirt, ridding them of their clamminess.

'Tell me, Hannah,' continued Hymie. 'Was he the soldier you were nursing at Doringspruit?'

Hannah nodded mutely, anger, relief and frustration coursing through her.

'I thought so. Shortly after you took him in, I met a sergeant on the road. After buying all my tobacco and two bottles of gin, he told me, very foolishly I might add, what had transpired. I told him not to spread the word; the commando would get wind of it and no one would be any the better for it.'

'Thank you, Hymie,' said Hannah, at last.

'Will you be on your way now?' he asked, with concern. 'Will you be all right? Aye, you were as pale as death itself, but the colour has come back to those beautiful cheeks.'

'What will you do now, Hymie, now that the war is over?'

'Aye, I have given it a lot of thought. I am giving up the wagon. Sweet Jesus, Hannah it can get lonely. There is going to be a depression. Look around you. Yes, the British government is putting a lot of money into the country, but it will take decades to restore things.

'Who is going to have money to buy stuff from a wandering smous? Aye, Hannah, I have thought about this. I am going to Johannesburg and I will find myself a little shop. Where there is gold there is money. Once I have the shop, I'll find a good wife. Aye, in the past I could not offer a woman a life in a wagon. In Johannesburg, there are many Jews, and I must marry a woman of my own faith.'

'Whoever she is,' said Hannah, 'she would have found herself a good man.'

Hymie reached out and kissed Hannah briefly on the cheek, and then swung down from the cart. Hannah watched him cross the street. His black cotton trousers were crudely patched and the mustard-coloured waistcoat that he wore had seen better days. Hannah knew she probably would never see Hymie Rosenberg again.

She thought of the length of fine lace he had given Marike, and the image of the last time she had seen it, tied around Marike's waxen face.

This was the man who had been sensitive to Marike's need to be loved. This was the man who had given them Honnie, and this was the man her father called 'a dirty Jew'.

Hymie turned and raised his hand in a wave, put on his hat and disappeared around the corner.

Hannah turned the empty Cape cart around and headed home; forgotten were the monthly supplies. She clenched the reins, twisted in her hands, till her knuckles were white and bloodless. Rage surged through every vein, every capillary and throbbed behind her eyes, and at the base of her skull.

She spared the Boer ponies from her wrath and kept them at their usual plodding pace, her thoughts deep and bitter. She reflected on her life at Doringspruit; it had been controlled and manipulated. No books or magazines ever graced their lives; they had to learn to read from the family Bible. Hendrik lived according to the Scriptures, quoting at every opportunity. As a child she accepted his religious fanaticism as a way of life, only when she went to live with Aunt Magda did she learn there was a life beyond the Holy Book.

Her father had showered them with love, but that love had now proved to be conditional, and she, his youngest daughter, whom he called his little lamb, had not met with his conditions or approval.

The afternoon shadows of the wattles and gums cast mottled patterns across the dirt road. The Cape cart bounced across the irregular corrugations, the wheels churning the dust, which glowed in the sunlight. Flies buzzed lazily about the ponies and about Hannah's face. Doves rose up from the gravel road at the sound of their approach, their grey wings shining like silver in their flight.

As the cart pulled into the yard, she saw her Pa, his large frame bent over a rudely fashioned workhorse. A long plank of wood was clenched in his powerful hand, while he hammered at it with the other.

She saw him as a crude peasant. His unkempt, thick yellow hair jutted out from beneath his slouch hat, which was covered with wood dust.

She climbed down from the cart and hurried over to where he worked, her skirts swishing with her quick steps. He looked up over his shoulder when he heard her approach.

'Why did Pa not tell me that the English captain, Tristan, came to Doringspruit?'

Hendrik released his grip on the plank and it clattered to the ground, sending the dust into small clouds about his feet. He turned and faced her, throwing the hammer down.

'You did not earn the right to know. You gave up that right when you supped with the devil, and took the enemy into my home.'

'You had no right not to tell me of his visit, no right at all.' Hannah's words were clear and rang with rage. 'He was a dying man, it was the Christian thing to do.'

'And the love?' bellowed Hendrik. 'Is it Christian to love a man who has taken up arms against your nation? No, Hannah, it is treason.' Hendrik's thick neck was corrugated with angry tendons and veins, which jerked as he spoke.

'Pa lied,' her voice was now controlled and hoarse. 'Pa lied about the death of his own daughters. Is that a Christian thing to do?'

'The Lord knows I lied to protect my child from the enemy… and from herself.'

'The war is over, Pa. There is no enemy. It's over.'

Hendrik raised his hand and pointed his thick finger to the heavens. 'You have shamed us, Hannah. Before the eyes of God, you have shamed this family. While your nation was out fighting for our independence, you were harbouring the enemy, making him well so that he could return to the battlefields and order the cannons to be fired against us. The Lord has seen the Judas in you.'

'We are to be married. I love him, and in the eyes of the Lord, love is not a sin.'

Hendrik's face was incandescent with rage. A thick blue vein pulsed across his forehead. 'No child of mine, no blood of my blood, flesh of my flesh, will wed the enemy.' His voice resonated like a fervent prayer.

'You are the daughter of a commando, and as such you will marry a commando. You will do your duty and give him many children so that we can build our nation once again.'

'I will leave here and find my English captain,' replied Hannah, her voice a mere whisper. 'He came back for me, so I do not doubt his love.'

Hendrik's face was grotesque in anger. Small beads of sweat glistened on his skin, and small specks of saliva were trapped in his golden beard.

'Thou shalt honour thy father.' His rich voice echoed across the yard.

'I have no father,' she cried. As the words left her lips, she wished she could snatch them back. The windows to the map of his mind opened, and she saw she had taken the road of no return.

She turned from him and walked across to the makeshift bench Hendrik had built beneath the apricot tree. Along the branches, bright, tender leaves, luminous in the afternoon light, stood side by side with the fading blossoms. She brushed the petals from the seat and sat down, dropping her face in her hands.

He came back, she told herself. He came back. Her anger was such that tears escaped her. She pushed the loose strands of hair back from her face and stared at the ground. A lizard scurried across the sand and darted into a dark opening in the rocks. She looked out across the veld, painted with the golden glow of the late afternoon sun. Had it not been for Hymie, would she have ever known?

She heard footsteps in the brittle, dry grass. She turned and saw Katrina walking towards her.

'Don't worry about your Pa,' she said, as she sat down beside Hannah, not bothering to dust the petals away.

'Your Pa is angry, he has been for a long while. Anger is like a boil, day by day, it is more painful, but today that boil has opened and the pus has run free. Now the boil can heal.'

She leaned forward and rested her crossed arms on her knees and stared into the distance. 'From the first day I saw you in the camp, I saw you were different.' Katrina spoke as though she was speaking to herself alone.

'You were always working in the hospital, befriending the English nurses, reading English books. You were never one of us.'

Hannah watched the lizard reappear from between the rocks. It stood motionless, head raised, then darted from view into the dry grass.

'No matter what side of the war you're fighting,' said Hannah. 'You believe your cause is just.'

'It has been a bitter blow to our men, Hannah, but they made their choice. They decided to go to war, to fight to the bitter end, no matter what the cost. I could understand their cause, but I could not understand their stupidity.'

Hannah leaned back on the bench. 'I did not choose to fall in love with him. It is something that simply happened. Pa has no right to choose what kind of husband I must take.'

'You are right, Hannah, your Pa does not have the right. After all, it isn't your Pa who will have to bed your husband each night.'

Katrina now sat back but continued to stare into the distance.

'This war has changed things; our men went to war and left us to fend for ourselves. They entrusted their farms to their women. They cannot now tell us we are incapable of making our own choices. Things are different now. We have a voice. Look what that English woman did for our cause, Miss Hobhouse. Look how she stood up to her government and to those in high military ranks, Kitchener and such like.

'We must not be led like blind sheep. We must do what we think is right for us. We are women. Sometimes there is no reason in what our heart tells us, but we must follow the path it tells us to take.'

'Sunette is lucky to have a mother like you, Katrina,' replied Hannah. 'I have wondered so often what my mother was like, if life would've been any different. My sisters were good to me while I was growing up, particularly Marike, because she was the eldest. Palesa was like a mother to me too, and the other servants, so I was fortunate in that respect. I miss Palesa as much as I miss Marike. They have both gone, so what is left for me here at Doringspruit? A father who will never forgive?'

'I love your Pa, Hannah. He will get over this disappointment. I haven't seen my blood for seven weeks, and if I am to bear him another child, this joy will dilute his anger.'

Katrina turned and faced Hannah. She reached out and gently put her hand on Hannah's shoulder. The gesture opened the doors to her desperation and anger; Hannah buried her face in her hands and wept.

'Tomorrow, I will take the Cape cart and we will ride into Pretoria,' said Katrina. 'Pack your things and you can catch the train to Cape Town. You can stay with Hendrik's sister, your Tante. And then you can decide what to do. But you will never find your man if you stay here at Doringspruit.'

Katrina dropped her hand from Hannah's shoulder and stared into the distance once again. 'Life is different for each one of us. Some of us are swallows and some of us are chickens. Hannah, you are a swallow amongst the chickens. We, like chickens, are happy to scratch a living from the soil, but you Hannah, need to fly. You must now fly north, like the swallow, and find your mate.'

Katrina sat quietly till Hannah finished weeping. The sun sank low on the horizon, setting the sky alight with its fiery colours. The crepuscular calls of the crowned plovers and the francolin echoed across the veld beyond. A cricket began its incessant shriek, crying out to the world that darkness was falling.

Katrina stood up to leave; she brushed the dry petals from her skirt and began to walk away.

'Katrina,' called Hannah. Katrina turned and faced Hannah. 'Don't let Pa make a chicken out of Sunette,' she said. 'Make her a swallow, Katrina, and let her fly.'

Hannah watched Katrina walk away, her skirts swaying with her sensuous gait. A swallow swooped past. It dipped in the air, feeding on the wing, rose up and was gone.

Hannah sat till the darkness fell across Doringspruit. The moon rose up beyond the far, roofless gable of the house, shining yellow against the blackness. In the distance, she heard the family preparing the evening meal over the fire outside the tent. The ring of cooking pots and their lids, and the clatter of the plates, reminded Hannah of the concentration camp. Was this any better? She asked herself.

She stood up and walked over to the house and hurriedly went inside.

Hendrik had made a temporary roof over two bedrooms of the house by chopping down some wattle trees and securing them to some of the twisted corrugated iron sheets. The two rooms provided shelter for his daughters and the children, while he and Katrina shared the tent outside.

Hannah walked into her room, and lit the lamp beside her bed. She dragged the trunk away from where it stood against the wall, and hastily dug away the sand unearthing the biscuit tin, which contained the diamonds.

She sat down and tipped the diamonds from the leather pouch onto her blanket. She selected three of the largest stones and two small ones and put them aside. She scooped up the balance and put them back into the pouch, and then put the pouch back into the biscuit tin.

Tipping out all her clothing from a carpetbag, she put in the biscuit tin, and a few selected items of clothing and repacked the bag. She opened the trunk and took out her coat, and began pulling away at the stitching of the hem, releasing the gold sovereigns. There was enough money to pay for her train fare to Cape Town and any extras that should be needed.

The arc of light from Sannie's lamp floated past her doorway as Sannie made her way to her room, which she shared with Gideon and Sunette.

Hannah gave her enough time to get the children settled, and then picked up the diamonds and went into Sannie's room.

Sannie was brushing out her thick, golden hair. She turned to Hannah, her eyebrows raised with a look of surprise.

'Katrina is taking me into Pretoria tomorrow. I'm leaving for Cape Town, I'm going to Tante Magda.'

'I know,' said Sannie, dropping her hand, which held the brush. 'I'm sorry it has come to this, Hannah. But you knew the price you would have to pay. You took the path of your carnal desires; there is no going back. You could never have had both Pa, and the Englishman. You have made your choice.'

'I love Tristan, Sannie. I must write to him and tell him that Pa lied, then he can make his choice. Pa has found happiness in another woman and will start a new life, a life apart from us. We must do the same.'

Sannie tossed the brush onto her bed and fastened the buttons of her nightdress. Hannah looked across at the sleeping children. Little Gideon lay on his back with his arms outstretched, the palms of his hands facing upwards with his fingers curling inwardly. He was a beautiful child.

She looked across at Sunette. Her bird-like frame lay on its side in a foetal position with her face turned towards the lamp. The weak yellow glow caught her high cheekbones, which in turn darkened the sockets of her sunken eyes. Her wild hair, which was so much like her mother's, fanned out across the pillow, shining like spun silk in the lamplight. She hoped one day that this child would fly from the restrictions of this claustrophobic, God-fearing life of Doringspruit.

'I won't be coming back to Doringspruit, Sannie,' continued Hannah. 'I know when a decent time of mourning has passed, Willem Prinsloo will ask you to be his wife. I won't be here to see that happy day. I won't be here to see your dreams come true.'

Hannah took Sannie's hand and dropped the diamonds into her palm. 'I want you to take these into Pretoria and sell them. Take the money and spend it on whatever Soetwater needs, a new roof, a new barn, whatever you think is fitting. And take a small amount and buy something pretty, a bone china tea set, a good rug or maybe a fancy chair. Something special that you can remember me by.'

Sannie looked down at the diamonds shining in the palm of her hand. She remained silent for some time.

'Although we have never been close,' she said eventually. 'I will miss you, Hannah. You know...you know... that Pa has forbidden any correspondence between us.'

'When you are Willem's wife, Sannie, you will be Mevrou Prinsloo, not Sannie Van Vuuren. You must not let Pa tell you what to do. We have made sacrifices, Sannie. We have not fought our own private war of survival to let our men-folk treat us like children. I will write to you via Willem Prinsloo, and I am sure he will pass the letters onto you.'

Sannie threw her arms about Hannah's neck. 'I wish you well,' she said. 'I hope your plans for the future work out. Even though I cannot understand your love for an Englishman, and I will never forgive them for what they did to our nation, I hope he makes you happy. After all, we spring from the same womb. God, in his generosity, will forgive you.'

Hannah turned and left the room, leaving Sannie standing holding her fist, which was clenched around the stones, against her heart. She returned to her room and dropped down onto her makeshift bed and wept. This war, in its evil aftermath, was like a pernicious cancer creeping across the land, seeping into homes and private lives, contaminating everything it touched.

***

Hannah lay down on her bed but sleep escaped her. She relived her moments with Tristan, every touch and every word. The moon cast a shaft of silvery light through the windowless opening in the wall. A water dikkop screeched, breaking the silence of the night. It was the sound of Doringspruit and the sound of her childhood nights.

She thought of the happy times at Doringspruit. She thought of Palesa with her loving admonishments and the lyrical sound of her Sotho language, the warmth of her skin and its gentle smell of soap and wood fire. She remembered the day Palesa explained how the calves, in the far paddock, were made and how they were born, and that humans were created in the same way. This was a subject that her sisters would never approach.

She remembered her shock, when she found her first blood on her nightdress and on the sheets, and the stickiness of it between her legs; it was Palesa to whom she had turned. Palesa had wept for joy and told her that something very special had happened. She was now no longer a child, but a woman.

Hannah got up off her makeshift bed, wrapped her shawl around her shoulders, and went through the house and out into the yard. She made her way round to the apricot tree and sat down on the bench. The night sky overhead sparkled with the brightness of the Milky Way and the moon hung in the sky like a polished silver ball.

She sat alone with her thoughts, her fears, her hopes, until the grey dawn rose up from beyond the distant kopjes.

She went to her room, picked up her carpetbag and then made her way round to the side of the house, where the Cape cart was kept. It was not long before Adam appeared with the ponies, and began to harness them to the cart.

The grey dawn sky had dissolved into shades of pink when Katrina came out and greeted her.

'Adam will ride with us, Hannah,' she said, as she placed a basket on the back of the cart. 'It's a long way, and it's better for us not to be alone. The countryside is still full of opportunists with no scruples.'

Adam took the reins, swung the Cape cart around and headed for the northern track. As they left the yard, Hannah briefly looked back. Hendrik stood watching them, the dawn light shadowing his face. He never raised his hand in farewell; he simply stood with his arms at his sides, and then the image of him receded, and disappeared into the russet cloud of dust that plumed beneath the wheels of their cart.

Chapter Twenty-Four

Hannah's journey to Cape Town on the train was a pleasant one. She shared the compartment with two middle-aged spinsters, who had travelled up to Pretoria to fetch their orphaned niece, and were now returning to the Cape. The child reminded Hannah of Sunette; she was thin and had the appearance of most of the children who had survived the concentration camps. The child seemed contented and at times, lifted the maudlin mood that Hannah found herself in.

When the train pulled into the overcrowded station in Cape Town, promises to visit and addresses were exchanged. Hannah, after bidding her farewells to her travelling companions, and unencumbered by luggage, hurriedly made her way to the waiting carriages.

The smell of the salt on wind and the screech of the gulls made Hannah feel as though she had returned home. She remembered Aunt Magda telling her that the Cape always called one back, and seeing it now in all its floral glory, she knew it to be true. She felt an exhilarating sense of freedom, the shackles of the Scriptures evaporated and the sense of guilt lifted from her soul. She was free.

She gave the coachman the address in Wynburg and settled back against the warm leather. Where was Tristan? Was he still in the Cape or had he sailed back to England? What were his feelings? What was he thinking of now, at that very moment? The carriage bounced its way through the busy streets and out onto the road to the suburbs. The spring air was bright and clear and the wild flowers were beginning their dramatic showcase of colour. Table Mountain, wearing its cloak of cloud, stood proud against the flawless sky.

***

Magda Hetherington was at her walnut davenport writing letters, when her young Malay servant announced that a Miss Van Vuuren was in the hall and wished to see her.

Magda pushed back her chair in surprise, dropping her pen, resulting in a fine spray of ink on the highly polished yellowwood floor. She stood up hastily, as she was not expecting any of her nieces. Her first thoughts were of Doringspruit, and what catastrophe had transpired for one of Hendrik's daughters to arrive unannounced. She hurriedly left her small library and found Hannah standing in the sitting room, a dirty carpetbag at her side.

'Hannah. This is such a wonderful surprise,' she cried, as she ran to embrace her.

'I hope you don't mind Aunt Magda. I simply had nowhere to turn.'

'Come child, and sit down,' she said, ushering Hannah towards the couch. 'Maisie,' she called. 'Tea, and lots of it. Make it in the big pot. I think we are going to need it.'

***

'How preposterous,' exclaimed Magda, after Hannah had finished relating the situation, 'but so predictable. Hendrik knows only one rule, and that is his rule. He is so much like our father, only my father, at least, gave Harold the opportunity to prove himself. But you are here now, and that is all that matters.'

'I cannot express how thankful I am to have you, Aunt Magda. It's like…like…finding an opening in a dark room through which I can escape. Each day seemed to bring further problems. Everyone at Doringspruit had their role to play. I knew I was the outcast, but was never told why. It was only when I met Hymie, all the pieces fell together.'

Magda saw the years of hardship etched across Hannah's face. She looked tired, the brightness in her expressions had faded; somewhere behind her vivid blue eyes lay the untold stories of her time in the concentration camp.

'All I want,' Hannah continued, 'is to find peace, a sanctuary. Somewhere where I can feel secure and wanted…valued. I don't want to feel like the child of the devil that contaminates everything it touches. I want to feel the warmth of the human spirit. I never again want to hear the cry of a hungry child. I never want to feel the icy wind against my skin as it slices through my clothing. And never again do I want to look at my father and see the hatred in his eyes.'

Magda stood up from her chair and went and sat beside Hannah. She reached out her hand and placed it over her niece's.

'We were sheltered here in the Cape,' she said. 'We had the newspapers to tell us what was happening, but they were written with a slant. Stories reached us by word of mouth from the British and the burghers themselves. I cannot begin to tell you, Hannah, how concerned I've been about you all. I did a lot of relief work for an organisation in Strand Street, Marie Koopmans-De Wet. We worked hard; it was all we could do for the war effort. The harbour was choked as ship after ship arrived carrying thousands and thousands of troops from all across the Empire. Cape Town thrived. It is so sad to see so many prosper while others suffered, but that's the nature of war.'

Hannah put her plate down with a half-eaten scone. 'Thank God, it's all over now; we can begin to rebuild our lives. And thank goodness, Aunt Magda, I have you. Some people are not so fortunate.'

'Before we go any further,' said Magda, trying to lighten the conversation by tapping her fingers lightly on Hannah's hand. 'I think the first thing we need to do is fit you with a new wardrobe of clothes. You must take time to rest and fatten up.'

Hannah gave her a half smile and reached out for the fine porcelain Coalport teapot to refill her cup. 'It's so good to have a nice cup of tea.'

'Help yourself to another scone.' Magda lifted the plate of fresh scones, which were heaped with jam and cream. 'Goodness, you need a lot of fattening up. Look at you.'

'No thank you, Aunt Magda, I could barely finish the last one.'

Hannah looked across the room and out through the window at the far end. Outside, in the bright Cape sunshine, the doves fluttered about in the oak tree. Hydrangeas stood large and round in the shade of the oak, their promised blooms still green and tender. Everything was green and vital from the winter rains; green, a colour that had almost faded from her memory. In the far corner of the garden stood an apricot tree, and at once Doringspruit came to mind. Everyone and everything at Doringspruit had either been touched or destroyed by the war. They had lost Marike, they had lost the farmstead, they had lost their livestock, their crops, their orchard, and of course, beloved Honnie. The only thing that had survived the ravages of war, had been the apricot tree.

'I must write to Tristan and explain that Pa had lied, and that I am still alive,' she said, bringing her mind back to the present.

'Why write child, when you can be on that very boat that will carry the letter?'

'No,' said Hannah. 'I must write. I cannot present myself like this. I have no clothes for travelling…I simply have nothing at all.'

'Well, first thing in the morning we'll take a trip to Mrs Walford, my new seamstress. I will tell her that several dresses are urgently required, winter ones, as it will soon be winter in England. She will have them done in less than a week. I will travel with you as you cannot travel alone. You need to be chaperoned. Once our staterooms are booked, I will cable William, Harold's only surviving brother. He and his wife will probably travel down from London to meet us in Southampton.'

'But Aunt Magda, a letter will at least prepare Tristan,' she said, looking down at her hands. Her nails were torn and the Doringspruit soil had embedded itself into every crevice. Her knuckles, now large with the lack of flesh, were red and cracked with the dryness of the Transvaal winter and the harsh manual labour. 'I can't arrive unannounced. I must send a letter.'

'Nonsense. Absolute nonsense. What if the letter goes astray? Would you know? You would simply think he no longer cared. By the time he receives a letter, he will have to reply or book his passage to South Africa. Precious time will be wasted. No, you must go to him so that once he sees you, the past will revisit him. We can be on the water within ten days, and in England, three weeks after we sail. In a little over a month we will be in London.'

***

The request to have seven dresses made in seven days by Mrs Walford and her team of seamstresses was met with a barrage of impossibilities. It was finally agreed that six dresses would be made in ten days but there would be a greater emphasis on the trimmings and details. Once they were in London, explained Magda, they would go on a shopping trip and no expense would be spared.

But bookings for good staterooms on one of the Castle line ships proved to be almost impossible. Many officers and their families were still returning to Britain. Magda pulled every influential string she could muster and finally procured a booking for a date that was suitable for their arrangements. Maisie, the young Malay servant girl would be travelling with them.

***

The voyage was uneventful. Apart from the occasional game of deck quoits, when the weather permitted them to be on deck, Hannah and Magda found the long days at sea boring. Hannah spent most of her time reading. She had purchased a large collection of books, both fiction and non-fiction, all to inspire her and to broaden her knowledge of the country to which she was travelling.

As the ship steamed north, the weather changed. Blue skies were exchanged for grey. The colourless sea turned choppy, making the ship roll and tip, forcing Magda to remain in her stateroom with a bucket at her bedside. The short stop at Madeira made a pleasant break despite the inclement weather. Magda once again found her sea legs and began to enthuse about their forthcoming arrival in England.

The Hardwick Castle docked in Southampton on the coldest and dampest day November had to offer. The docks were filled with a cacophony of shouting stevedores, gulls, vendors, and the general upheaval of arriving passengers. The quayside was slippery, forcing the women to step cautiously through the milieu of passengers and onlookers. Both Hannah and Maisie trailed behind Magda; their eyes round with bewilderment. The smell of the docks with its stinking fish and rotting food was repulsive, and for the first time since she had left Cape Town, Hannah felt nausea rising up from the pit of her stomach.

William Hetherington had sent his coachman to meet his sister-in-law and her niece as influenza had made it impossible for him and his wife to make the journey themselves.

It was heavenly as the carriage pulled away from the docks. Within minutes they had reached the quiet country lanes. Through the small circle in the misted carriage window, which Hannah had wiped clear with her handkerchief, she saw the country she had dreamed about. It lay lush and green beneath an overcast sky. Thick hedgerows lined the roads, oak trees stood in green fields, their naked branches resembling the limbs of some strange contortionist. This country was of a gentle climate, it was serene on the eye, but juxtaposed to this gentleness was its vicious hunger for power.

As the carriage made its slow way up to London, Hannah's mind was filled with thoughts of Tristan. This was his country; these never ending green fields were familiar to him. Had he travelled this very road? Had he seen these very trees? Was he in London? How would he react when he saw her? As the coach laboured its way through the rain, its wheels throwing up the mud in their wake, Hannah began to feel the first trembling thoughts of uncertainty. She should not have listened to Aunt Magda, she should have written. Now that she was on his territory, in his own familiar environment, how would he see her? Yes, she should have written.

On their arrival in London, they were welcomed with great warmth and enthusiasm by the Hetheringtons. A variety of teas were served along with a mountain of cake, while Maisie was shown to her quarters by a young, fresh faced kitchen maid who was the same age as herself.

William Hetherington was a mild-natured man with a nondescript face and watery eyes, a far different man to his younger brother, Harold. Harold had always been the dashing adventure seeker, handsome without the arrogance that so often comes with good-looking men. Frances Hetherington, William's second wife and the mother of his five children, was a stout, upright woman, corseted in such a manner, that she looked permanently ill at ease. Her fine grey hair was parted down the middle, and scraped back into a small, lack-lustre bun in the nape of her neck. She was a gracious hostess, and was pleased to have the opportunity to discuss recent events in Africa with those who had actually lived through the war. The Hetheringtons had a great affection for Magda since she was an avid correspondent, and had been faithful to Harold's memory.

***

'The Dunn-Caldwells? Yes, of course, we are familiar with the family,' said William, over dinner that evening. 'Godfrey Dunn-Caldwell sits in the House of Lords, and is quite active in many respects. He has had a sterling political career.'

William helped himself to a third helping of Brussel sprouts.

'We don't socialise with the family, but we had the occasion to meet them at a charity do several months ago. I do believe the son, the only son, is in a family partnership of criminal lawyers. It is rumoured that he will follow his father and go into politics himself one day.'

Frances Hetherington rang the bell for the servants to clear the table, a gentle reminder to her husband that he had had enough to eat.

After dinner, Hannah excused herself, the journey and the excessive amount of food had made her tired. She bade everyone goodnight and made her way up to her beautifully appointed bedroom.

She slipped between the white, lavender scented sheets and immediately, she was sucked into a deep and uninterrupted sleep.

She woke to the rousing call of a street merchant. The room was still dark, only a small, pearl grey chink of light escaping from behind the heavy, brocade curtains. She crossed to the window, pulling back the curtain allowing more light into the room. She looked across at the small carriage clock on the mantle and was shocked to see it was past nine thirty. Hurriedly, she dressed for breakfast and ran down to the dining room, embarrassment flaring in her cheeks.

The table had been cleared of all the used breakfast dishes, but the jams and butter still remained. On the far side of the table, a place had been neatly set for one. Hannah left the room and made her way to the drawing room from where she heard the cheery voices of the Hetheringtons.

'Good morning,' she said, on entering the room. 'I do apologise for rising so late. I had no idea of the time.'

'Sleep was what you needed, my dear,' said Frances, as she rang for the servants. 'Fuller will have breakfast ready for you within five minutes. You must eat, my dear. You are far too thin. Come sit with us till it is ready.'

William Hetherington put down his Times and began to fold it into a precise square. 'I will have a note sent to the Dunn-Caldwell residence at Connaught Square, telling Tristan Dunn-Caldwell that you are a guest here in our home. I am sure he will make arrangements to meet with you.'

'No,' snapped Magda. 'We will call in later this morning. If he is not home, we will call another day. Hannah wishes to surprise him.'

'But Aunt Magda…I think it wise that he is aware that we are in London and we can wait for his invitation.'

'Nonsense, Hannah dear. Don't you want to see the look of surprise when he sees you for the first time? No, we will call this morning. Hannah, after you have breakfasted, we will take a carriage. Dress warmly my child, it is quite chilly out.'

'Oh, how exciting,' said Frances with a sigh. 'He will be so surprised to see one of the sisters who had nursed him, and such a pretty one at that. Do you look alike…the sisters I mean?'

'Yes, you can see we are sisters. My late sister, Marike, was very much like my father whereas Sannie took after my mother, or so I believe. I, on the other hand look like Aunt Magda.'

'Twins my dear,' said Frances. 'You could be twins.'

'Flattery,' retorted Magda, wagging a long elegant finger at her sister-in-law. 'Is that payment for the diamond earrings I gave you?'

Everyone laughed just as Fuller announced that Hannah's breakfast was ready.

***

As Hannah stepped from the carriage she looked up at the house on Connaught Square. Had Magda not been right behind her, she would have retreated back into the anonymity of the dark interior of the Hetherington's black upholstered carriage.

'Take control, child,' said Magda gently. 'Never show that you are nervous. It puts you at a great disadvantage. You must do the talking at the door, from the beginning you must be in charge of the situation.'

Hannah raised the highly polished brass knocker and tapped twice. The door was opened almost immediately by a portly, intimidating butler.

'Good morning,' said Hannah, with a confidence she did not feel. 'We are here to see Captain Tristan Dunn-Caldwell.'

'Do you have an appointment?'

'No,' replied Hannah, removing her gloves, pulling one finger at a time to hide the trembling of her hands.

'We are presently residing in Kensington with relatives. We are from South Africa and thought we would surprise Captain Dunn-Caldwell.'

'I'm afraid, Madam, that Mr Dunn-Caldwell is away for a few days. It's the start of the hunting season and Mr Dunn-Caldwell and his fiancée have journeyed up to Tylcoat. If you would like to leave a visitor's card, I will be sure to give it to him on his return.'

Hannah, for one second, reeled at the word fiancée, but she was quick to cover her shock. 'Thank you, but no. We were hoping to surprise him. Perhaps we will call again over the next few weeks. Good day to you.'

Hannah stepped into their awaiting carriage. Magda climbed in, sat beside her, and reached out her hand and rested it on Hannah's arm.

Hannah stared out through the carriage window, but it was not the wet London streets that she saw; she was back in Africa with Tristan's face close to hers. 'Who knows what tomorrow will bring?' he had said. 'We must live every precious moment that we have. I love you, Hannah. I will always love you.'

The carriage rocked as it began to move. Hannah felt Magda's hand gently squeeze her arm.

'We must leave for Tylcoat as soon as possible, Aunt Magda. You were right to surprise him, but unfortunately, I am the one who has been surprised. Obviously Africa was a short adventurous interlude for Tristan. Oh, what a difference a few minutes can make in your life…in your dreams. I wonder when he proposed. When he stepped off the ship?'

***

The uncertainty and the vulnerability of being in a foreign land with strangers evaporated. As the carriage made its way back to the Hetherington's residence, Hannah's anger gave birth to a confidence that was beyond her comprehension. He had taken her for a fool. She was nothing to him but a toy to pass the time with. She had put her family at risk; she had put herself at risk. Through him, she had lost her family and the respect they held for her. No, she would not rest until he knew how she felt. Yes, he had returned to Doringspruit to find her, but how long did his grief last?

Magda saw the change in her niece. Gone was the uncertainty and apprehension, now a flame burned behind her vivid blue eyes. Her cheeks were high with colour and the fine flesh of her nostrils flared as thoughts raced through her head. The spirit of Hannah Van Vuuren had returned.

In her mind, Magda tried to assess the situation. Had this man turned to another woman in his despair and loss as men so often do? In his weakness, did he try to shut out that chapter of his life by plunging himself into another relationship? Or was he seduced by the glamour of war, as men believed it to be, and lived every moment to its best, feasting on the opportunities the less fortunate had to offer? She was well versed in the ways of men. Her life in Kimberley had taught her many things; most of all, things were never what they appeared to be. She had met men from all walks of life, some rich and some poor. Some were poorer than the dirt under their feet and became as rich as kings, and others, who were rich and had thrown it all away in the sleazy gambling dens of Kimberley. Some men were adventurers, moving from one Empire campaign to the next; these men would never be tamed. Was Tristan Dunn-Caldwell one of them?

Magda knew how this society worked. She had travelled to England many times while she was married to Harold. If it were the beginning of the hunting season, parties and balls would be held. Weekends of fun and scandalous affairs would take place behind closed doors.

Their unannounced arrival would be met with curiosity. Hannah and her chaperone would be invited to stay purely out of gratitude for what she had done for the son of Godfrey Dunn-Caldwell. They would seize the opportunity to debate political matters concerning the war, since it was still a matter on everyone's lips. Matters such as tax implications and the costs of the war, the huge financial drain on the tax payer for the mass repatriation and rehabilitation of the conquered Republics, would be topics heatedly discussed around the dinner table.

As the carriage stopped outside the Hetheringtons residence, the coachman swung down from his lofty seat and opened the carriage door.

'Sorry, Hayes,' said Magda, with a sincere ring of apology in her voice. 'But I have, right this minute, decided to take Miss Van Vuuren shopping. First, we'll take lunch at the Ritz if you could drive us there. Thank you.'

As the carriage pulled away, Magda patted Hannah's hand. 'We'll buy you some frocks that will stun the Midlands society. You will walk into Tylcoat dressed as fashionably as European royalty. You will leave everyone agape at your beauty and taste.'

Hannah smiled. Yes, thought Magda, no one will look upon us as coarse Boers who know nothing but a simple pastoral way of life, or, whose beliefs lie in the ludicrous idea that the Earth is flat. They will see us at our best; no woman will match our beauty or our diamonds, no woman will match our spirit.

***

They caught the early train from St Pancras Station two days later. Dress alterations were the main cause for the delay, but Magda was wise enough to know that arriving on a weekend would be to their best advantage.

From the first class carriage window, Hannah watched the English countryside slide past in all its verdant beauty. Cattle stood fat and contented in green fields and the sheep, warm and round in their woolly cocoons, grazed peacefully on the slopes of the rolling hills. Crows, with their untidy flight, lifted into the air at the sound of the steaming engine. A weak winter sun broke through the sparse cloud casting long shadows at midday, a strange phenomenon for those who were strangers to this land.

Small villages with their church steeples and stone cottages came and went as the train steamed north. Tristan, Tristan, Tristan, was the litany of the wheels.

Hannah's mood changed from anger to fury. Fury at Tristan, fury at her father and his lies, fury at her own foolishness and weakness.

The train pulled into Leicester Station with a symphony of steam and screeching metallic brakes. Coach doors swung open with a clatter and porters rushed about, as luggage was hastily transferred from train to trolley. With the sound of slamming doors, the hissing of steam and the station master's whistle, the train pulled away from the platform, leaving Hannah and Magda running after the young porter, who was effortlessly wheeling their luggage towards the awaiting hackney carriages.

'So rushed, everything is so rushed,' exclaimed Magda, with annoyance.

Magda gave the coachman the address of a small but exclusive hotel in the neighbouring village of Quorn, which had been recommended to her by William Hetherington.

'It's too late now to visit Tylcoat,' whispered Magda, once they were seated in the carriage. 'We will rest tonight, and my goodness, am I going to rest. We'll set out after morning tea.'

Chapter Twenty-Five

The carriage crossed the river Soar and wound its way along the country lanes. The winter sun highlighted the dry-stone walls dappled with lichen. The smell of the damp air and rotting autumn leaves drifted through the open window of the carriage, as the road meandered through the woods. The carriage lurched as it took a sharp turn, and then passed through the gates of the Tylcoat estate. Hannah sat silently, as they made their way up the long drive lined with century-old elms. In the distance she saw the lake; the lake in which his sister Katherine had so tragically taken her own life. On its smooth surface were two swans, their startling whiteness contrasted against the dark water. They passed the formal garden with its clipped hedges of yew and box. Then, through the trees, she caught her first glimpse of the house, standing on a gentle rise, in all its majesty.

***

From the far end of the rose garden, where Godfrey Dunn-Caldwell was walking his dog, he saw the carriage making its way up the drive. Curiosity cut short his walk, and he hurriedly made his way back to the house, arriving just as the carriage came to a standstill in front of the sweeping stairs. He waited for the coachman to open the carriage door, and then he stepped forward and assisted his unexpected guests in alighting.

'Thank you,' said Hannah. 'We were hoping to meet with Captain Tristan Dunn-Caldwell.'

'My son,' said Dunn-Caldwell, with a certain reserve in his voice. 'He is out at the present time. He should not be long. Would you two kind ladies care to wait, or can I be of any assistance?'

'I am Hannah Van Vuuren from South Africa, and this is my dear aunt, Mrs Hetherington. We have been visiting relatives in Kensington and since we were doing a little sightseeing, we thought a trip to Leicestershire would be exciting.

We were hoping to surprise Captain Dunn-Caldwell. My sisters and I nursed him for a few weeks on our farm, Doringspruit.'

Dunn-Caldwell tapped his walking stick against his boot and his dog came to his side.

'This is no place to discuss such matters. Please, do come inside and have some tea.' He turned and led the way followed by his arthritic, black Labrador.

As they entered the great hall, Dunn-Caldwell turned to a butler, who appeared from no-where, and ordered tea and sandwiches to be brought to the drawing-room.

Hannah and Magda swept across the flagstones behind Godfrey Dunn-Caldwell. He was a tall, angular man who exuded an air of cautious disdain. He was not friendly, yet he gave no reason for Magda and Hannah to feel they were not welcome.

He did not speak until they were settled in the drawing-room. Waving his hand, he intimated that they should take a seat. Hannah, ignoring his gestures, moved over to the tall windows, which overlooked a gravel drive and the rose garden beyond.

'I was led to believe, or should I say, my son was led to believe, that all the Van Vuuren sisters perished in one of the refugee camps.'

Hannah turned to face him and said, 'Concentration camps, we were not refugees. My eldest sister, Marike, died from the measles. Both myself and my sister Sannie survived.'

Dunn-Caldwell eased himself into a winged chair and remained silent for a short period. She watched his fingers massage the top of his dog's head as he sat dreamily beside his master. In the uncomfortable silence, Hannah studied the room. On the walls hung a pale turquoise chinoiserie silk. Although soft and subtle, it was this design that dominated the room and everything in it. Magda sat on a small Queen Anne sofa with her hands resting elegantly in her lap.

'So you have come to England to visit Mrs Hetherington's relatives?' said Dunn-Caldwell at last.

Magda spoke for the first time. 'My late husband was Major Harold Hetherington; he fought at the battle of Majuba.'

Her voice was clear and confident; leaving Dunn-Caldwell in no doubt that this was a woman who was in charge of her own intentions.

'I have visited England on many occasions, since his family is very dear to me. But unfortunately, this war in South Africa has prevented me from doing so over the past few years. I have spent my time in Cape Town, doing work for the war effort.'

At that moment, a tray of tea was brought in along with several large platters of neatly cut sandwiches. Dunn-Caldwell stood up and leaned over the platters, silently assessing their fillings. He hooked one out with a bony finger, and gave it to his dog.

'Arthur likes salmon,' he said absently. He turned from the platters on the long table and paced backwards and forwards with his hands clasped behind his back.

'Do you intend settling in England now the war is over, Mrs Hetherington?'

'Goodness, no,' laughed Magda. 'Don't misunderstand me. I do love the country but I could never settle in such a climate. The Cape is my home. Everything pales by comparison.'

Hannah turned back to the tall windows and stared out to the countryside, glowing in the pale winter sunshine. Green, everything was green, even the trunks of the oaks were green with moss. In the flowerbed beneath the window, the ivy grew thick and green, reaching up and clinging to the walls encasing the window with its green vigour.

The pacing stopped. 'You are aware that Tristan is engaged to be married?'

'Yes,' replied Hannah, turning from the window to face Tristan's father. 'I learnt of the engagement whilst in London. You must be very happy. Congratulations.'

Dunn-Caldwell moved back to the sandwiches, pulled another from the pile, and fed it to the waiting Arthur.

'We are all very grateful for your dedication to Tristan. It could not have been easy. I know...I know Tristan felt a certain fondness for you...and gratitude.'

Gratitude. The word was the equivalent to that of an obscenity. She stared at this stranger standing before her. The sunlight from the window highlighted his unruly, greying eyebrows, which grew in a thick, tangled hedge either side of his narrow aquiline nose. His eyes were deep-set, their colour indefinable. His steel grey hair grew low on his forehead, now lying in all directions, styled by the elements whilst out walking his dog.

Her mind turned to her father. Two men from different continents, enemies at war, yet their hearts thrummed to the same patriarchal, controlling beat. Her father's words were direct; no innuendoes or underlying tones, that was the way of Africa. Here Dunn-Caldwell's words were spoken with sweetness, but beneath the sweetness, the taste was threatening. She turned away from him, hiding her tears of anger and looked once again through the tall windows. Green, yellow-green, purple-green, blue-green, the world beyond the panes was clad in green. Suddenly, she longed for the warm, textured colours of Africa, where shadows and meanings were clear and defined.

'You believe that I have come to England to undermine the engagement,' said Hannah without turning to face Dunn-Caldwell. Her voice was clear and controlled. 'Your judgement of me is so far from the truth. Being a politician, you will know more than most about poor judgement, for it is through poor judgement that politicians send men to war.'

At that moment the door swung open and Tristan strode into the room.

***

Tristan had gone out early that morning to confirm the details of the hunt to be held the following day. Walter Shaw was the Master of the Quorn Hunt, as well as the organiser of the annual Christmas fair to be held on the Tylcoat estate. He was overly conscientious with any project he undertook, and it was this enthusiasm that had run away with him, keeping Tristan out for most of the morning.

On his arrival back at the house, Burns informed him that he had two guests, ladies from South Africa, who were waiting for him in the drawing-room. Tristan thought nothing of it, assuming it was relatives of a fallen comrade, who wished to know the final hours of their loved one.

As he entered the room, his eyes fell on the woman standing with her back to him, looking out the east windows. Her blond hair was swept up into swirls on top of her head revealing the gentle curve of her slender neck. She turned and faced him.

'Hello, Tristan.'

For a brief shuddering moment, Tristan's world turned into a kaleidoscope of disbelief. The room spun in shards of colour, spinning and spinning until he reached out and steadied himself on the back of a Venetian armchair.

'Christ almighty…it can't be,' he whispered. 'Hannah?'

The winter sunlight slanted into the room, catching the sun-bleached golden strands of her hair. Her face was flushed and her eyes were moist. The fine flesh of her nostrils flared, a small peculiar nuance that he remembered so well. She was dressed in pale apricot, a colour that gave her skin a warm, fresh glow.

'Hannah…I thought…I thought. Christ almighty!' He strode over to where she stood. He reached out his hand and touched her shoulder. 'I cannot believe what I am seeing. Your father told me…he told me that you and your sisters perished in the concentration camp.'

Hannah swallowed back her tears. She wanted to reach out and touch his face, the face that had never left her thoughts, the face that was forever in her mind. She wanted to run her fingers through his strong dark curls. She wanted to feel his breath against her skin.

'Marike died. Sannie and I survived,' she said softly.

'But why did he tell me you had all perished? Hannah, I cannot comprehend all this. Christ almighty, is it really you?'

'You know why, Tristan. I don't have to tell you. You know only too well. You have fought a war, and you know the bitterness that has washed over our nation. But I am not here to discuss all this, what's done is done. I am here to wish you all the best on your impending marriage.'

Hannah heard Dunn-Caldwell's voice from somewhere in the room.

'Mrs Hetherington, I have a superb collection of botanical specimens from the Cape in my conservatory. Would you like to see them?'

Hannah heard the movements of Magda's skirts as she stood up from the Queen Anne sofa. 'Thank you, yes. That would be most interesting.'

Dunn-Caldwell moved across the floor, walking considerably well without his walking stick. He was followed by the stiff-legged Arthur, and in their wake came Magda, a small smile playing at the corners of her mouth.

Tristan waited till he heard the soft thud of the closing door before he reached out and took Hannah in his arms.

'Hannah, Hannah,' he whispered against her cheek. 'Thank God you're alive. You have been in my thoughts. Hannah, you have no idea how I have struggled to deal with…with your death.'

Hannah stepped back, easing herself from his grip and turned away from him, once again looking out through the tall windows.

'Struggling so much, Tristan, that you got yourself engaged almost immediately?' she said. 'Did our relationship mean so little that you could move into another in a matter of months…weeks? Or was it days?'

'It was not like that, Hannah, you know that.' Tristan moved over to the small sofa, which Magda had just vacated and sat down. He rested his elbows on his knees and dropped his face into his hands running his fingers through his short dark curls. He looked up at her and continued.

'That day when I left your father, I was devastated. I made my way to the Cape and resigned my commission. Hannah, my world had collapsed. Those first few days, that train journey to the Cape, I was existing in a world of such…such broken emotions. Guilt, Hannah. The guilt I felt was overpowering. I thought of those camps, I thought of you every day, every hour, every minute. Hannah, our future together is what got me through the tragedies of war. Losing you… was like…like wrenching out my heart. It was the final blow to my faith…in life… in humanity. The guilt of not being there when the colonial troops came to Doringspruit. You had saved my life, while I was powerless to help save yours. But the guilt was only a shadow of the loss. I knew I had lost more than the woman I loved, I had lost our dreams…I had lost the children I had dreamed of…your children…our children. Losing you was losing everything. I can't remember the voyage back to England. My emotions were as turbulent as the seas on which I was returning home.

'When we docked, I stepped from the ship onto familiar soil. I told myself…Africa, the war, will be locked away in the recesses of my mind. That was the only way I was going to deal with my loss, to lock it away. I travelled straight up to Tylcoat. Felicity was here to welcome me home. She has always been in love with me…ever since we were children. She and Katherine had been best friends…they were so alike…Katherine and Felicity. As I told you in Africa, Langsby and my father are old friends, it was always hoped that we would marry, so it was the natural thing to do… to propose. She was the balm I needed. She was a part of the past, a past that was away from the nightmare of war, and away from my memories of you. With Felicity, I knew there would never be passion; therefore, there would never be pain.'

He stood up and moved over to the window where Hannah stood. She could feel the warmth of his body against her back.

'Where do we go from here?' she said, without turning to face him. Outside a pheasant ran across the gravel drive, its feathers shining purple-bronze in the winter light.

'I don't know, Hannah.'

She turned to him, her eyes once again moist with unshed tears. 'I should've written. I should not have put myself in this position. I saw it in your father's eyes. Gratitude, he said, that's all it was, gratitude.'

He reached out to take her in his arms, but she moved away with the swiftness of a hunted animal.

'Hannah, you know…you know what we have only comes once in a lifetime.' He reached out and tugged at her arm, turning her to face him then pulled her into the circle of his arms. 'Your father lied, my father lied,' he whispered.

She pulled back. Looking up into his eyes she saw what she wanted to know. His feelings had not changed; he still loved her.

***

The door opened and Magda entered the drawing-room.

'Your father has invited us to spend the weekend here at Tylcoat,' she said with a broad smile. 'He has sent for our things at the hotel, and of course, Maisie.'

Tristan was pleased at the invitation as it gave him a further chance to talk to Hannah alone. Felicity and her parents were due to arrive shortly, and he needed to change out of his riding clothes and gather himself together. Felicity was sensitive to his moods, over the years she had learned to read him like a book. He excused himself and hurried from the drawing-room.

Once the door was shut behind him, Hannah turned to her aunt and said, 'Aunt Magda, it's not in anyone's interest to spend the night. It will simply make the situation impossible.'

'Come, come, my dear,' replied Magda, as she moved over to the long table and helped herself to a sandwich. 'How could he not invite us? After all, look what you had risked for his son. Not to invite us to the dinner party this evening would have been unashamedly rude.'

Magda wiped her hands on a small linen napkin, which had been placed beside the platters of sandwiches.

'I think,' she said, as she dabbed the corners of her mouth, 'that Godfrey Dunn-Caldwell was favourably impressed with my connections at the Cape. He was surprised to know that I had been a regular guest of Cecil Rhodes, when, of course, he was Prime Minister of the Cape Colony. I told him I had spent many an enjoyable evening at Groote Schuur. He was keen to learn of my acquaintance with Lady Sarah Wilson, who was also a regular guest of Cecil's. You know Lady Sarah, the youngest daughter of Lord Randolph Churchill. At one time, we had been on quite friendly terms. Godfrey was not to know that I thought her quite insufferable. But since she had made quite a name for herself during the siege of Mafeking, any connection to this meddlesome woman never fails to impress. And, of course, he was quite overwhelmed by my knowledge of his specimens in his conservatory. I offered him some quite sound advice on his lilies, particularly his Disa lilies. I think, my dear Hannah, he now has a slightly different opinion of us. We are not the country bumpkins he perceived us to be. He was a difficult man to win over, but it is connections that capture this man's attention. Once he had learnt of my connections at the Cape, charming him was quite simple.'

***

Once the chambermaid had unpacked their luggage and Maisie was shown to her quarters, Hannah and Magda had time to rest. Their rooms, furnished in impeccable taste in sage green and pale cream, were adjoining.

'You must rest for a few hours, my dear,' said Magda, as she moved about Hannah's room, scrutinising every detail, from the heavy satin curtains to the smallest ornament on the mantel. 'We don't want to look fatigued and washed out. One must be fresh in the mind and fresh in the face, when one goes into battle with fellow dinner guests. For that is what this will be, a battle. The war, even though it is over, is stinging every pocket of this land.'

Hannah dressed for the evening. She brushed out her golden hair and Maisie helped her to twist it into a fashionable design at the back of her head. She chose a dress of dove grey silk, simple in cut and discreetly trimmed in the same colour lace. The austerity of the colour offered no distraction to her flawless beauty. Below the small hollow of her throat blazed the ten-carat diamond necklace Magda had given her.

'Hannah, my dear, you are quite breathtakingly beautiful,' exclaimed Magda, as she entered her niece's room.

'I can honestly say the same of you, Aunt Magda. You are simply stunning.'

Magda Hetherington wore a dress of deep maroon velvet; a shade that gave colour to her cheeks and offset the creaminess of her skin. Hannah found it difficult to believe that her Aunt was only ten years older than Sannie. Magda Hetherington looked no older than thirty.

On Magda's insistence, they were the last of the guests to enter the drawing-room. Together they swept in. Hannah's appearance was of clear, understated sophistication. Magda, on the other hand, glittered with her diamonds. Her appearance told the world she was successful and confident, and a woman of the new age.

At once Tristan made his way across the drawing room with Felicity Langsby on his arm.

'Miss Van Vuuren, Mrs Hetherington, may I honestly say it is a great honour to have you as my guests tonight, a very small compensation for your kindness and charity that you showed me in Africa. May I introduce you to my fiancée, Miss Felicity Langsby.'

Felicity Langsby's brown eyes were wide with curiosity. 'This is truly a great honour,' she said kindly. 'We are all so very grateful for the kindness that you have shown towards Tristan. We are greatly indebted to you and your family.'

She was dressed in cream satin, a colour that did little for her sallow complexion. Her fine brown hair, although neat, was unfashionably styled. Her features were soft and feminine, and when she smiled, her cheeks dimpled in childish fashion. No one could say Felicity Langsby was beautiful, but she had a sweetness about her that made it impossible for her to be disliked.

The glow of the chandeliers gave the drawing room a totally different appearance. The candlelight bounced off the Irish crystal glasses and shimmered on the creamy white shoulders of the women. The room was filled with muted laughter and genteel conversation. Large arrangements of roses, blowsy chrysanthemums and lilies, interspersed with fern, stood on pedestals in the four corners of the room.

'May I interrupt?' came a voice from behind Tristan.

'Of course, Aunt Lavinia,' replied Tristan, stepping aside to allow his maiden aunt into the circle of conversation. Hannah knew instantly that Tristan's Aunt Lavinia was Dunn-Caldwell's sister. She was small where her brother was tall, but she had the same unruly set of eyebrows either side of a prominent nose. Where Dunn-Caldwell's long face was harsh, his sister's was soft, but both bore a stamp of eccentricity.

'So these are your guests from Africa,' she said, with wonderment in her frail, yet unrestrained voice. 'Who would have thought I would meet a real live

Boer. You know, I was in London on Mafeking night. Oh, it was so exciting. There was cheering and singing everywhere. Everyone was hugging and kissing each other. The celebrations went on for days. Bunting filled the streets and there were fireworks. Oh, Baden-Powell was our hero. My, what a dashing man he is.'

As she spoke, she moved her hands in an expression of awe, spilling her champagne down the front of her bold-coloured, lilac satin dress. 'And now I get to meet two Boers. I can't wait to tell my friends. This is all so very exciting.'

Everyone laughed politely. 'And I thought they were all so ugly and crude. Well, that's what the Daily Mail told us.'

'I think,' said Tristan with embarrassment, 'we need to take our places in the dining-room'

***

Godfrey Dunn-Caldwell sat at the head of the long mahogany table, which seated the eighteen guests with ease. On his right sat Magda Hetherington and on his left, sat his future daughter-in-law, Felicity Langsby. Next to Felicity sat Tristan, and next to Magda sat Hannah. On Tristan's left sat his Aunt Lavinia, whose small jet black eyes never strayed from Hannah. On Hannah's right sat one of Tristan's university colleagues, Robert Bouchard, a man well known for his wealth and exceptional good looks. Further down the table sat the jingoistic General Langsby and his long-suffering wife, Violet. Other guests included the Portmans and the Smyth-Gibbons, both families from neighbouring estates, as well as the Manson family from London.

Robert Bouchard had difficulty keeping his eyes from the diamond pendant glowing against Hannah's skin. After a few spoonfuls of soup, he gave in to his curiosity.

'Miss Van Vuuren, that is some sparkler you have around your neck. How many carats? Ten, twelve?'

'Ten, and flawless,' replied Hannah with pride. 'A gift from my Aunt Magda.'

'Mrs Hetherington, if I owned such a diamond, I would never part with it,' replied Bouchard, craning his neck past Hannah. 'It was very generous of you.'

Magda smiled. 'Hannah… Miss Van Vuuren is more than a mere niece to me; she is my closest friend. And besides, I have had my pleasure from it.'

252

Felicity Langsby leaned forward over the table and in a hushed, shy voice asked, 'Tristan tells me you were in one of the many concentration camps. It was frightfully brave of you. What was it like?'

With a feeling of uncertainty, Hannah glanced nervously towards Tristan. Should she be honest with Felicity, or should she shroud her reply in sketchy untruths.

'It…it was difficult. We had no time to gather our things, and what we did not take with us was burnt along with the homestead. So what we managed to pack in a few minutes is what we had to make do with in the camp, which was the bare necessities.'

'I presume you took that smashing sparkler with you?' said Bouchard, taking a long sip of his wine.

'Our treasures, we buried at the onset of war. We had anticipated looting and general bad conduct from the khakis, and we had no knowledge of how safe our valuables would be in the camps,' replied Hannah, with a salting of resentment flavouring her words.

'But how awful,' exclaimed Felicity. 'I cannot imagine such a violation. It must have been dreadful. Simply dreadful.'

'What were the lavatories like?' asked Tristan's Aunt Lavinia, leaning as far as she could across the table. 'So many people. Were there enough lavatories?'

'Lavinia,' snapped Dunn-Caldwell.

'But Godfrey dear, one must ask these questions, if one is to know how they lived.' Lavinia's eyes moved back to Hannah's face. They remained fixed as though she was examining a strange curiosity. Hunched over the table, her hands fidgeted with the edge of her plate. Her fingers were bent with age and were adorned with several rings, one of which was a large, deep purple amethyst.

'How many people were in your tent?' asked Lavinia, but did not wait for Hannah to reply. 'I believe the women and children were filthy. The papers, particularly the Daily Mail, were full of stories.'

'We had two buckets of water per tent, Miss Dunn-Caldwell. With those two buckets we had to wash, cook and make tea and coffee. Sometimes there were fourteen to sixteen women in one single tent.'

Dorothy Smyth-Gibbons broke her bread roll in half, and then looked up and said, 'I have a friend who is related to one of the women on the Fawcett commission. Apparently, it was difficult to find camp superintendents with the right qualifications and training. I mean, these men had to supervise women who were not used to being housed in such cramped conditions. The superintendents had to have some knowledge of business administration, along with many other issues, such as sanitation, supplies and all the rest. They were thrown into these positions and had no idea that the camps would become so overcrowded. Sometimes, the job was totally beyond their capabilities. Kitchener himself did not do his sums properly.'

'Poppycock,' blurted Langsby. 'We were doing these people a favour. We were looking after the Boers' womenfolk, and their children, while they were running amok with their Mausers. They should have been grateful.'

Magda Hetherington ran a long elegant finger across the rim of her glass. 'If I may just add,' she said quietly, 'these womenfolk did not need looking after. Life alone on a farm was not new to them; their mothers had done it, and their grandmothers. They had their servants, their children and their farm animals. That's all they required to lead a full and contented life. The sole purpose of the scorched earth policy was to denude the land of any sustenance that the commandos needed, to continue the guerrilla war. To say it was for their own protection is ludicrous. One must not forget that it is estimated that 28 000 non-combatants died in these camps, most of them children.'

General Langsby face reddened. 'My dear Mrs Hetherington, perhaps you are not aware that marauding bands of natives were sweeping across the land, raping and slaughtering everything in their path. Womenfolk alone on the farms were vulnerable.'

'How very generous of the British Government to think that these women needed their protection,' she continued, 'But why, then, were there just as many black concentration camps? Did these people need protection from their own kind?'

Louisa Portman leaned back in her chair. She had never liked the pompous Langsby and took this opportunity to side with his opposition.

'Imagine losing everything that is dear to you; watching it consumed by flames, and in the case of farm animals, slaughtered. Then these poor, defenceless people were herded into camps. What was Kitchener thinking? And we like to think we are a civilised nation.'

The soup plates were cleared and a host of vegetable tureens were placed on the table. Large meat platters, bearing roasted lamb and beef, were strategically placed so that everyone had access to them.

Dunn-Caldwell reached over with his fork and stabbed a thick slice of lamb. He pulled it from the fork with his fingers, and then dropped it into the mouth of Arthur.

'Godfrey,' snapped Lavinia. 'I do wish you wouldn't feed that confounded dog at the table.'

Dunn-Caldwell leaned over and repeated the procedure, only this time it was a slice of beef.

Felicity leaned over towards Hannah and in a conspiratorial whisper asked, 'Why did they not put the black people with the white people? Why did they have to have separate camps?'

Before Hannah could answer, Dunn-Caldwell received another sharp reprimand from his sister Lavinia for feeding Arthur another slice of meat.

'It's all so barbaric,' continued Louisa Portman. 'Rounding people up like cattle, whatever next?'

General Langsby, smoothing down his thick, golden moustache, took the bait. 'I am of the same opinion as Joseph Chamberlain, our Colonial Secretary. He believes the British race is the best governing race the world has ever seen, and he believes that there are no limits to its future. What we did in South Africa was best for the Empire and all the King's subjects. We have won the war and we owe it to our very brave military.'

Tristan watched Hannah. He greatly admired her calm demeanour, as the debate was a sensitive one. He knew, too, that Louisa Portman despised the obstreperous Langsby, and the political jibes would go on all night. Louisa was a feminist and a suffragette.

'And that brave, brave woman, Emily Hobhouse. Did you have the good fortune to meet her, Miss Van Vuuren?' asked Louisa, whilst pushing her food around her plate.

Hannah leaned forward at the same time Bouchard leaned back, so that Hannah's view of Louisa Portman was not obscured.

'No. Unfortunately, Miss Hobhouse was not able to visit any of the camps in the Transvaal. But I must add that we were truly thankful for the pressure she brought to bear on the British Government. Things greatly improved after her visit to South Africa.'

'Meddlesome woman,' Langsby sneered. 'Some women will do anything for notoriety.'

Ignoring General Langsby's remark, Diana Manson put down her empty glass of wine and said, 'Louisa dear, I had the honour to meet the woman. I attended a meeting in London at the women's branch of the SACC; you know, the South African Conciliation Committee. It was purely out of curiosity that I went. It must have been around June 1900, about nine months into the war. Their main cause of concern was the government's bad policy of war against two small states, and even at that stage, already 20, 000 of our brave men were either dead, wounded or missing. It was at this meeting that concerns were expressed about the women of the Transvaal and the Orange Free State.'

'There were many pro-Boers,' replied Louisa Portman. 'But being pro-Boer also meant you were pro-Englander, for the very reasons you have stated; the Government's bad policy of war. It was purely a matter of justice and humanity.'

'You forget,' bellowed Langsby, with a commanding voice. He spoke as though he was addressing his troops. 'The Boers rode across the country burning the farms of their own compatriots purely, on a whisper of a rumour of spying. Kruger was denying the Uitlanders the vote, yet he was quick to take their taxes. And where was Kruger when tide turned against the Boers? He was on a ship sailing to the safety of Switzerland. Desertion, that's what it was, desertion.'

Ignoring the conversation at the far end of the table, Lavinia Dunn-Caldwell leaned forward. 'You have not answered my question, Miss Van Vuuren,' she said, her small black eyes glimmering in the light of the candles. 'What about the lavatories?'

'I think, Aunt Lavinia,' interjected Tristan. 'That is a question you may ask Miss Van Vuuren, when the gentlemen retire for cigars. I am quite sure she will oblige you with an answer.'

There was a long whine from Arthur, which was immediately rewarded with another slice of meat.

The political banter continued. Dessert was served but did little to sweeten the mood of the guests. Copious amounts of wine was drunk which loosened tongues, making the debates more heated. Lavinia Dunn-Caldwell's eyes stared at the rim of her glass.

Once the men retired from the ladies to smoke their cigars and circulate amongst each other with a glass of good vintage port, Felicity moved across to Hannah and sat down beside her.

'Tristan tells me you had such wonderful servants. He said they were so good to him, even though he couldn't speak their language. How are they? Did they too, go to one of those black concentration camps?'

The room shimmered with the sparkle of crystal and silverware, the candlelight danced off the fine china and reflected in the windowpanes. Amongst all this, Hannah saw Palesa, her eyes round with terror, running after Honnie with her arms outstretched, as she chased the wagon bearing them off to unimaginable sorrow.

'I'm sorry,' continued Felicity. 'I really didn't mean to upset you.'

Hannah shook her head silently and then replied. 'I…we don't know what happened to them. Yes, they did go off to the camps, but we have no knowledge of what happened after that. The authorities did not keep records of names in the black camps…or any records of those that perished, not like they did in the white camps. We will never know.'

At that moment Hannah saw, to her relief, Lavinia Dunn-Caldwell being led away on rather unsteady legs.

'Oh, Aunt Lavinia has once again had too much of the good spirit,' said Felicity, with fond affection in her voice. 'I must say, Miss Van Vuuren…Hannah, your aunt is truly a beautiful woman, and if I may dare to say, you are so much like her. You could be sisters.'

The atmosphere of the evening had been oppressive. Hannah stood up and excused herself from Felicity. She wanted to run from the stuffiness of the room, to tear herself away from the prying eyes and probing questions. The day had been too much; her emotions were raw, from the first confrontational words with Tristan's father, to the overpowering, insensitive conversation at the table. Why had she put herself in this position? To be dissected like a rodent under a microscope, analysed and examined. She looked across the room to Aunt Magda, who was at that point disengaging herself from the animated Louisa Portman. To Hannah's relief, she saw her aunt making her way towards her.

Magda Hetherington took Hannah's arm and steered her away from Felicity Langsby.

'Do excuse us, Miss Langsby. I need to have a quiet word with my niece.'

Once out of earshot, Magda turned to Hannah and said, 'I have a note from Tristan. He asked me to tell you to meet him in the library at 12.30. By that time, most of the guests will have retired or carriages would've departed.'

***

Tristan sat in the winged chair in the library. The lamps cast small pools of light and the fire, which burned in the grate, gave the room a warm, orange glow. He had gone easy on the wine that evening, drinking only one glass of white and, later, declining the port, as he wanted a clear head to think things through. While he waited, he thought of Hannah. She had been born on a farm in Africa and raised on the vast openness of the veld, but this was where she belonged, amongst the culture and glamour of the new Edwardian age. Magda Hetherington shone with all the qualities of success, but Hannah's serene beauty had eclipsed her. Every eye was fixed on the young Boer woman, shining like a brilliant light amongst the mundane; she was like a glowing Phoenix that had risen from the ashes. Hannah. His Hannah, the Hannah he loved, the Hannah that had cared for him, risked her safety for him, the Hannah he could not have as he was duty bound to honour a commitment.

The hands on the tall longcase clock standing against the far wall showed it was past 12.30. He took out his pocket watch and noted that the longcase clock was five minutes slow. The logs in the grate collapsed, sending a shower of embers across the hearth. Silence filled the room, a painful agonising silence, which fed wild and dangerous memories. Memories of shared moments at Doringspruit, memories of their laughter, their quiet private jokes, memories of their love making. He relived once again his time at the farm and he thought of the servants now lying in nameless graves. He thought of the farmstead, standing amidst broken rubble and charred wood, its soul buried in sorrow.

A small French carriage clock struck the quarter hour. The door to the library opened, and Hannah stepped into the room.

'Thank God, you're here,' he said, as he stood up and hurriedly crossed the room to where she stood. 'For a dreadful moment, I thought you weren't coming.'

'I'm leaving in the morning, Tristan. I've come to say goodbye.'

'Hannah, if only we could turn back the clock.'

'But we can't, Tristan. If we could turn back the clock, there would've been no war, no lives lost.'

From the moment she had heard of his impending marriage, something inside of her had changed. The months working in the camp hospital had taught her many things about people, and above all, she discovered many things about herself.

'Tristan,' she continued. Bitterness glittered in her eyes as she spoke. The strain of the evening had chipped away at her patience. 'We can't hide from what has happened. After the war, I had to deal with the aftermath of my betrayal to my family. It wasn't easy, but I dealt with it. I faced it. I didn't have to hide, like you did, in the arms of another.'

He stepped towards her and reached out and rested his hands on her shoulders. 'I know I have failed, Hannah, I know I was weak, but I have made a commitment to Felicity, which I'm duty bound to honour.' He dropped his hands and moved away from her, hiding the emotions he felt.

'The war,' he continued softly, 'the sadness, the unspeakable grief, I often told myself if I got through the nightmare, I would never again fail a commitment. I would never lie, I would become the do-gooder in society, anything, so long as I didn't die in some God-forsaken, foreign land and be buried in a grave that no one would remember.'

He moved across to the fire and dropped down on his haunches to throw on another log. He watched the flames splutter, then stood up and moved back to the chair in which he'd been seated. He stood silently for some time, deep in thought, and then continued.

'I was riding beside two gunner officers. Behind us were our wagons with our supplies. Out of nowhere, came a rapid burst of fire. The Boers had entrenched themselves along the kopje and were obviously watching us as we approached the river. The gunner officer on my left fell from his horse. I knew he was dead the moment he hit the ground. My horse floundered and then fell; I knew it had been shot. The sound from the dying animal was unbearable, a sound that will live with me forever. I went down with the horse but was uninjured, just a minor spraining of my wrist. Everyone was running in all directions and then we began to return the fire. Very few of us survived the skirmish. I had been spared whilst many others around me had perished. Some lived for hours in the most unthinkable pain. The veld was strewn with broken bodies. The wind picked up and began to blow the letters clutched in the hands of the dying men; photographs of young children, young women, and mothers. These were people who would never see their loved ones again. It was then, Hannah, I made a covenant. I would never fail my duty to others; whatever was asked of me, I would deliver. I was spared, Hannah, 22 000 colonial troops died during that war, and I was spared. I wasn't meant for war; I stayed on in South Africa purely because I knew you were there. I couldn't leave the country and leave the woman I loved.'

Hannah crossed the floor and stood before the fire. She watched the logs glowing in the grate, giving off its warmth to an otherwise cold room. Above the mantle hung a portrait of some long forgotten ancestor, her lips curled in a sad and lonely smile.

'You had the choice, Tristan,' she said softly. 'To go to war or not. You chose to join a regiment and you went to war. But what choice did we have? We had no choice. We were rounded up like sheep and taken to camps. I saw cruelty. I saw death every day. I also saw death in the faces of the living. I saw young children, brittle as winter grass, surviving on little more than their mother's love. I saw how the war changed people. Every soldier on the battlefield, living or dead, had the choice. Do you know what image lives with me, the image I see before my eyes before I sleep at night? It is the image of Marike's body, wrapped in a worn blanket, lying in six inches of muddy water at the bottom of her shallow grave. What choice did loving, kind Marike have? Marike, who never thought ill of others. There were no coffins left, no wood to make a coffin. Marike was just another number in the camp. She was not a loving sister, she was merely a number. I close my eyes at night and I see her body beneath that worn blanket, and all I want to do is reach out and hold her. What had she done in the world to deserve that? Tell me, Tristan? You and your soldiers had the choice. Don't expect me to feel remorse for you.'

'Every young man lusts after the glamour of war,' said Tristan after some time. 'Little does he know of the horrors. I know we had the choice, but that does not make my burden any lighter.'

Hannah moved away from the fire. The dove grey silk of her dress caught the orange glow of the flames. For a fleeting moment the colours reminded Tristan of the last dying minutes of an African sunset.

'Do you love her, Tristan?' she said softly.

'I love her like I loved Katherine.'

'Katherine was your sister. No man should love his wife like he loves his sister. That is a cruel and unkind love, a patronising, humiliating love. You cannot bring Katherine back by marrying Felicity.'

Tristan came and stood beside her. 'Many VCs were won for ultimate acts of bravery during the war. What you did for me was the ultimate act of bravery.

At any one time, the commandos could have called in, and had your farm burned and you and your sisters raped and shot. Hannah, I have thought about that over and over again. I will always be forever indebted to you. It is that strength, that spirit, that I fell in love with.'

She turned and faced him, and for the first time she looked directly into his eyes.

'You are duty bound to honour your commitment. A woman like Felicity does not deserve a commitment through obligation or duty. No woman deserves such humiliation. Felicity is a good woman; she deserves more than an obligation. She deserves to be the first and foremost in any man's life. She does not deserve to be second best. She deserves to be loved with passion, the kind of passion a man should have for the woman with whom he is going to share his life. She is above pity. To honour a commitment. Honour is about truth and honesty. There is no truth in your love for her, and there is no honesty. If you can dishonour a truly good woman in this fashion, then you have failed in your covenant. The war has cast shadows over us all, it has changed us all. What I did for you, I would have done for any other man, the difference is, I fell in love with you. We had a passion, we had a commitment. Felicity is your conscience for all the wrongs of war. You must look long and deep into your soul and ask yourself if you are doing what is right by her. And if the answer is 'yes' then you have failed in your pledge to yourself.'

She turned from him and left him standing beside the fire. Without looking back, she opened the door and left the room.

***

Hannah and Magda Hetherington rose early the following morning, long before the Tylcoat guests had left their beds. A carriage was summoned, and with as little fuss as possible they left the Tylcoat estate, and made their way back to London. Hannah had made it her business that she would not set eyes on Tristan again.

***

The voyage home was a lacklustre event. Once they had passed the Equator, the weather turned to sunshine and blue skies. Hannah and Magda improved their game of deck quoits and were much in demand for drinks and conversation. In the back of her mind, Hannah locked away the last few gruelling weeks. She refused to revisit the events that had sucked away every fibre of emotional strength from her. The war was over; this was a new age. It was time to move forward. Yesterday was the past, today was the present, and tomorrow would bring whatever she willed it to bring.

Chapter Twenty-Six

Tristan sat on the Chinese wooden bench, which overlooked the lake on the Tylcoat estate. Overhead, the sky shimmered with the colours of mother of pearl. The sun, weak and watery, tried to break through the fine cloud that lay heavily across the fields. The lake lay, flat and motionless, like a solid sheet of frosted glass, and on its banks, the ducks and geese sat hunched against the cold.

It had been four weeks since Hannah's departure from Tylcoat. Their meeting, although brief, had said more than a lifetime of words. Was she now back at Doringspruit? No, he remembered her words that she could never return to the family she loved. The family that she had forfeited the day she took him into her bed. She was in Cape Town. What was she doing, and what were her plans?

He thought back to the war. Many VCs had been won for acts of bravery, but there would be no medals, no military honours for the sisters of the Van Vuuren household. He knew of the ruthless principles of the Boers; they did not take kindly to treason. Hannah's, Sannie's and Marike's selfless act of kindness would go without recognition or reward.

In the distance, the rooks took flight, screeching their discontent at an unseen predator. Tristan stood up and hurriedly made his way towards the stable block. He needed to see Felicity and he had no desire to make the pre-required appointment.

***

Yates showed Tristan into the drawing room, where Felicity sat at her harp, tutoring her young cousin.

'Tristan!' she said, surprised. 'This is unexpected.'

She turned to her young cousin and said, 'dear Phoebe, I think that's quite sufficient for today, you've done so well and I'm so proud of you. Run along and ask Mrs Stewart to give you some biscuits and a glass of milk.'

Once the child had left the room and the door had closed firmly behind her, Felicity turned to Tristan. 'Contrary to what I said earlier, this visit I have been expecting.'

'Felicity...'

'No, Tristan, let me speak first. I know what you're about to say. From the moment you returned from Africa, I saw that the war had changed you. And from the moment Hannah entered the drawing-room that night at Tylcoat, I knew your feelings towards her.'

Felicity's cheeks flamed as she spoke, her eyes were bright and with each sentence she drew in her breath sharply. 'I will not suffer the indignity of being jilted for the second time. This time, I am breaking off our engagement. I shall make the necessary announcement to my parents and to your father within the next few days. It would please me greatly if you delayed your visit to Africa for a few weeks to quell any gossip that may arise.'

She pulled the bell-rope and Yates silently appeared. 'Mr Dunn-Caldwell is leaving, could you please show him to the door.

'Felicity....'

'I have nothing more to say to you, Tristan. Please leave.'

Felicity watched Tristan as he turned to leave. At the door he looked back over his shoulder, his handsome face pale and drawn. He smiled briefly, and was gone.

You cannot lose what is not yours, she thought, *and Tristan has never been mine.*

***

The Cape glistened in the summer sunshine. The wild flowers and silver leaf trees shimmered in the breeze. The turbulent turquoise seas crashed against the rocks, sending white foam flying high into the air before settling on the pristine white beaches. Table Mountain, with its virginal mantel of white, sat like an awaiting throne for the goddess of beauty.

Christmas came with a frenzy of invitations from Magda's well-connected circle of friends. The year of 1903 was seen in with fountains of champagne and dancing beneath the bedecked ceilings of the Governor's mansion.

Long summer days slipped by. The oaks began to turn from green to gold. The last of the summer flowers had begun to fade when a letter from Sannie arrived. In it, she had written of the hardships of the Transvaal. They had had difficulty obtaining draught animals to plough the fields, but once the fields had been ploughed and the crops planted, the rains did not come. Their crops were pitifully poor. She and Willem Prinsloo had married two days before Christmas and she now lived at Soetwater. At her time of writing, she fervently hoped that she was expecting her first child, for all the signs were there. Little Gideon had grown and was a happy, contented child. Katrina had given them another sister. The baby was born a month early, but was a strong, healthy infant resembling Sunette. She had been named Marikie, after their sister, Marike. The baptism would take place the next time they went to nagmaal in Hemel. She had sold the diamonds and they had fetched a good price in Pretoria. The money had helped towards building materials and she took a small portion of the money, as Hannah had suggested, and bought a magnificent framed mirror so that she could see that she always looked good for her husband. On her last trip to Hemel, she had managed to buy a rose bush for Willem. Even though the rains had been poor, the bush had survived and had even rewarded them with two blooms. She had taken this as a sign from God, like the rainbow after the floods, that all would be well again one day soon. Her letter ended with her best wishes for Hannah's happiness and that she would write again soon.

She read the letter over several times. Sannie's words painted a picture of optimism and hope.

Hannah sat in the garden, as it was a particularly warm day for the month of April. The morning sunlight slanted across the shrubbery, casting defined shadows across the lawn. The rain from the night before had seeped into the soil, and the air had a sweetness about it.

She looked up from her sewing and saw Marie hurrying across the lawn towards her. Marie had been with them for only three days, and Hannah was in the process of training the young woman in the duties of a housemaid.

'There is a gentleman to see you, Miss Hannah,' she said nervously.

'That will be Mr Buxton, Marie,' she said kindly. 'He was meant to call only this afternoon, but, since he is a man of senior years, I will forgive him for this unscheduled visit. Show him out into the garden, and be sure to address him by name.'

The petite housemaid nodded in confused concentration and turned to leave. 'Oh, and Marie, prepare a tray of tea for us. See there are plenty of biscuits. Mr Buxton has more than a generous appetite.'

Hannah had been working closely with the elderly and pompous Mr Buxton, raising funds for the displaced in the Transvaal. Together with the church, they had organised many fund raising events, and had recruited the skills of many of the women's organisations. They had become known in the Cape social circles as a formidable team.

Hannah gathered up her sewing and folded the linen napkin, on which she was embroidering a simple motif of apricot blossoms. Haphazardly, she collected the coloured skeins of silk and placed them neatly on the folded linen napkin. She took the small pair of sewing scissors, which had once belonged to Marike, slipped them lovingly into their soft leather sleeve, and tucked it safely into the side pocket of her sewing basket.

As she reached out for the wooden reel of white cotton, she looked up and saw with disbelief, Tristan crossing the newly mown lawn. The reel of white cotton dropped from her fingers, and clattered and rolled along the surface of the garden table.

She stood for a few moments, drinking in his presence. He seemed taller, leaner than she had remembered. He walked with long relaxed strides behind the young housemaid who hurried across the lawn, her feet barely touching the ground.

'It's alright, Marie, you may go,' said Hannah, with a sharpness that was not intended.

'How are you, Hannah?' he asked softly, once the housemaid had retreated and was out of earshot.

'Well, Tristan, this is a surprise,' she said, steadying herself with one hand on the edge of the garden table. 'How long have you been in Africa?'

Tristan saw the intensity in Hannah's vivid eyes as she spoke, but was unable to read her thoughts.

'My ship docked last evening.'

'What brings you to Africa? I thought you had resigned your commission.'

'My return to Africa has nothing to do with my commission. You brought me back to Africa,' he said, stepping closer towards her. 'Only you had the power to bring me back, Hannah. I need…to put things right between us.'

'You could've written, Tristan. It would've spared you the long journey.'

'Yes, I could've written but what I wanted to say to you could not be said in a letter. A letter could be lost, a reply could be lost, and nothing would be resolved.'

For a few moments, there was silence between them. Hannah bent down and picked up the reel of white cotton and hurriedly dropped it into her sewing basket.

'There is nothing to resolve, Tristan. What we needed to say was said.'

'No, Hannah. After you left, I had time to think. What you had said was true. Felicity deserved to be more than my conscience. My behaviour that night was irrational and unreasonable…'

'Tristan,' she said quickly, raising her hand in a gesture to stop. 'I had a long time to think on the sea voyage home. I needed to make sense out of this madness. War is many things to many people. For the Empire, it was power, for the Boers it was pride. For you, it was a cowardly act to extricate yourself from a less than exciting marriage, and for me…it was tragedy. That sets us apart.'

'Hannah, what is done is done. We don't have the power to change things…'

'No,' interrupted Hannah. 'We can't change things and for that very reason, Tristan, we were never meant to be. At Tylcoat I saw a man so different to the man I knew at Doringspruit. I saw the pious man you had become. Remember, Tristan, I've lived with piety all my life, it's a trait I despise.'

'Hannah, everything happened so quickly. The woman I loved and believed to be dead was there, in my home.'

'And so was the woman who was soon to be your wife,' interjected Hannah.

'That night…that night in the library, it haunts me. Hannah, what we had was extraordinary.'

'What we had, Tristan, was a hungry need to block our minds from reality. It was a love born out of circumstances.'

'We can work this out, Hannah…'

'There is nothing to work out, Tristan, nothing.'

Hannah saw Marie crossing the lawn with the tray of tea. She waited till Marie had placed the tray on the table and left before she continued.

'It's over, Tristan. I'm sorry you've wasted your time travelling back to Africa. But it's over.'

'I never stopped loving you, Hannah. I returned to England a broken man. I found sanity at Tylcoat. I felt safe, the harshness of Africa and the savageness of war were a million miles away. Felicity was waiting. Sweet Felicity, who knew not to ask questions, because she knew there were answers she didn't want to hear, and for that I was grateful.'

A sudden breeze lifted the coloured skeins of silk and blew them to the ground. The corners of the folded linen napkin fluttered momentarily.

'Hannah' he continued, his perfect hands were upturned, his fingers splayed in an expressive manner.

'I returned to Tylcoat a broken man. Everything about Tylcoat was familiar and safe. It was where I spent a happy childhood. No screams of dying men, or other unspeakable horrors of war. Tylcoat was my haven.'

Hannah's eyes never left Tristan's face. His features were taut with emotion and his green eyes were bright and intense. 'We've both witnessed more than any human should witness,' he continued. 'It's left its mark on both of us. Hannah, I'm asking you to come back to England, to Tylcoat, as my wife.'

'No,' she whispered. 'No, Tristan. This is where I belong. How can I sit in the elegant drawing rooms of England, knowing that my family, my nation, is eking out an existence on the farms, destroyed by the power hungry elite of the Empire? My conscience won't allow it.'

They stood in the silence of the morning for a brief moment. She could feel the breeze against her skin and the loose strands of hair as it swept across her cheek.

'War divided a nation, and it divided my family,' she continued. 'Now that the fighting has ended, the war will continue, not with bullets and cannon fire, but with human emotions and bitterness. Besides, would I be accepted as your wife? Each time there was a social event, a dinner party, a charity ball, or whatever, would it turn into another freak show, like the time I was at Tylcoat. Would I be rolled out like some curiosity to be examined, scrutinised, dissected and insulted?'

She looked across the lawn to the shrubbery beyond, avoiding his eyes. 'Too much has happened, and yes, we have both witnessed too much.'

He stood silently. The morning light caught the angle of his cheek and gleamed on his dark curls.

'We can try, Hannah,' he said softly. 'You need time to heal.'

She reached out and brushed his arm lightly. 'Yes, we could try, Tristan, but it would never work. This is where I belong. My people are in desperate need of funds. Families in the Transvaal are destitute. Many of them are women with children who have lost their husbands in the war. There is nothing for them. How are they to rebuild their lives? My father is one of the lucky ones. He has savings and he is healthy and strong; he will rebuild Doringspruit. My people need people like me who can, perhaps, make a difference. Many families are still in the camps as they have nowhere to go, they rely on the charity that others are prepared to give.'

He stood silently in the morning sunshine. He knew the peace that surrounded them in the garden, with its birdsong and lush foliage, was a far cry from the drought-ridden Transvaal.

'I'm sorry, Tristan,' she continued, 'that this hasn't worked out for us.'

'I'll wait for you, Hannah. I know in time you might think differently.'

'No, Tristan. We both know that life is too short to wait, and I know I will not change my mind.'

He turned to leave, then looked back and said, 'I will be forever grateful to you, and your sisters, for giving me care in my hour of need. I will always love you, Hannah.'

She watched him walk away, his lean back, straight and upright.

She sat down at the table on which the tea tray was placed. She had no inclination to resume her sewing. Somewhere in the depth of the purple shade of the shrubbery, the coucal began to call, reminding her of Doringspruit.

She thought of the home of her childhood, and as it stood now, with the veld around it, empty and desolate. She thought of the day they returned to Doringspruit after the war. The walls of the farmstead were still standing, but without the roof and the windows. She remembered the wall of the veranda against which a handful of crimson zinnias were flowering; no doubt they were descendants of the seeds Hymie had once given Marike. She knew, at that moment, Marike was still with them. Everything seemed so incomplete.

The house had lost its soul and they, as a family, had lost Marike. She remembered, as they walked around to the side of the house, and there, standing, untouched, was the apricot tree. It stood so tall and proud, its winter branches stretching towards the sky. Everything around them had changed, they as a family had changed, yet the apricot tree had stood steadfast, waiting for their return.

She thought of the harsh winter that year. Her father had the money to buy food, but there was no food to be bought. They worked hard; every moment was a moment not to be wasted. The spring came and the apricot tree burst into a cloud of blossom reminding them that another season had dawned, and life would go on. The blossoms were a symbol of hope.

She knew she would never return to Doringspruit. Through the madness of war and the madness of love, she had lost much. But she would always have cherished memories of her family and the veld, and the unyielding spirit of the apricot tree.